T0382015

Praise for A. A. Dhand

'Outstanding – relentless, multi-layered suspense
and real human drama'
Lee Child

'Timely, and a compulsive page-turner'
Liz Nugent, author of *Strange Sally Diamond*

'This man knows how to keep me up into the
early hours. Relentlessly thrilling!'
Vaseem Khan, author of *Midnight at Malabar House*

'A fireball of an opening chapter and it just gets better
and better. A. A. Dhand is a gifted writer'
Steve Cavanagh, bestselling author of *Thirteen*

'Another thrilling page-turner from A. A. Dhand . . .
This might be his best yet'
Alex Caan, author of *Cut to the Bone*

'Intense, gripping and impactful'
James Delargy, author of *55* and *Vanished*

'An adrenaline-filled ride'
Ajay Chowdhury, author of *The Waiter*

'I doubt I'll read a better thriller this year'
M. W. Craven, author of *The Curator*

'Deserves attention for its sheer inventiveness
and unbridled energy'
The Times

'An author to keep an eye on . . . Dhand is a fearless writer'
Sunday Times

'High octane drama from one of Britain's freshest crime voices'
Phil Williams, BBC Radio Five live

A. A. Dhand is the author of several novels, and has been shortlisted for the CWA Steel Dagger Award. His DI Harry Virdee novels have been adapted for TV by the BBC. He was raised in Bradford and spent his youth observing the city from behind the counter of a small convenience store. After qualifying as a pharmacist, he worked in London and travelled extensively before returning to Bradford to start his own business and begin writing. The history, diversity and darkness of the city have inspired all his novels.

As a pharmacist, A. A. Dhand was surrounded by drugs, dealers, and incredible stories of maverick drug deals, which on one hand blew his mind in their ingenuity, and on the other sickened him with how easily they preyed on the most vulnerable. His experiences inspired the writing of *The Chemist*.

For more information about A. A. Dhand and his books, follow him on X @aadhand, and on Instagram @aa_dhand.

Also by A. A. Dhand

Streets of Darkness
Girl Zero
City of Sinners
One Way Out
Darkness Rising
The Blood Divide

THE CHEMIST

A.A.DHAND

ONE PLACE. MANY STORIES

HQ
An imprint of HarperCollins*Publishers* Ltd
1 London Bridge Street
London SE1 9GF

www.harpercollins.co.uk

HarperCollins*Publishers*
Macken House, 39/40 Mayor Street Upper
Dublin 1, D01 C9W8, Ireland

This edition 2025

1
First published in Great Britain by HQ,
an imprint of HarperCollins*Publishers* Ltd 2025

ISBN: HB: 978-0-00-864585-4
TPB: 978-0-00-864584-7

Set in Sabon by HarperCollins*Publishers* India

Printed and bound in the UK using 100% Renewable
Electricity at CPI Group (UK) Ltd

For the Dhands.

*And for all the independent community pharmacy
contractors out there. The struggle is real.*

Author Note

Whilst I have used the real world of community pharmacy as a vehicle to tell this thriller, *The Chemist* is a heightened world and not procedurally factual.

For the purposes of drama – policies, drugs and doses have been manipulated to facilitate fiction.

Prologue

Police helicopters overhead and the sight of armed snipers on the rooftops of neighbouring buildings alarmed Idris Khan.

It wasn't every day that the staff and patients waiting inside his pharmacy bore witness to a hostage situation.

Across the street, inside Dare Café, customers had been lined up against the large floor-to-ceiling windows; a human shield concealing what was taking place inside.

Nobody knew what that was except for Idris.

He glanced at his reflection in the window. A black eye was in the infancy of healing.

Idris ran his hand across his torso, gently massaging his ribcage, which was still bruised from what had happened the night before. He felt certain that if he lifted his shirt, he would find a wound seeping with fresh blood.

He shuddered and glanced at the floor. The black tiles were spotless, gleaming almost.

Nobody could tell that, twelve hours before, they had been stained with Idris's blood.

He sighed and focused on the drama unfolding outside the café.

Another police car arrived, two more officers exited the vehicle and urgently ushered people away from the café.

A police cordon was hurriedly established and overhead, the helicopter made another pass.

Idris knew who the hostage taker was – a man whose circumstances had forced his hand.

A man who would do *anything* to survive.

But murder? Shit, Idris hadn't seen that coming.

He should have, though. Again, his hands indiscriminately moved to his ribs.

Jemma, Idris's assistant manager, arrived by his side, auburn hair in his periphery, her dark blue uniform smelling potently of a lemony-scented perfume.

He didn't turn to face her and after an awkward silence, Jemma finally tucked a small bottle of medication inside Idris's hand.

Behind them, two elderly patients continued to speculate about what was happening outside. *Shouldn't the pharmacy be closed? Clearly, it wasn't safe out there.*

'Don't,' Jemma said finally. 'Just . . . don't.'

Idris remained silent. He was struggling with what to do, time working against him. Soon, more police cars would arrive, order would replace chaos and the cordon would become impenetrable.

If Idris was going, it was now or never.

He examined the small plastic medicine bottle Jemma had given him.

Methadone, 1mg/ml sugar-free solution – 100mls.

Idris slipped it inside his pocket and opened the door.

Jemma put her hand on his shoulder.

'You can't do this, Idris, it's madness. Think of Mariam? Think of . . . what might happen,' she whispered, fearful, desperate.

Idris smiled weakly at her, ignored the fear crippling his insides.

'I'm the only person who can stop this, Jemsy,' he replied and then walked out of the pharmacy.

It was fifty short yards to the entrance of Dare Café.

Headingley was one of the busiest areas of Leeds – full of students who attended the nearby universities. They were in full swing of the legendary Otley Run: a pub-crawl from Otley into the centre of town. Seventeen pubs along the way with a pint in each one.

The police were heavily outnumbered by students who were simply far too drunk to realise what was happening.

Idris took his opportunity, walked urgently towards the security cordon, ducked underneath it and immediately raised his arms in surrender to show the officers rushing towards him that he was no threat.

'Stop, armed police,' screamed a male voice.

Idris froze outside the door of the café, turned his head and stared down the barrel of a machine gun.

'Back away from the door. Now,' hissed the officer, his face concealed behind a black protective mask.

'My name is Idris Khan. I'm the pharmacist who works over there . . .'

Idris nodded behind him towards the pharmacy.

'You need to trust me. I know what's happening inside. I'm the only one who can stop this.'

'Back away from the door, I will not ask again.'

The officer's radio crackled.

Idris heard the message: 'Sunflower negative. Repeat, sunflower negative. Apprehend suspect.'

'There is no threat to life and I am not armed. Now, I'm going inside. You shoot me if you must but with all these people watching? With all the phones recording it? You can't pull that trigger,' said Idris firmly.

Around them, seemingly everyone was recording the clash on their mobile phones. This shit was going viral.

The Chemist who entered an armed siege.

Idris's heart was racing. He had never been so close to a gun before, never mind been forced to stare down the barrel of one.

Not even last night.

If you don't get inside, Idris, you're dead. They will come for you. And Mariam. And . . . Rebecca.

Idris's life depended on entering the café, to defuse whatever was happening inside and then to somehow put into play what he had been forced to agree to the night before.

Idris grabbed the handle, braced for a bullet and opened the door. The officer's radio crackled loudly again, this time, the voice more urgent.

'Sunflower negative. Repeat, sunflower negative.'

'I promise I know what I'm doing,' said Idris and as the helicopter roared overhead once more, he gathered every ounce of courage he had and stepped inside the café.

Part One

Chapter One

Two days earlier

Idris Khan was driving through Headingley, on his way to work, at 5 a.m.

The sun was yet to rise and Idris felt calm surrounded by the darkness, feeling like it camouflaged him from the world – something he could not do in his job as a pharmacist which involved interactions, whether with members of the public or related to the drugs he supplied.

He preferred the kind with drugs because in most instances, he could manage those.

But people? They were unpredictable and unpredictability was not something Idris enjoyed.

He pulled his car into the medical centre car park, and nestled into his usual space, adjacent to the pharmacy.

He exited, seeing the usual evidence from the night before. Empty beer cans, half-eaten takeaway containers and the odd discarded fancy-dress costume littered the streets.

And, as always, there was vomit, intermittently soiling the pavement.

Students.

The main campus of the University of Leeds was nearby

with several halls of residences within walking distance of the pharmacy.

Monday night was always two-for-one in the local pubs which meant today, the pharmacy would be more chaotic than usual, seemingly every student in Headingley attending for a miracle hangover remedy.

Over the years, mostly by trial and error, Idris had created what he now simply referred to as 'the cure'. Esomeprazole to settle the acid in the stomach, a tube of oral rehydration tablets and a couple of paracetamol for the headache.

It had become so well known that nowadays students simply walked in and asked for it. Occasionally, if the student had also been smoking weed, Idris sold them a bottle of cleansing eye drops to counteract the redness in their eyes.

Idris was now commonly known within every student residence simply as 'The Chemist' and while it was a professionally inaccurate term, he accepted it with fond affection.

Idris now used an electronic fob to raise the shutter, the metal joints creaking loudly as it opened. He unlocked the doors, stepped inside and hurried towards the alarm panel, deactivating it.

Idris didn't switch on the main lights, preferring the ambience of dim emergency lighting. It felt like the darkness outside had followed him in and for Idris, there was comfort in that.

He lowered the shutter and looked around the dispensary: a large, square clinical area with four workstations, each one stacked with over a hundred dosette boxes. They were filled with specific medications for different patients. Each box told a detailed story, holding at least six medications. Anxiety, cholesterol, blood pressure, pain and the most popular ailment which required treatment these days: depression.

A box had seven horizontal slots, each one labelled with a day of the week and four vertical compartments: breakfast, lunch, teatime and night. Pharmacy dispensers would pop relevant medications into specific time slots and once complete, the tray would be checked by a pharmacist.

Idris had three hundred patients on dosette boxes and the completion of each set of trays was an arduous, labour-intensive task. Yet Idris enjoyed it, finding the process a cathartic one, working alone, in almost darkness, just a small table lamp highlighting the bench. The pills were his companions, different colours, shapes, sizes, each one telling Idris a distinct story.

Idris did the same thing he did each morning: he put on some classical music, brewed a pot of coffee and got to work.

Two hours later, with the time approaching 8.30 a.m., Idris had finished. He rubbed his eyes, vision now blurry from the hundreds of pills he had checked.

He stretched and released a loud, animated yawn.

Christ, he felt brain dead.

Idris glanced to his side, at his in-tray, full of unopened post and a bold scribbled note from Jemma on top of it.

IF YOU DON'T SORT THESE, THEY'RE GETTING BINNED!

Idris gently leafed through the top few envelopes. They all displayed the same bold red stamp – URGENT – and all were from his main pharmaceutical wholesaler.

An anxiety he was all too familiar with tightened his chest a little.

So far, his staff had not realised that the pharmacy's fixed drug quotas had been reduced. Idris was close to going bankrupt, a result of draconian cuts made by the government to the NHS pharmacy budget. Each month he continued to trade, his finances worsened and the demands for him to settle his debts increased.

Idris kept telling himself that a good flu and COVID vaccination season was all he needed and with that period just about to start, it gave him a fighting chance to fend off the wolves.

A last chance before his pharmacy closed for good.

8.50 a.m. Idris was lying on one of the comfortable, padded benches in the main waiting area of the pharmacy. Outside, he could hear a familiar growing commotion from three distinct queues of customers.

First, and always the most animated group, were his 'blue scripts', those patients prescribed methadone whom Idris had to supervise as they consumed their daily doses. They were called blue scripts because their NHS prescriptions were blue and not green or white like standard ones.

The second queue were other patients who had secured 8 a.m. appointments at the GP surgery, located above the pharmacy inside the medical centre. They had probably seen Idris's wife, Mariam, who owned the practice and were now impatient to get their medication. He could hear their voices outside.

'Says on the door 9 a.m., what time is it now?' said an irritated male voice.

'It's 8.55,' whispered Idris, eyes still closed, listening intently.

Finally, the third line – his staff and certainly the most reluctant to step inside the pharmacy to begin another Groundhog Day of supplying medications and answering queries.

At 8.58, the silence was shattered by the ringing of the first of four telephones in the pharmacy.

Then the second handset.

And now, the other two.

At exactly 9 a.m., Idris got off the bench and raised the shutter.

As bright, hostile sunlight splintered the darkness, Idris unlocked the doors.

Showtime.

Chapter Two

Rebecca Fury was sitting at her desk, inside her office at The Elizabeth Projects, a government-funded organisation designated to look after sex workers. Located in Beeston, it was only two miles from the centre of Leeds.

Might as well have been two hundred.

While the centre was full of high-rising luxury apartments, fancy gourmet restaurants and vogue night clubs, Beeston housed the first and only legalised red-light district in the country and with that, came everything specific to that world.

Drugs.

Pimps.

Abuse.

Etched in large silver letters, across the side of the building were the words PEACE, COMPASSION, RESPECT.

Empty words in an empty world.

Rebecca's office was a skeletal affair; a desk, a couple of chairs and a bookcase full of literature focused on safeguarding, sexual health and drug abuse. The walls were covered in brash, uncompromising posters which warned of the risks of sex work.

Rebecca leaned back in her chair and allowed the sun's rays, streaking through a window, to caress the side of her face.

She closed her eyes, raised her feet onto the table and imagined that she was anywhere but here – that outside, she was not surrounded by pimps, vulnerable girls and . . . criminality.

The Maldives.

That's where she'd escape to if she ever got the chance. She'd have a small bar with a limited selection of food – quality over quantity – and she'd spend her evenings creating maverick new cocktails.

In these dreams, there was always the same man, dark-haired, olive-skinned, kind eyes.

A teenage love affair which had turned into a rebellious fight to be together, and when everything had been going so well for them, tragedy had struck.

Her hands went to her stomach, to where she'd carried their baby.

Where she'd also lost it.

Flashes of blood, panicked nurses and doctors who had been forced to restrain her in order to administer drugs.

The phone on her desk rang sharply, knocking her back to reality. Startled, she took a moment to get herself together.

Always the same daydream – what if? What could have been?

She answered the phone, listened to the message and said, 'Send her in.'

Rebecca was sitting opposite Amy Starr, with her head in her hands.

The girl just would not listen.

And she was just that, a nineteen-year-old girl. She had her blonde hair in pigtails, a slight frame and a naivety which was rare, especially in Beeston.

For almost an hour how, Rebecca had been warning her

against hitting the streets outside, where even at this early morning hour, sex workers were loitering in the cold.

'Lots of other girls do it,' said Amy defensively.

'You're just a kid,' replied Rebecca, looking at her intensely. 'You've an innocence about you which these streets will strip away. This game's not for you.'

'Liam says . . .'

Rebecca's rebuttal was instantaneous, her words tinged with poison. 'Liam is a parasite.'

Amy's response was equally quick. 'Liam loves me,' she said defensively but looked away, her words empty and hollow.

'He's a pimp and he has at least six other girls working for him.'

'So? He looks after them, doesn't he?'

Again, she was unconvincing; needy even.

'At least try and sound like you believe that, Amy.'

'Look, I'm going out there. Now, are you going to give me the free condoms or not?'

Rebecca opened a desk drawer, grabbed a handful of them and slid them across the table.

'Finally,' said Amy, snatching at them and stuffing the condoms inside her bag before jumping out of her chair.

'Sit back down,' said Rebecca firmly and pointed at the chair.

Amy remained stoic, disinterested now she had got what she needed.

Rebecca opened a different drawer, removed an envelope and pulled a blue prescription from it. She waved it at Amy, who immediately retook her seat, expectant, eager.

'Blue script arrived this morning. You start today – if you still want it?' said Rebecca.

'I want it. That council bitch said that if I goes on it, she would help us get, like a new flat or summat.'

Rebecca replaced the prescription in the envelope, scribbled a hasty note and slipped that inside too. 'The blue script gives you access to methadone. Methadone gets you off the drugs, allows you to function and puts you in control. That – not a new flat – gives you control, Amy.'

Rebecca pushed the envelope across the table. Amy stuffed it roughly in her handbag and stood up to leave.

'I'm gonna be OK, you know,' said Amy, trying to act determined but with no real authority to her words. 'I work the streets a bit, get me some monies, get me some options, innit.' She pointed to the window, where outside, sex workers continued to toil by the side of the road. 'I'm not gonna be like the other girls, still here in fifty years or whatever.'

Rebecca came around the desk and perched on it, casual, calm. 'That's what everyone says, Amy.'

'Yeah, but I got a plan.'

Rebecca lifted a business card from her desk and handed it to Amy. 'My number. If you're out there and you feel afraid, vulnerable or at risk, then you call me. It's what I'm here for.'

Amy slipped the card into her bag. 'You said there was a chemist who would take me on for my methadone?'

Rebecca smiled warmly and said, 'At the pharmacy, ask for Idris.'

Chapter Three

Six patients waiting. Two pending consultations. Three hundred and eighty electronic prescriptions waiting to be dispensed.

And as always, the phones were ringing.

A bullish male patient was complaining about having to wait fifteen minutes for his medication.

Idris stirred his tea and whispered to himself, 'You'll wait twenty minutes for a Costa but not your meds.'

Jemma waltzed past Idris, carrying a basket full of medications.

'Costa? Chance would be a fine thing,' she said, picking up Idris's tea and taking a sip.

'Damn it, woman, that's the second time this morning,' he said, grabbing another mug.

'The Mews called, they want their PPE ASAP.'

'It's in my car,' he said.

In the waiting area, an irritable male voice snapped at one of Idris' counter staff. 'How much longer is this going to take? I've a gym session booked in twenty minutes. It's always the same in this bloody chemist. I mean, how long does it take to stick some pills in a bag?'

Idris watched, as Vanessa, his pharmacist manager, her face flushed, her Spanish temper firing, stepped across to Jemma and said, 'Which one is gym freak's script?'

Jemma handed a small red basket to Vanessa, who duly

looked at the prescription and discreetly whispered, 'Urgent for Viagra. Typical man.'

Then, as she always did when a patient was acting like an ass, she placed the basket to the bottom of the queue.

Idris glanced into the waiting area and had a quick look at the guy. Rugged, early thirties, power suit, power tie, *power prick*, he thought. He saw a blue script, Al-Noor, enter the pharmacy, pointed towards the consultation room and gave Al-Noor a hand signal, indicating he'd be five minutes.

Idris stepped into the consultation room to find Al-Noor sitting at the desk, smiling as usual. He was Idris's favourite blue script, a forty-eight-year-old Syrian refugee who unlike most of his addicts, looked healthy and was always in a positive mood despite living in one of the most dangerous areas in Leeds.

'How's things, Al?' asked Idris, taking a seat.

'Mr Idris, I am OK. And you?'

Mr Idris.

No matter how many times Idris had corrected him, Al-Noor still added 'Mr' to Idris's name. It was a term of endearment and Idris was fond of it.

'Al, I need a holiday,' said Idris, removing the dose of methadone from a prescription packet and sliding it across the table as if he were a bartender sliding a shot towards a customer.

Al-Noor caught it in his hand, unscrewed the cap and immediately drank the green methadone solution. He then poured a little water into the container and drank that before sliding the bottle back across the table to Idris.

'Hit you again?' said Idris, jovially.

Al-Noor grimaced. 'One day, Mr Idris, Al-Noor will not be sitting here. He will be free and not just from methadone but also from The Mews.'

The Mews. A dystopian estate housing five nightmarish tower blocks, each one accommodating a mixture of drug addicts, convicts on probation and the largest community of illegal immigrants in Yorkshire.

Al-Noor was a prisoner inside The Mews, working for a kingpin who controlled everything which took place there, Jahangir Hosseini.

Al-Noor had the most important job in The Mews.

He was 'the runner', in charge of supplying heroin to the addicts who would pay him, and in turn, Al-Noor would pay Jahangir. Not that this position meant Al-Noor had any power. He remained a slave to the system, the only luxury afforded to him being that nobody would dare cross him. Messing with the runner was akin to disrespecting Jahangir personally and no resident dared to do that.

The Mews: a place few dared to go, yet the most important location Idris visited every day.

Idris was known there as The Chemist and like Al-Noor he had complete, secure access to all areas, supplying the residents with legal prescription medications and clean needles and syringes so they could administer their heroin safely.

'Mr Idris, I know I will be seeing you later but please, tell me what this says.'

Al-Noor removed a brown envelope from his bag and pushed it across the table towards Idris. It had a Leeds City Council stamp on it and was marked STRICTLY PRIVATE AND CONFIDENTIAL.

Having helped Al-Noor to fill out a specific application form several weeks ago, Idris knew what this was about.

He read the letter then laid it flat on the table. He frowned at Al-Noor, dismayed. 'Shit, Al, I'm sorry but it's bad news.'

Al-Noor looked at the floor. 'They said no, didn't they?'

'They did.'

'Please. Read it to me.'

Idris picked up the letter and read it aloud.

'*Dear Mr Qadri,*

We are in receipt of your letter requesting emergency accommodation away from the Mews for you and your son, Faris Qadri. We are afraid to inform you that, at this moment in time, your request cannot be considered as we await the outcome of your claim for asylum. We understand you will be disappointed, but we look forward to revisiting this request on successful receipt of a positive outcome of your immigration status.'

Idris returned it to Al-Noor who whispered, 'Still a slave, Mr Idris.'

He pointed at the empty bottle of methadone and waved at Idris. 'To this. To The Mews. To Jahangir.'

'Keep the faith, Al. The transfer will happen. I know it's tough.'

'I don't care for me, Mr Idris. Faris is all I worry about.'

Faris, Al-Noor's fifteen-year-old son, was something of a maths prodigy. He was, as far as Al-Noor was concerned, his best chance at getting his asylum application approved.

Al-Noor reached into his bag and removed a maths textbook. He turned to a specific page and showed it to Idris. 'Please, check Faris's working for me.'

Idris did so, much like he did most days when Al-Noor asked him to mark the extra work he encouraged Faris to undertake.

'I could do these sums in my dreams if they were in Arabic,' said Al-Noor.

'I bet. Not many addicts on my books with a degree in engineering, Al.'

'I miss those days, Mr Idris. Working in Syria. It is all I ever wanted to do with my life. Math, technology. I want the same thing for Faris. For that, he must excel at math.'

Al-Noor had fled Syria when the war had proven too dangerous to remain there. He had made the perilous trip to the UK across land and sea and lost his wife to the English Channel during that ill-fated trip.

It had been organised by Jahangir Hosseini who had done what he always did with adult refugees he helped to arrive in the UK. He had forced Al-Noor to use heroin, ensuring he became addicted; guaranteeing that Al-Noor would remain a slave not only to the needle but also to Jahangir.

The Mews was full of refugees who shared this story.

Idris checked Faris's work, circling one incorrect answer.

'Same as yesterday, Al. Tell him to look at this one again.'

Idris handed the book back to Al-Noor who stood to leave.

'How long, Mr Idris?' asked Al-Noor.

'The Mews?'

'Yes.'

'Maybe half an hour.'

Idris watched Al-Noor leave, aggrieved that his request for emergency housing had been rejected.

Jemma knocked on the door and slipped inside, bringing with her a dose of methadone.

'New blue script,' she said to Idris.

He looked at her, puzzled. 'But we're not taking on any new blues,' said Idris, annoyed.

Jemma slid an envelope onto the table and Idris recognised the handwriting immediately.

'It's from Rebecca, you still want to refuse?'

Idris shook his head and Jemma stepped out of the room and called out Amy Starr's name before escorting her into the consultation room to meet Idris.

Chapter Four

Amy Starr sat in front of Idris, meek, shy, with her sleeves pulled over her hands and fidgeting in her seat. Her blue script said that she was nineteen years old, but she looked more like a child than a teenager, her eyes shining with an innocence Idris had never seen before in a patient presenting with a blue script.

There was nothing hardened or streetwise about her.

Alarmingly, she'd come in accompanied by Liam Reynolds, who was an addict and someone Idris had barred a long time ago for aggressive behaviour. Liam was also an alcoholic and a pimp who ran girls in Beeston.

'You want a drink of water before we do this or one afterwards?' asked Idris, reading the confidential note which had been addressed to him.

TAKE THIS ONE ON FOR ME, PLEASE. SHE NEEDS US . . . RX.

'Afterwards, innit,' said Amy, her childlike voice matching her appearance.

Idris scrunched up the note from Rebecca and threw it in the bin. He filled out a methadone contract with Amy's name and date of birth and listed her address the same as it was displayed on her prescription; NFA – *no fixed abode*.

'Where are you living?' he asked, sliding the form across to Amy so she could sign it.

'Sorta between places at the mo. Wiv Liam.'

Idris winced. He'd heard this spiel before.

Amy looked at the contract, puzzled. 'What's this?'

'Methadone contract.'

'But like, what's it say?'

Idris paused, realised that she was illiterate. 'Would you like me to read it to you?'

She nodded, still not making eye contact with him.

Idris read it to her, highlighting the important parts: that his pharmacy would supply her with methadone liquid, supervise her drinking it and then give her a glass of water afterwards to ensure she'd swallowed it; that if Amy arrived in a timely manner, was a polite and respectful client then she would be treated the same as any other patient.

'I got it,' she said and signed the contract, writing carefully.

'The most important thing on this contract is the rule of three. You know it?' asked Idris.

Amy shook her head.

'If you miss three consecutive doses of methadone, I have to cancel this prescription. No more methadone, you got it?'

She shrugged and looked at the methadone suspiciously. 'What's it taste like?' she asked.

Idris liked her immediately. He smiled and said, 'Like medicine.'

'Me nan used to give us a lollipop when we were little and had some medicine.'

'Is she still around, your nan?' he asked, unscrewing the cap from the medicine bottle, and putting it in front of Amy.

She nodded. 'I was livin' wiv her before . . . ya know.'

She used her hand to simulate shooting a shot of heroin into her forearm.

'How long have you been on the needle?' asked Idris.

'Like, seven months maybe.'

'How'd you start?'

She shrugged. 'Just sorta did.'

'Weed?'

Another nod.

'Gateway drug for everyone who ends up in here.'

'How many you got?'

'A lot.'

'How many's a lot?'

'Three hundred.'

She finally looked at him, beautiful soft green eyes and again, he was struck by how irreproachable she looked.

'Wow. Three hundred?'

'We look after The Mews.'

'Oh. Figures then, innit.'

She leaned forward, plonked her elbows on the table, rested her chin on her hands and smiled. 'Your sorta nice, ya know? Rebecca said you would be.'

Idris leaned back in his chair, relaxed. 'What did you expect?'

'Dunno, like a teacher or summat.'

He laughed and kept the smile on his face. 'I can be a militant son of a bitch if people fuck around in my chemist's.'

She frowned at him. 'Never heard a chemist swear before.'

Idris pointed at her methadone dose.

'Thirty millilitres. Starter dose. Spill it and there's no more. Rules and regulations, all that boring shit people love.'

Amy picked up the bottle and smelled the contents.

'How many people have you seen come off heroin with this?' she asked, carefully waving the bottle towards him.

Idris wanted to tell her that he couldn't remember because the number was so high. He knew exactly how many.

Zero.

'One step at a time,' he replied and nodded for her to drink the methadone.

Amy put it to her lips and paused.

'Neck it in one, like a shot. Best way,' said Idris.

Amy did so, replacing the bottle on the table and grimacing. She lifted the glass of water and took a sip.

'It's horrible,' she said.

'Try make it same time tomorrow, kid,' said Idris.

'How do you know Rebecca?' she asked.

For the first time, Idris was hesitant, and Amy saw it. The next thing she said was alarmingly close to the bone. 'What is she, like your ex or summat?'

Another pause from Idris and then he said, 'Why do you say that?'

'She wrote a kiss on that envelope,' said Amy, pointing towards the bin.

'That's a leap,' he said, a little too quickly, because again, Amy saw it.

'Nah, there's summat there,' she said, smiling innocently. 'Amy don't know much about much but when there's summat there, Amy sees it.'

Idris stood up and opened the door to the consultation room. 'We're all done here, let me walk you out.'

Amy extended her hand. 'Nice to have met you, Mr Chemist.'

Idris stared at her hand, at dirty fingernails and broken nail varnish on splintering nails. He shook it. 'Welcome to Headingley Pharmacy,' he said.

'Thanks for taking me on. I promise, I won't be no trouble.'

24

Chapter Five

Idris lifted a large orange tote box containing fifty medication parcels which he – and only he – was responsible for delivering to Pavilion Mews.

'Here,' said Vanessa, handing him a magnetic vehicle tracking device, which was warm to the touch. 'It's fully charged.'

'Thanks,' he replied, taking it from her and placing in the tote.

Vanessa pulled him discreetly to one side and lowered her voice.

'Jahangir was rude to staff yesterday. Can you have a word again? I don't understand why we need to put up with his shit.'

Christ, if only she knew, thought Idris.

He placed the parcel into the tote box, smiled at her and simply said, 'Sure.'

Seeing that it was raining outside, Idris slipped on a heavy raincoat, and pulled a waterproof sheet over the tote box.

He was set to leave when Daniel Fury entered the pharmacy, his clothes dripping wet, having been caught in the downpour. He brushed excess water from his coat, walked to the counter and slammed a thoroughly drenched blue script on it, hints of a dark tattoo creeping over his knuckles.

Jemma glanced at the script and shook her head. 'We can't accept that. It's ruined.'

Daniel fixed her with a cold stare, veins on the side of his temple bulging as his face tensed. 'It's raining outside.'

This time when Jemma spoke, her words were a little shaky. 'I know. But that script is unreadable. You'll have to get another.'

'You want me to walk three miles back to Armley, in this rain, and get a new script? Are you daft? Let's say I did that. It'd still be raining, meaning the new script would also be ruined.'

Idris moved to the counter, stood beside Jemma in solidarity, ready to intervene.

'Daniel, Jemma is only doing . . .'

Daniel didn't look at Idris, just raised his hand and stuck it right in front of Idris's face, keeping his pernicious gaze on Jemma.

'I'm. Talking. To. Jemma,' he said slowly, purposefully, still without looking at Idris.

This was Daniel through and through.

Angry. Edgy.

Jemma stood her ground.

'The law is the law, Daniel. If we dispense from that, we'd be breaking it.'

'Breaking the law,' whispered Daniel to himself, mocking her. 'Tell you what, Jemma, I'll leave that shitty script here and go outside and score some shitty street heroin. But first I'll need money so I'll rob some little old dear who was on her way to buy some milk from the supermarket so she could brew a tea while watching Judge Rinder. I'll traumatise the poor cow, get nicked, fuck my probation and end up back in a cell but you, Jemma, you'll still be here, acting like the pompous bitch that you are.'

Jemma shoved the blue script back across the counter, turned to Idris angrily and said, 'This is why nobody wants to serve him. You deal with it.'

Jemma stormed off, leaving Idris one on one with Daniel.

'That was rude,' said Idris.

Daniel stood stoic, water still dripping from his coat onto the floor.

'Apologise to Jemma and I'll sort you a new script.'

Daniel thought on this for a beat, weighing up his options. Then, he looked to where Jemma was in the dispensary and shouted, 'Sorry for calling you a bitch,' before retreating and taking a seat in the waiting area.

Outside the pharmacy, Idris loaded the tote into the boot of his car, next to two large cardboard boxes of PPE which were also intended for The Mews. Then he dropped to his knees and attached the magnetic tracking device to the underside of the vehicle. It was an insurance requirement, nothing more.

He saw a taxi pull up outside the pharmacy and a familiar care worker leaped out and rushed towards his pharmacy.

A new blue prescription for Daniel.

Idris hadn't waited for it to arrive, and had just given Daniel his dose of supervised methadone, technically breaking the law.

He was distracted by the sound of Daniel's voice behind him.

'Thanks for sorting that. You off to The Mews?' said Daniel.

Idris looked at him and nodded.

'Grab a lift?'

'Depends.'

'On what?'

Daniel opened the passenger door and Idris said, 'On whether you're going to call me a bitch.'

'As my former brother-in-law, I'm thinking that if I did, it'd probably be warranted.'

The drive to The Mews took around twenty minutes and for the first ten, neither Idris nor Daniel said a word.

'Why'd you act like that?' said Idris finally.

'You know why.'

'Jemma isn't in a position of power. She's not part of the system.'

'Everyone's part of the system. Including you. Standing over me, watching me drink methadone like I'm a five-year-old. Fuck that and fuck you.'

Idris sighed and tried to change the topic. 'You seen Rebecca lately?' he asked.

'You know I haven't. You're the only one who sees her these days.'

'For her methadone,' said Idris defensively.

Daniel laughed mockingly. 'Not even you're dumb enough to believe that.'

'It's true.'

Idris could feel Daniel's gaze piercing the side of his face. 'All the chemists in the world and your ex-wife chooses you. What's she on nowadays? Twenty millilitres? Ten? That isn't a dose. It's a ploy so you can keep seeing each other.'

Idris fell silent. Because deep down, he knew it was true. 'She's still part of your family.'

'Only family I got is the green stuff and the odd needle when I need it.'

'Christ, man, you got people in your life. You just got to engage.'

'You mean apologise.'

'Maybe. What's wrong with that?'

'I tried to help Rebecca.'

'You gave her the needle,' snapped Idris.

Daniel slammed his hands on the dash and then unceremoniously pulled on the handbrake forcing the car to a halt.

'Are you crazy?' said Idris, annoyed.

Daniel opened the door and got out. 'The hell with you, Idris,' he said, slamming it closed.

Idris pursed his lips and exhaled deeply, watching Daniel disappear inside The Mews.

'You've got people who still care,' whispered Idris, aggrieved and drove towards the entrance, pulling up outside.

Ahead of him were high-rise tower blocks to each side of a winding road which stretched deep into The Mews. There was only one way in and the entrance, as ever, was covered by thirteen-year-old Samir, a wiry Middle Eastern boy with a toughness to him which was years ahead of his age. He was sitting comically on an orange sun lounger and on seeing Idris, hopped off it and walked coolly across.

Idris lowered the driver's side window. 'Morning, Samir.'

'Good morning, Mr Chemist.'

'Twenty-two parcels. Blocks A to E.'

Samir scribbled it down inside a scruffy notebook, removed his mobile phone and dialled a number, speaking bluntly as soon as the call connected.

'Chemist coming in. A to E.'

Another young boy rushed across to Samir and whispered something in his ear.

Samir stepped away from Idris's car then unashamedly slapped the boy across the face, forcing him to fall chaotically to ground.

'You lose a wrap, you pay for it,' snapped Samir. He kicked the kid, who hurriedly got to his feet, nodded respectfully, then disappeared inside The Mews. The change in Samir's demeanour was frightening and instantaneous. He was as hardened as any of Idris's blue scripts.

Samir walked to his sun lounger, pushed it aside and allowed Idris to drive into The Mews.

Idris parked in the centre of the courtyard, got out of the car and looked around anxiously before opening the boot. He removed the tote box full of prescriptions, an electronic signature device and one of the boxes of PPE. He placed everything on the ground, closed the boot and scanned the area.

The Mews was full of activity – teenage boys running product into the towers. They had been constructed in the 1980s and looked like they should have been demolished years ago. Towering, nightmarish ruins with rising damp visible across external walls. Dozens of windows were boarded over and on almost every balcony, clothes had been hung out to dry.

There was graffiti everywhere – one key message repetitive and unambiguous painted in bold red: VIDEO THE TOWERS, YOU LOSE THE PHONE AND A FINGER . . .

Samir ran across to Idris, and stopped him from starting his deliveries.

'Mr Idris, what for me today, please?' he asked, politely.

Idris kicked the box of PPE. 'First things first, Samir, how many boxes of PPE do you want? One or two? I've another in the car.'

'Just one. I will take to Jahangir later, no problem. So, give me a riddle. Today, I am sure I will solve it,' he said excitedly.

Idris took a moment, faked being a little stuck then nodded theatrically.

'Samir, you're in a race and you pass the person in second place. What place are you in now?'

Idris started a thirty-second timer on his watch.

Samir grinned, took a few beats then said, 'Easy. If I pass the person in second, then I'm in first place.'

Idris frowned and said, 'Eighteen seconds left. Use them. Listen again.'

Idris put the tote box down, crouched to be at eye level with Samir. 'Think about it. You're in a race and *you pass the person in second place*. What place are you in now?'

Samir kept his eyes on Idris who could see the boy was desperately replaying the riddle in his mind.

Samir smiled just as Idris's watch started to bleep.

'Time's up,' said Idris.

'If I pass the person in second place, then I am now in second place not first.'

Idris ruffled the boy's hair, and stood up.

'What for me today, then?' asked Samir again.

Idris removed a small bar of chocolate from his pocket and handed it to the boy.

'Samir, you run the courtyard to The Mews. Earn good money but still always want a chocolate bar from me. Why?'

Samir smiled. 'Because it is free. Free is good. And your riddles keep me sharp. One day, maybe like you, I also become a chemist.'

'To become a chemist, you need to go to school. Pass exams.'

Samir slipped his hand in his pocket and pulled out several sleeves of street heroin and a large bottle of blue pills which, to Idris, looked to be diazepam, a popular drug abused by addicts.

'What you need, Mr Idris? I am a street chemist.'

Idris picked up his tote, ready to set off on his delivery round.

Samir's phone rang and he answered, listened to the short instruction and then waved for Idris to stop.

Samir closed the gap, lowered his voice, his tone now serious, solemn. 'Mr Idris, Jahangir wants to see you before you start your round. He is not happy.'

Chapter Six

Jahangir Hosseini stood on the roof of tower block A, the first one located inside The Mews, and stared across his vast kingdom.

While for many, The Mews was a jungle, full of drug addicts, ex-convicts and illegal immigrants, for Jahangir it was simply home.

He was comfortable here, festering in other people's misery. Being cruel came easily to Jahangir, something which had served him well throughout his lengthy incarcerations, in tough prisons in Syria. As far as Jahangir was concerned, life was about the survival of the cruellest. Once people knew what he was capable of, they usually fell in behind him.

When the war had kicked off in Syria, the prison he had been inside had been attacked. All the prisoners had escaped. Jahangir was one of three brothers, all of them incarcerated at the same time and all of them on life sentences for murder.

Now, they controlled the immigrant routes from Syria into the UK.

His oldest brother, Jawat, had remained in Syria. Next in line was Mawt who ran their operations in Calais, which left The Mews for Jahangir.

Each time a new international conflict ignited, the Hosseini family knew the refugees would come. They were new types of warlords, preying on people's vulnerabilities, promising them kindness – money, food, accommodation, but ultimately, the only thing they delivered was a lifetime's addiction to heroin.

The trade here was simple, cocaine, marijuana and mostly heroin. The narcotics came from Afghanistan, through Turkey, across Europe to France and then on boat crossings from Calais into Dover. From there, they made their way to The Mews.

Jahangir had ruled here for five years now; it was the most coveted location for anyone who dealt in drugs.

He had only one competitor, Thomas Mead, head of the other notorious cartel family in Yorkshire. Their respective crews clashed frequently on the streets, and Jahangir was constantly having to defend The Mews from possible infiltration.

While Jahangir had only a fraction of the footprint Thomas did, The Mews was the base for a regional drug empire with a gross annual turnover of £500 million. Thomas Mead had twice the geographical footprint but did not come near to that level of influence.

The Mews, the ultimate location for any kingpin.

Jahangir glanced below into the sprawling courtyard to see that The Chemist had arrived. His focus was distracted by the teenage boys dealing product. As soon as a transaction was complete, they would go back to playing football, celebrating scoring goals like they were world superstars.

He eyed them greedily, feeling a little aroused; they were superstars – *his little superstars.*

Idris waited outside Jahangir's door. He could hear a conversation being spoken in Arabic, the sound of Jahangir's deep, vulgar laugh and then finally, Idris heard his name being called.

He stepped inside to find Jahangir sitting shirtless on his bed, counting a large stack of cash. A cigarette burned in an ashtray and there were several half-eaten takeaway containers on a decrepit-looking table.

Jahangir's henchmen, two thugs called Elyas and Majid, were in the corner of the room, dressed in white PPE gowns, cutting pure heroin with a bulking agent, to create five- and ten-pound heroin wraps.

Al-Noor was also there, waiting obediently, eyes on the money, seemingly counting along with Jahangir.

Jahangir peeled off a couple of ten-pound notes and handed them to Al-Noor, who accepted them and duly left the room, nodding at Idris politely as he walked out.

'Chemist, I need an inhaler. My chest is tighter than a baby's asshole before it takes its first shit,' said Jahangir and started to laugh, his eyes never leaving the money which he continued to sort.

'It'll be with you tomorrow,' replied Idris, wanting to leave.

'Money?'

Begrudgingly, Idris put his hand in his pocket and removed five hundred pounds in crisp twenty-pound notes. He stepped forward and put them on the bed next to Jahangir.

'Five hundred.'

Jahangir grabbed the cash, didn't count it and added it to the pile. 'Chemist, Jahangir thinks it is time we negotiate a new deal.'

Not wanting to sound desperate, Idris replied respectfully even though he thought the demand was absurd. 'What were you thinking?' he said.

'One thousand. From next month.'

Idris grimaced, kept his cool and replied, 'I can't afford double.'

'Maybe I find a new chemist then?'

'Maybe you do,' said Idris, feeling that if he didn't push back, more demands would arrive and in much shorter periods of time.

Jahangir looked at Idris, annoyed but also surprised.

Idris held his gaze. If he'd learned anything working inside The Mews, it was that when challenged you didn't look away.

Jahangir smiled. 'How much do you think we should settle on?'

'I think that five hundred is plenty. People trust me. I know the rules. A new chemist will take time to fit in here and might not be able to do the job. If you feel like the deal we have is not a fair one, then I accept you will find someone else, but I can't increase the money. Times are tight for me.'

Idris was bluffing. His thoughts went to the dozens of final demand letters he avoided opening.

Shit, if he lost The Mews, his business was done.

The methadone supervisions and the additional scripts he delivered to The Mews accounted for a significant proportion of his business.

'Seven fifty,' said Jahangir. Idris realised that this wasn't really about the money. Jahangir must have had ten grand sitting on his bed.

This was about power.

'OK,' said Idris, just wanting to get on with his round.

'Good. We backdate to this month so tomorrow, on your round, you bring Jahangir an extra two fifty.'

What a bastard, thought Idris.

Truthfully, he doubted that he had ever hated a man more than Jahangir.

Idris turned to leave again.

'Hey, Chemist,' said Jahangir just as Idris reached the door. He stopped. Waited.

'Tomorrow, remember. My inhaler,' he said.

Chapter Seven

At eight thirty, Idris locked the main doors to the pharmacy and opened the out of hours emergency hatch, a separate cubicle accessible from outside but which didn't allow patients into the main floorspace. A thick protective glass screen separated Idris from the customer much like a cashier inside a bank. He'd never had any problems but since he serviced The Mews, the hatch ensured that working until 11 p.m. would not compromise his safety.

The daily methadone measure or, as Idris called it, game time.

Idris meticulously lined up over a hundred glass medicine bottles on the dispensary bench, in perfect symmetry, and filled the Methasimple machine, an ingenious device which automatically measured doses of methadone. With classical music playing softly, Idris got to work, preparing the following day's doses for The Mews addicts.

Each dose would be signed, bagged and the blue script attached to it, ready for the patient the following day.

It was an immense task, taking real concentration. Spillages of methadone were not acceptable, anything over a few millilitres needed witnessing by a police officer.

*

Two hours and several cups of coffee later, Idris was exhausted.

He thundered into a chair, closed his eyes, taking a few minutes' rest. It wasn't a physically demanding job, but the attention needed to ensure the doses were correct was mentally taxing.

Idris rubbed his eyes and rested his head on the back of the chair, slouching a little to make himself more comfortable. His thoughts inevitably went to Jahangir.

Another two hundred and fifty a month.

Always cash.

Always untraceable.

Idris was breaching every rule of owning a pharmacy by having entered into a financial agreement with Jahangir who might have been many things, but first and foremost was Idris's patient.

He remembered the inhaler Jahangir had requested, moved to his computer and emailed an order to the surgery.

With closing time approaching, Idris placed the completed measures of methadone into five large yellow trays and secured each one inside a controlled drug cabinet, bolted securely to the wall.

He then started the worst job of the day: completing the record keeping of methadone doses which addicts had collected.

There was a faster electronic way of doing this but Idris preferred pen and paper. It reminded him who had and had not collected.

A few minutes before 11 p.m., Idris was finished. He put the kettle on, lined up two empty mugs and put a teabag in each one.

She was normally here by now.

Idris glanced to the bench where a solitary blue prescription remained attached to a small parcel. The name on the script said, REBECCA FURY.

Idris checked the time again: 23.01.

Dismayed, he picked up his phone, accessed his favourites and dialled Rebecca's number. It went straight to voicemail.

That was unusual. Rebecca hadn't missed her methadone in over a decade, albeit, what she was prescribed wasn't really therapeutic – a mere 15mls.

While neither Idris nor Rebecca had ever spoken of it, they both knew that she attended the pharmacy each day to see Idris.

Most men might have hated their ex-wives, but Idris was not part of that gang.

Much like Rebecca, he too looked forward to seeing her, both of them still comfortable with each other.

Idris tried to call her again. Nothing.

'Goddamn it, get off the streets, woman. You can't save them all,' he whispered to himself.

At 23.15, Idris unfolded Rebecca's blue prescription and, on the side, where pharmacists had to sign that they had supervised a dose, he wrote three letters he always hated.

DNA. *Did not attend.*

Idris was in the middle of securing Rebecca's dose in the cabinet when he paused.

This wasn't like her. In fact, this was totally out of character.

Idris changed his mind. He returned to the script and crossed out the DNA.

He slipped the bottle of methadone in his pocket, grabbed his keys and headed out of the pharmacy.

Chapter Eight

Driving through the red-light district in Beeston felt surreal after the vibrancy and bright lights of Headingley.

This specific area was all about despair – abandoned warehouses, aggressive graffiti tags and everywhere he looked, Idris saw shadows and secrets. The only illumination came from some of the neon outfits the sex workers were wearing.

Idris ignored the lurid appeals from girls who tried to flag down his car and parked outside TEP – The Elizabeth Projects.

He waited a while, observing the dozens of vehicles frequenting the area. Some were clearly habitual visitors, several girls feigning excitement at seeing their regulars.

It was the newbies who got Idris's attention – those punters who drove slowly, watching, and then veered away too afraid to engage. He wondered which event in their lives would make them transition from window shopper to actual punter.

Idris approached the front door of TEP and tried it.

Locked. Lights off.

A CCTV camera, high up on the external wall, rotated slowly towards him.

Idris veered away from the building, towards the road, calm, assured of his presence here. He knew most of the girls because they were on his books for methadone and the majority lived inside The Mews.

He saw Clare Glass, whom he had supplied methadone to a few hours before. While many of the girls tried hard with their appearances, Clare didn't give a flying fuckeroo. She had a perpetual snarl across her face, reeked of marijuana and Idris genuinely could not understand how anyone could pay her for sex. The streets had made her bitter and the more she worked, the angrier she became.

'Have you seen Rebecca?' asked Idris.

Clare ignored his question and simply said, 'Slow night.'

Idris sighed. 'Seriously, Clare?'

'Got bills to pay.' She nodded towards a young girl who was in conversation with a taxi driver. 'Can't compete with these young 'uns.' She smiled, her teeth long ago rotten by her drug use.

'Bet it's like shaggin' a corpse. He'll have a shit punt and come back to Clare. They always come back home.'

Idris, familiar with Clare's lewd personality, removed a ten-pound note from his pocket. She looked at it, disinterested.

'Thought you chemists were rich, like.'

'Don't mess about, Clare. A tenner to answer a few questions is better than some limp cock in your mouth.'

'No one's cock is limp in here.' She turned her face to Idris, stuck her tongue in the side of her cheek and mimicked giving a blowjob.

Idris put the tenner in his pocket and removed a twenty.

Clare tried to take it from him, but Idris moved his hand away.

'Rebecca?'

'She was out here earlier, bein' a nosy cow, trying to save the world one hooker at a time.'

She eyed the money in Idris's hand, greedily.

He handed it over and Clare stuffed it inside her pocket before removing a crumpled-up packet of cigarettes. She lit one, took a drag and blew smoke in Idris's face.

'Yer know, all these years I been comin' to you for meth and never once have you ever wanted a good time.'

'You're not my type.'

She flipped him the finger, took another drag on her cigarette.

'It won't take much to take that twenty back off you.'

'I'd like to see you try it, Idris.'

Idris changed the tone of his voice. Harsher now. Tired of her bullshit.

'Then maybe your methadone's a little light tomorrow. Sixty millilitres instead of eighty.'

She smiled. Even though it was a bluff, it got Idris the answer he needed.

'Like I said, she was 'ere, then got called off to some shitshow wit' that new 'un. Amy Starr. Know her?'

Idris nodded.

'She's too young for this game,' said Clare, offering him her cigarette.

Idris declined. 'How long ago did Rebecca leave?'

Clare shrugged. 'Like, what time is it now?'

Idris glanced at his watch. 'Just before midnight.'

'Maybe, like, ten thirty, then.'

'She got a place? This Amy?'

Clare nodded. She glanced at Idris's pocket again.

He folded his arms across his chest and waited.

The silence hung a few seconds and then Clare said, 'Her fella, Liam, got her a share on one of them vacants on Turney Street. Dead man's cul-de-sac. End house. Red door.'

'The Vacants? What's a newbie doing going down there?'

'Free, innit. Loadsa shitty rooms to fuck in.'

Idris sucked his teeth. He didn't want to go there.

'Yer want me to come wiv yer? Fifty quid would do it.'

'I've got this,' said Idris and walked away a little quicker than he had arrived.

The Vacants.

A run-down housing estate, long since abandoned and now a breeding ground for drug dealers and sex workers.

Not quite The Mews but not far away.

The streetlights didn't work, the tarmac on the roads was badly decaying and every single house was boarded up.

Idris saw Rebecca's car outside the house with a red door and pulled in behind her. Parked on the other side of the road was a gleaming BMW with blacked-out windows.

Idris didn't like that; wrong part of town for a car like that.

He tried to call Rebecca but again got her voicemail.

Idris got out of his car.

The doorframe was rotten, multiple holes in it revealing an absolute darkness inside. Idris used the torch on his phone to try and figure out how to open it. The hinges were corroded so Idris stuck out his leg and simply kicked it open.

The torch wasn't powerful enough to provide any clues as to the details of the hallway. He stepped inside, his feet immediately crunching on something metallic. He crouched, shining the torch along the floor and saw it was littered with empty nitrous oxide canisters; the new buzz-drug, cheap to buy and it gave a powerful if short-lived high.

Idris moved to the kitchen. He tried the light and was surprised to find that it worked.

More nitrous oxide.

Used needles, empty condom sleeves, cheap lighter fluid and discarded cans of cider.

Every junkie's dream combination.

There was an entrance into a living room, the door missing, and again shrouded in darkness. Idris moved carefully to the doorway, looking for a light switch and found only naked wires.

Dismayed, he stepped into the space, raised his phone high in front of him and scanned the room.

Again, nothing but clutter and drug paraphernalia.

Then a sudden hand on Idris's shoulder.

He screamed and turned around but he was mistaken, he'd simply veered into some shelving.

'Christ's sake,' he whispered and moved back into the hallway.

He looked towards the staircase and was about to call out for Rebecca when he heard voices upstairs.

He called out, his voice shaky, 'Rebecca? You up there? It's Idris.'

Silence.

Had he heard voices or was he imagining it?

Slowly, he crept upstairs, taking them two at a time, adrenalin coursing through his veins.

More crunching on metallic canisters.

The landing was unremarkable – a diseased wilting carpet, a ceiling covered in damp and litter everywhere.

What kind of desperate freak wanted to have sex with someone in a nightmarish space like this?

There was a lone door at the end of the landing. Idris pushed it open and stepped inside.

Blood.

Pooled on the floor and glimmering in the moonlight which snaked its way through a cracked windowpane.

Quiet sobbing came from the corner, where Idris saw Rebecca, her arms wrapped protectively around the child-like body of Amy Starr, both women huddled on a bed with blood splatters across their bodies.

Lying in the middle of floor was the body of an obese, clearly dead white male, a knife sticking out of his back.

Idris breathed out slowly, trying not to panic.

Carefully, he moved towards the bed, kneeling in front of Rebecca. Her eyes were wide, almost glaring at him. Messy dark hair was strewn across her face and her lip was bleeding.

Idris asked her the only question he immediately needed an answer to.

'You? Or . . .'

He nodded at Amy.

Rebecca didn't need to reply; her eyes screamed a truth Idris desperately didn't want to believe.

Slowly, he put her hand in his, grasped it tightly and said, 'I'm here. I've got you.'

Rebecca's eyes darted to a wallet lying on the bed. She nodded towards it, her teeth chattering.

Idris grabbed it but it was too dark to examine the contents, so he took it across to the window and used the moonlight. Expensive leather, bursting with cash – mostly fifties.

He removed the driving licence and stared at it in disbelief.

Idris brought it closer to his face, almost believing his eyes were playing tricks on him, then glanced back at the victim, hoping to learn something which contradicted the evidence in his hand.

It made it only more conclusive.

He turned to Rebecca, horrified.

'What the hell have you done?' he whispered.

Chapter Nine

They had made their way to the kitchen and Idris was slouched in a chair, head in his hands, trying to figure out what to do next.

Opposite him, crying quietly, Amy was being comforted by Rebecca. If they didn't calm the girl down, they'd lost already.

'Idris, just go. We'll call the police,' said Rebecca but there was little conviction in her voice.

She wanted Idris to stay; *needed him to*.

Idris scratched five-day-old stubble on his face and looked at her, serious, focused.

'He's Patrick Mead, the biggest kingpin in Yorkshire. Nobody is walking away from this unless we cover it up. You know how this will go. They'll find you, then Amy, then me.'

Rebecca's eyes darted between him and Amy, imploring him to stop talking.

Idris shook his head. 'She needs to hear this.'

'We need to calm her down first,' said Rebecca.

Idris removed Rebecca's dose of methadone from his pocket and slid it across the table.

Rebecca looked at it, surprised.

'You don't miss doses, that's what got me here,' said Idris, nodding at the bottle.

Rebecca picked it up, unscrewed the cap and gave it to Amy. 'Here. Take this sweetheart. It'll take the edge off.'

Amy hesitated a second, glancing between Rebecca and Idris. 'What's in it?'

'Fifteen millilitres of methadone,' said Idris.

Amy looked at him distrustfully.

'I'm your chemist, for God's sake. I'm hardly about to poison you. Drink it.'

Amy did so.

A half hour later, with Amy now a touch calmer, the plan was set – one which Rebecca didn't like. She and Idris had moved into the hallway to continue an argument they'd been having for the last few minutes.

'Enough already,' snapped Idris.

Rebecca was equally short-tempered. 'This is madness!'

'No. Madness is thinking they won't come for us.' Idris grasped her hand. 'It's already in play. Out there somewhere, one of the Mead family is wondering where their recently released from prison, fuck-up of a family member is. We clean the scene, you take Amy some place safe and I'll . . . do the rest.'

Rebecca sighed. She pressed the palms of her hands against her eyes and groaned. 'God, what have I done?'

Idris said nothing.

Rebecca continued, reliving the night's events. 'Amy called me, panicked, in a mess. I got here and he was . . . forcing himself on her. He had the knife at her neck.'

She stopped talking but Idris could figure the rest of it out.

Rebecca moved her hands away from her face and stared at him, a deep rage brewing behind her eyes.

'I just went back to . . . to . . .'

Idris held her face in his hands. 'Let's not do this now. I've got you. Trust me, that's all you need to do.'

'You know I trust you. I just can't put you at risk, you're all I've got.'

'Then do what I say. Help me,' said Idris and told her exactly what they were going to do.

Outside now, Idris worked quickly.

The Vacants remained deserted but Idris was afraid that another working girl would soon arrive with a punter and discover what he was attempting to do.

He opened the boot of his car, thankful to see the lone box of PPE which Samir had not taken from him inside The Mews.

Idris lifted it, setting it down on the pavement and with the cover of darkness, stripped out of his clothes to his underwear and then changed into a full body PPE gown, including gloves and plastic shoe wraps. He had lifted Patrick's car keys from the dead man's trouser pocket and now used them to get inside the BMW.

Idris slipped into the driver's seat.

A discreet dashcam was attached to the windscreen. Idris immediately disconnected it then searched the rest of the vehicle.

Nothing.

Satisfied, he pushed the car's boot-release button then went to inspect it.

Shivering in the bitter cold, the plastic gown providing little cover, Idris stared at a large black bag in the corner of the boot.

He pulled it towards him, wincing at the weight of it.

Unzipping it, Idris looked inside and found it to be full of cash.

'Shit,' he whispered.

It appeared that Patrick had either been on his way to pay somebody, or since they were talking about the Mead family, more likely, he had just collected it.

Idris zipped the bag closed, took it with him and secured it in the boot of his own car. If Rebecca and Amy needed to run, the cash might give them a fighting chance.

Inside the bedroom, Idris dropped the box of PPE on the floor.

'Strip,' he said to both women.

They had been briefed on the plan and immediately started to remove their clothes.

'Not your underwear,' he said to Amy who had taken his direction literally.

He handed them both thick PPE gowns, waited until they had put them on.

'Anything which puts you here – hair, clothes, items with prints on – lift it and put it in this.'

He handed them a large PPE waste disposal bag used for soiled garments.

Amy didn't move.

'Problem?' asked Idris.

'He was . . . you know . . . inside me. Some of me is gonna be on his . . .'

'Don't worry about that.'

'But . . .'

'I said don't worry about that. I'll sort it.'

Rebecca took Amy gently by the arm. 'Trust him, Amy. He's smart. Idris knows what he is doing.'

Amy shook her head. 'Like how? He's just a chemist.'

Rebecca shared a nervous glance with Idris. 'He just does. Come on, we've work to do.'

51

Thirty minutes later, having cleaned as best they could, Idris stood by the open doorway and examined the room.

It wasn't good enough.

The room was a chaotic shit hole and there was no telling if hair, blood or other traces of DNA might still be lingering.

An option Idris had not wanted to explore was now the only one he had.

Rebecca slipped into the room. 'We're ready,' she whispered.

'You go. I've got to do more.'

'More?'

He stared at her, cold, animalistic, until she got it. 'More,' he repeated.

'Let me help you,' she said.

'Can't have you anywhere near this. They can link you to Amy through work. Like Amy said earlier, I'm just The Chemist. Nothing links me to this part of town.'

He crouched, removed a piece of PPE from the box and handed it to her. 'Put this across your number plates, it'll mean ANPR can't read them. Do the same to my car.'

She took the PPE from him. 'I'm scared to leave you.'

'Get the girl safe. She's our weakest link. She folds and we're both done. Can you do that?'

Rebecca nodded, determined, and then for no other reason than she needed to, moved towards Idris, and kissed him.

'I'm sorry, I just . . .'

Idris put his arms around her and hugged her, comfortable, familiar, *secure*.

Idris was standing by the window, watching as Rebecca carefully fixed the PPE across hers and Idris's number plates and then got into her car and drove away.

He sat on the bed, his PPE gown slippery against the mattress. He stared at Patrick's body, at the knife still in his back.

Idris needed to remove the weapon.

On the floor by his side was a box of nitrous oxide – NOS canisters he'd lifted from the kitchen, along with a can of cheap lighter fluid; standard items in a drug den to give junkies quick highs.

NOS was highly combustible and would ensure that the fire Idris was about to start would burn red hot and hopefully obliterate every piece of DNA left in the room.

Not the blade, though; steel needed a much higher melting point.

Crouched over Patrick's body, Idris grabbed the handle of the knife firmly, took a moment to compose himself and then in one clean movement, pulled it free.

He stared at the blade, blood dripping from it, and suppressed an urge to vomit. Quickly, he wiped it on the side of the mattress then slipped the knife into a PPE disposal bag which also contained Rebecca's, Amy's and his own clothes.

He then placed dozens of NOS canisters around Patrick's body.

Now, for the final and most difficult part.

Idris crouched by Patrick's face and carefully forced his mouth open, glad that rigor mortis had not yet set in. He pushed a canister inside Patrick's mouth, knowing that once the fire was raging, this specific canister would ignite and blow Patrick's jaw to pieces, hopefully making dental identification impossible.

Idris pushed Patrick's mouth closed, the sound of his teeth hitting each other making Idris shudder.

Finally, Idris poured lighter fluid in a trail from Patrick's body to the bedroom door.

He used a lighter he had taken from Amy to set it alight then grabbed the bag of soiled PPE and walked out of the room.

Chapter Ten

Outside, Idris hurriedly accessed Patrick's car again and poured the remainder of the lighter fluid inside, also throwing in a dozen canisters of nitrous oxide before setting everything alight.

He got into his car, drove a short distance and pulled over, now looking in his rear-view mirror. A few minutes later he saw the flames inside the house, almost at the same time as Patrick's car exploded.

Idris pulled away from The Vacants, hoping that he had done enough to cover his tracks.

He kept to the side roads which, he hoped, wouldn't be covered by traffic cameras. He knew the clear plastic across his number plates would ensure ANPR could not decipher his vehicle registration, having gleaned the trick from one of his blue scripts.

Idris cut through north Leeds quickly, the late-night hour providing little traffic resistance, and arrived in Kirkstall, at the twenty-four-hour gym he was a member of. He parked in a corner of the car park, a row of trees shielding his car in darkness.

Idris opened the boot and removed his gym bag, hurriedly changing into his sports gear. He stuffed the PPE he had been wearing into a PPE disposal bag then carefully removed the knife. He wrapped it in a new piece of plastic before slipping it inside his gym bag.

This late-night trip was all about the knife.

Idris entered the gym, wearing a face mask, and swiped his access card through the reader, logging his entry, giving him an alibi.

Inside the changing rooms, he put on his swimming shorts, concealing the knife inside a towel, and made his way to the wet area of the gymnasium. The pool was deserted and while there were several men inside the jacuzzi, the place Idris needed to be, the steam room, was empty.

Idris threw some cold water onto the sensor, ensuring piping hot steam would pour into the room, and sat by the steam inlet, one foot either side of it. Carefully, he removed the knife from the towel and held it in front of the outlet so that the steam thoroughly cleansed the blade and with it, any traces of DNA.

Idris rested the blade on the tiles, balancing it against the outlet, and tried to relax. He closed his eyes, wondering whether this might be the last time he had any peace.

Rebecca.

Anyone but Rebecca.

Their history was a chaotic one.

They had met at thirteen inside the corner shop his parents had once owned. Rebecca had been one of the paper girls and quickly caught Idris's eye. She was from a tough travelling family, and he had been taken by how fierce she was – red hair, redder temper.

By fourteen they were dating and by nineteen they were married. For six perfect years, until a tragedy had changed everything.

Images of Idris cradling a stillborn flashed across his mind;

Rebecca screaming in agony as the midwife administered drugs to sedate her.

Idris opened his eyes, breathing heavily, the intense heat of the room was making it hard to breathe.

He got to his feet and stumbled, the sound of the knife clattering onto the tiles behind him.

He was going to faint.

Idris dropped to his knees and crawled towards the door, pushing it open and almost collapsing in the doorway

He heard shouts from nearby – the men in the jacuzzi – and looked towards them, his vision still fuzzy, and saw them hurrying towards him.

Christ, company. This was the last thing he needed.

Idris took large, desperate gasps of cooler air and scrambled onto his knees, waving his hands towards the men, trying to convince them that he was fine.

'Hey, you OK?' said the first guy, arriving by Idris's side.

Idris replied confidently, his voice steady even if his balance was not. 'I'm good, I was just stepping out and slipped. Seriously, no drama.'

The second man simply gave him a thumbs-up and returned to the jacuzzi, satisfied there was no threat to Idris's safety.

'Too hot in there, stripped the brown right off my face,' said Idris.

The first man laughed, and Idris put his fist out for a bump which was duly honoured.

Idris regained his composure and returned to the steam room.

At 2 a.m. Idris arrived home, later than usual, but knew his wife Mariam would be asleep. She had got used to the fact that Idris was a perpetual night owl.

Idris carried his gym bag, containing the soiled PPE and the knife, into the garage and threw it into the corner, then returned to the kitchen looking for the one thing he needed to ensure that tomorrow he would be able to discard the evidence in a unique, untraceable manner.

Idris found Mariam's handbag on the dining table, opened it and removed her purse, deftly taking her NHS smartcard.

Dr Mariam Khan, general practitioner.

Idris slipped it inside his pocket and walked out of the kitchen.

Tomorrow morning, unbeknown to his wife, she was about to help him incinerate evidence of the murder of one of the most feared men in the north of England.

Idris was certain he'd covered his tracks.

He was wrong.

Chapter Eleven

Rebecca was parked outside Liam's house where Amy was currently staying.

She had spent the last fifteen minutes rigorously convincing Amy that coming here was the right move, yet Amy remained uncertain.

'Everything needs to be normal. You open the door, run into your bedroom, get changed and hide the PPE,' said Rebecca finally.

Amy was fidgeting furiously with her hands, scratching them angrily. 'What if he's in the bedroom?'

'Then you go into the bathroom. Liam is going to be drunk or high, right?'

Amy nodded.

'There you are, then, don't overthink it.'

'Why can't I come home with you?' asked Amy, pleading.

Rebecca felt an increasing pressure inside her head. She needed to get out of here because the façade of calmness she was desperately trying to show Amy was slipping quickly.

Images of blood, the knife, Patrick's dead body swirling through her mind.

'Because it will raise suspicions and we can't have that,' she snapped.

Amy looked at her, ready to cry.

Seeing that the girl was slipping, Rebecca quickly took Amy's face in her hands, reassuring, confident. 'Darling, we're going to have to double down here and be brave. If you tell anyone about what happened tonight, we're all dead. You know who the Mead family are. Everyone does,' said Rebecca.

Amy hugged Rebecca, tight, needy.

Rebecca kissed the side of her face. 'You'll be fine. Just do what I said.'

'Can I call you if I need to?'

'Of course,' replied Rebecca, even though she desperately did not want that.

Amy took a few moments, composed herself and then got out of the car.

Rebecca watched her leave, anxious, afraid. She pulled the car away, praying that Amy would be able to hold it together.

Liam Reynolds finished the spliff he was smoking, necked his can of extra-strength lager and watched Amy get out of Rebecca's car.

Her first night as a working girl and she had called that interfering bitch, Rebecca.

Her punt must have got heated.

Amy should have called *him*.

Liam could deal with men who wanted to use their fists rather than their cocks. All it really meant was a hike in the price they paid and ensuring they didn't break any bones. Scars healed quickly but more serious injuries meant his girls coming off the streets.

Rebecca intervening meant that Amy might not have earned anything. Liam unbuckled his belt, removed it and held it by his side.

The front door opened. He could hear Amy taking off her heels then she immediately ran upstairs. He heard the shower being switched on and the bathroom door slamming closed.

Maybe the daft cow had earned a few quid after all.

Liam lit another joint, grabbed a fresh can of beer and waited.

Amy leaned against the bathroom door, relieved she hadn't seen Liam. She removed her coat, then peeled the PPE from her clammy skin and stuffed it inside the bin. She jumped in the shower and yelped.

Cold water.

'Shit,' she cried, darting out of it.

Liam obviously hadn't topped up their gas meter, again. Yet she bet there was a new eight-pack of beer downstairs.

Amy forced herself back inside the shower, she had to get clean.

She scrubbed her skin hard – trying to rid herself of the stink of Patrick Mead.

What the hell had she and Rebecca done?

Patrick Mead was a notorious gangster which meant he would have dangerous connections. Soon, when his family realised he had been murdered, they would surely come looking for those responsible.

Even though Amy had not been the one to stab him, *she* had called Rebecca, and together they had covered up his murder.

Amy turned the cold water off and jumped out of the shower, grabbing a towel, and was dismayed to find that it was damp.

She buried her face into it and released a furious scream.

Why didn't anything work in this house!

She dried herself, wrapped the towel around her and

unlocked the door to find Liam standing there, holding a can of beer, his eyes bloodshot red.

He leered at her.

'Did yer break yer cherry?' he said, a slight slur to his words.

Amy nodded. 'I was, just, you know . . . washing.'

Liam made a gesture for money with his hands and smiled wickedly.

Christ. *The money*. She had meant to ask Rebecca for some.

'I . . . I . . . haven't got any. He tried to rape me. I had to call Rebecca,' she said, panicking.

'I saw.'

The leer vanished from Liam's face, instantly replaced by a look of deep annoyance.

'Babes, he was, like proper mental. Had a knife and everything. Wanted to cut me!'

'So?'

'What?' she said, incredulous.

'I said, so what? He wants to get a little freaky, what do you do?' Liam glared at her, awaiting a response.

'I charge more,' whispered Amy.

'You charge more. So, let's us get this right, you 'ad a golden ticket wiv someone we could 'ave done propa business wiv, got propa cash and you called Rebecca?'

Liam removed his hand from behind his back to reveal he was holding his belt.

'No, Liam, that isn't fair,' she said, desperately wishing that she wasn't naked. The belt hurt when she was fully clothed. It would strip the skin from her bones now.

'Fair? I give you a roof over yer head, food, tries to help you make a little money . . .'

'By pimping me out!'

Liam slapped her, sending Amy's head a full ninety degrees

to the side. She tripped over a bathmat and went crashing to the floor.

'What did you call me?' he said, stepping into the room.

Amy scrambled for her coat and slipped it on, needing to put layers between her and the belt.

'Please, Liam. I'll be good to you. I'll do whatever you want. Be, like, propa good to you.'

'A fuck? That's what you think I want?'

'I don't know what you want,' she said, trying not to cry.

He pointed at her, the swaying of his body a little more exaggerated now that he wasn't leaning against the door. 'What I want is money, little girl. Same thing the other girls give me. I look after you better than them. Know why?'

Amy shook her head and hunched her knees towards her chest, trying to make her body smaller and leave only her arms and legs exposed to the belt.

''Cos, I love you, Amy.'

'And I loves you too, Liam. Like propa love. Like . . . I want to get married and shit and 'ave babies wiv you kinda love.'

He smiled at her but did not drop the belt.

With sudden, devastating ferocity he lashed the belt at her, striking her arm.

Amy screamed, her eyes wide and terrified as Liam recoiled the belt ready for another go.

Desperate, Amy pulled her phone free from her coat pocket and waved it at Liam. 'Look! I . . . got something to show you! Something, like, we can use,' she screamed.

Liam raised the belt for another swing.

Amy quickly accessed the video library on her phone, raised the handset high above her head and showed Liam the clip she had secretly taken at The Vacants.

A clip of Rebecca stabbing Patrick to death.

A clip nobody knew anything about.

Liam glanced at it, then dropped his belt. He took the phone from Amy, holding it in front of his face, mesmerised.

Liam sank to his knees and now lovingly wiped tears away from Amy's face.

'Baby girl, you just made sure that you and I are never hittin' dem streets ever again.'

Chapter Twelve

Idris opened his eyes to be met by the beautiful green eyes of his wife, Mariam, who was staring at him.

'Must have been some dream you were having,' she said, running her hand through his hair, affectionately.

'Was I sleep-talking again?' he asked, wondering if the night's events had just been some vivid nightmare.

She shook her head. 'Just making distressing groaning noises.'

Idris forced a smile. Everything about his marriage was forced. It was a union of convenience borne out of the bullshit that came with both he and Mariam being divorcees, something still seen as a taboo in the South Asian community.

'Maybe you were taking advantage of me in my sleep?' he said.

She laughed and ran her hand under the duvet, down his chest and slipped it inside his boxer shorts.

'And it's not even my birthday,' said Idris. This was the last thing on his mind.

She leaned across the bed and lifted her stethoscope, wrapped it around her neck and shot him a sultry stare. 'Want to start the day with a spring in your step?'

Idris got out of bed, needing to buy himself a little time. 'I'll meet you in the shower. If you're going to take advantage of me, then I'm going to need a coffee first.'

Downstairs in his office, Idris sat at his desk and turned on the computer. While waiting for it to load, he opened a drawer and removed a hidden sleeve of Viagra tablets, quickly popping one into his mouth and washing it down with a glass of water. His marriage had been through a testing couple of years when Idris had discovered that Mariam had been having an affair. Not wanting to be two-time divorcees, they were attending couples therapy sessions. It wasn't working for Idris, and while Mariam was intent on saving their marriage, Idris was simply going through the motions and needed the Viagra when it came to intimacy.

In earnest, he had never fully committed to the marriage; his emotions always with Rebecca which was why, when he had found out about Mariam's affair, he had partially blamed himself.

Idris pulled the laptop closer to him and typed, 'Local Leeds news' and hit search.

He scrolled through multiple hits until he found the one link he was looking for.

BODY FOUND IN BEESTON HOUSE FIRE . . .

Idris clicked on the link and hurriedly read the news article, scrolling through generic details he already knew but little more.

The news was out – nothing he could do now except wait and pray that he'd covered his tracks.

His thoughts went to his bag, hidden in the garage. The cash inside it. The soiled PPE and most importantly, the damn knife.

Idris turned off the computer and headed upstairs, towards the sound of his wife singing in the shower.

Idris walked hurriedly away from his car, past the pharmacy, and stepped inside the adjoining medical centre, carrying his gym bag tight across his shoulder.

On the fourth floor, he used Mariam's NHS keycard to gain access to the medical waste room, which contained large yellow clinical bins, each one able to store over a thousand litres of waste, everything from blood-soiled dressings to used needles. Each bin had a robust one-way chute meaning once an item was deposited, it could not be retrieved.

Idris wheeled one of the bins towards the door blocking it, ensuring that he could not be disturbed, and then set quickly to work.

He removed a pair of gloves from his pocket, slipped them on and dropped to his knees, unzipping his bag. Carefully, he removed the bag of soiled PPE and the knife and proceeded to push both items through the chute of the yellow bin and then, vitally, Idris sealed the bin closed, ensuring no more deposits could be made.

He closed his eyes, and tried not to listen to the voices screaming inside his mind.

What was he doing?

Just call it in. Rebecca acted in self-defence.

But that voice was not nearly as strong as the loudest one.

Patrick Mead. Patrick-fucking-Mead.

Idris removed a black bin liner which contained the money he had taken from Patrick's car. Hurriedly he counted a handful of twenties into a thousand-pound bundle and then guesstimated how many stacks he could make.

Christ, maybe a hundred.

A hundred grand.

His thoughts went to his unpaid drug bills, of the final reminders and threats of court action.

Idris climbed onto a yellow bin, carefully removed a ceiling tile and pushed the bag into the void, before replacing the tile.

He jumped off, realigned everything as it should have been and left.

On his way down the stairs, Idris removed his phone, scrolled to a number and hit 'call'.

He spoke quickly and calmly. 'Good morning – is that Medical Waste Solutions? I'd like to arrange a priority collection of yellow bins.'

Chapter Thirteen

DCI Brian Pitchford was lying in bed, frozen, unable to move, his eyes wide open.

The same position he found himself in every morning.

While he had got used to it, he could still feel his heart racing and his mind, as ever, carried an anxious whisper.

What if it doesn't work today?

What if today is . . . the day?

He had heard his partner, Marcus, on the phone with a HC-MET detective, then heard him writing down details of an incident which required Brian's attention; a dead body had been found at The Vacants.

HC-MET: Homicide and Criminal Major Enquiry Team.

An 'incident' usually meant murder.

Brian's eyes darted across the room, where Marcus was undertaking a routine he did every morning. He watched Marcus open a bottle of tablets – Sandofar dispersible – and dropped four into a tumbler of water, disturbing the glass, encouraging the tablets to dissolve. He grabbed a straw and came across to Brian.

'Here we go,' he said, using one hand to gently lift Brian's head from the pillow and with the other, he ensured the straw found its way into Brian's mouth.

Brian's swallow reflex was still unaffected by his Parkinson's disease, so he was able to drink the solution, albeit slowly.

Marcus lowered Brian's head back onto the pillow, smiled reassuringly and moved back around the bed, slipping beneath the covers and holding Brian's hand reassuringly.

Now, the wait; around forty-five minutes, a time Brian spent the same way every morning, thinking on how he wanted to meet his end.

Aged sixty, he had the rarest of forms of Parkinson's.

Most patients who suffered an overnight seizing of their movements were at the end stages of the disease, unable to work and generally had to rely on full-time carers to assist in their day-to-day living.

Brian was one of only a dozen patients known globally to suffer from an atypical form of the disease. While he had daytime symptoms, his disease largely affected him overnight to the extent that he could not function.

The Sandofar tablets were taken to replace dopamine in the brain, which was the hormone vastly depleted in Parkinson's patients. It also acted as a neurotransmitter and was vital in people being able to move. Once the tablets kicked in, Brian would be able to slowly get himself out of bed and with Marcus's help, shower and get ready for work. His second dose of the tablets was a hefty, slow-release formulation, the medication being released gradually, not an instant hit like the dispersible ones. The effect of these daytime doses generally lasted until he went to bed, ensuring he could keep working as a senior detective.

The clock, though, was ticking.

He had maybe a couple of years left before the disease left him in a wheelchair; before his memory started to fade and he entered a stage of the disease which would painfully strip away every inch of his honour, and force Marcus to stop his own work as a freelance journalist, to ultimately become Brian's full-time carer.

That day would never arrive.

Brian refused to die that way.

While the UK had no routes to assisted dying, the government was discussing opportunities for patients with terminal conditions to choose how they might die.

With dignity, was all Brian cared about.

In control of his own destiny.

He tried to move his fingers, felt them twitching and slowly, applied pressure to Marcus's hand.

The first signs the Sandofar was working.

His mind started to become less fuzzy, his thinking more focused.

A potential homicide at The Vacants.

The first thing Brian thought of was that it must have been a sex worker or an addict. The Vacants were a notorious hot spot for both.

Brian felt a stronger sensation throughout his body and moved his other hand.

And now came a warmth in his face and the ability to slowly smile.

He opened his mouth, and whispered to Marcus the same thing he said every morning, 'Thank you.'

Late in the morning and after finishing his home-based routine of taking pills and gentle physiotherapy, Pitchford arrived at The Vacants in his colleague DS Darcy Black's car. He had surrendered his licence the year before after failing a stringent DVLA medical assessment.

Darcy parked outside the property with the red door, which was teeming with scenes of crime officers.

Pitchford slowly got out and stared in amazement at the house. His movements were slow, measured but stable and he used a cane to support himself when he walked.

The building was structurally intact, just a top-floor window blown out or, more accurately, the wooden board which had been covering it turned to ash. The fire crew had long since gone, releasing the site to the police, leaving a charcoaled mess of rubble, ruin and . . . one dead body.

Pitchford took a brief glance around the area, one detail immediately grabbing his attention.

A burned-out 5 Series BMW was parked across the road and clearly something to do with what had gone on. A car like that didn't end up at The Vacants by chance. Pitchford made an instant, logical deduction – whoever owned the car was the dead person inside. He also reckoned that he'd been a punter or, more likely, a drug dealer. Derisive, perhaps, but after forty years working as a detective, he found these deductions came quickly.

He remained where he was while Darcy logged them in with the uniform officers and then went and spoke to SOCOs, the scenes of crimes officers.

The street was maybe a quarter mile long, thirty or so houses on each side, each one derelict, and seemingly uninhabitable.

'One body, upstairs bedroom,' said Darcy, coming back to him.

'Anything else?'

She nodded towards the BMW. 'Victim's car, I'm betting. Pimp or dealer. Take your pick. Place your bets. Choose your evil.'

A new idea seemed to ping into her mind, and she added, 'Or an out-of-town shmuck, here on business who wanted to get his dick wet before he returned home.'

'Cynical as ever,' he replied, bluntly.

'Being cynical is half the job. Your words, if I remember correctly.'

Pitchford liked Darcy. She was no-nonsense, dressed in the same black suit and white shirt each day, brunette hair tied neatly, and what he loved most about her was that she wasn't a snowflake like so many of the newer officers he had babysat as they climbed the ranks.

She also didn't try and care for him, something apparent in her next statement. 'You going to manage the stairs, or shall I get the fire crew back to crane your wrinkly old ass through the window?'

'Is that your one for the day?' he asked.

'Was pretty soft. If you start shaking on me like a crackhead on LSD, I might have another pop at you later.'

He pointed his cane towards the house. 'I'd race you if I thought you'd keep up. Don't want you breaking one of those ridiculous heels and snapping your ankle.'

Pitchford climbed the stairs carefully, putting both feet together on each step before attempting the next one. At the top of the landing, he took a few minutes to get his breath back then made his way carefully to the bedroom, which was now a burned-out shell.

He didn't look at the body first, never did. Always the location, then the victim.

The room was nondescript, black charcoal everywhere. There were the remains of a bed and the floor was largely still in situ.

What focused his attention were dozens of tiny silver canisters dotted around the floor.

He identified them immediately. Nitrous oxide.

The city was suffering an epidemic of the damn stuff, seemingly every street was littered with empty shells.

'Addict? Punter? Both?' said Darcy who was crouched by the side of the victim.

Pitchford made his way to her but didn't crouch.

The body was a completely charred skeleton. Not a patch of flesh left. It would have been bizarre had it not been for the nitrous oxide canisters everywhere, which Pitchford imagined had helped to create a much hotter inferno.

He removed a torch from his pocket and used it to inspect the body in more detail.

He kept the beam on the victim's face, stepped a little closer and focused intently on the victim's jaw.

'Darcy, get me a pair of Magill's forceps from SOCO,' he said.

She stepped out of the room and returned a few seconds later, waving the forceps at him.

'Victim's mouth, there's something inside.'

Carefully, Darcy used the tweezers to gently tease an unexploded silver canister of nitrous oxide from the victim's mouth. She stood up, slipped it into an evidence bag and waved it at Pitchford.

'What do you make of that?' he asked her.

'Someone wanted to destroy the jaw structure, to conceal the victim's identity.'

'Smart. Doesn't strike me as something a junkie or a sex worker would be mindful to do after killing a man,' replied Pitchford, making his way around the body towards the gap where the window had once been. He pointed his cane at the torched BMW. 'Find out whose car that is, Ms Darcy. That is the key to this case.'

Chapter Fourteen

Idris lowered the pharmacy shutters as soon as Rebecca arrived, closing a touch early at 22.35.

They had exchanged several cryptic texts earlier in the day but now that she was here, Idris wanted to ensure they had a plan of action.

She sat on the bench, and waited until the shutter was fully closed. Rebecca started to speak when Idris put his finger to his lips, shook his head and pointed to the ceiling. 'Tonight, we need a view. You grab the tea, I'll bring the methadone,' he said.

Idris used his keys to access the surgery on the top floor. He and Rebecca made their way to a staff room which had a large window, one which allowed them onto the flat roof.

The roof was usually reserved for impromptu summer drinks sessions or, more frequently as a safe space for staff to have a quick cigarette. Now Idris and Rebecca found themselves sitting on its shallow perimeter wall with their legs dangling off the edge, hundreds of feet above ground.

It provided a stunning view across Headingley, stretching far and wide. From here, they could see luxury apartment buildings in the centre of the town but also, towards the south, the high-rises located within The Mews.

Two sides of the same city yet vastly separated by class, opportunity and wealth.

Idris wrapped his hands around his mug of tea, which was cooling quickly in the icy, winter air. He'd borrowed a stray blanket from the tearoom and now draped it across both his and Rebecca's laps.

'How is the marriage therapy going?' asked Rebecca, wanting to delay speaking about the night before.

Idris forced a laugh. 'Shit. Apparently, my lack of concern about Mariam's affair means I'm dead inside.'

'You're not dead inside. Far from it.'

She looked at him and smiled.

'It is what it is. Financially, divorce isn't on the cards so we both pretend like we have a marriage. Can we get off this topic?' said Idris, uncomfortable.

'Did Amy show today?' asked Rebecca, changing the subject to the thing they needed to speak about.

Idris shook his head. 'DNA.'

'You call her?'

'Tried. No answer. You?'

'Same. Was going to go and visit her but didn't want to do anything which was off routine.'

'Think she's run?'

'Doubt it. She's broke. Not like Liam is going to front her any money.'

Idris set his tea down on the wall, pulled Rebecca's dose of methadone from his pocket and handed it to her. 'Amy had your dose last night. You miss it?'

She accepted the bottle from him, opened it and swallowed the dose in one before handing it back. 'Didn't sleep. But it wasn't due to missing my dose.'

'Fifteen millilitres might not seem like a lot but your body will be missing it. Did you feel sick today?'

'All day. But again, I don't think that was anything to do with the methadone.'

She turned to him, waited till he looked at her and said, 'Where did you go last night?'

'Gym for a while. Needed an alibi but also used the steam room to clean the blade then dumped it and the PPE in the medical clinical waste bin. Collection is scheduled for tomorrow, so we're clear.'

'That's what I call "Idris smart". What now?'

'I don't know.'

Rebecca pointed into the distance, her fingers shaking from the cold. 'Out there, someplace, do you think they're coming for us?'

Idris shook his head. 'I've replayed it so many times in my head. Biggest risk was some random cop stopping my car. Since that didn't happen, I don't see how they find us. The house and car were reduced to ash, and once those yellow bins get collected, we should be golden.'

Rebecca put her hand on Idris's. 'What you did for me last night. It was . . . incredible.'

He squeezed her hand. 'It was necessary.'

Idris told her that he had used the pharmacy computer to research Patrick Mead and found a week-old news article from the Yorkshire *Evening Post* which documented that Patrick was being released from prison on parole.

'He came out recently, meaning he didn't wait long before picking up Amy.'

'That's what every convict wants as soon as they're released. A fuck.'

'What happened in that room?' asked Idris without looking at Rebecca. She was less likely to tell him the truth with his eyes on her.

She told him that Patrick had picked up Amy and they'd driven to The Vacants. Amy had told him that it was her first time, that she was nervous, and he'd been delighted to hear it, pressuring her that since she was new to this, he didn't need to wear a condom. He had tried to pay her more but Amy had refused and Patrick had got angry.

Amy had excused herself, gone to the bathroom and discreetly called Rebecca to come and rescue her.

On arrival, Rebecca had found Patrick beating Amy and trying to rape her.

'Where did the knife come from?'

'Patrick had it. At Amy's throat. Threatening her. I walked in and he came at me. We fought—'

'Did he hit you?'

Rebecca nodded. 'Stomach. Took the wind right out of me. Amy was on him, but he just shrugged her off. He dropped the knife momentarily and I grabbed it. He came at me again and . . . it just happened.'

A lie.

A blatant lie.

Idris looked at her and waited for Rebecca to realise it for herself.

The silence lingered and this time, she didn't break it.

'First time you've lied to me, in . . . I don't know how long,' said Idris.

Rebecca opened her mouth, seemingly to protest her innocence but then stopped.

Idris waited.

Rebecca picked up her tea and threw the remainder off the ledge of the building.

She doubled down on the lie. 'I told you what happened.'

'He came at you?' said Idris.

'He came at me.'

'So why was the knife in his back?'

Oh.

So simple.

So utterly damning.

Rebecca turned away, looked towards where The Mews were and took her time to compose herself. 'What do you want me to say?'

'Considering I saved you from a prison cell, how about the fucking truth?' said Idris, annoyed.

She turned to face him, angry, upset. 'The truth? Really?'

'What's that supposed to mean?'

She tried to kiss him, planted her lips on his but he didn't reciprocate.

She withdrew, looked away and said, 'The truth that you still love me. That we both made the wrong move by leaving each other. That if I found a different pharmacy to get my methadone from, you'd be heartbroken. That the real reason you put your life on the line last night was not to save me from prison but because the thought of never seeing me again is more painful than anything that happened last night.'

She had him.

Idris took her face in his hands and kissed her, and for a few minutes they returned to a time when nothing else had mattered except being with each other. Breaking all the rules; casting aside religious, social and racial divides.

Idris pulled away from her and composed himself.

'Now, the truth,' said Idris.

Rebecca told him that for the briefest of moments, she had returned to that night when she had been brutally attacked. Pregnant with their child and at the mercy of two criminals who had wanted to hurt her, for no other reason than to avenge a feud which had nothing to do with either Idris or Rebecca but to do with her brother, Daniel. That in that instance, she had released a rage she had been storing for years.

Her eyes narrowed and she almost hissed her words.

'I saw myself back there. On the ground. Helpless, afraid. Only, this time, I was the one holding the knife. He was beating on Amy and I just . . . I don't know . . .'

She stopped talking, looked away, balled her hands into fists.

Idris didn't push it. He, like Rebecca, hated thinking of those memories, of what that night had cost them both.

Idris put his hands on hers and she relaxed the tension in her fists. 'I asked you this before and I'm asking it again. What now?' said Rebecca.

Idris thought on his response for almost a minute then quietly said, 'There is only one way we get caught. Amy is our loose cannon. You need to find her and together, we get her the hell out of Leeds.'

Chapter Fifteen

Adel was one of the poshest suburbs in Leeds and the Adelphi nursing home, a five-million-pound luxury facility, catered for the affluent elderly population providing bespoke care to its residents.

Thomas Mead had named the facility after the Greek for 'brothers' because this endeavour had been built by both him and his brother, Patrick.

The fees were high but the ageing clientele had the means, often selling their expensive homes to own a share in the apartments they now resided in.

And uniquely, Thomas accepted cash which meant that he was also able to wash considerable sums of money through the care home, using it as a route to launder drug money.

Business was booming, the care home at capacity and he had plans to open another facility nearby.

Thomas had been busy authorising payments to suppliers when he had been notified that two detectives were waiting downstairs, in reception.

He had immediately gone to view the CCTV footage and was looking at an old white man with a walking stick to hand, standing next to a much younger colleague.

Thomas was alarmed.

Christ, his brother had only been out of prison two days

and here the police were, ready to no doubt throw more shit at his family.

He had tried to call Patrick, who hadn't come home last night, but Thomas had not been particularly surprised or worried about that. Patrick had told him that he was going out to visit an old flame, and that he'd probably be gone a few days – until he'd got ten years of abstinence out of his system.

Thomas again tried to call Patrick and again, the call went to voicemail.

An anxiety that Patrick might have already got himself into trouble and screwed his probation flickered across Thomas's mind. It had taken him eighteen months to engineer a scenario whereby the ironclad details of Patrick's probation would satisfy the relevant parties.

Shit, they hadn't even got his tag in place yet, the company responsible for doing it still processing some bullshit paperwork.

It was why Patrick had taken his opportunity to abscond.

Was that what all this was about? It seemed the most likely solution.

But the detective had said they were from HC-MET.

Homicide and Criminal Major Enquiry Team.

The same team which had arrested this brother ten years before for manslaughter after Patrick had killed someone, he claimed in self-defence, when a drug deal had turned sour.

Thomas had been given the detectives' names by his receptionist and now used his computer to google them quickly, finding their details on the HC-MET website.

Brian Pitchford was top dog – a DCI.

The woman, Darcy Black, his junior.

Still, the fact that a DCI was on his doorstep was a bad

omen. Thomas had already called his barrister and told him to be on standby.

He was debating which room to take the meeting in. How comfortable to make the detectives. Whether to play good cop or be standoffish?

He tried to call Patrick for a third time and when it proved fruitless, he called his receptionist and asked her to bring the detectives up to his office.

There was a knock on his door and his assistant, Chantelle, dressed in a conservative light-coloured suit, opened the door and showed the detectives inside.

Thomas got to his feet and waited as both Pitchford and Black made their way towards his desk. The old man walked slowly, putting his weight through his walking stick as he made his way across. Black remained by his side, taking measured steps, seemingly so that if the old man fell over, she'd be there to intervene.

An odd combination, he thought.

He extended his hand and shook firstly Black's hand and then Pitchford's, surprised that the old man had a firm shake and solid, rough hands.

'Thomas Mead,' he said, gesturing for them to sit down.

'DS Darcy Black.'

'DCI Brian Pitchford.'

'I'd like to say it's a pleasure but when the Mead family gets visitation from HC-MET, it usually means a headache.'

He watched as Pitchford carefully placed his feet, used his hand to feel where the back of the chair was and sat down cautiously.

The detectives shared a look, ostensibly figuring who was going to lead.

Black leaned forward, and said, 'Thank you for seeing us as such short notice, Mr Mead.'

'Thomas, please.'

She nodded and said, 'Last night, there was an incident at a house in The Vacants in Leeds. A house fire destroyed the building. Are you familiar with this area?'

He nodded. Waited for more.

'A body was found inside the house and I'm sorry to have to tell you that we believe it to be your brother, Patrick Mead. A car – leased in his name with you as guarantor – was found outside the property and a preliminary forensic analysis also suggests it to be him. I am so sorry.'

Thomas thought on all the unanswered calls he had made to his brother, yet still said, 'You must be wrong. My brother would never visit The Vacants.'

'I know this must be very difficult to hear,' said Black, her tone and demeanour full of professional sympathy.

Pitchford then added the one detail which made Thomas believe it could be true.

'I'm afraid he was murdered, Mr Mead. Your brother suffered a fatal stab wound.'

Thomas clenched his teeth, jaw muscles tensing.

'You said it was a house fire,' he said quietly.

Pitchford shook his head. 'It would appear that the fire was started post-mortem, we believe to try and conceal the identity of the victim or at least make identification harder, but also to potentially try to cover up the fact that he was murdered.'

'Who would do such a thing?' asked Thomas, knowing damn well the list was an endless one.

'Well,' said Black, losing her previous sympathetic tone and replacing it with a more authoritative edge, 'we were hoping to speak to *you* about that.'

'Let's not beat around the bush. My brother was a career criminal. If you're looking for people who had beef with him, there are plenty. He had been out of prison only two days. Off the top of my head, I'd suggest you start with his previous known enemies. I'm sure the police have a robust database they can refer to.'

Pitchford took a moment, and really looked at Thomas, hard enough and long enough that it made Thomas feel uncomfortable.

'We are indeed pursuing those lines of enquiries. I wonder, did your brother tell you where he was going last night? You're listed as his next of kin and Probation Services have you documented as his key contact.'

'He told me he was going out to get laid,' said Thomas truthfully, seeing no reason to lie about it.

He watched as Black made a note in her book.

'Getting laid anywhere in particular?'

'An ex, he said. But considering you found his body in The Vacants, we all know which group of people trade from there.'

Pitchford nodded and said, 'We do. And the next place we are going to visit is Beeston.'

Chapter Sixteen

Idris was by the front door of the pharmacy, watching as the yellow clinical waste bins were loaded into a large artic lorry, which had the words MEDICAL WASTE SOLUTIONS etched in large black letters across its side.

He closed his eyes, took a deep breath.

That was the end of it.

All of the evidence gone.

The bins would be taken straight to an incinerator and eviscerated.

Idris retreated a few steps and sat on a bench, next to an elderly man who was waiting for a prescription.

'Sitting out here with the common folk. Are you OK, Idris?' said Malcolm, a seventy-year-old patient who visited the pharmacy every week to collect his dosette box.

'If I go back in the dispensary, I'll end up either answering the phone, checking prescriptions or more likely, making the staff cups of tea.'

Jemma strode out, walking towards them carrying Malcolm's dosette box. 'You make us a cup of tea? Hell will freeze over before that happens.'

Idris feigned a look of hurt and replied, 'You see, Malcolm. That's why I'm sitting out here with you. Less abuse.'

Malcolm chuckled, accepted the box from Jemma, thanked them both and duly left.

Jemma nodded towards the front doors. 'Speaking of abuse, Clare Glass is en route.'

Inside the consultation room, Clare, dressed scantily in readiness for her shift in Beeston, swallowed her daily dose of methadone, staring at Idris in a manner which unnerved him.

She slammed her empty medicine bottle on the table, turned to leave and hesitated.

She turned back to Idris who was annotating the right-hand side of her blue script. 'Something else?' he asked, not realising that Clare was smirking at him.

'Maybe,' she said.

'I'm listening.'

'Cops came to Beeston today,' she said, sitting down opposite him.

Idris did exactly what he shouldn't have. He stopped writing and looked at her, unable to hide the tension in his face.

Her smirk widened. 'There it is,' she said, cockily.

Idris realised his error and went back to writing on her script.

'They were asking about The Vacants. Who trades from there. We all heard there was a fire there last night and that they found a body.'

'Shit happens,' replied Idris, trying his damnedest to sound casual.

'Thing is, Idris, you were in Beeston last night askin' 'bout Rebecca and Amy. And I sent you to them Vacants.'

Idris had finished the entry on her script but kept his pen there not wanting to look at her.

'Amy and Rebecca weren't there,' he replied calmly.

'Funny, tho, innit. Like one a 'dem coincidences.'

'Yup,' said Idris and folded Clare's prescription neatly. He forced a smile. 'Life's full of coincidences.'

Clare's eyes looked as if they were shining, as if she'd consumed something other than methadone.

'Did you tell the detectives about this coincidence?' he asked, needing to know the answer.

She shook her head. 'I don't tell the pigs nuffink.' She paused and added the word, 'Yet.'

'You should tell them whatever you're happy with,' said Idris confidently.

Clare leaned forward, giving Idris a view down her chest, almost as if she were attempting to be provocative.

'Lend us fifty quid, would you, Idris?' she said coldly.

There it was. The nonchalant blackmail demand.

Idris stared at her. It felt like a game of chess. She had checked him and was awaiting his move.

'Piss off, Clare. I'm not a bank,' he said and once again, gave her a broad, confident smile.

She leaned back in her chair. 'How's about a twenty, then?'

It was becoming more awkward, the tension palpable. Idris doubled down, he couldn't get into this.

'There's a cash machine outside Sainsbury's. Give that a try.'

Clare stood up, the moment over, and winked at him. 'God loves a trier, Idris, innit.'

'You keep trying, Clare. Keeps you sharp, love,' he said and stood up, opened the door for her to leave and followed her out.

He watched her disappear, feeling like he'd dodged a bullet and then saw Liam loitering inside the pharmacy, bullishly standing in the retail area, holding a can of deodorant and spraying it casually underneath his clothes like he owned the joint. In his other hand, as always, he was holding a can of extra-strength lager.

Idris marched across to him, annoyed. 'Liam, you're barred. What are you doing here?'

Liam removed the can of deodorant from under his clothes, kept hold of it and said, 'Need to speak to a chemist.'

'Find somewhere else or shall I call the police?'

Liam's eyes narrowed, a snarl now across his face. 'Nah. You don't wanna call the pigs, Idris. Last people's you wanna see.'

They looked at each other and right there, Idris realised that Liam knew.

'I'm busy, Liam.'

'I know. Like, late-night busy, Idris. Makes a man wonder.' Liam pointed towards the consultation room. 'Fink you and I need to go and 'ave a sit-down in there.'

'I don't think so,' replied Idris. He'd outmanoeuvred Clare and was intent on doing the same thing to Liam.

Liam finished his can, threw it into a bin and removed his phone from his pocket. He accessed a file then handed it to Idris.

'I've muted it, 'cos, fing is, Idris, the shit you can hear on the footage?'

Idris took the phone and stared at a clip of Rebecca stabbing Patrick Mead to death. Horrified, he immediately stopped it and looked around nervously to make sure nobody else had seen it.

Liam shifted closer to him, smelling of booze, and dropped his voice to a whisper. 'Get in the fucking room, Chemist, you and I need to talk.'

Chapter Seventeen

Idris had undertaken many uncomfortable conversations in the pharmacy's consultation room, none, however, quite like this one.

Liam sat slouched in a chair, legs wide open, with a shit-eating grin across his face.

'I'm reckonin' we start with a grand a week,' he said.

Idris pursed his lips, took a breath, racking his brains for how to respond.

'Whatsa matta? Big bad Chemist man got nuffink to say?'

Liam leaned forward, sudden, aggressive, bloodshot eyes glaring at Idris. 'How 'bout you bar me now? Tell me you're gonna call the police?'

Liam burst out laughing, clearly revelling in every moment. 'One large a week. And I need to get clean. Fuckin' drug centre won't take me on so I need fifty millilitres of methadone from you a day. I want ten days' supply, five hundred millilitres. I'll collect it tonight.'

Christ, the longer Liam talked, the more outrageous his demands were becoming.

Idris pointed to Liam's phone, resting on the table between them. He'd been tempted to smash it to pieces but assumed the footage wouldn't have been the only copy.

'Patrick was trying to rape Amy,' said Idris, softly, calmly.

'So?'

Idris bristled at the bluntness of Liam's response.

'We saved your girl,' said Idris, trying to make it more personal to Liam.

Liam picked up the phone, watched the footage and said, 'Every time I watch it, I get a hard-on.' He grabbed his crotch. 'Reckonin' I'll be crackin' one out to this tonight.'

Idris wanted to lean across the table and punch the bastard.

'A grand a week. Due, let's be sayin' in a couple-a days. Gives you time to get down t'bank. But my meth, I need that tonight.'

Idris removed his own phone, accessed his internet banking app and held the phone high so Liam could see it. 'I'm holding two hundred quid in my account, Liam. Out there, I've got dozens of final demand letters to pay my drugs' bill. I'm about as broke as you are. Where the hell am I going to get a grand a week?' said Idris, adding a little edge to his voice. Clearly, playing nice was not going to work here.

'I don't be givin' a shit where you get it. All's I know is that the Mead family be bad men. Like, puttin' you six feet under bad men. And one large a week is the price to be savin' you and your bitch's life.'

'I've just showed you my bank balance.'

'Chemists be rich. Everyone be knowin' dat.'

Liam seemed to reconsider his options and said, 'Course, with all dem pills out there, you can be givin' me a gee's worth of it. Pregab, diazpam, morphine.'

'I can't do that. Everything's accounted for,' lied Idris, knowing that if he went down that path, it would quickly escalate.

'Cash it is, then.'

Liam stood up to leave. 'Methadone tonight. Cash in two days time. Ya get me?'

Idris put his head in his hands, broken.

Liam laughed. 'Hahaha, I'm gonna bleed you for everyfin' you got, Chemist. Gimme the cash from you wallet. I need funds.'

'What?'

Liam raised his voice, almost shouting at Idris now. 'Your wallet,' he barked.

Afraid patients or his staff outside might hear, Idris removed his wallet and handed Liam the thirty-five pounds it contained.

Liam stuffed it in his pocket.

'Amy's methadone. She ain't comin' in for it today. Gimme it. I need a hit now.'

'Liam, I've got staff out there. I can't be handing you her methadone. They'll see.'

Liam stepped closer, crouched to be at eye level with Idris. When he spoke, his breath stank of alcohol. He didn't speak his words, instead singing them, cocky, arrogant. 'Go-and-get-me-my-bitch's-methadone.'

And then, before Idris had any time to react, Liam slapped him.

Idris's head was sent crashing into the wall.

Liam stood up, backed off and raised his fists. 'Come on, beautiful, you's wanna dance?' He jumped up and down on the spot, teasing Idris, mimicking a boxer.

Liam laughed, lowered his fists.

Idris remained where he was, stunned, the skin on his face stinging.

'All these years, you been treatin' Liam like a bitch. And for what? 'Cos you gets to wear a shirt and tie and be all Chemist-like? Now, go and gets me Amy's methadone or I'll slap you again.'

Idris rubbed his cheek and suppressed a rage he knew all too well, then walked out of the room.

*

Idris weaved his way past patients, into the dispensary, and hurried towards the controlled drugs cabinet.

He unlocked it just as Jemma appeared by his side and said, 'Check this prescription, will you? Vanessa's busy with a patient.'

She stuffed a red basket into his hands, containing a solitary bottle of Gaviscon liquid.

Idris frowned at her. 'Check it yourself. What's the point in being a technician if you can't even do a Gaviscon?'

'I dispensed it. Hurry up, I've got six other reds waiting.'

Idris signed off on the Gaviscon.

Jemma took the basket from him, ready to leave when she hesitated. 'What are you looking for? And why is Liam bloody shitface in the consultation room?'

'There's nosy and then there's you,' he replied, trying to sound casual. 'For your information, I'm checking stock of oxycodone injections for an end-of-life patient at the nursing home. And Liam is begging for another chance to be allowed to use this pharmacy. I'm going to give it to him.'

Jemma was immediately irate. 'What? Last time, he stole the bloody charity box!'

'I know. His girlfriend, Amy Starr, the new blue script comes here. She said she'll keep him straight.'

'Then get rid of her too. I'm telling you, Vanessa is going to shit a brick if you take him on.'

'First time Liam messes about he's out. I've made the decision, deal with it.'

Jemma stormed off, muttering as she went.

Idris turned back to the controlled drugs cabinet, leafed through the uncollected methadone parcels and found Amy's. He took it, and walked away, stuffing it in his pocket as he went.

*

93

Idris re-entered the consultation room and handed Liam Amy's dose of methadone, watching as he brazenly swallowed it.

'Ahhh. Hit the spot,' he said, wiping his lips and throwing the empty container on the table.

'Amy's going to withdraw if she doesn't get her dose,' said Idris.

Liam removed the money Idris had given him from his pocket and waved it at him. 'We be goin' to get some good stuff now, better than methadone.'

Liam stepped closer to Idris, making him momentarily recoil.

Liam grinned, clearly revelling in every minute of this. 'Tonight. Nine p.m. Five hundred millilitres of methadone or bad things gonna happen to the footage, Chemist.'

'Liam, listen—' started Idris but Liam waltzed out of the room, laughing.

Idris had never felt so alone or vulnerable in his life.

His immediate thoughts went to Daniel, someone he knew who could help with Liam.

Idris removed his phone, scrolled to Daniel's number and was about to hit 'dial' when he stopped.

Daniel was just as likely to kill Liam as he was to threaten him.

Thoughts of Idris's chequered past with Daniel surfaced and Idris suddenly felt unsteady.

He turned the lights off in the room and thundered into a chair.

Darkness.

Chapter Eighteen

Thomas Mead sipped coffee and glanced across Leeds from the balcony of his city centre penthouse apartment. A cooling evening breeze massaged his neck and he now focused his attention away from the centre towards Headingley.

Towards Pavilion Mews.

The one place he and Patrick had never managed to infiltrate and the one area they coveted the most. Thomas had hoped that with Patrick being released from prison, they could have formulated a new, ambitious plan to secure The Mews.

A fitting recompense for the time Patrick had served.

Now, with his death, it would remain an unfulfilled ambition.

It pained Thomas who had always wanted to impress his older brother. Patrick had been more like a father figure than a brother to him.

For all the territory his organisation controlled, they would always play second fiddle to the city's main dealer, Jahangir Hosseini, leader of The Mews.

Not that he hadn't tried to gain control of it.

There was a racial element to his problem. The Mews was mostly inhabited by immigrants or, as Thomas called them, *foreign bastards*. It meant that the white population inside The Mews was an intimate group and difficult to infiltrate.

Christ, Thomas had sacrificed dozens of men trying to topple Jahangir, but the man was a formidable enemy with a reach well beyond the UK.

The Hosseini family originated from Syria but had left when the war had started. With generational links to Afghanistan, they controlled a large share of the drugs market across Europe and vitally, they also regulated the influx of immigrants across the channel with a powerful presence in Calais and Dover.

Their business model was impressive. Securing product was one thing. Ensuring that you had a desperate, endless stream of people forced to buy it was priceless.

Thomas envied Jahangir because Thomas's territory was slipping. It wasn't the quality of his heroin but the fact that Jahangir was undercutting the price to such an extent that Thomas could not compete.

The Mews . . . how to infiltrate it?

His thoughts were disturbed by Damon, his childhood friend and second in command of their organisation. Damon was the muscle, a formidable, former pro-boxer who had served almost as much jail time as Patrick for frequently hospitalising people who tried to fuck with their crews. Thomas controlled the business, Damon the streets.

He arrived by Thomas's side and stood peering into the distance, much like Thomas had been doing. Then he put his arm around Thomas and whispered, 'Brother, they are ready for you to see Patrick.'

The police autopsy room was a cold, clinical space – gleaming silver steel benches and smelling strongly of disinfectant, which didn't quite mask the odour of death.

Thomas stared at the charred remains of Patrick, blinking away tears. He covered what was left of the body with a plastic sheet and walked away.

Outside, in the corridor, he allowed tears to run down his face. Why hadn't he stayed with Patrick on his release from prison? Thomas should have realised the first thing Patrick would have wanted was a woman.

Finding the girl who had taken Patrick to The Vacants was key: only she could tell them how Patrick had died and who had stuffed a canister of nitrous oxide into his mouth.

That didn't seem like the modus operandi of a sex worker.

It was a smart, deliberate move to try and stop the identification of Patrick's body.

Calculating in its delivery.

His phone rang, Damon calling.

Thomas answered, didn't speak just listened to the devastating message.

It was murder; Damon had proof of it now even if they didn't have the identities of those involved.

As soon as Thomas had their details, he would see to this matter personally.

He stood up, glanced once more through the viewing window at his brother's body and whispered a quiet promise.

'On my life, brother, I will avenge your death.'

Having left the crematorium, Thomas had made his way across to Bradford, to a slaughterhouse which had been part of his family business for three generations. It was mostly defunct now, operating only for a handful of clients, but Thomas had kept it to remind him of his family heritage.

The Meads had been a powerful family at one time in

Bradford, before the city had crumbled due to the collapse of its wool trade. Like a lot of white people, Thomas and his family had moved to Leeds to create a new life there, but he'd kept the slaughterhouse to keep him from forgetting where his family had come from.

The location came in useful when dealing with his enemies, their screams confined to a dark, nightmarish area where sounds and life disappeared.

The smell of blood was overwhelming, the metallic taste of it tingling on his tongue.

Thomas was holding Damon's phone, watching footage of Rebecca, Amy and then later Idris, leaving the house where Patrick had been found murdered.

Thomas had installed a dashcam in Patrick's car, to keep an eye on him, and it had captured everything.

His men had downloaded it from the Cloud then deleted it so that nobody else could view it.

The police would never see this evidence because this was going to be dealt with in-house.

Thomas took multiple screenshots of the video, still captures of Rebecca's and Idris's car number plates. He couldn't make out their faces but that didn't matter. His organisation had several corrupt police officers on their books and in a few hours' time, Thomas would have the key information he needed.

He glanced around the slaughterhouse, at freshly washed down carcasses of cows and at blood soiling the drains.

'What do you want us to do?' asked Damon.

Thomas pointed to the carcasses.

'We will bring them here, string them up and make them suffer. That is how we avenge Patrick's death.'

Chapter Nineteen

Having closed the pharmacy for half an hour, Idris walked to his car, reached under the rear wheel arch and pulled free the magnetic tracking device. He slipped it inside his pocket, trudged down the street to a late-night coffee shop and completed a familiar routine of buying two hot chocolates.

Idris found Al-Noor sitting in his usual spot, outside Sainsbury's, his begging basket empty with a sign next to him which said, IN SYRIA I WAS AN ENGINEER. I AM ASHAMED TO BE HERE, BEGGING FOR MONEY BUT PLEASE, SPARE WHAT YOU CAN.

Idris had written the sign for him. He hadn't liked the wording, but Al-Noor had been insistent that people who gave him money needed to know that he was an educated man.

Idris sat down next to Al-Noor on a dry, clean piece of cardboard. This was something he routinely did, to break up the long evenings he worked.

'Evening, Mr Idris,' said Al-Noor, graciously accepting the hot chocolate from him and moving aside to create a little more space.

'Evening, Al,' replied Idris and acknowledged a regular patient of his who had exited Sainsbury's and peered at Idris, perplexed as to why their pharmacist was sitting on the ground, next to a beggar.

Idris enjoyed these moments, watching the world go by, seeing what Al-Noor observed first-hand.

'Anything exciting this evening?' asked Idris.

'Man having an affair with a young woman,' replied Al-Noor and took a sip of his chocolate.

'Tell me.'

'I have seen this man, many times at the bus stop. Always with his wife. They don't talk much. She catches a bus in one direction, him in another. Tonight, I saw him in a car, with a much younger woman. He dropped her to that house, over there,' said Al-Noor, pointing to a detached residence across the street. 'In the car, he kissed her quickly before she left.'

Idris smiled. He loved hearing of these stories. To most people, beggars were a nuisance. But Idris enjoyed listening to what they had seen.

'Family friend maybe?' teased Idris.

Al-Noor looked at him, cynical. 'We do not kiss our friends in such a way, Mr Idris.'

'Fair enough.'

'Are you OK tonight? You seem, I don't know, tired maybe?' said Al-Noor.

Idris scratched the stubble on his face. 'Long days, Al. Even longer nights but you're right, I'm not OK. In fact, I find myself with a bit of a problem.'

Al-Noor turned to face Idris, immediately concerned.

Idris forced a smile. 'I'm OK. For now.'

'Tell me, is there anything I can do to help you, Mr Idris?'

Idris removed the small metallic device and waved it at Al-Noor before discreetly placing it between them under the cardboard. 'This is a car tracking device, Al. I think that maybe, at some point soon, some people might come to see me at the pharmacy who won't be happy and will maybe try to ruin my business. What I'd like for you to do, is to move your pitch from here to the street opposite the pharmacy, in front of the café where I can see you and you can see me.'

'Why?'

'So that if I send you a text message, you can slip this device under the car which might bring these people to my pharmacy who want to do bad things to Mr Idris.'

Al-Noor looked horrified at the prospect. 'Who would want to do this? Mr Idris, you are the most kind, respectable person I have ever met.'

'That's good of you to say, Al, but looking after The Mews means sometimes dangerous people might try things with me – especially since I own a pharmacy.'

Idris wasn't speaking about Liam. That situation was an altogether different crisis. He was referring to the fact that if he hadn't covered his tracks in The Vacants, then perhaps one of the Mead family might come to see him *and if that happened*, there would be only one option. Idris would need evidence for the police that they had threatened him.

Admittedly, he was thinking of the worst-case scenario, but he was now in so deep that from this moment on, all his thoughts were focused on not only his and Rebecca's survival but also Mariam's.

'Mr Idris, I don't know who would want to do bad things to you, but Al-Noor is happy to help.' Al-Noor spoke his words hesitantly.

'Tell me what's on your mind, Al. I can see something isn't right,' said Idris.

'This spot is the best one in Headingley. People spend money in the supermarket and when they come out, they give their spare change to me. Opposite the pharmacy is the café. At night it is closed. I will not make any money,' he said, dismayed.

'How much do you make here, Al?'

He shrugged. 'Maybe ten pounds each night. On a good night, maybe twenty.'

'I'll cover that.'

Al-Noor shook his head. 'Mr Idris, please. I could not accept that. You already help me so much.'

'This time, it would be you assisting me.'

'How long would I need to do this?' he asked.

Idris shrugged. 'Maybe a week?'

'OK, Mr Idris. I will do this for you. But, my phone has no credit. If you message me, I will not be able to reply.'

Idris removed a twenty-pound note from his pocket and nodded towards Sainsbury's. There was something crucial Idris needed Al-Noor to purchase.

'You can top up your phone in there and while you're at it, Al, can you buy me a bottle of green food colouring?'

Chapter Twenty

Idris returned to his pharmacy with the bottle of green food colouring Al-Noor had purchased for him.

In the dispensary, by the sink, he removed an empty plastic methadone container from the bin, filled it with water then added a hefty dose of the food colouring. He shook the bottle and created a replica bottle of methadone.

Now, for the difficult part.

Idris removed the lid and took the open bottle with him to the bench and placed it next to several others, these ones all genuine methadone liquid.

Knowing he was in range of the pharmacy's CCTV cameras, Idris moved quickly past the bench, catching the fake bottle with his elbow, knocking it over. He walked into the retail area, spent a minute looking at the shelves, seemingly for a particular product, and then returned to the dispensary to find the five hundred millilitres of green liquid all over the floor.

He made a big show of acting devastated at this discovery then using his phone, took several photographs of the spillage.

He sent them to Vanessa, with a text which said, Gutted! Accidently spilled 500ml of methadone! Really, don't want to call the police to witness this. It's all on CCTV. Can I sign off that you were here and witnessed it? I'll fill out a 101 non-emergency police referral now.

Idris logged onto the 101 website and filled out an incident form detailing that he had spilled the methadone and that he was the pharmacist in charge.

The pharmaceutical regulations stated that in the event of a methadone spillage, a police officer needed to visit the pharmacy to witness the incident. In reality, the police rarely did so, an unofficial understanding in place that if another pharmacist witnessed the spillage, that would suffice as evidence.

Idris's phone beeped and he read the text message from Vanessa.

OMG! Gutted! Yes, of course. Document it in the register that I was there. I'll countersign it tomorrow. Happy cleaning!

Jackpot.

Idris grabbed the methadone register and completed an accidental spillage entry giving him 500ml of methadone he could now give to Liam.

He measured ten separate 50ml doses and labelled them all for a specific patient at the pharmacy who was firstly prescribed that dose but also had the rarest of privileges of being allowed to take the doses home with them.

Finally, Idris carefully removed the date from each bottle and then roughed up the labels, ensuring that name of the patient and the date it had been supplied were unreadable, making it look as though the bottles had been sold on the black market.

Idris looked at the doses, anxious. He had never broken the law before and felt sick at what he was being forced to do. His pharmacy was his sanctuary, but if he went through with this, it would become a place of criminality.

With his heart racing, and feeling light-headed, Idris dimmed the lights, put his head in his hands and thought about the money he had lifted from Patrick's car. It had been playing on his mind and he was conflicted about what to do with it.

He wanted to settle some of the final payment demands sitting in his drawer. Yet he couldn't use ill-gained cash to settle those debts. He would need a way to wash the money, so that he could bank it, and Idris had no such means.

Once he supplied Liam with methadone, where would the criminal acts he was forced to undertake end?

The doorbell sounded and Idris peered over the counter and saw Liam standing there with Amy.

Amy.

She was the key.

If he could *somehow* get her to see reason, *she could destroy the footage.*

Idris slipped the doses of methadone into a bag then took them with him to the out-of-hours hatch.

He didn't confine Liam to that space and instead allowed him into the main shop area, dismayed to see Amy remain outside.

'Yo, yo, yo, how's ma Chemist? You got summat for us?' said Liam, clearly drunk, holding his customary can of lager.

'First, let me speak to Amy,' said Idris.

'Nah.'

'I'm not giving you anything until that happens.'

The expression on Liam's face changed and he suddenly shoved Idris. 'I say it and you fuckin' does it, Chemist,' he shouted, loud enough that from outside, Amy clearly heard it. She stepped closer to the door, peered inside.

Idris doubled down. 'No. I need to speak to her.'

Liam removed his phone, accessed the clip of Rebecca

stabbing Patrick, showed it to Idris then loaded his Instagram account. 'Ten seconds then I'm sharing it.'

'Do it,' said Idris, bluffing.

'What?'

'You've got me and Rebecca. So we might as well hand ourselves in to the cops. You've got a golden egg here. I can give you this methadone and arrange some regular cash but first, I need to know Amy is all right. Let me speak to her or upload the damn clip and I'll go down to the police station right now.'

Liam stared at Idris, momentarily unsure.

The clip was useless without their co-operation.

Liam waved Amy inside.

'Alone. I want to speak to her alone,' said Idris.

'Don't push yer luck,' snapped Liam.

Amy shuffled inside. Liam pulled her towards him, kept her close and planted an aggressive kiss on the side of her face. 'Chemist wants to speak wiv ya.' Amy looked at Idris, uncomfortable, afraid.

'Are you OK?' asked Idris, his voice soft.

She nodded hesitantly.

'I'm glad. Rebecca and I were worried about you. Thinking of you.'

Again, she nodded.

Idris was certain that Amy didn't want to be part of this blackmail; she was almost recoiling from Liam.

Liam pushed her behind him, then unceremoniously shoved her out the door. He turned back to Idris and stretched out his hand. 'Meth. Now.'

Idris hesitated. He felt sick, his stomach churning and when he picked up the parcel, his hand was shaking.

Liam snatched the bag, looked inside. 'Yeah, baby,' he said, grinning maniacally. He removed a dose, opened it and while he might have been drunk, he had enough poise to just taste the methadone instead of necking it which Idris had expected him to do.

'Fifty millilitres a day and I's gonna be clean, Chemist man. I's gonna be making plans for that cash you's gonna be givin' me,' said Liam, slurring his words.

Liam sealed the bottle and dropped it back into the bag. 'End of the week. A grand large.'

'I already told you . . .'

'I ain't gonna be askin' you for it every week. I need a crib. A grand gets me a deposit. After that, you and I be talkin'. Makin' a deal. But you need to give us one gee.'

Liam stormed outside, grabbed Amy roughly by the arm and dragged her away, both of them cowering from the rain.

Idris retreated into the dispensary and slumped into a chair, a mess, his hands shaking.

There was no going back now. He had pissed on all of the pharmaceutical rules and supplied a highly controlled drug to a known addict.

What if Liam stupidly drank it all, ended up dying and there was an investigation? They might trace it back to Idris.

Visions of Patrick Mead lying dead in The Vacants now flashed across his mind.

How could everything have gone so badly wrong in only twenty-four hours?

Idris's thoughts were disturbed by the sound of the out-of-hours doorbell.

Christ, he didn't have the bandwidth for a night of tiresome consultations.

The doorbell sounded again and this time, kept ringing, incessantly.

Idris peered over the counter and saw a smartly dressed Caucasian man standing at the door, the hood of his coat pulled tight across his head, clearly trying to avoid the rain. He trudged reluctantly to the hatch, buzzed the patient inside and said flatly, 'How can I help you?'

The man kept his head bowed, his wavy dark hair partially obscuring his pale face, his hood dripping water onto the floor.

'I need some advice,' he said.

'You're in the right place.'

The man removed his phone. 'Got something to show you, a bit, you know, off the grid.'

Standard practice, thought Idris, images of some sort of rash, somewhere delicate, no doubt.

The man slid his phone across the hatch, an image on screen.

Idris looked at it momentarily confused and then, horrified.

Thomas Mead removed his hood, his eyes piercing Idris's face. 'Open the doors, Chemist, you and I got a lot to talk about.'

Chapter Twenty-One

Thomas Mead snarled at Idris, his breath crystallizing on the thick protective screen separating the men from each other.

'You thought you covered everything, didn't you? Except the Cloud footage from the dashcam in Patrick's car. It captured yours and Rebecca's number plates. I don't know who the other girl is, yet. A hooker, I'm reckoning. We'll get to that soon enough. If you want to see Rebecca again, open the doors.'

Idris locked eyes with the man and in that moment, realised the pain swirling in the man's eyes could only have come from a family member of the deceased.

Idris glanced at the phone again, a still image of him, outside the house where Patrick had been murdered, clear on screen.

Idris felt a wobble in his legs as if they would suddenly give way.

'Rebecca?' he said, his voice shaky.

'We picked her up outside The Elizabeth Projects. She's in the car.' Thomas stepped close to the protective glass screen and suddenly banged his fist on it, causing Idris to take a step back. 'Open the fucking doors,' he yelled.

'Let me speak to Rebecca,' said Idris, trying to sound calm.

Thomas removed his phone and made a call. 'Bring her,' he said and hung up.

Idris glanced outside, saw the door of a black Range Rover open and a muscular Caucasian man step out, dragging Rebecca with him.

He pulled her aggressively towards the pharmacy.

'The keys to the main doors are in the back,' said Idris shakily, his eyes never leaving Rebecca.

'Get them. No tricks. I see something I don't like; we leave with the woman,' said Thomas and pointed to a large CCTV monitor hanging from the ceiling in the corner of the pharmacy. 'Turn those cameras off.'

'The DVR is in the back storeroom.'

Thomas took a beat, eyes never leaving Idris. 'You have thirty seconds then we're gone.'

Idris moved quickly into the dispensary, his mind counting down the thirty seconds. He grabbed his keys and his phone.

He rushed into the back room where the DVR was and vitally, the police panic alarm. Idris urgently texted Al-Noor.

Al, bad people here. Pls, fit tracking device to black Range Rover outside pharmacy. DO IT NOW!

Ten seconds.

Idris switched off the CCTV cameras then put his finger on the red button.

If he pressed it, the police would arrive but then what? He and Rebecca would surely go to jail. If he didn't press it, Thomas could do as he pleased to them.

Twenty seconds had passed.

Idris applied pressure to the panic button just as his phone beeped with an incoming text message.

A reply from Al-Noor.

Mr Idris, I am coming.

Idris didn't hit the panic button.

He had to somehow deal with Thomas.

Amy.

That's who Thomas needed.

That is who they would pin this on. And Liam.

Thirty seconds.

Idris rushed out of the storeroom back into the retail area to find Thomas, Rebecca and Damon retreating towards the Range Rover.

He unlocked the main doors, stepped outside and shouted, 'Hey, I'm here.'

They stopped.

Idris remained where he was, the rain cooling his face which felt flushed and hot.

Thomas turned around, stared at Idris then whispered something in Damon's ear.

They started back towards the pharmacy and Idris could see that Rebecca had a gag around her mouth.

He retreated inside, leaving the door open.

As the men entered the pharmacy, behind them, Idris saw Al-Noor step out from the shadows of Dare Café into focus.

The men looked at each other, just as Thomas, Damon and Rebecca entered the pharmacy. She looked unharmed but her eyes screamed of a terror Idris knew all too well.

Idris closed the door and dropped the shutter, watching as Al-Noor disappeared.

He closed his eyes, took a beat and turned around.

He didn't see whose fist it was, just felt it smash into his face, and as Idris hit the floor, he could taste blood inside his mouth.

Chapter Twenty-Two

Idris's vision was blurry, and he could hear Rebecca's muffled voice, trying to scream.

He curled into the foetal position, anticipating another blow.

When it didn't happen, he lifted his head and saw Rebecca, not only gagged but with what looked like cable ties securing her wrists. She was sitting on a bench and looked unharmed.

'Listen, it's not what you think,' started Idris but Thomas didn't let him finish and thundered a brutal kick into Idris's side. It knocked the wind out of him, and Idris lay on the floor, crumpled in a heap trying to get his breath back, desperate, urgent. Thomas removed a cable tie and secured Idris's hands behind his back.

Idris glanced at Rebecca who was crying, and his memory shifted to a darker place, of her in a hospital bed, blood covering her thighs as their stillborn child was taken away to be resuscitated.

Always that memory, always the screaming.

With them both restrained and the CCTV now defunct, Thomas took a slow walk around the pharmacy, past the retail area and into the dispensary where his attention was immediately taken by a drawer overflowing with unopened envelopes marked URGENT.

He opened a few and read the final demands for payment from suppliers and the threats of court action.

The Chemist was broke.

Thomas moved towards the shelves and looked at the hundreds of medication packets before stopping outside the controlled drugs cabinet. It was open and he analysed several of the pre-packed measures of methadone. On each one, after the patient's name, was the word (MEWS) in brackets, printed in bold capital letters.

To the side of the cabinet was a large, detailed map. Thomas, still holding a dose, looked at it, eyes widening.

The Mews.

Christ, did The Chemist have access?

He spent several minutes looking at the map, taking in the specific details it held, noticing that each tower block had a four-digit numeric next to it.

Entry codes to the buildings.

Thomas removed his phone, took a few photos of it and then undertook another, slow analytical walk around the dispensary, this time focusing on several medications.

Diazepam.

Viagra.

Cialis.

Pregabalin.

These were drugs Thomas knew had a value on the black market.

For the first time since he had learned of his brother's murder, he smiled. This information changed everything. Perhaps there was something different to be done here.

Thomas saw a lone blue script sitting on the counter,

attached to an uncollected prescription parcel. The name on it surprised him.

Rebecca Fury.

He moved towards it, tore it open and inspected the medication it contained: a small bottle of methadone. Thomas could hardly believe his luck, a slow smile spreading across his face.

He walked back towards the secure drugs cabinet, searched the shelves and found the drug he was looking for.

Thomas knew exactly how to manipulate what he had learned and not only punish Idris and Rebecca but make them slave to his business interests.

Idris was slouched against the shutter, watching as Damon played with a knife he was holding.

Idris was desperately thinking of what he could offer Thomas to escape this crisis.

Money?

There was the stash he'd taken from Patrick's car, unless Thomas already knew about that.

Idris watched, afraid, as Thomas took a seat on a bench in front of him.

'We didn't do it,' started Idris.

Thomas raised a finger to his lips. 'Idris Khan. Pharmacist. You supply drugs to The Mews?'

Idris nodded, surprised at the question.

'Methadone?'

'Yes.'

'To how many?'

'All of them.'

'How. Many?'

'Three hundred.'

'And you have unrestricted access to The Mews?'

'Yes.'

'To Jahangir Hosseini?'

Idris hesitated. He didn't like talking about Jahangir to anyone.

Thomas smiled. 'Your face says it all. How often do you see Jahangir?'

'Every day.'

'Here? Or at The Mews?'

'Both.'

Thomas looked at Damon and put his hand out for the knife. 'Chemist has access to The Mews. Interesting, no?'

Damon handed it to him.

Thomas cut the cable ties loose from Idris's hands, then handed him a packet of diamorphine 30mg ampoules, which Thomas had lifted from the controlled drugs cabinet, and a new syringe.

'Make me a shot of diamorphine,' said Thomas, pointing to the packet.

'Why?' asked Idris.

Thomas turned and slapped Rebecca, sending her body careering off the bench to the floor.

'Hey,' shouted Idris, aggrieved.

'Ask why again and she gets more than a slap. Now do it, Chemist.'

Idris snatched the diamorphine from Thomas and the needle.

'I can't like this. I need some water for injection.'

'Get it.'

Thomas turned to Damon, pointing for him to go with Idris.

Idris struggled to his feet and walked alongside Damon into the dispensary.

Thomas now focused on Rebecca who was using her shoulder to massage the side of her cheek where Thomas had slapped her.

He removed her dose of methadone from his pocket and waved it at her.

'Rebecca Fury, you're an addict?'

Rebecca's gaze flickered from Thomas to Idris who returned carrying the water for injection and hovered near Thomas, who removed the gag from Rebecca's mouth.

'Answer me, are you an addict?'

'I used to be,' said Rebecca.

'An addict is always an addict, no?'

She didn't respond.

Thomas turned to Idris. 'Diamorphine. Legalised heroin, right? Just 100 per cent pure?'

Idris nodded.

'Make me a thirty-milligram shot,' said Thomas, pointing at the medication.

Idris opened his mouth to ask why but stopped when Thomas added, 'Ask me why again, and you'll regret it.'

Reluctantly, Idris used the water and the syringe to create a 30mg dose.

'Place it on the floor.'

Idris did so.

Thomas lifted it, waving it at Idris, like it was a pencil.

'Tell me how it works. You and The Mews.'

'Addicts come in here and I supervise them taking methadone. That's it.'

'So why do you go to The Mews?'

'To deliver other medications.'

'Such as?'

'Pregabalin. Diazepam.'

116

'How many deliveries a day?'

'Maybe twenty.'

Thomas's eyes narrowed, more questions brewing in his mind. 'How long have you been doing this?'

'Couple of years.'

'Nobody has access to The Mews. Why you?'

Idris thought of the delicate deal he had struck with Jahangir. He didn't want to tell Thomas about it, but the bastard was sharp.

'Money,' said Thomas smiling, letting out a dry laugh. 'Chemist has lots of debts to pay. Some deal with Jahangir, no?'

Idris looked to the floor unable to meet Thomas's gaze.

'I know a little of how a pharmacy works. Addicts come to you, you give them drugs, you get paid, no?'

Again, Idris didn't respond.

'Jahangir sends all his addicts to you; gives you access to The Mews, and you make some money. What's his cut?'

'Twenty-five per cent,' said Idris bitterly.

'How do you pay? Drugs?'

Idris shook his head. 'I would never do that. I give him cash.'

Thomas snorted in derision. 'Ethical man. No drugs. But . . . murder is fine.'

'We didn't murder your brother,' snapped Idris.

'The hooker?'

Idris had to lie. 'Yes,' he replied.

'What is her name?'

Idris paused but he had little option. 'Amy.'

'Amy what?'

'Amy Starr.'

'Does she come in here for methadone?'

'She just started.'

Thomas walked back into the dispensary where he spent another few minutes speaking with Damon.

'Are you OK?' whispered Idris to Rebecca.

She nodded. 'I'm scared, Idris.'

Idris looked around desperately searching for anything to use as a weapon.

He wondered about Al-Noor outside. Maybe he had called the police? Christ, Idris hoped so. He had been mistaken in not activating the panic alarm.

Thomas and Damon returned from the dispensary and stood in front of Rebecca. Damon was now holding the syringe of diamorphine in his hand. Without warning, he suddenly descended on her, grabbing her arm and instantly stuck the needle in it.

'No,' she screamed, unable to stop him with her hands tied.

Idris tried to stand up but Thomas removed a gun from his pocket and pointed it at Idris's head.

Idris didn't stop, fear now forcing him into fight mode.

He tried to get near Rebecca, knowing that if they injected her, if the dose didn't kill her, it would certainly awaken the addict inside of her.

Thomas cracked his gun into Idris's neck, sending him crashing to the floor.

'One more fucking move, Chemist, and I'll put a bullet in you,' hissed Thomas.

'Please, don't do this to her,' said Idris.

Damon put his thumb on the barrel of the syringe, primed to inject Rebecca with diamorphine but stopped, waiting for the final command from Thomas.

Thomas crouched beside Idris. 'You must really care for her, Idris. Time to see just how much she means to you.'

Chapter Twenty-Three

Al-Noor had watched the men disappear inside the pharmacy, dragging with them a Caucasian woman he had never seen before. He had immediately realised that they were powerful men, the way they had carefully scoped the building, before entering.

He pulled on his raincoat, tightening the hood, and walked away from Dare Café, ambling slowly, in a non-threatening manner towards an expensive-looking black Range Rover.

Al-Noor wanted to assist Idris. By nature, he was someone who enjoyed helping people, especially those who had shown him kindness, yet he was also fearful of getting dragged into a situation which might make his life more complicated than it already was.

The engine of the Range Rover was purring smoothly, but Al-Noor could see nothing inside the car, the panes blackened out. He knocked on the driver's side window and waited.

Nothing.

He tried again, knocked a little harder.

The window was lowered a few inches and the driver, who did not look at Al-Noor, said, 'What?'

'Brother, it is a cold evening. Please, give me some change so that I can go and buy a warm drink,' said Al-Noor, quietly, softly.

The window was immediately closed.

Al-Noor had got accustomed to people saying no to him and simply knocked again.

The window was lowered, and the man shot out a hand, holding a solitary one-pound coin.

'Piss off,' he said, annoyed.

Al-Noor accepted it but immediately dropped it on the ground.

'Oh, sorry, brother, I will get it and leave you in peace.'

Al-Noor dropped to his knees and searched for the money while at the same time removing the tracking device Idris had given him from his pocket. Using the cover of darkness, Al-Noor thudded his body against the car to cover any noise fitting the tracker would make and attached it to the underside of the car.

Now, using the torch on his phone, he hunted for the pound coin, found it quickly and stood up, tapping it on the window while animatedly thanking the man.

Al-Noor retreated across the street, making a mental note of the number plate of the vehicle.

He had a feeling Mr Idris was going to need it.

Chapter Twenty-Four

'Please stop,' screamed Idris.

'You have one chance to save both your lives,' replied Thomas, calmly retaking his seat opposite Idris.

'Take the syringe out,' shouted Rebecca, looking horrified at it.

Damon remained unmoved, his hand wrapped around the plastic barrel of the syringe, primed to inject Rebecca with pure diamorphine.

Thomas raised his hand stopping Damon, then threw four packets of medications he had lifted from the dispensary to the floor.

Diazepam, pregabalin, Viagra and Cialis.

'These drugs you stock interest me. Tell me about them,' said Thomas.

'No,' said Idris vehemently, gritting his teeth, furious.

Thomas pointed to the syringe sticking out of Rebecca's arm. 'I reckon that size hit either kills her or gives her the best fucking high she's had in years.'

'It's too much, it'll kill her,' said Idris, panicking.

'How long have you been clean?' he asked Rebecca without turning to face her.

'Nine years,' she whispered.

'And yet, you've still not managed to come off the

methadone. If I hit you with that shot, what do you reckon it does? Puts you back to day one, right?'

His words might have been intended for Rebecca, but Thomas's eyes remained fixed on Idris. He saw immediately that the girl meant more to him than just an addict on his books.

'You love her, don't you?' he said to Idris and broke into a knowing grin. 'This shit just gets better and better. Pillar of the community chemist . . .' He stopped, corrected himself and added, '*married* pillar of the community chemist falls in love with an ex-junkie.'

Idris was sick of this. He struggled to his feet, stood in front of Thomas who remained calm and seated.

'What do you want?' said Idris.

'Three things. First, I want you to kill Jahangir Hosseini. I can't get near that cockroach but you seem to have the keys to the kingdom. Second, I want you to run *my product* through this pharmacy and distribute it in The Mews using those three hundred addicts who come here for methadone. Lastly, I want you to supply me with unlimited quantities of these four drugs,' he said and used his foot to push the drugs towards Idris. 'Do that and you both live.'

Idris took a beat.

He wanted to tell Thomas that he was insane. That what he was asking was impossible. He wanted to reach over and kill the son of a bitch for allowing his henchman to stick a needle in Rebecca's arm.

Instead, he simply said, 'OK.'

Thomas laughed. 'So easy.'

He grabbed Idris by the throat now and pinned him to the wall. 'Do I look stupid? We leave and the first thing you'll do is either squeal or do a runner.'

Keeping his hand firmly on Idris's neck and without turning to face Damon, he gave the instruction Idris had been dreading.

'Inject her,' he said.

Idris couldn't speak properly and croaked a weak response. 'Please, it will kill her.'

Thomas said, 'Half dose.'

Idris looked at Rebecca and could do nothing but watch in horror as Damon pressed the barrel and injected half the diamorphine into Rebecca's arm.

'No!' she screamed but Damon simply used his other hand to pin her against the floor.

'You bastards,' whispered Idris, trying not to cry.

Thomas let him go and Idris rushed to Rebecca who was slipping into unconsciousness.

'I'm sorry, Idris,' she said, fading quickly as the diamorphine started to take effect. 'I should never have got you into this.'

And then, her eyes closed, and she fell unconscious.

'Please, let me give her a reversal drug,' said Idris, worried that Rebecca would immediately overdose. He pushed her onto her side, into the recovery position so that if she vomited she would not choke on it.

'No,' said Thomas.

Idris faced him. 'If she dies, I'm doing nothing for you!'

'She won't die. She's a junkie. But it's on you to keep her alive. We're taking her with us, and each day Jahangir lives, we'll hit her with a daily shot of heroin. And not that clean stuff we just gave her. Black-tar shit. If you leave it too long, we'll get her hooked so bad that a few days from now, she'll be willing to work the streets in Beeston for a hit.'

Thomas nodded for Damon to grab Rebecca.

Idris tried to intervene, but he was no match for Damon

who simply shoved Idris to the floor and thundered a vicious kick into Idris's ribs.

Idris screamed and tried to get up but Thomas pointed his gun at Idris. 'That's enough.'

Damon lifted Rebecca's body and slung it over his shoulder. He grabbed the keys from the bench, raised the shutter, unlocked the door and left with her.

Thomas stepped towards Idris, malicious, spiteful and in complete control.

'Jahangir dies. You run The Mews. You supply me with product. Those things happen, you get the girl back. You blab, go to the pigs or do anything I don't like, Rebecca dies. Then your wife Mariam upstairs.'

Idris stared at him in disbelief.

Thomas grinned. 'NHS website, Idris. Old newspaper article about how The Chemist and his doctor wife started up a new business in Headingley. We know everything.'

Thomas paused by the door and hissed a parting shot. 'She's a good-looking girl, Idris. You leave it too long and maybe instead of a needle, we'll have some fun with her.'

Chapter Twenty-Five

Liam was lying in bed with Amy, both naked, post coital, feeling fucking pleased with himself. Soon, he'd have the money he'd demanded from The Chemist, a grand, more cash than Liam had seen in years.

He was setting The Chemist up for much more. Liam had bigger plans, he was going to ruin Idris until he had nothing left.

But a grand would get Liam a crib, the hell away from the shit hole he had lived in for the last few years.

Liam ran his fingers down Amy's bare chest, circling where her heart was.

'Fings are gonna be changin' for us. New crib, get us some wheels, maybe even book that holiday we's been talkin' 'bout for ages.'

'That would be somefin',' replied Amy but there was little conviction to her words, something Liam instantly picked up on.

He sat up, frowned at her. 'What's up wiv you?'

'Nuffin'.'

'That's crap. I can see it in yer face.'

Amy looked away, out of the window. 'Just . . . yer know, Rebecca and Idris did save my life.'

Liam's tone was immediately sour, the edge to his voice unmistakable. 'Fuck them. And fuck you if this is what yer gonna be like.'

Amy turned to him, immediately remorseful about what she had said. 'No, I just mean that . . .'

Liam got out of bed, slipped on his boxer shorts, his temper well and truly stoked now.

'That Chemist has been up our asses foreva. Mr Fuckin' credit to society but why do you fink he helped that bitch Rebecca? *Cos he's screwin' her, Amy,* that's why. The twat is married to some doctor in that surgery at the medical centre, did you know that? He's no better than dem men who shag girls in Beeston every night.'

Amy, realising that Liam was becoming increasingly irate, said, 'Yer right, love. He's just like that twat Patrick Mead who tried to rape me. We shoulda let the Meads sort Idris out. He'd be a dead man.'

Her words seemed to calm Liam's temper.

Amy, buoyed by being able to change his mood, went one step further.

One step too far.

'Imagine what the Meads would do if they saw that footage we got.'

As soon as Amy said it, she saw the instantaneous shift in Liam's demeanour.

'Babes, yer right! Yer goddamn right! Why didn't I think of that?' said Liam, excitedly.

He hurriedly started to get dressed, pulling a black top over his skeletal frame, clearly thrilled at the idea. 'I show the Meads the footage of Rebecca killing Patrick and forget The Chemist, we got a propa millionaire willing to give us real loot. I'm finkin' like . . . millions!'

Amy jumped out of bed, grabbed her dressing gown, mortified at what Liam was suggesting.

'Babes, I'm on that video too,' she said.

Liam slipped on a pair of dirty jeans and pointed at Amy. 'They ain't gonna care about that, they're just going to wanna know who killed Patrick!'

Liam was so excited he could barely stand still, hopping around the room, giddy.

Amy rushed to him, desperate to undo the idea she had created.

'Liam, please, if The Chemist gives us a grand a week, that's plenty!'

Liam snorted at her. 'I ain't no debt collector, going to see that cunt every week. I want a mill, so that I can get the hell out of Leeds and down to London where the propa rich people live. Get me a phat crib down there.'

Amy did not miss the fact that Liam was speaking entirely about himself. The ruse about blackmailing Idris had meant that she would always have had a part to play. But with the Meads, Amy realised she too would be in the firing line.

She had taken Patrick to The Vacants. She had called Rebecca.

Amy was certain that Liam would trade her life for an obscene amount of money in a heartbeat.

Liam slipped on his trainers, snatched his jacket, seemingly ready to head out.

'Where are you goin'?' said Amy, alarmed.

'To go see Thomas Mead, sort this deal out.'

'Liam, please, just fink about this. It might go badly for us. How do you even know how to find him?'

'I bought gear from their crew before. I'll see one of their dealers, tell them I've got intel about his brother's death, maybe show a little clip of that video and bam! I got me an audience with the boss.'

With that, Liam stormed out of the room.

Amy saw him disappear down the stairs, heard the front door slam closed, and just like that, in the space of only a few minutes, she found herself alone, abandoned and once again, at the mercy of what she and Rebecca had done.

Amy started to cry.

She felt just as helpless and alone as on the night of Patrick Mead's murder.

She wiped tears from her face, thought desperately on who might possibly be able to help her.

There was only one person she could think of.

The Chemist.

Chapter Twenty-Six

Idris was slumped on the floor, broken and bloodied but more than anything else, lost. The syringe which had been used to inject Rebecca was lying beside him, a drop of her blood still hanging from the tip.

The diamorphine would have lit up Rebecca's insides. When she started to crash, her body would crave more and Thomas would give her dirty street heroin, full of impurities which would potentially do more harm than the pure heroin.

His thoughts were disturbed by a banging on the shutters and the sound of a familiar voice outside.

'Mr Idris, it is Al-Noor. Are you OK?'

Idris rolled onto his side, feeling like his ribs were on fire, hoping that Damon hadn't cracked one of them. He struggled to his feet and hobbled towards the front door, raising the shutter and allowing Al-Noor inside.

'The tracker. Tell me you fitted the tracker, Al?' said Idris, desperately.

Al-Noor looked aghast at the state of Idris's face and the mess across the shop floor.

'Al, the device? Did you fit it?' said Idris, grabbing him firmly.

'Yes, Mr Idris, I did it,' replied Al-Noor.

Idris rushed into the dispensary, switched on the computer,

tapping his fingers impatiently on the bench as the screen loaded.

Al-Noor remained in the retail area, statuesque, confused about what to do next. Hesitantly, he made his way towards Idris, crossing the invisible barrier which separated the dispensary from the waiting area.

Idris typed his password into the computer, loaded the home page and accessed the tracking software.

Al-Noor arrived by Idris's side, hesitant.

'Mr Idris, is OK if I stand here?'

'Fine, Al,' replied Idris, waiting for the tracking device to reveal its current location.

Leeds Road, Bradford.

'Got you,' whispered Idris, relieved he had the location but at the same time, dismayed that the battery life of the tracker was showing only 52 per cent.

'Please, Mr Idris, tell Al-Noor what is going on. Should we call the police?'

Idris finally met his gaze. 'No, Al, that's the one thing we cannot do.'

Both men were now in the retail floorspace. They'd cleared up the mess and Idris was gently applying anti-inflammatory cream to his ribs.

The location tracker showed Thomas Mead's vehicle had stopped at an old slaughterhouse on Leeds Road in Bradford.

Idris knew where it was and was mulling over whether he should visit to see if there were any opportunities to get inside.

And do what?

Idris was a pharmacist, not a hero. And if he were caught, it would surely result in Thomas killing both himself and Rebecca.

Instead, mostly because he needed to get it off his chest, he confided in Al-Noor that Thomas Mead was trying to blackmail him into supplying drugs but didn't give any further details. While Idris trusted Al-Noor, he was still very much aware that Al-Noor's loyalties lay with Jahangir, where he earned his money.

'Mr Idris, I cannot believe what you are telling me. Ms Rebecca being taken is surely a reason to go to the police. In this country, they will help. They will arrest these people who are blackmailing you.'

Idris shook his head, finished applying the cream to his ribs and placed it by his side.

'Even in this country, Al, some people are more powerful than the police.'

'Then what will you do?'

'They asked me to do something to get Rebecca back.'

'What?' asked Al-Noor, taking a seat across from Idris who was looking intently at him.

Idris thought on the demands Thomas had made to kill Jahangir. He couldn't tell Al-Noor about that.

'They want money,' said Idris, looking away, afraid that Al-Noor would see that Idris was lying.

Killing Jahangir was one thing – a singular, horrifying act – but running The Mews was something entirely different.

For that, Idris was going to need the *one man* who ran product throughout The Mews, who had the address book, the knowledge and the trust of the residents.

Al-Noor.

Chapter Twenty-Seven

After repeated assurances from Idris that he was OK, Al-Noor had left, and Idris finished tidying his pharmacy, removing any trace of what had happened with Thomas.

He grabbed one of the instant-use icepacks he sold, cracked it open and using medical tape, secured it around his ribs, screaming as he did so.

The pain was unlike anything he had experienced.

Idris moved into the dispensary, grabbed a bottle of liquid morphine and swallowed a dose, hoping it would dampen the pain crippling his insides.

He switched off the lights, leaving just the emergency perimeter lighting on and glanced ruefully at the blank CCTV monitor. Damon had smashed the DVR and taken it with him, meaning there was no record of what had happened. And Idris didn't have a Cloud backup, something Damon would have realised looking at the antiquated CCTV system.

Idris was sitting in front of the computer and launched the pharmacy PMR: the pharmaceutical medications record software.

He typed his password then inputted Jahangir Hosseini's details and accessed his medication record.

While it was mostly supplies of methadone tablets, there

were other entries for Viagra, diazepam and the one thing which instantly triggered Idris's imagination.

A salbutamol inhaler.

Jahangir was an asthmatic.

He remembered Jahangir's demands for Idris to organise a new inhaler for him.

Idris tapped his fingers against the bench, deep in thought.

Was he seriously looking at ways to kill Jahangir?

His thoughts turned to Rebecca.

Alone.

Isolated, in some shit hole of a location, and when she woke up, what would be her first response? A massive shock and withdrawal from the diamorphine probably. And the hope – the single and only hope that Idris would somehow come and rescue her . . . *again.*

His thoughts turned to their shared past; of Rebecca lying on a hospital bed, covered in blood, screaming while their stillborn child was taken away.

Of Rebecca looking at Idris, only one question in her eyes: *Why didn't you save me, Idris? Why weren't you there?*

Idris opened his eyes and slammed his fist on the table, hard enough that it split the skin across his knuckle.

Blood on the white dispensary bench.

He grabbed a tissue, pressed it across the wound and stemmed the bleeding, watching as it turned from white to red. He grabbed another and applied more pressure to the wound until the blood started to clot.

Idris glanced at the computer screen, at the one button flashing green, which he needed to press but was struggling to do so.

The ACR button: Abbreviated Care Records.

Hitting it would allow Idris into the GPs' official full medical records and give him access to Jahangir's comprehensive file: reasons Jahangir had attended appointments, outcomes of those consultations and any prescriptions which had been issued. Blood results, too, and sometimes other sensitive data such as any restrictions on the supply of medications which the GP had put in place.

But accessing the records also meant that an auditable entry would register on the NHS ACR database, showing that Idris had accessed Jahangir's record including the date and time.

Idris glanced at the clock on the wall.

00.05.

What possible reason could he have for accessing Jahangir's record so late?

He thought on it, checked the last time that Jahangir had received a supply of salbutamol, and was relieved to see that it had been over two months before.

This piece of data was his 'in'. Idris created a false record of an emergency supply of the inhaler, which was reason enough to access Jahangir's ACR record, something he now did.

Idris removed the tissues from his knuckle and, satisfied the bleeding had stopped, grabbed a pen and some paper.

He scanned Jahangir's NHS record, knowing every webpage he accessed would leave a trail. He scrolled through pages of records, becoming increasingly frustrated with each entry he read.

Addiction.

Impotence because of it.

Asthma.

The odd supply of painkillers.

Nothing useful he could use.

He was about to log out of the ACR portal when he paused. Next to the small cross which would have closed the webpage was a square box, with an entry written in bold red ink.

Idris stared at this, eyes widening.

One single piece of intel which changed everything.

Idris knew how to kill Jahangir but more importantly, how to get away with murder.

Chapter Twenty-Eight

With the rain continuing to fall, Al-Noor had returned to his place outside Dare Café, sitting on a now waterlogged blanket. He was shocked at what had happened to Mr Idris but felt helpless to do anything about it.

Al-Noor knew who Thomas Mead was, everybody inside The Mews did. The only rival to Jahangir Hosseini and by all accounts a man equally as ruthless.

Al-Noor could not understand why Thomas was targeting Mr Idris. He may well have had access to The Mews but didn't have any power.

There were many things Al-Noor did not understand but one thing was clear to him, Mr Idris was a good man. Yet, he had also realised that Idris had not been telling him the complete truth.

Maybe, if Mr Idris had told him more, he might have been able to offer solutions. Al-Noor was now well versed in the ways criminals operated, having witnessed almost every criminal act within The Mews.

Dismayed at the night's events, Al-Noor packed up his belongings and headed home.

Outside The Mews, Al-Noor breezed past Samir, whose eyes were now clearly bloodshot, the smell of marijuana lingering potent. They both acknowledged each other and went about their business.

Al-Noor was accosted by three separate Mews residents, all high on heroin and all enquiring whether Al-Noor had another supply on him. He bluntly told them he hadn't, and they let him be.

He made his way into the tower block – the door, as usual, unsecured – and took the stairs to the fourth floor, spying – as usual – empty heroin wrappers on the stairwell and several used needles.

How he wished that he could have taken his son away from here.

But the letter he'd received yesterday morning – the one Idris had read to him – made it clear that for now, Al-Noor was trapped inside The Mews.

He unlocked the door to his apartment and stepped inside, surprised that the lights were on.

Then he saw why.

Jahangir Hosseini was sitting on the couch, Faris dressed in pyjamas, by his side, his homework book on his lap.

'What is going on?' asked Al-Noor, startled.

Jahangir raised his hand, impassively, and spoke softly, something which unnerved Al-Noor. 'Faris was afraid. He woke up, you were not here, and he came outside into the corridor. I found him, brought him back here,' said Jahangir and tapped the maths book resting in Faris's lap. 'Faris was explaining to me things I did not know. Smart things. Intelligent things.'

Al-Noor looked at Faris, afraid, visually checking that his boy was OK.

'Abba, I woke up and you were not here. I walked outside into the corridor and Uncle Jahangir was there and said he would stay with me until you returned.'

Al-Noor looked at Jahangir who again gave him a wry smile, one which made Al-Noor's blood run cold.

'That is very generous of Uncle Jahangir, but now that I am home, he can go back to his evening. It is not right that we have disturbed him,' said Al-Noor nervously.

Jahangir slipped a lecherous arm around Faris and squeezed the boy's shoulder.

Another smile.

Another uncomfortable beat.

'There is no burden in looking after those we care about, Al-Noor,' replied Jahangir but there was something in the way he said it which was unnerving.

In fact, Jahangir's piercing gaze was anything but reassuring.

'Jahangir, sir, thank you for doing this. I am home now so, please, you are free to go.'

Jahangir didn't move, kept his pernicious gaze on Al-Noor.

'Little man, time for adults to speak and for you to go back to bed,' said Jahangir to Faris.

Faris closed the maths book, placed it beside him and jumped from the couch.

'Abba, will you please come and tuck me in?'

'You go to sleep, my prince. I will be in later and sleep beside you. OK?'

Faris nodded. 'One hug before bed, Abba?'

Al-Noor embraced his little boy, kissed the top of his head then gently pushed him towards his bedroom, waiting until he'd closed the door. He turned back to Jahangir who was now standing stoic, with his back towards Al-Noor.

A shift in the atmosphere of the room.

Quieter.

Edgier.

'Thank you for your time this evening, Jahangir sir,' said Al-Noor, a little needy, and certainly afraid.

Something was wrong.

'Ungrateful, tricky little bastard,' hissed Jahangir, keeping his back towards Al-Noor. His words sent a sharp jolt throughout Al-Noor's body. His legs buckled a little.

'Sir?' he said and waited.

Jahangir turned around, holding the brown envelope from Leeds City Council, which confirmed that Al-Noor's application for emergency rehousing had been refused.

The one thing nobody was allowed to do: *leave The Mews*.

In his other hand, Jahangir was holding his mobile phone and waved it at Al-Noor, saying, 'Elyas is coming.'

Elyas was Jahangir's second in command and a barbaric son of a bitch.

Al-Noor stepped closer to Jahangir, afraid, desperate to stop this situation before it escalated.

'Sir, please, there is no need for Elyas,' he started but his words were cut short by his front door flying open and Elyas stepping inside, his clothes as always tight-fitting revealing a muscular torso and his dead eyes glaring at Al-Noor.

Jahangir stepped towards Al-Noor, now toe to toe with him.

'You will come with us now, quietly and without protest or . . .' Jahangir nodded towards Faris's bedroom door, 'Faris will pay the price.'

Chapter Twenty-Nine

The slaughterhouse, located off Leeds Road in Bradford, was a damp, squalid place. It had once been the prized asset of the Mead family back when they had significant control over the city.

Now, it was simply referred to as The Pit.

In the late Eighties, they had owned several slaughterhouses supplying meat across the whole of Yorkshire, but the main arm of this business had been inside Bradford.

The collapse of industry within the city, notably the wool mills, had put paid to any sort of future. The population changed, an ever-growing South Asian population who wanted halal produce.

The Meads had tried to accommodate what at the time had been a niche market, but it had been a futile effort. Competitors had squeezed them out of the market, price wars had erupted, margins decimated, and they had been forced to look to other areas to grow their burgeoning business.

Drugs had never been on their agenda.

But they had made poor investment choices. Two luxury hotels in Bradford had taken them close to bankruptcy.

The Nineties were all about change and the Mead family had not kept their eye on the market. They had realised the money which had once been confined to Bradford was now being moved at speed across the city towards Leeds, which started to boom.

The white population left and took with them all the money.

By the time the Meads adapted, they were way behind in the game and their losses started to strip away all the money they had made.

Assets were seized.

Bank accounts frozen.

And the final, bitter blow which forced them to look for alternate ways to make money: their five-bedroom manor house, home of a former Jewish aristocrat, was repossessed to pay off a crippling bank loan.

The Meads found themselves homeless, penniless and experiencing struggles like those they had suffered when they had first arrived in Bradford.

And then came . . . the solution.

Heroin.

Thomas's father, Jonathan Mead, had realised that the drugs market in Yorkshire was on the rise. While he didn't have connections to the main route of supply – Afghanistan through Pakistan – he did have European connections, from when he had sold meat to international suppliers.

Jonathan already had the import and distribution contacts and had entered the world of class A drug importation.

He had been the first one.

Seized the market.

Started what would become, for Yorkshire, a problem of epidemic proportions.

The market had spread quickly and with it the Mead family

had reinvented themselves. Patrick had taken it to the next level, ruling the market with an uncompromising, ruthless mentality.

Thomas stopped looking around the skeletal structure, his attention broken by Damon who said, 'We just leave her here?'

Damon unceremoniously dumped Rebecca's body onto a wilting old grey couch.

Thomas pointed to a shitty-looking red blanket, lying despondently on the ground. 'Put that over her.'

Damon hesitated, clearly not wanting to afford Rebecca any such comfort.

'She needs to stay alive. Do it,' said Thomas.

Damon lifted the blanket, cursed that it was soaking wet and dropped it back on the ground. A rat scurried away from it, into the shadows.

'This thing will give her pneumonia,' he said.

'Your jacket, then. Put that around her.'

Damon shook his head. 'This is a two-grand Canada Goose original.'

'Do I look like I give a shit?' snapped Thomas, wanting to get the hell out of here.

Too many memories of a failing business which had nearly broken their family.

Damon reluctantly removed his jacket and placed it over Rebecca's body.

'Now what?' said Damon.

Thomas thought on it. 'Get a crew here to babysit. Twenty-four-hour watch but they don't touch her,' he said firmly.

'Why not? She's dead anyway, right?'

'Nobody touches her. She's the key.'

'To what?'

'The Mews?'

'A two-bit junkie?'

'A two-bit junkie who The Chemist loves. Did you see that shit in his eyes tonight? Don't know what their deal is, but there's history there. Equity we can use.'

Damon wasn't seeing the bigger picture and was clearly frustrated at having to arrange a watch over the girl. 'Use for what? You think The Chemist can bring down Jahangir Hosseini? Are you crazy?'

Thomas chewed his lip, once again glancing around the building. 'You know what this place is, right?'

Damon nodded. 'The Pit. The place you won't sell, to remind us that if we take our eyes off the ball, we could lose everything.'

Thomas shook his head. 'That's what I tell you it's about. It's not.'

'So, what then?'

'It's a reminder that if you don't constantly grow as a business, keep moving forward, then you're stagnant. And this,' he said, pointing around the building, 'is what happens to things which remain stagnant. Nobody gives a crap about what they once were, only what they are now.'

Damon shrugged, not getting Thomas's point.

'We need The Mews. It monopolises our empire. The Chemist can give us that, but he can also help us run product throughout that shit hole.'

'He's a chemist, a geek who shagged the white girl and got himself in a mess.'

Thomas shook his head. 'You're wrong. He's much more than that.'

He kicked at the couch where Rebecca was lying. 'The way

he went to The Vacants to save her? Torched the house. Used the nitrous oxide? He's clever, more than just a chemist.'

Thomas stepped closer to Damon, serious.

'The Chemist is that one golden opportunity we've been waiting for.'

Chapter Thirty

Idris was sitting in darkness at his kitchen table, holding an icepack across his ribs. He'd taken another dose of morphine before leaving the pharmacy, mostly for the pain but also because otherwise, he wasn't sure how he was going to sleep.

He'd pushed thoughts of Rebecca to the back of his mind and told himself that the diamorphine would keep her sedated until morning.

He also consoled himself with the fact that if any harm came to her, what Thomas needed Idris to do would be off the table.

For now, though, Idris need to tell Mariam what had happened.

He'd created a story, one he thought plausible, and as he heard Mariam's footsteps coming down the staircase, he braced himself for her reaction.

Hurriedly, Idris removed the icepack from his ribs and put it across his face.

Mariam stepped into the kitchen, saw the state of him and rushed towards him, startled.

'Oh my God, what happened?' she said, immediately touching his face and taking a closer look at Idris.

'Calm down, it's not as bad as it looks,' he replied, hoping that the lies he was about to tell her would hold.

'Who did this to you?' she said, moving across to the light switch and turning all the spotlights on.

The light was blinding and Idris turned his face away.

'Mariam, calm down, I can explain.'

She held his face in her hands, inspected the damage: the bruising around his eye, the wound on his lips and his eyes, badly bloodshot from the force of the blows he had suffered.

Idris spoke quietly, calmly. 'A new blue script kicked off, I'd forgotten to lock the main doors and he came in as high as a kite. He wanted to take his dose off site, I refused, and he got physical. I hit the panic alarm, the police arrived and snatched him up.'

'Physical is an understatement,' she said, pulling a chair closer to him and sitting opposite.

'I gave as good as I got.'

Mariam inspected Idris's hands, which were unmarked. She stared at him, the lie obvious.

'OK, well, I tried.'

'We need to get you to A&E,' she said, standing now to seemingly go and get changed.

'Mariam, please,' snapped Idris, a little harsher than he had intended.

She stopped, momentarily taken aback.

Idris closed his eyes; he didn't have much left in the tank.

'I'm sorry. I just don't want to waste hours waiting in A&E. We're both aware of the signs of concussion. If I start throwing up, lose my balance or suddenly forget your name, you can triple-nine me, OK? For now, I just want a shower and to go to bed.'

146

Mariam's eyes narrowed and she took a moment to reflect on what he had said.

'I take it you're pressing charges?'

Idris shook his head.

'What's the point? He's NFA, and I'm not wasting months pursuing him for fifty quid in compensation.'

'He should be going to prison, Idris.'

'He is. When the police searched him, they found some heroin. Screws his probation and back to prison he goes. I don't need to do anything.'

Christ, the lies just kept rolling off Idris's tongue. But Mariam seemed to relax.

'I really don't like that we're not getting you checked over.'

'I'm married to a doctor. Christ, if you can't look after me then why did I marry you?'

She rolled her eyes but was softening.

'Can you climb the stairs, or do you need some help?' she said.

'Piggyback.'

She smiled. *Finally.*

'I don't like you working at the pharmacy so late every night.'

'I've been doing it for years. One bad incident doesn't suddenly make it unsafe.'

Slowly, Idris got to his feet. The world was a little hazy, but he put that down to the morphine.

'Have you booked a locum for tomorrow?' she asked him, clearly expecting him not to go into work. It caught Idris off guard. He had to go into work to attempt to resolve what had happened with Thomas.

He blurted out another lie. 'Sure I have,' he said.

Chapter Thirty-One

Al-Noor was cowering in the corner of the room, deeply afraid, alarmed Jahangir had ordered Elyas to lock the door. His heart was racing, his thoughts on Faris as Jahangir showed the letter from Leeds City Council to his two main henchmen, Elyas and Majid.

Majid did not possess the physical presence of Elyas. He had an altogether different skill – using unique implements of torture which he had brought over from Syria to terrorise people.

The atmosphere in the room was tense, Al-Noor searching for any way to explain the letter. He did the only thing he could think of and, in desperation, said, 'It was not my doing, Jahangir sir. The Chemist filled out the forms for me and told me to sign. He said this place is no good for Faris.'

Jahangir took the letter from Elyas, dropped it to the floor and stomped on it until it was nothing but fragments.

'You lie,' he hissed and nodded to Elyas.

Elyas grabbed Al-Noor, pinned his hands around his back and said, 'You are nothing more than a slave.'

'Please, Jahangir sir, I have served you loyally. I have never stolen, always turned up for work!'

Jahangir was sneering at Al-Noor, a sudden change in his face.

Darker.

Anarchic.

He removed a sleeve of cocaine from his pocket, tapped some onto the table and snorted a line.

Jahangir closed his eyes, welcoming the rush.

He looked at Al-Noor, eyes now seemingly lifeless, frightening.

'You are just a slave,' he whispered.

Al-Noor knew that he had only one chance.

To fight.

'I am not a slave. I am Al-Noor, former chief engineer of the Syrian defence system and I will not work for you anymore,' he said defiantly.

Then he threw his head back, butting the rear of it into Elyas's nose, who screamed and released Al-Noor who charged at Majid, the two men grappling with each other, engaging in a desperate struggle.

'Slave, how dare you act this way,' hissed Majid who was easily the stronger man. He pushed Al-Noor away before landing a brutal kick between his legs.

Across The Mews, in an opposing tower block, Daniel was sitting at his desk, having taken a brief pause from writing a novel about this life, one he had been working on for over a decade.

For most of the evening, he had been mulling over his argument with Idris, annoyed about a truth Daniel seldom acknowledged. That he had been the cause of Idris's relationship with his sister Rebecca breaking down and while she had tried to reach out to him several times, Daniel had not responded.

Guilt.

He had been a shit brother and there was too much traumatic history between them; too much liability on his part.

Daniel glanced at his novel again; he had over eighty thousand words but still didn't have a title, something which continued to needle him.

He had stopped writing because his focus was now on the top floor of A block.

Jahangir Hosseini's flat.

Usually, the curtains were drawn, giving no clue as to the criminal activities taking place inside. Tonight, though, they were open, and Daniel was watching the struggle taking place – Al-Noor taking a savage beating.

Shit, not Al-Noor, he thought.

He might have been the only decent man inside The Mews.

Daniel squeezed the pencil in his hand until it snapped in half, frustrated at what he was witnessing.

A decade before, he might have been the man inside of that flat dishing out such a beating. The difference was, Daniel had only done it to those who deserved it. Runners who had tried to steal from him. Addicts who had underpaid.

And the worst sort, those who thought they could encroach on his and his previous business partner Zidane's territory.

Zidane was now a guest in the most secure facility in the north of England – Wakefield, a Category A prison, reserved for the most serious offenders. His sentence for being a former kingpin had been twenty years. His sentence for a double homicide Daniel had helped him to commit had been life.

Daniel thought of Zidane now, probably sitting inside his cell, alone, and Daniel hoped, at peace.

Zidane who was nothing like Jahangir. Who had run the game with morals, and a robust code of honour.

Honour: not a word Jahangir understood.

150

Events inside Jahangir's flat were getting worse and having infrequently, rather voyeuristically observed what happened before to victims inside of Jahangir's flat, Daniel wanted to close his curtains and save himself from that horror show.

Yet, he did not, instead hoping for a miracle which was unlikely to land.

'I will not work for you anymore,' shouted Al-Noor, switching to Arabic so that he could fully vent at the men. He remained in a heap on the floor, having taken several violent blows from Elyas and Majid. 'You promised to bring me here and set me free! I have worked for two years, for little money, and all the while, you,' he spat, pointing at Jahangir, 'lord it over us as the devil you are. No longer, you hear me! Fuck you and fuck your Mews!'

Jahangir had heard all this before, from the men who had done Al-Noor's job before him. There came a natural point in this game where the chief runner became bitter at the imbalance of power.

'Almost ten years I have run The Mews, like this,' hissed Jahangir, closing his palm into a fist until his knuckles cracked. 'You think you are the first to think you can leave? That you can take all this knowledge you hold about me and The Mews outside of these walls?'

Jahangir nodded at Elyas who lifted Al-Noor from the floor, punched him in the stomach and then bent him over a table in the centre of the room.

'A slave, you said,' whispered Jahangir, stepping closer to Al-Noor, whose hands were now pulled across the table by Majid and held solidly. 'A slave is what I will make your boy, Faris. Remove him from school. Allow him into Uncle Jahangir's room.' He leaned over the table, whispering now into Al-Noor's ear, the stink of his stale breath across Al-Noor's face. 'Everyone knows what happens in Jahangir's room.'

Jahangir removed his belt from around his trousers and handed it to Elyas who wrapped it around Al-Noor's neck, pulled his head back, constricting his breathing.

Jahangir yanked down Al-Noor trousers, then his underwear and slapped his bare ass.

Then, as he had done so many times before, Jahangir lowered his own pants and said, 'This is where I show you what being a slave really means.'

Daniel couldn't watch anymore and pulled his curtains closed. He'd been holding the stub of his broken pencil so hard that the jagged end had pierced his skin and drawn blood, which now soiled the latest pages of his novel.

He looked at it discolouring the pages and ruining the words he had so carefully written.

And in this instance, he found his title.

He closed the notepad, opened the very first page and in large, bold letters, wrote, *The evil tyranny of men.*

Chapter Thirty-Two

The morning after the night before.

Idris had slept poorly, partly due to the pain in his ribs, mostly due to fear over what was happening to Rebecca.

Several times, he had woken feeling as if he could not breathe. A combination of the damage to his ribs and the crippling anxiety of having got himself into such an impossible situation.

Sitting alone at his dining table, Idris continued to think on how to kill Jahangir Hosseini, convincing himself that he would be doing the world a favour. That Jahangir deserved it.

But Idris was not a murderer.

He had Patrick's cash, he could make a run for it. To where, though? And leave both Mariam and Rebecca to face Thomas's wrath?

Every avenue Idris explored led him to only one devastating conclusion.

Jahangir Hosseini needed to die, and Idris needed to recruit Al-Noor to help him run Thomas's product throughout The Mews.

Perhaps, if they did this, Thomas would lessen his grip on them, find another way to distribute his product. And let Idris and Rebecca go?

Not a chance.

Had Liam and Amy not had the footage of what had happened two nights ago, Idris might have been able to push the blame towards them.

Christ, Liam.

Idris was certain that situation was only going to escalate.

Thomas might have been an evil bastard, but he was in control of his senses.

Liam was a boozed-up addict which brought only reckless uncertainty.

Idris stared at his phone, at the tracking software. He could see that Thomas's car had left the warehouse at midnight, visited a well-known shisha bar in Leeds, then finally arrived at a location Idris assumed to be Thomas's home in Adel, a posh suburb of Leeds.

All data which was interesting and perhaps would serve a purpose later.

Idris closed his eyes, pushed the pain in his ribs out of his mind and thought of what to do.

Al-Noor was the key here.

Idris needed him.

Idris was standing in the retail area of the pharmacy, listening to an elderly patient complain about their recurring headaches but not really paying attention.

Once again, he had covertly taken a shot of morphine liquid, feeling it warm his insides. The pain subsided but Idris knew that in a few hours' time, he'd be taking another dose.

Christ, he was becoming increasingly like his blue-scripted patients, he thought.

Drug dealers, dead bodies and now . . . drug abuse.

He had seen Al-Noor bypass the pharmacy and head upstairs to the GP surgery.

Unusual.

Idris was worrying about Rebecca, his eyes unable to leave the spot where she'd been lying the night before, unconscious.

Had she come around yet?

Had Thomas and his men made good on their threat to inject her with shitty street heroin?

She couldn't go back there, that struggle had nearly killed her.

Idris had phoned The Elizabeth Projects and reported Rebecca as being ill and unable to work for the rest of the week.

Daniel entered the pharmacy, pointed at Idris and then the consultation room.

Inside the room, Idris handed Daniel his methadone, watched him swallow it and then passed him some water.

Daniel drank it and said, 'Hell of a shiner,' nodding at Idris's black eye and returning the empty bottle before sitting down.

'Gym accident.'

Daniel raised his eyebrows, clearly not believing it.

'Perfect black eye,' said Daniel. He reached across and tapped Idris's ribs.

Idris nearly fell over and stifled a scream.

'Must have been a bad gym session for it to injure your face *and* your ribs.'

Idris looked at him, confused as to how Daniel had known.

Daniel pointed at them. 'You keep massaging them. Don't even know you're doing it, do you?'

Idris moved his hand away from his ribs. He so desperately wanted to tell Daniel about Rebecca but was certain that would make the situation a lot worse.

Daniel may have been a lot of things but above everything else he was a hot-headed, impulsive addict. And looking at him now, eyes reddened and pupils dilating fluidly, he was obviously on something more than the methadone he had just consumed.

'What do you want?' asked Idris.

'You heard about Al-Noor?'

Idris shook his head.

'When's the last time, you saw him?'

'Just now. Gone upstairs to the surgery.'

Daniel took a moment, thought on what he was going to say next. 'You know why?'

Idris shook his head.

'Jahangir and his men ran a train on him last night. Beat the shit out of him too.'

Slowly, like the life had suddenly been sucked out of him, Idris sat down.

'Man's gonna be a mess. Giving you the heads-up 'cos I know you two are close.'

'A train?' whispered Idris, knowing full well what that meant.

Gang rape.

Daniel scratched thick stubble on his face. 'Al-Noor must have tried his hand. Cash must have been light. Everyone knows you don't touch the stack with Jahangir.'

Idris shook his head. 'No way Al-Noor was skimming.'

His thoughts immediately went to what had happened the night before. It seemed too close to the bone to be a coincidence.

Yet it couldn't be related to Thomas. Nobody knew about that.

Idris thought of Faris, whom Al-Noor doted on and

156

sacrificed everything for. He felt sickened that if this *was* something to do with what Idris had pulled Al-Noor into, then it was two lives and not just one which were at risk.

'I told you what I know. Now is maybe about time you tell me the truth about your face,' said Daniel.

Idris looked sheepishly at him, touched his black eye, shrugged and said, 'Fell down the stairs.'

Daniel fixed him with a cold, patronising stare. 'You fell down the fucking stairs.'

Idris felt immediately foolish for such a blatantly weak lie.

'I opened the door into my face. Or maybe, I walked into a lamppost. No, I've got it,' said Daniel, mocking Idris cruelly, 'I just woke up like this.'

He leaned across the table, dropped his voice and said, 'Don't lie to me. Are you caught up in some shit you shouldn't be?'

Idris took a beat.

This was the moment.

To tell the previous joint kingpin who once ran The Mews the truth. To engage him and glean from him the right way to handle this.

No, he's high, Idris. You know that he will make this worse. Much, much worse.

'Someone hit me. A new blue script. Not one from The Mews,' said Idris.

Daniel considered this a beat, his eyes never leaving Idris's, but he seemed to buy it, standing to leave and heading for the door.

'Listen,' said Idris, a little more desperately than he wanted to sound.

'Yeah?' said Daniel without turning around.

'Is ... er ... Thursday breakfast club still happening today?'

157

'It is. Why?'

'No reason.'

'Why?' said Daniel again, more forcefully.

'Just thinking it's probably best to keep Al-Noor away from it, after last night?'

Daniel opened the door to leave. 'The last place Al-Noor is going is to Thursday breakfast club.'

If only that had been true.

Chapter Thirty-Three

Al-Noor's eyes were bloodshot red, his face heavily bruised, as he pushed a lone, handwritten green prescription across the pharmacy counter and then disappeared into the consultation room.

Idris looked at the prescription. GLYCERYL TRINITRATE 2 PER CENT OINTMENT.

It was a specialist cream for anal injury.

Idris sighed and placed it inside a red basket, then to the top of the waiting pile, and went to get Al-Noor's methadone.

Idris loitered by the side of the controlled drugs cabinet, Al-Noor's methadone to hand but he didn't want to take it to him.

Of all the people this could have happened to.

Over the years, Idris had known many runners within The Mews. They were usually the guys whom the kingpin trusted the most – not too savvy and always with some collateral which could be leaned on.

For Al-Noor, this was Faris, who, as yet, had not succumbed to The Mews.

Idris leaned against the cabinet, his mind a mess.

Jemma came to him, pulled him to one side and said, 'We've got calls coming in from The Mews. You're never this late in leaving. And when are we going to talk about what really happened to your face? Where's the DVR from the back room? Why isn't the CCTV working? What's going on with you?'

She had worked with Idris for over twenty years. There wasn't a chance she was going to buy into any nonsense.

Idris remained quiet.

'Do I need to go upstairs and ask Mariam?' she asked bluntly.

'No,' said Idris a little too forcefully. 'Everything is fine, shit, we're all allowed an off day.'

'Not when it comes to The Mews, we're not. Go give that dose to Al-Noor and then, bluntly, get your ass out of here. I'm sick of them calling us.'

Idris was standing outside of the consultation room.

He could not believe that forty-eight hours after rescuing Rebecca and Amy from The Vacants, he was now faced with this.

One single, stupid night of consequence.

He tapped his head on the frame of the door lightly, building his courage to enter and then hesitantly did so.

Al-Noor was sitting in his usual position, facing forward, not looking at Idris.

Idris noted he was not sitting in the chair but perched at the end of it.

He grimaced, slid the methadone dose onto the table and remained standing.

Al-Noor drank his methadone, replaced the cap on the bottle and passed it back to Idris, neither man looking at the other and all of it in silence.

'Please. Sit down, Mr Idris,' said Al-Noor softly.

Christ, that was the last thing Idris wanted to do. 'Al, I've really got to get back to the dispensary . . .' began Idris but

Al-Noor simply kicked Idris's chair towards him and glared at him. 'Sit down.'

Idris did so.

Al-Noor kept his eyes on the table, unable to look at Idris.

'Today, when Faris finishes school, he will come here. It is my hope that he will understand why his father cannot be here to collect him. That his father is a good man who was forced to do something he did not want to.'

Idris didn't like where this was going. Nor had he ever heard Al-Noor speak in such a manner with so much pain to his voice.

Idris thought on what had happened – how could anyone recover from such an ordeal?

'Why won't you be here, Al?' asked Idris gently.

'I must do something.'

'What?'

'By this afternoon, you will know.'

'Al, Faris needs you.'

Al-Noor finally looked at Idris and he saw the anarchy swirling behind his eyes. He was no longer the Al-Noor Idris had come to know.

'He needs to be away from The Mews. He *must* be kept away from The Mews.'

Idris thought to this own traumatic past; of blood and loss and of Rebecca screaming in a hospital bed.

There were some things you could simply never recover from.

'When Faris arrives, you will call these people,' said Al-Noor, removing a scruffy piece of paper from his pocket and pushing it across the table towards Idris. 'Social services. They will take Faris into their care, away from The Mews.'

'Where will you be?' asked Idris, anxiously.

Al-Noor stood up to leave.

Idris also got to his feet and stepped in front of Al-Noor, afraid.

'Move aside, Mr Idris.'

'I won't. I don't like how you're talking.'

'Don't worry, Mr Idris,' said Al-Noor, 'your secrets about Thomas Mead wanting you to push his product in The Mews will never be spoken of.'

Idris froze, shocked at what Al-Noor had just said. The threat, while softly veiled, was clear.

'Yesterday, I did something for you, Mr Idris. I planted the device on the car. Al-Noor hopes that after today, you will keep a little eye on Faris. You will make sure he does his maths homework and studies hard.' Al-Noor stretched out his hand. 'Shake my hand, Mr Idris, let me go, and do as I ask with Faris.'

'Al, please. Whatever is going on, let me help you.'

Al-Noor stared at Idris, cold, then at his hand.

Reluctantly, Idris shook it.

Al-Noor walked out of the consultation room.

It would take only eleven minutes for Idris to regret allowing him to leave.

Eleven minutes which would dictate the rest of Idris Khan's life.

Chapter Thirty-Four

The slaughterhouse Rebecca was being held captive inside was freezing, with dark pockets almost everywhere she looked. She had woken with a severe headache, and felt horribly sick. She wasn't sure if it was the diamorphine causing that, or the rancid, crisp smell of decay.

She had been awake just over an hour and was sitting huddled in the corner of the couch, cold, feeling scared and vulnerable, looking at Damon who was on the phone. Rebecca heard Thomas's name mentioned several times and wondered whether the boss himself was going to make an entrance when he did just that, walking onto the expansive, derelict floorspace dressed in a smart blue suit, no tie and with pristine tan-coloured shoes.

He looked every inch a respectable businessman not the cruel kingpin he really was.

'How are you feeling?' he asked her, placing a cup of coffee and a croissant on the couch beside her.

She looked at it suspiciously and didn't move.

'There's nothing in there except coffee,' he said, smiling warmly, unnerving her with how easily he managed to switch from a vicious kidnapper into a seemingly caring human being.

'Enjoy it,' said Thomas, sitting down on a wooden stool. 'Might be all you get today.'

Rebecca lifted the plastic container, removed the lid, inspected the contents and smelled the coffee.

She closed her eyes, enjoying the scent and welcoming the warmth from the cup.

'So, to my earlier question, how are you feeling?'

Rebecca took a small sip of coffee and said, 'I have a headache.'

'Is that usual after a diamorphine hit? You'll have to educate me.'

'I was almost ten years clean,' she said bitterly.

'Let's hope you get to hit that milestone again.'

Rebecca took a larger sip of coffee and replied coldly, 'You're going to kill Idris and me, the first chance you get.'

Thomas smiled and it made Rebecca want to scream – the sheer ease with which he transitioned from dark to light.

'I could have done that last night.'

'Why didn't you?'

'I think we can all work together.'

'We will never work for you.'

'You already do.'

'Idris is a good man. He doesn't deserve what you are doing.'

'I'm glad you said that. It's why I'm here. Tell me about him.'

Rebecca had a momentary urge to throw the coffee at Thomas's face. She wondered how badly it might burn him, but she quickly reined in the urge.

'He's just a chemist,' she said quietly and looked away from his piercing gaze.

He laughed. 'I love how everyone keeps saying that.'

'It's true.'

'So, how come you looked away when you said it?'

'You're not pretty enough for me to spend my time looking at.'

Another laugh. 'That's good. I like that. I think we might get along when this is all done.'

She shot him daggers. 'When all what is done?'

'When Idris kills Jahangir Hosseini.'

'What makes you think that he could do such a thing?' said Rebecca, perplexed.

'He loves you.'

She tried her hardest to be dismissive. 'Don't be so stupid.'

'So, going into The Vacants to save you and the whore was – what? Charitable work?'

Rebecca said nothing.

Thomas continued, probing for details. 'You fucking him?' he asked bluntly.

'No.'

'You've got a tattoo of his name on your arm. Idris, Ethan and Rebecca. Who is Ethan?'

Just hearing Thomas say her late son's name made her nearly throw the coffee at him. She gripped the cup harder, crimpled the edges.

'He was my son. Idris and I were married. A long time ago.'

'How long?'

She thought on it and said, 'Twelve years.'

'What happened?'

'Life.'

'Life happens to us all. What happened to you two?'

Rebecca glanced into the darkness of the warehouse. She no longer wanted the coffee, a sickly, painful feeling in her stomach.

She threw her drink on the ground, the container bouncing

on the concrete floor, the coffee spilling across it. She kept her focus on the shadows in the corner of the room.

Again, Thomas simply waited.

'We lost our child. After that, we lost . . . each other.'

'That's tough.'

His patience and the pity of his responses finally ignited a rage in Rebecca. 'Fuck you,' she said. 'Tough is being clean for almost a decade and having some cunt stick a needle in your arm.'

The slur momentarily removed the passive look from Thomas's face.

'I'm not telling you any more. Do what you want.'

Thomas leaned back on his stool and removed a brown paper bag. He opened it and waved a syringe at her.

'Please. God. No,' she said.

'I keep my promises. I told Idris the rules last night.'

Rebecca raised her hands in despair, pushed her body as far back into the couch as she could. 'Anything but the syringe. I'm clean. I was clean!'

Thomas removed the protective cap from the needle, pointed it at her.

'It's happening. The only thing up for negotiation is the dose.'

She heard a noise behind her and turned to see Damon standing there, holding what appeared to be a stun gun.

'Easy way or hard way? Your choice. Now, you were telling us about you and Idris.'

Her voice broke but she stopped herself from crying. 'What do you want from me?'

'I told you already,' snapped Thomas, his previous gentle demeanour vanishing. 'Everything you know about The Chemist. Everything there is to know about you and him.'

Rebecca thought on their past, the struggles she and Idris

had suffered simply to be together – racial, religious – of their decision to alienate themselves from their toxic families and to follow their own path, one which had eventually led to murder.

And to the disintegration of their relationship.

To a reconnection with her brother, Daniel, and the darkness within that relationship.

Rebecca told Thomas none of this, only that she and Idris had been married and that the relationship had ended after they had not recovered from the trauma of losing their newborn son.

And she absolutely didn't tell Thomas about . . . Zidane.

Never about him. Simply conjuring up his name sent a shiver down her spine.

Thomas would surely have killed her and Idris if he found out about that skeleton.

When she was finished, Thomas seemed satisfied.

'Please, don't give me another shot,' she said, hating the fact that her voice was weighted with desperation.

'And the hooker? Amy. What about her?'

'She's gone. Don't know where. She was scared.'

'Where can we find her?'

'She's an addict. And a sex worker. Your guess is as good as mine.'

Thomas seemed to accept this. He nodded at Damon who removed his phone, hit record and then quickly plunged the taser into the back of Rebecca's body.

She screamed, her body convulsed, and within a few seconds she was unconscious.

Thomas removed a black balaclava from his pocket, slipped it over his head and ensuring Damon was videoing, pushed the needle into Rebecca's body and injected her with impure street-level heroin.

He backed away, ensuring Damon had stopped recording and removed the balaclava.

'Send it to The Chemist,' said Thomas.

He watched as Damon did so and then said, 'Details on him?'

'We did a deep dive. Nothing showing. Like everyone keeps telling you, he's . . .

'Just a chemist,' finished Thomas.

Damon nodded. 'He's not going to kill Jahangir.'

Thomas pointed towards Rebecca. 'He was married to her. They had a child together. He will do whatever it takes to get her back. Where are we on the wife, Mariam?'

Damon shrugged. 'Waiting for you to greenlight it.'

Thomas took a moment, seemed conflicted and then said, 'Send him that footage as well.'

Chapter Thirty-Five

Eleven fateful minutes.

That was all it had taken for Al-Noor to leave the pharmacy, walk across the road to Dare Café where the weekly Thursday morning breakfast club was underway. Organised by the local community, it was a heavily subsided full English breakfast for only two pounds and while mostly for homeless people, many Mews residents also attended.

One of them was Jahangir Hosseini who always had a fixed place there. It was the one location he was guaranteed to be, unarmed and without his usual henchmen.

Idris had watched as Al-Noor had seemingly entered the café and taken the whole place hostage.

Idris's thoughts went to the conversation he had just shared with Al-Noor.

Look after Faris, Mr Idris.

Christ, Al-Noor was going to execute Jahangir inside the café!

With Jemma's concerns falling on deaf ears and with Headingley now teeming with armed police, Idris had rushed out of the pharmacy, past the police cordon, to the front door of the café and entered.

Idris hovered inside the doorway, looking incredulously at

Al-Noor who was towering over a bloodied Jahangir Hosseini, gun raised, pointing it at his head, ready to execute him.

Idris glanced at the two dozen or so members of the public, lined up against the windows as a human shield and smiled reassuringly at them. He recognised all of them as being patients registered at his pharmacy.

'Mr Idris, what are you doing here?' shouted Al-Noor.

Idris wished he knew the answer.

And Christ, the scene unfolding in front of him could make it all so easy. If Al-Noor killed Jahangir, the first demand Thomas had made would be realised.

Idris had forced his way inside because he needed Al-Noor to help him distribute Thomas Mead's product throughout The Mews, something which would prove impossible if Al-Noor killed Jahangir.

While he had been standing inside the pharmacy, witnessing the unfolding drama at the café, Idris had, for the first time, realised what he needed to do.

His plan was an audacious one but if he could get Al-Noor to stand down, Idris had a chance to do what Thomas had asked of him. And, after learning what Jahangir had done to Al-Noor, Idris was more determined than before to kill the bastard.

'Al, I need you to put the gun down,' said Idris.

Al-Noor kicked at Jahangir's body and said, 'I will kill him. Then I will kill myself.'

Idris pursed his lips and took a calm, measured breath.

'What if I could make this all go away, Al?' said Idris.

'You can't. Mr Idris, please, turn around and leave.'

'I can't do that, Al. I need you to listen to me.'

Al-Noor took a step back, a crazed look on his face, and

waved the gun haphazardly at Idris who instinctively raised his hands to protect himself.

'Get out,' shouted Al-Noor.

'Not until you give me five minutes to talk to you, alone. I promise I can help. Please, Al, give me just five minutes. After that, I will leave, and you can do whatever you want.'

Idris could see that deep down, Al-Noor was just as afraid as he was.

Idris nodded at Jahangir who, like everyone else inside the café, looked perplexed at Idris's arrival.

Idris spoke confidently, resolute in his ambition to stop Al-Noor. 'Let me tie Jahangir up so we can talk, before you do something which is going to affect the rest of Faris's life,' said Idris, trying his best to sound assured. 'Can you really afford not to give Faris that chance to live his life alongside his father? A chance for me to save you from this?'

Idris could see that Al-Noor desperately did not want to pull the trigger. That rage, humiliation and shame had got him this far but now, with the gun in his hand and Jahangir's life at his fingertips, Al-Noor had come to realise that it was not so easy to pull the trigger.

Al-Noor retreated a few steps and told Idris to secure Jahangir.

Idris and Al-Noor were standing in the far corner of the room, speaking quietly. Idris had given Al-Noor his dose of methadone, an act which he hoped would pay dividends later when he attempted to explain to the police why Al-Noor had done this.

Idris had brazenly told Al-Noor of the plan he had formulated. Even as he said it, he could hear the scale and absurdity of it, yet it was the only solution to the problems they both were facing.

'This is madness, Mr Idris,' whispered Al-Noor.

'I can make it work. I promise.'

'How?'

'I just told you.'

'It is not possible.'

'I'm The Chemist. Everything is possible.'

'And why would you do this?'

Idris sighed, exasperated at having to explain himself again. Each second they wasted in here would make what he had to do that much harder.

'I will do this to save Rebecca. You will do this to protect Faris. That's why we are here.'

Idris could see that Al-Noor was not entirely convinced by the plan. If Idris were being honest, neither was he.

'Can you do what I asked, Al? Take yourself to that place. Convincingly. If the armed police outside don't buy it, this entire plan fails.'

Idris looked intensely at Al-Noor, searching his face for a resilience he needed to see.

And, for the first time, he saw it.

Al-Noor did have it within him. Moreover, he wanted out of this terrible situation.

'I will do whatever I can to protect Faris,' said Al-Noor.

'Let's take this one step at a time. First, release the hostages. It will make the police relax, show them that I have helped you and that you are capable of being reasoned with. We keep Jahangir until the end.'

Al-Noor seemed reluctant.

'We don't need the hostages. Everyone will be a lot calmer if we release them,' repeated Idris.

Al-Noor nodded, clearly out of his depth.

Idris stepped back into the main area of the café, hurried to the door and called out to the hostages.

'Everyone out, now!'

There was a momentary hesitation. Several of them looked to Al-Noor who nodded for them to leave, keeping the gun by his side.

Idris opened the door and the hostages moved quickly, stepping outside where armed officers ushered them away to safety.

With the last one gone, Idris closed the door and turned to face Jahangir.

'Al-Noor will let you go on one condition.'

Jahangir was unresponsive.

Idris continued, trying to keep his voice measured. 'Faris leaves The Mews. He comes to stay with me. You leave him alone.'

Jahangir smiled and nodded warmly. 'Of course.'

Idris knew it was a lie. There wasn't a hope in hell that Jahangir would leave the boy alone after what had happened in the café.

Jahangir had a reputation to protect and Faris would be the first casualty.

It didn't matter that Jahangir was lying. Idris just needed him to believe that he had negotiated his release so he could gain a little equity with him.

Idris nodded at Al-Noor who didn't move. Idris could see he was having second thoughts.

'Al, remember what I said. You trust Mr Idris.'

Al-Noor walked towards him, passed Jahangir, and paused.

Idris saw that his hand had tensed around the gun. That he

was replaying what had happened to him the night before in his mind.

'Think about Faris and the future you want him to have,' said Idris urgently, needing to refocus Al-Noor's mind.

Idris stretched out his hand and slowly, calmly, placed it on the gun and gently prised it away from Al-Noor then nodded for him to go into the kitchen.

'I'll give you a few minutes to get your head right. Then, I'll leave with Jahangir,' said Idris.

Al-Noor pulled Idris to one side, away from Jahangir and dropped his voice. 'Swear to me, Mr Idris, that you will protect my boy and get me out of this nightmare.'

'I swear to you.'

Idris handed the gun back to Al-Noor. 'Remove the clip for me, Al. I don't know how to do it.'

Al-Noor did so and returned it to Idris. Then he disappeared into the kitchen.

Idris placed the unloaded gun on the table and put the clip inside his pocket. Then he freed Jahangir, helped him to his feet and pointed at the front door.

'You have magic in your words, Chemist,' said Jahangir, smiling as if he'd won the lottery. 'I think that tomorrow, you and I speak more about our deal. That Jahangir gives you a better one. And maybe a promotion.'

Idris didn't look at him, terrified that Jahangir would see his deceit.

'Let's get out of here. We're going to step outside, raise our hands and they will come for us,' said Idris, pulling Jahangir towards the door.

Idris hesitated, delaying until he could hear the one thing he needed.

The sound of Al-Noor screaming.

Chapter Thirty-Six

Even though it was daytime, and a bitter chill was in the air, the red-light district in Beeston was teeming with illicit activity.

Liam was sitting on the pavement, smoking a joint, watching some of his girls engaging with punters. He was feeling pleased with himself, with a clear plan of how he was going to bleed the situation with Idris and Rebecca for everything he could get.

Liam had called a mid-level dealer who worked for the Mead crew, told them that he had intel about Patrick's death and said that he wanted to meet the boss, Thomas. His contact had said that he would arrange it but that if Liam was bullshitting, the consequences would be severe.

Right now, Liam felt like the most powerful man in the world, manipulating this situation like a proper don.

Liam was going to engineer a bidding war for the footage of Rebecca killing Patrick.

The Chemist against the Meads.

Who could raise the most amount of cash in the quickest time?

Liam wasn't naïve to the fact that once the Meads knew he had the footage, he too might be in the firing line.

They were unlikely to meet his demands. What Liam needed was to apply more pressure to the Chemist.

He looked across the street, at Clare Glass, one his most experienced working girls, who smiled at him.

Liam winked at her, everything set for his imminent meeting with the Mead crew.

He was realistic about the amount of cash either party could raise in the timeframe Liam was going to give them; too long and the Meads would be able to engineer a plan to seize the footage from him by force.

A hundred grand; that's what he was going to ask for, more than enough to set him up somewhere decent. Maybe enrol in a detox programme and then, invest that money in setting himself up as a serious player in the drugs market.

Yeah baby, Liam Reynolds was going places, all right.

And that skank Amy wouldn't be coming with him. She was always whining, constantly holding him back. The bitch hadn't even been able to work the streets to earn her keep.

A dark Range Rover pulled up across the road and flashed its lights at Liam. His phone started to ring – an unknown number.

Liam answered, didn't speak first, just waited, his eyes never leaving the vehicle.

'Liam, come over to the car,' said a voice he recognised as his contact.

Liam hung up, stubbed out his joint and made his way confidently towards the car. He opened the back door, had a final look at Clare who nodded knowingly at him, before getting inside.

Liam was met by a wave of cool, icy air-conditioning. He marvelled at the luxurious leather interior of the vehicle and saw his contact, Trevor, sitting in the passenger seat.

The doors were locked, the sound momentarily making Liam nervous.

'Yo, Trev, long time, man,' said Liam, extending his hand to a street dealer who he had frequently done business with.

Trevor remained still, and when he spoke his voice had a nervous edge to it. 'What have you got, Liam? You better not be messing us around. This is serious.'

Liam withdrew his hand, glanced at the rear-view mirror, at Damon, whose eyes remained on Liam.

'Fing is, yeah, I know who killed Patrick Mead.'

'So do we,' replied Damon coldly.

Liam removed his phone, scrolled to a few stills which he had screenshotted of Patrick lying dead on the floor.

Liam wasn't stupid; he needed to drip-feed the intel to them, only revealing the complete footage when a deal was firmly in place. He handed the phone to Trevor who looked at the images then passed the phone to Damon.

'Where did you get these?' asked Damon.

'From the hooker who was in that room with Patrick.'

'Amy Starr,' said Damon.

Liam was momentarily stunned; *how did they know her name?*

Damon spoke in a controlled, clinical manner. 'We already know Amy killed Patrick, that situation is in hand.'

Liam instantly made the connection to how they knew.

Idris. Rebecca.

Christ, the Meads had already somehow got to them.

Liam also realised that Idris had done the only thing he could have: thrown Amy under the bus.

He smiled to himself, this shit just got better and better.

'The Chemist tell you that crap?' asked Liam.

A narrowing in Damon's eyes. Colder. Meaner.

'I know what happened that night. What if I told you it was Rebecca, not Amy, who killed Patrick?' said Liam.

'I'd need to see proof.'

'I have a video clip.'

'Show it to me.'

'For a price.'

'How much?'

'A hundred large, in cash.'

Damon snorted, unlocked the car doors. 'Get the fuck out.'

Liam didn't move, holding his nerve. 'You got some deal with The Chemist, right? Only reason he's not dead. I show this footage to the cops and him and Rebecca go to jail. Whatever plans you have are over.'

There it was, Liam's power play. He had been around long enough to know that the Meads would want complete control of this situation.

This time when Damon spoke, his tone was softer. 'OK. You give us the footage and we'll give you a hundred grand. But we want the other girl as well. The hooker, Amy,' he said.

Liam had no issue with this, it saved him the problem of killing Amy himself. 'Timeframe?' he asked.

Damon handed Liam's phone back to him and thought on his answer. 'A few days. We got your number. We'll call you.'

Liam made to leave the car.

The doors were suddenly locked again.

He glanced nervously at Damon, his heart racing.

'You mess us around, Liam, and it won't go well for you. Understood?' said Damon, a real menace to his voice.

Liam nodded.

The car doors were unlocked, and Liam hurriedly got out.

He had barely closed the car door when the Range Rover pulled away aggressively.

Liam watched it leave, heart still racing.

Clare came across to him, stood by his side, smoking a cigarette. She offered one to Liam who took it.

'Did you get all that?' asked Liam.

Clare showed him her phone, the clip of Liam getting into the Range Rover, of Damon and of Liam, and one of him leaving.

'Send that to me,' he said, using a lighter to spark up his cigarette.

He watched as Clare did so, removed two twenty-pound notes from his pocket and handed them to her.

Liam knew the Meads were not going to pay him anything, certainly not a hundred grand.

No, this was all about Idris and tightening the noose around that bastard's neck.

'What was all that about?' asked Clare.

'Leverage,' replied Liam and walked away from her.

Chapter Thirty-Seven

Stepping out onto the pavement, Idris and Jahangir were confronted by chaotic scenes.

Armed police.

A helicopter circling overhead.

There was a sniper on the roof of a building opposite and everywhere Idris looked, he saw police uniforms and the blue lights of multiple squad cars.

What had he got himself into?

'On the ground,' yelled armed officers, rushing towards them with their weapons raised.

Idris took a wider scan of the road, at the yellow police cordon, and scores of people, most of whom he recognised as patients, staring in amazement at their local chemist dropping to his knees and raising his arms in surrender. He struggled to do it, the pain inside his ribs excruciating.

It became so much worse when he was set upon by two armed officers who frisked him then cuffed his hands behind his back and yanked him to his feet.

He swallowed the scream, closed his eyes, desperately not wanting to throw up.

The officer found the loaded clip in his pocket, removed it, and seemed to think this made Idris their prime suspect.

He spoke urgently into his radio that they had found Idris to be armed.

He should have left the clip inside.

'I took the clip with me to make sure there was no threat,' shouted Idris, still grimacing, but trying his hardest to sound confident.

'I'm not the guy who was holding the café hostage. I'm the pharmacist from across the road. I went inside to help. The man you need is inside, he's called Al-Noor. He is a patient of mine and is having a psychotic episode. He's unarmed. The unloaded gun is on the table.'

Idris faced the officer who had tried to stop him entering the café thirty minutes before. 'You saw me go in. I'm not the hostage taker,' pleaded Idris.

Along with Jahangir, who Idris thought must have surely been known to the officers, Idris was marched towards a police car, ashamedly glancing at members of the public he recognised.

As he reached the vehicle, he glanced in the direction of the pharmacy and saw that Mariam was also there, looking terrified, and staring incredulously at him.

He tried to give her a reassuring smile but wasn't certain that she had seen it as the rear door of the police car was opened and Idris was thrown roughly inside. He landed heavily, and screamed loudly, his ribs feeling as if they were on fire.

Idris stopped when the driver got into the car. He remained flat on the back seat, suddenly mindful that everyone witnessing his arrest had been holding their mobile phones, recording it.

As the car pulled away, Idris closed his eyes, listening to the driver's radio; the message that armed officers had now entered the café.

His thoughts turned to Al-Noor.

Could he deliver on what Idris had asked him to do?
He hoped so.
Their lives depended on it.

Al-Noor continued to scream as armed officers rushed into the kitchen, their weapons raised, and surrounded him.

'On the ground, now!'

Idris had given Al-Noor one very clear instruction. To remember his journey across the English Channel, to recall in vivid detail the ferocity of the waves, the bitter chill of the air as his wife, Rima, had fallen out of the boat and disappeared below the water. Of how Al-Noor had shielded Faris's face so that he could not witness his mother's death.

Later, Al-Noor looking at the ground, imaging it was the ocean and continuing to wail in agony, pointing to the ground, and screaming psychotically. 'Help my Rima, she is in the water. She cannot swim; you must save her!'

Al-Noor released an animalistic scream, bringing to the surface an agony he had long since confined to the darkest parts of his memory.

As he was grabbed forcefully by armed officers, he started to thrash, imagining that he was in the ocean, trying to stop his wife from slipping underneath the water.

Then, he felt the hot, painful sensation of a taser in his back.

Everything faded to black.

Chapter Thirty-Eight

The police interview room was cold, clinical and clichéd.

Magnolia walls, a desk fixed to the floor, four chairs and above Idris's head, an air-conditioning unit continued to blow sickly stale air down onto his body.

Idris had refused the offer of a lawyer to be present while he was interviewed by the two investigating officers, DCI Brian Pitchford and DS Darcy Black. He felt that this would have surely shown the detectives that he had nothing to hide.

They didn't seem satisfied with Idris's answers to their questions, the same ones fired at him repeatedly.

'Let's go through it all one more time,' said Pitchford. Idris noticed that the old man had a slight tremble in his hand which he clearly tried to hide by placing his other hand on top of it.

Idris sighed. He was tired, wanting to get back to Mariam, to somehow explain to her why he had entered the café. The way she had looked at him when the squad car had taken him away was still etched vividly across his memory.

Hurt.

Fear.

Yet, even when he finally returned to her, he would be unable to tell her the truth.

Idris took a sip of water, tried to relax and said, 'Can you turn the air-conditioning off? It's not warm air or cold air, it's just air.'

Black left her seat, turned it off then returned.

Idris then repeated the lie he had already told them, choosing his words carefully.

'Al-Noor is a patient of mine. He had missed three days of his methadone supply, a hundred millilitres a day which is significant, and I had to cancel his prescription. I saw him just before he entered the café and he was suffering from withdrawal psychosis. He was irritable and not his usual self and I was in the process of organising a new prescription for him when he entered the café and took everyone hostage.'

This time when he said it, he heard just how far-fetched it sounded. But the detectives were not medics. They wouldn't know that he was bullshitting.

Pitchford again repeated an earlier question. 'Why would you need a new prescription for Al-Noor?'

Idris snapped. 'Are you deaf? Or is the arthritis in your hands bothering you?' said Idris, pointing at them, annoyed, frustrated.

Pitchford replied calmly, 'Not deaf. No arthritis. Just like to hear it again.'

'If you miss three days of methadone you need a new prescription from the clinic.'

'Yet you gave him a dose inside the café? Isn't that breaking the law?' asked Black.

Shit, Idris hadn't considered this angle.

'The cancelling of a prescription is a good practice arrangement not a legal one. I used my discretion in giving Al-Noor his dose to try to end a serious threat to the public. And it worked.'

'Why didn't you arrange a new prescription the day before?'

'I didn't see Al-Noor the day before.'

'Did you know that he was carrying a gun when he came into the pharmacy?' asked Pitchford.

'I've already told you that I didn't.'

'Odd, no? This man, whom you have told us repeatedly is a good, honest, decent human being, was walking around Headingley carrying a loaded gun? Not exactly something you can walk into a shop and purchase.'

Idris took another sip of water. 'Al-Noor is the main runner within The Mews. Obtaining a gun would not have been difficult for him.'

'Why carry one into the café, though?'

'I believe he was replaying his voyage from Syria in his mind. Thought that the people smugglers were onto him, tracking him inside the café.'

Idris now added something he had not said previously. 'I'm sure you guys know that Jahangir Hosseini and his family are major players in people smuggling and heroin distribution. That's why Al-Noor went after him.'

Pitchford's eyes had not moved from Idris. Almost as if the old man was looking through him, not at him.

Black scribbled something onto a notepad, showed it to Pitchford who nodded and then said, 'Jahangir Hosseini. Tell us about him.'

'I can't.'

'Why not?' said Black, suddenly becoming more alert at the mention of Jahangir's voice.

'He's a client of mine. Patient confidentiality,' said Idris.

'Wow, that didn't seem like such an issue when speaking about Al-Noor,' said Black.

Idris's answer was immediate and confident. 'That was different.'

'Why?' she said.

'Because I have Al-Noor's consent.'

Pitchford lifted his right hand away from his left, which had not stopped twitching. 'Can you tell us about that?' he asked.

Pitchford was smart, using all open questions ensuring that Idris did most of the talking. Ensuring that they gave him the maximum opportunity to let something slip.

Idris took a moment, kept his voice calm and said, 'I told Al-Noor inside the café that once we exited, I would be taken into custody and that with his consent, I would speak about his case with the police and, if needed, a psychiatrist.'

'That was *very* calm of you. Very professional considering the circumstances,' said Black.

Christ, Idris felt an imaginary noose tightening across his neck. The more he spoke, the more absurd his story was starting to sound, even to his own ears.

He could feel beads of sweat trickling down his back.

'I'm a pharmacist. We're always calm under pressure,' he said.

'Why a psychiatrist?' asked Pitchford.

'I was assuming that one would be sent to assess Al-Noor's mental capacity. He is not lucid.'

Pitchford looked at Black and, in that look, they shared something Idris could not decipher. It made him uncomfortable.

'Seems like you thought of everything,' said Pitchford.

Idris didn't like the way he said it. 'What do you mean?' he asked.

Pitchford shifted a little in his chair, leaned in a little closer and said, 'Well, you are, as you have said repeatedly, just a chemist. Yet you found the courage to enter an armed siege, disarm a suspect, engineer everyone to be released without

186

harm and,' he said, smiling broadly now, 'even had the clarity of thought to gain Al-Noor's consent in order to discuss his medical situation with us.'

Pitchford started to clap theatrically. 'Well, Mr Chemist, I have to say, I think I'd like to sign you up for the fast-track system to join our team. That is quite some forward thinking.'

Idris met Pitchford's gaze and saw that he had not convinced the old man of anything other than the fact that he was lying.

Idris took another sip of water, his mouth again parched.

Pitchford nodded at Black, who stepped away from the table to a water-cooler in the corner of the room, filled another plastic cup and brought it across to Idris, placing it in front of him.

Fed up now, Idris left it where it was and said, 'I'm tired. I'd like to go home.'

Pitchford pointed to the door and again Idris saw the smallest of tremors in his hand. 'Please. You've been more than helpful.'

'Very helpful,' added Black, the sarcasm in her voice obvious.

Idris got up slowly, desperately not wanting them to see just how much pain he was in, and went for the door, opening it.

He stopped when Pitchford said, 'One thing, Idris, if you'll permit a final question?'

Idris stopped, heart beating faster than before. 'Sure,' he said, turning around to face them both.

'The black eye you're sporting. How did you get it?'

Nightmarish visions of Thomas injecting Rebecca with heroin flashed across Idris's memory.

Idris answered quickly.

'A new addict wanting a methadone supply at the pharmacy punched me. I barred him. No big deal.'

Pitchford got to his feet, stepped across to Idris, keeping one hand on the table, using it almost as a support.

'That's what Jemma told us too. At the pharmacy.'

Idris said nothing, waited for the trap. He could see it so clearly but there was no way out.

'She also said that you told her that you'd called the police and reported it. Even gone to the trouble of writing down a police crime reference number.'

Idris wanted to run. He felt the room closing in around him. Sweat prickled on his temple.

'A fake police crime reference number,' said Pitchford, now close enough that Idris could smell stale coffee on his breath. 'Because you never did report such an incident, did you, Idris? I find that peculiar. Don't you, Ms Black?'

'Very peculiar,' she replied, resuming her previous sarcasm.

'It's not peculiar at all. I lied,' replied Idris, confidently and again too quickly.

Another careless error. Sweat tricked down his back.

'Tell me about that *lie*,' said Pitchford, emphasising the word *lie*.

'I have access to The Mews. They hear that I called the police 'cos one of theirs was acting like a twat and maybe other addicts want to stop using my pharmacy. Bad for business. But staff need reassurance, so I told them I'd reported it and that the addict was barred. Simple.'

Pitchford seemed satisfied with the answer. 'Addict's name?' he said.

Idris smiled, tried to make it look as confident as possible and shook his head.

Pitchford said the answer before Idris did. 'Patient confidentiality, right?'

'You learn fast,' replied Idris and shot Black a courteous smile before stepping out of the interview room.

Pitchford made his way back to his chair, sat down and let the silence linger a moment.

'He's lying,' said Black.

'Hmm.'

'Why?'

Pitchford turned to her. 'Find out, DS Black. Cross reference all agencies. I have a feeling our chemist is involved in something far beyond his control.'

Chapter Thirty-Nine

Idris traipsed towards his pharmacy, visions of Rebecca being marched into Thomas's car replaying inside his mind. He had tried to call her mobile, but there was no connection.

Idris glanced ashamedly towards the yellow police cordon, still in situ around the café. His feet felt leaden and in earnest, all he wanted to do was run away from the accusations and questions which would be thrown at him over the next twenty-four hours.

What had he done?

And the loudest voice:

How was Rebecca?

Idris approached his pharmacy when he heard a wolf whistle close by. He turned and saw Liam standing beside his car, grinning maniacally.

Idris could hardly believe it. *When was this godforsaken day going to end?*

He walked reluctantly to Liam who was concealed in the shadows, hidden by an overbearing oak tree.

'Liam, it's not a good time,' said Idris, stopping in front of him.

'It's a great fucking time,' replied Liam, unashamedly smoking a spliff and blowing smoke towards Idris. He nodded towards the café. 'That was some shit you pulled off today. Propa spy agent stuff.'

'What do you want?'

Liam removed his phone, scrolled to the two short clips of him getting into and leaving a black Range Rover and showed them to Idris.

Idris's face drained of the little colour it had. His chest tightened and his ribs suddenly started to throb.

He recognised the driver – Damon.

'The fing is, Idris, I got buyers for the footage of Rebecca killing Patrick and here's the real kicker, you're gonna love this. These guys . . .' Liam pointed at the phone, 'think that Amy killed Patrick.' Liam started to laugh. 'I mean, where are they gonna get that from?'

Idris stared at Liam.

'Checkmate,' said Liam, snarling at him.

'I gave you the methadone and I'm trying to get you a grand a week,' said Idris, desperate.

'Fings have changed. The Meads see that footage and Rebecca is dead.'

Liam slid his finger across his throat, ominous, cocky.

'I want a hundred grand, Idris. Or I'm selling the footage to Thomas Mead.'

Idris stepped closer, Rebecca's situation now more perilous than ever. 'Liam, please . . .'

Idris was cut short by Liam aggressively pushing him away.

'I don't want hear shit from you except that you're willing to pay the money.'

Idris looked away, this situation feeling more desperate than anything which had happened over the past forty-eight hours.

Liam continued, uncompromising, bullying Idris with every

word he said. 'Sell yer car. Yer wife's too. Then get a loan, you pros can get money like that,' said Liam, clicking his fingers.

'You're insane,' whispered Idris.

'Insane is finkin the Meads ain't gonna kill you and Rebecca.'

Liam stepped past Idris, whispering in his ear. 'You's got two days max, Idris. Get me my dosh or Thomas gets the video.'

Then he walked away, discarding his spliff into the air as he went.

Idris stepped through the doors of his pharmacy, pleased that it was empty with just Jemma and Vanessa working in the dispensary.

He glanced at his watch.

20.00.

The end of their shift and he needed them to leave so he could take a dose of morphine liquid for the ache in his ribs. It was the only reason he had returned here.

He stepped quietly into the dispensary and stood, uncomfortably alone, waiting for Jemma to notice him. When neither she nor Vanessa did, Idris cleared his throat and sheepishly said, 'Hey.'

They both turned towards him.

'Oh God, you scared me,' said Vanessa, theatrically putting her hand on her chest, feeling her heart rate. Then she stepped towards him and hugged Idris.

He winced, it was the last thing he needed. His ribs felt ready to crumble.

'God, are you OK?' she said.

Idris stepped away from her, swallowed the pain.

'I'm OK,' he said, grimacing, struggling not to scream.

Vanessa broke the embrace, stepped back and then slapped her hand against his shoulder.

More pain ricocheted throughout his body. 'What on earth were you thinking, Idris? Are you crazy?' she said.

Idris was tired, so terribly exhausted from the day's events. He didn't know what to say and simply shrugged. 'Another time. I'm tired. Did you book a locum?'

Vanessa shook her head. 'I was going to do the hours. Bill you double time.'

'I got it. Go home,' he said.

'Are you mad? You can't work a nightshift after what happened today.'

'I'm going to close early.'

Jemma, who still had not looked at him, finally spoke, keeping her attention on the work she was doing. 'Have you called Mariam?' she said bluntly.

'I will,' he replied, feeling that she wanted to discharge her anger at him. She'd tried to stop him and importantly, having known Idris for over two decades, Jemma seemed to know that he was withholding things from her.

'I'm not letting you work,' said Vanessa, vehemently shaking her head in disapproval.

'Vee, I just need to sit here a while, alone, and think on what I'm going to say to Mariam. Lock the doors on your way out, I won't even put the hatch into play. I just need an hour to get my head right.'

She looked at him, measuring whether he was being serious or not.

'Honestly, I'm fine. I just need a brew, a couple of co-codamol and a little time.'

Jemma finished dispensing the dosette box she was working on, swiftly grabbed her coat and marched towards Idris, still having not looked at him.

He grabbed her arm as she passed him.

She swiftly slapped it away. 'Don't. Just . . . don't,' she snapped.

'I'm sorry, Jem,' he said, genuinely.

Vanessa looked at them both, seemed to realise they needed a moment and grabbed her things. 'I'll leave you both to it. Idris, honestly, I'll drive past here on my way back from the gym and if you're still here, I'm going to be pissed.'

She left Idris and Jemma to it and promptly walked out.

Idris waited until she had gone, then stepped in front of Jemma. 'Seriously. I'm sorry.'

'What the hell has got into you lately?' she snapped.

'Nothing.'

'There you go again. The lies just roll off your tongue, don't they?'

She put her bag down, clearly prepared for an argument. 'I'm not leaving until you tell me what is going on.'

'With what?'

Jemma reached out a hand and touched the side of his face. He flinched away from her. 'How about we start with that black eye? The truth. Do you really think I'm that naïve?'

Christ, he wanted some quiet time and instead he'd walked into a hornets' nest. 'And Mariam. Did you even, for one second, think about her? What is it about Al-Noor that needed you to go into the café so badly? What have you got yourself into?'

Idris sat down on a stool, deflated, his head now pounding from a headache. He remained silent, unable to find the right words.

Jemma seemed to realise that perhaps, he'd had enough for one day.

'Do you . . . I don't know . . . want a tea?' she said finally.

Idris kept his eyes rooted to the floor and simply said, 'Yes.'

Jemma popped two strong codeine tablets onto the bench beside Idris, next to his tea. 'You're definitely closing up, right?' she asked. 'This strength will knock you for six.'

He popped the tablets into his mouth, swallowed them with a sip of tea and rubbed his eyes. 'Yes, I'm closing,' he whispered.

Jemma put her hand on his shoulder, her previous fierceness now gone. 'You really need to call Mariam.'

'I texted her when I left the station.'

'She reply?'

'No.'

'You might avoid telling me why you went into the café, but you will need to tell her. I've never seen her so upset.'

'I know.'

Idris wrapped both hands around his mug of tea, welcoming the warmth.

'Do you want me to stay with you?' she said softly, again seeming to realise that he was at rock bottom.

'No.'

'Doesn't feel right to leave you like this.'

'Trust me. Being alone is what I need right now.'

'Give you a piece of advice?'

'Always.'

'Tell Mariam the truth.'

'I will,' he replied, and he meant to. If the day had proven one thing to Idris, it was that he was out of his depth.

Jemma grabbed her things, checked one final time that he didn't need her and left him alone, locking the outer door as she exited.

Even though he'd taken strong painkillers, Idris still grabbed a bottle of morphine liquid and took a dose. His ribs were killing him.

He returned to his bench and saw two blue scripts which had yet to be collected: Rebecca's and Jahangir's.

His phone pinged.

A disappearing WhatsApp message from an unknown number.

Usually, he would have deleted it without hesitation, yet something told him that this was from Thomas.

He opened the file and let out a small, pained cry, looking at a photo of Rebecca, comatose on a grey cement floor, a syringe sticking out of her arm.

Idris slammed his phone down on the counter.

'Fuck!' he shouted.

Another disappearing message arrived.

He didn't want to look it, feeling sick at the sound of it.

This time it was a photo of Mariam, arriving for work that morning.

Another one arrived – Mariam outside their home, it must have been that evening.

Shit, they were watching his house, the intent clear.

If Idris didn't kill Jahangir, everyone he cared about was dead.

Idris felt dizzy, vision blurring, his mind throwing conflicting thoughts at him.

He craved for the normality his pharmacy had always given him – routine, purpose, meaning.

Idris picked up his phone, the decision made, one he should

have actioned as soon as Thomas entered his pharmacy: to call the police, report what had happened.

He was going to be struck off the register, lose his licence and his pharmacy business and in all probability, receive a jail sentence.

Idris dialled 999 and was about to hit 'dial' when the out-of-hours doorbell sounded.

Idris peered over the counter, and saw Jahangir Hosseini standing there, smiling.

Idris retook his seat and glanced at the phone in his hand, 999 still on screen.

He looked at Jahangir's blue script for methadone tablets, still waiting to be consumed.

Idris thought to the patient data he had accessed the night before. The vital intel which, in the right hands, *in Idris's hands*, would be fatal.

Idris deleted the number from his phone, closed his eyes and took a beat.

The doorbell sounded again, followed by the sound of Jahangir tapping on the door.

Idris thought about what Jahangir had done to Al-Noor.

Shit, what about Faris? Where was he? Idris had not been here to greet him, that was if Faris had even come to the pharmacy after he'd finished school. Idris had sworn to Al-Noor that he would look after his son.

There was only once place Faris would have gone.

Home. The Mews, the place Jahangir would be going next.

Idris was certain that after what Al-Noor had done earlier, Faris was in danger.

He needed to get the boy to safety.

Idris, with a steely resolve now, started to internalise his anger, accessing darker memories of his past with Rebecca and a night which changed everything for them both.

Of rage and guilt and being unable to save her from trauma.

But Idris could save Faris and in a way, redeem himself from what he had done so far.

'Jahangir is a parasite,' whispered Idris to himself. He moved his hand to his ribs, took a breath and then pushed his knuckles into them, the searing pain making him yell in agony. But he needed this – to feel anger, bitterness and most importantly, *rage*.

Idris took a final glance at Jahangir's blue script then walked out of the dispensary to the retail counter. He acknowledged Jahangir's presence with a wave of his hand and quickly scanned the shelves for a particular drug; one which anyone could buy without a pharmacist's supervision.

A medication routinely available from corner shops and petrol stations.

A medication with no restriction to people being able to buy it.

A medication which was about to cost Jahangir Hossieni his life.

Chapter Forty

Rebecca rubbed her eyes, her mouth parched, her head feeling light.

Where was she?

Rebecca looked around the decrepit building, shadows and darkness everywhere, hints of towering steel columns and beams running high across the ceiling.

She tried to sit up and felt suddenly horribly sick.

Shit, she was going to throw up. Hurriedly, she leaned forward – and did so, all over the floor.

The weight of her body forced her to lose her balance and she slipped off the couch, falling onto the floor, thankful to avoid the area where she'd been sick.

God, where am I?

Male voices to the side of her were distorted, their words sounding like they were muffled.

She scrambled around on the floor, tried to stand up. Her hands and feet were secured with cable ties making it hard to move.

Her mind cleared and it all came back to her.

Thomas Mead.

His henchman, Damon.

The needle in her arm, full of impure street heroin.

Rebecca felt strong hands suddenly lift her from the ground and place her back on the couch.

She couldn't make out what the men looked like, the darkness seemingly wrapping around their faces, everything merging into an undecipherable mess.

She stared at them, again unable to understand what they were saying, everything sounding muffled.

'Water,' she said, her own voice sounding alien to her.

One of the men disappeared and returned a few seconds later with a bottle of water. He forced it into her hand, then retreated into the darkness. He was wearing a balaclava. Both men were.

Rebecca struggled with the cap of the plastic bottle, the cable ties making it difficult.

'Please, can someone help me?'

Help arrived; a man opened the bottle for her.

Rebecca slowly took a sip. Cautious, careful. Last thing she wanted was to vomit again.

She poured a little water across her face, it trickled down her temple, over the bridge of her nose.

She slumped into the couch, afraid, distraught at what she had brought not only upon herself but also Idris.

It felt like history was repeating itself.

Her hands went to her stomach to visions of her blood all over a hospital bed, Idris by her side, holding her hand as the doctors took their stillborn child away from them.

She started to cry, terrified that Thomas might have killed Idris.

If that were the case, why was she still alive?

Her vision cleared a little, still a touch blurry but she could make out more details of where she was.

A sprawling concrete floor, steel and cement, shadows of what appeared to be old machinery, for what exact purpose she wasn't sure. And that smell – metallic, rancid.

She had another sip of water, allowing it to trickle down her throat, then put the bottle aside.

Discreetly, she checked her pockets, hoping to find something which might help her. But they were empty.

She tried to remain calm, think on solutions.

Thomas didn't know just which circle she and Idris had grown up surrounded by. *That was key.*

She whispered her next thought, as if manifesting it. 'Please, call Daniel, Idris.'

Who else could help them?

But Daniel was an addict now, not the same man he used to be.

He is. He never changed.

Or . . . had Idris gone higher to . . . *him.*

Rebecca closed her eyes. A name neither she nor Idris had mentioned in over a decade was now firmly etched in her mind.

Loud.

Clear.

Crucial.

How else were they going to escape this nightmare?

Rebecca suddenly realised what the metallic taste on her tongue was.

Blood.

Suddenly more afraid than she had been, she glanced around the expansive warehouse, looking for clues as to why she could smell blood.

Her eyes narrowed, her vision adjusting well to the darkness now.

And now she saw it.

And screamed.

The dead, skinless shape of what appeared to be a cow, blood dripping from its headless body onto the concrete.

Rebecca immediately repeated her earlier action of leaning over the couch and again, threw up all over the floor.

This was what they had in mind for her and Idris.

A goddamn guillotine.

As she continued to wretch, her stomach now empty, her mind again went to Daniel.

Idris must have called him.

Which other move could he possibly have made?

Chapter Forty-One

Idris was standing behind the pharmacy counter, staring at Jahangir who was sitting on the same bench that Thomas had been perched upon the night before, smiling devilishly.

The two most feared gangsters in Yorkshire, face to face with Idris within twenty-four hours.

'Come, sit, Mr Chemist, we have much to talk about,' said Jahangir and for the first time ever, he sounded earnest, not full of his usual pomp.

An idea was forming inside Idris's mind. He had saved Jahangir's life – there was a debt to be repaid. Could he simply play Jahangir off against Thomas and get them to take each other out and then he and Rebecca could simply walk free?

He dismissed the idea as quickly as it surfaced; too risky.

If Jahangir came off second best, then Idris and Rebecca would certainly be killed.

Jahangir tapped a space beside him on the bench.

Idris hesitated, struggling with so many conflicting thoughts.

You know how to kill him. It's untraceable. Do it now. Save Rebecca.

'I need to . . . get your methadone,' said Idris.

'It can wait. First, we talk,' said Jahangir, again tapping the bench.

Idris didn't sit next to Jahangir, but opposite him.

'What you did today, Mr Idris. *Very big thing.* You know what I am doing on my way over here?'

Idris shook his head, continued to look at the floor, deflated.

'I called my older brother, Mawt Hosseini, in Calais. He is a big man over there. He can get his hands on many things. I tell him what Idris does for Jahangir and he tells me to give you a reward. Show our – how you say? – appreciation. So, tell me. What is it you want? Girls? Cocaine? Maybe a little of both,' he said, laughing.

Idris was feeling sick. Engaging in this bullshit was making what he needed to do so much harder.

'I don't need anything.'

'Everybody needs something.'

Idris looked at Jahangir. 'I'm not from your world. I don't deal in things like that.'

Jahangir laughed and pointed towards the dispensary. 'You have all the drugs in the world. You and me? We are same.'

'We are not the same,' spat Idris.

'Look at what you did today for Jahangir. We are lions.'

'I did it for Al-Noor,' said Idris, honestly. Perhaps the only honest thing he'd said all day.

'Al-Noor?' said Jahangir, with a sudden, obvious bitterness.

'I didn't want him to kill you and go to jail.' Idris fixed Jahangir with a purposeful stare. 'He's been through enough, no? Losing his wife. Forced to become an addict. Looking after his son.'

Jahangir met Idris's gaze, seemingly figuring out if Idris was being serious or engaging in some sort of joke with him.

'Al-Noor came to kill me,' said Jahangir.

'You ran a train on him,' Idris shot back.

'Al-Noor knows what the punishment is for those who try and leave The Mews.'

'He is a good man. He didn't deserve that. Nobody deserves that.'

Idris could tell he was starting to irritate Jahangir, but he was past caring. The bastard needed to hear what Idris had to say.

'Al-Noor will go to jail. And when he is inside, Jahangir's friends will make sure he never comes out.'

'Why?' said Idris, thinking now in detail about what he needed to do, running through the sequences inside his mind, growing more resilient with each passing second.

Patrick Mead dead on the floor.

Rebecca being taken.

Al-Noor being assaulted.

And Jahangir, now sitting cockily in front of Idris, like he'd won the lottery, revelling in how he had survived the scare at the café.

Idris stood up. 'I'm tired, Jahangir. Let me sort your methadone then let's both get home. We can talk more tomorrow.'

'Tea,' said Jahangir.

'What?'

'I want a tea. Three sugars. You make for me along with my methadone. Makes Jahangir happy.'

Hot tea.

It would make the tablets dissolve quicker. They would have a faster effect. Idris didn't want that, though. He needed Jahangir to die near or ideally, inside of The Mews.

Drop him home, Idris.

Collect Faris from Al-Noor's flat.

Kill two birds with one stone.

'Sure,' said Idris and retreated into the dispensary.

*

205

First, he made Jahangir a cup of tea and left it to cool, wanting him to drink it quickly so that they could leave as soon as he had taken his medication.

Idris also had another dose of morphine liquid, his fourth of the day, each one making his pain that little bit more bearable.

Now, for the switch in Jahangir's medication.

Idris popped eight methadone tablets into a small dish.

Jahangir was the only Mews resident who consumed methadone tablets and not the green liquid everyone else was prescribed. He claimed he couldn't stand the taste of it and had played merry hell until the clinic had finally given in and switched him to tablets.

Idris thought there was a darker reason.

Jahangir was allowed to take his weekend supply of methadone away with him. Idris was certain that Jahangir was selling the tablets on the black market, where they had a decent resale value.

Either that, or he was crushing them and mixing them with some other drug to snort.

Whatever the reason, Idris found it ironic that Jahangir's insistence to be prescribed tablets would now be the one thing which would cost him his life.

Idris removed the packet of medication he had lifted from the shop – a packet of common aspirin tablets – from his pocket, opened them and popped a single tablet into the dish where it landed next to the methadone tablets.

One tablet or two, Idris?

He wanted to use two tablets, for no other reason than to ensure the outcome he had anticipated would happen.

It might be too quick, Idris.

He might die in the car.

Idris removed a single white methadone tablet from the

dish and switched it with a single aspirin tablet, ensuring that he would still hand Jahangir exactly eight tablets, the same as he always did. Both aspirin and methadone tablets were white, with a central scored line down the centre. The only difference was that methadone tablets were marked with a small M5 branding and the aspirin with A300.

Undetectable to the naked eye unless you really knew what to look for.

One aspirin mixed with the seven methadone tablets.

Poison.

Idris removed a small prescription packet from a drawer – a new salbutamol inhaler which he had dispensed after viewing Jahangir's ACR and engineered an emergency supply for him.

Idris opened it and removed the full canister of the drug from the device. He then grabbed an empty one from a recycling bin and made the switch. Idris removed the label from the inhaler, ensuring there was no date showing when it had been supplied.

He put the inhaler on a tray, next to the methadone tablets and the cup of tea, and carried them all to Jahangir. He set the tray down, handed Jahangir his tea then tipped the tablets chaotically into Jahangir's hand and pointed to the inhaler left on the tray.

'Salbutamol inhaler you ordered is ready too.'

He watched, holding his breath as Jahangir popped the tablets into his mouth and swallowed them with a large gulp of tea.

'I'm closing early. You want a lift home?' asked Idris.

Jahangir grabbed the inhaler and said, 'Of course.'

Chapter Forty-Two

The drive to The Mews was awful, though it was fitting, thought Idris, that Jahangir's final resting place would be where he believed himself to be untouchable.

Idris had missed three calls from Mariam and didn't know how he was going to explain this day to her, never mind why he still had not arrived home.

For now, his focus was solely on Jahangir, who was subdued.

Idris kept glancing at him, wondering when the aspirin would kick in, wondering when it would force a cataclysmic internal reaction which would kill him.

Idris saw Jahangir run his hand across his chest and rub it.

There it was, the first sign of the reaper.

'I am not feeling too good,' said Jahangir.

'Long day,' replied Idris, pulling into The Mews and being waved inside by a lone boy who was on duty.

He parked in his usual spot, exited hurriedly then moved to the passenger side door and opened it.

Jahangir remained inert.

Idris tapped Jahangir who looked at him, in obvious distress. 'Mr Chemist, I am not feeling well. My chest feels very tight.'

Idris grabbed hold of Jahangir by his shoulders and helped him out of the car, pulling at his body to ensure he didn't fall back inside.

The aspirin was working.

There were many drugs brittle asthmatics like Jahangir could not tolerate. Ones which caused their airways to constrict and could trigger a fatal response.

When Idris had accessed Jahangir's medical history via the secure NHS Abbreviated Care Records, he had seen that Jahangir had a serious sensitivity to aspirin. Most asthmatics had to be careful with the drug but for a select few, those who suffered from a severe form of the disease, vasoconstrictors like aspirin could elicit a fatal adverse reaction. Jahangir had been admitted to hospital several years before after suffering from a severe reaction to the drug.

It had almost killed him. To Jahangir, an aspirin was akin to the deadliest poison.

As Idris pulled Jahangir out of the car, he heard a deep, severe wheeze from Jahangir.

'Get yourself home,' said Idris, patting him firmly on the shoulder and gently pushing him towards the towers before walking away quickly, head down, oblivious that Jahangir was trying to get his attention.

The first thing to suffer within the body during a catastrophic asthma attack was the voice box, the airways squeezed, the individual unable to speak.

Jahangir had no voice.

Jahangir stumbled towards his tower block, feeling as if his lungs were being compressed. He had suffered his fair share of asthmatic attacks and recognised this immediately as a merciless one. He kept moving, determined to get inside, away from the cold air which always made it harder to breathe.

Halfway to his front door, he stopped walking as the one thing he feared the most seized control of his body.

A dramatic, powerful contracting of his airways which forced him to drop to his knees, wheezing terminally.

Jahangir could not speak, never mind scream. In the darkness, he searched desperately for someone to help him.

The Chemist: that's who he needed.

Jahangir struggled to turn around, where in the distance, he could see nothing but blurry images of The Mews's foreboding towers.

Jahangir remembered the new inhaler The Chemist had given him. Urgently, he pulled it free from his pocket, removed the cap, put it to his lips and pressed the canister.

Nothing happened.

He tried it again.

The outcome was the same – the inhaler was empty.

He looked at it, horrified, and now back towards where The Chemist had disappeared.

Could it have been him? Had The Chemist done this to him?

As Jahangir's body collapsed onto the ground, wheezing morbidly, he peered into the nothingness of The Mews for help which was not coming.

Jahangir stared into the night sky, at a clear, full moon, the twinkling of distant stars, and took his final breath.

Faris had allowed Idris into their apartment and was busily packing his bag, Idris having told him that he would be staying with him because his father was poorly and in hospital.

Faris returned to the living area and collected his schoolbooks. He hesitated, looked at Idris uncertainly.

'Mr Idris, will I be coming back here soon?'

'Of course. As soon as your father is better. But it might be a few days.'

'When can I see him?'

'Tomorrow, I hope. If not, the next day.'

Faris again hesitated.

'Do you trust me, Faris?' asked Idris, gently, smiling at the boy but needing him to move faster. Outside, in The Mews courtyard, Idris could hear a growing clamour.

'You are the only person my father and I trust. He always says that you have kindness in your heart, Mr Idris.'

'He's a good, kind man, Faris, and he's going to be fine.'

Idris took Faris's bag from him. 'Are you sure you have everything you need?'

'How long will I stay with you?' he asked.

'Tonight, maybe tomorrow then I will introduce you to a friend of mine and she will take care of you until your father is better.'

Idris was banking on Rebecca being released and helping him look after Faris.

Faris nodded and Idris was again struck by the resilience of the boy. He supposed that having escaped a war-torn Syria, crossed the seas, and lost his mother in the process, temporarily moving home was a small thing to adapt to.

Outside, Idris quickly led Faris to his car, very much now alert to the sound of panicked voices in the distance, close to the tower block where Jahangir lived. He saw covert activity in the shadows, the glowing ends of cigarettes as they were being smoked and of people running in a panic.

Idris ushered Faris into his car, quickly got inside and sped away from The Mews. For the first time ever, there was nobody on watch at the entrance, everyone seemingly rushing towards a dramatic event happening inside.

Idris drove away aggressively.

In the distance, approaching him at speed, were the blue lights of an ambulance, its siren screaming with urgency.

Chapter Forty-Three

Idris closed his front door quietly and heard the television playing Mariam's favourite movie, *The Hangover*, a comedy she watched when she was upset.

Idris ushered Faris upstairs, accompanying him into the spare bedroom where he told him to get changed and then to try and sleep.

Faris asked Idris if he could leave the bedside lamp on as he hated the dark.

'Of course you can,' said Idris and gave the boy a reassuring smile before leaving him to head downstairs.

Idris saw that Mariam was sitting inside their conservatory, in silence, the movie having been switched off with his arrival home. He wasn't sure what to say to her, only that he was going to have to divulge snippets of the truth intertwined with a heck of a lot of lies.

He momentarily considered telling her everything, including about Rebecca.

Mariam had admitted to having an affair with an ex-colleague of hers. Perhaps this was Idris's opportunity to tell her about his difficult past.

Maybe this was the time for all truths to be laid bare.

He decided against it; Idris just didn't have the bandwidth to go there.

His thoughts drifted to Rebecca now. Had her situation changed now that Jahangir was dead?

How long would it be before Thomas made contact and made good on his promise?

What if they were now coming for Idris to fully close off the truth of what had happened with Patrick?

The noises inside his head were deafening, every avenue he seemed to explore full of toxic possibilities.

Idris opened the doors to the conservatory, slipped inside and sat down opposite Mariam. She didn't look at him, but he could tell she was furious.

He started with, 'I'm sorry.'

She gave him no response; didn't look at him.

Idris put his hands together, passively, as if he were in prayer.

'I did something stupid. I tried to help Al-Noor move out of The Mews, to escape from Jahangir Hosseini. I filled out emergency accommodation forms for Al, tried to put some pressure on social services to get him and Faris away from The Mews into safe accommodation. Jahangir found out and . . . punished Al-Noor.'

Mariam finally looked at Idris, seeing that amidst all the questions she had been obsessing over, this sounded like truth or the start of it anyway.

Idris continued, buoyed by the fact that her expression had softened a touch.

'You saw Al-Noor in the clinic today. For what?' asked Idris, wanting Mariam to realise it for herself. Perhaps throw in a little professional guilt that she had missed a serious assault. It was a shitty thing to do, but he needed to deflect some of the hurt onto her. Maybe even a touch of the responsibility.

'He had an . . . anal fissure,' she said, her voice a touch shaky, nervous.

Idris looked hard at her, waited for her to see it.

Which she did.

'Oh God, he wasn't?' she whispered.

'He was assaulted by Jahangir, Elyas and Majid.'

Mariam put her head in her hands, devastated.

Idris felt bad for her, knowing that she was wondering whether she could have stopped what had happened at the café by urgently referring Al-Noor to adult protection services.

'After seeing you, Al-Noor came to see me and told me he was going to kill Jahangir. Asked me to look after Faris until social services took care of him. I tried to talk him out of it, but I didn't have time to make an intervention. He just walked out of the pharmacy, into the café and took the whole place hostage.'

Mariam moved her hands away from her face and looked at Idris.

'So, you decided to put your own life at risk?' she said.

'I just . . . did it. I knew I could talk Al-Noor down.'

'You knew you could talk a drug addict, who had just been assaulted, out of killing his abuser? That's some reach for a pharmacist, Idris. Did you ever once think about me? About us?'

'I didn't think at all. I just acted on impulse.'

'I don't believe you. There's more. What are you not telling me?'

Idris hesitated and she saw it.

'I swear if you withhold anything, I will walk right out that door, right now.'

I didn't walk when you told me about your affair, he thought.

Because I don't love you. I love someone else.

Idris couldn't get into that now. Instead, he held up both hands, palms open, trying to calm the spiralling situation. 'There is more. I did it for us,' he said, desperately trying to buy more time, think on his next statement to her.

'For us? What do you mean?'

A truth she needed to hear.

The coup de grâce.

'We're going bankrupt, Mariam,' he said.

She looked at him, stunned. 'What?'

'I'm three months behind with creditors. They're threatening me with court orders and bankruptcy unless I pay them, but we don't have the money.'

'What are you talking about, Idris?'

He took a long beat, rubbed his eyes, felt a slight twinge in his ribs.

Idris told her bluntly that the government funding cuts to community pharmacy had plunged the pharmacy into debt. That he had maxed out their overdraft facility and now had nowhere left to go.

'I don't understand what this has to do with what happened today,' she said.

'If Al-Noor had killed Jahangir, it would have plunged The Mews into chaos. Mariam, I make over thirty per cent of my money from The Mews. Jahangir gives me access; the addicts all use the pharmacy. If I lose *that* contract, we'd be shut down within a month. I was making plans to make some of the money we owe by doing a large amount of flu and COVID jabs. I had a plan. But if we lose The Mews, Mariam, we're done.'

She finally got it.

The reality of a complex business decision they had made a decade before. Also the reason Idris had not divorced her when he had found out about her affair.

'Oh God, the bank loan is secured by the medical practice,' she said, her voice shrill, panicked.

He nodded. 'If the pharmacy goes bust, it would drag you under too. We'd lose everything.'

Mariam looked away, took a deep breath. Fidgeted with her hands.

'I'm sorry, I know it's a lot to take,' said Idris quietly.

'Why didn't you tell me this before?'

'What would have been the point in stressing you out too? I was making plans. COVID and flu will clear a month's debt. I had everything organised and then Al-Noor went in to kill Jahangir. I freaked out, saw everything I had been planning potentially go up in flames, and I rushed to stop him.'

Idris moved to sit next to her, feeling like the barriers had come down a little. He put his hand on hers. 'And I did stop him. Everything worked out OK.'

She looked at him, pained, and for the first time not angry. 'You put everything on the line to save our business? There is always a way out, Idris, but if you lose your life, that's it.'

Mariam hugged him and while it should have felt like he was winning, it instead simply spiked the pain in his ribs, and he bit his lip to stop himself from screaming.

He pulled away so she wouldn't see the agony in his face.

He felt no comfort from the embrace, wishing, instead, that it was Rebecca's arms around him.

'I'm . . . so sorry for all of this. When I got inside the café,

217

it was just so . . . surreal. Hostages, Al-Noor with the gun and Jahangir, cocky as always.'

'They really assaulted Al-Noor?' she asked incredulously.

'It's The Mews, Mariam. You know what that place is like. You know what Jahangir is like.'

'God,' she said, grasping his hand tightly.

He looked back to her now; kissed her cheek.

'I'll never do anything like this again and now that I've told you everything, maybe we can put our heads together and see if there's a way out of this mess.'

She took his face in her hands. 'We'll do it together, Idris. We'll figure it out.'

Idris stood up, braced to tell her the final piece of the puzzle. 'There is one last thing.'

She waited for it, her expression once again anxious.

'Al-Noor's boy, Faris, is upstairs in the spare room. He needs to stay here until tomorrow when I'll phone social services. He's a good kid. Clean. Not one of The Mews dealers.'

'How do you know?' she said, immediately suspicious. 'Every kid in that place is a dealer.'

'Not Faris. Trust me, I see him inside the pharmacy most mornings. Help him with his homework. He's good as gold.'

'OK,' she said, relaxing a little.

Idris leaned back into the couch and took a deep breath. 'God, my head is all over the place. I need to clear it. Mind if I hit the gym? Just need to burn off some energy. Get the noise out of my head.'

'Are you crazy? It's been a hell of a day. You need to rest and to reset.'

'What I need is the heat of the steam room, a jacuzzi and to just sit and relax. I won't be long. You OK with Faris? He won't leave his room. Shy. Reserved.'

Mariam nodded. 'I'll be waiting up for you, Idris. Please keep it to under an hour.'

'I'll be back in ninety,' he said and left, heading to only one place.

Back to The Mews.

Chapter Forty-Four

It may have been approaching midnight, but The Mews was alive, reacting to the news that Jahangir Hosseini was dead.

Idris, cloaked in a gym hoodie, had effortlessly walked into the compound without being challenged, the only time he could ever remember doing so.

It felt like the entire population housed inside The Mews were now in the courtyard, whispering, gossiping. Idris knew that while many would celebrate Jahangir's untimely death, the majority would be anxious about one thing; what impact might this have on their supply of heroin?

Idris checked his phone, perhaps for the dozenth time. He had sent a message to the number which had been sending him images:

Listen to the grapevine . . .

He could see that the message had been read twenty-six minutes ago.

Idris had lived up to his end of the deal. Would Thomas make good on what he had said?

Idris's heart was racing as he observed The Mews, wondering if changes were already being actioned. Elyas and Majid would take over for now. But they were not leaders.

He wondered how quickly Jahangir's replacement would be appointed and whether that would give Thomas enough time to infiltrate The Mews and take over.

There was no loyalty among addicts. They would buy product from whoever had it.

But with both Al-Noor and Jahangir now absent, The Mews was certainly exposed.

Idris's phone pinged with a message, the unknown number now familiar to him.

He read it instantly.

Pharmacy. Thirty minutes.

Idris felt a sudden, sharp ache in his ribs, as his body tensed.

Were they bringing Rebecca to the pharmacy?

Idris considered, for what seemed like the hundredth time that day, calling the police.

Yet now, that was impossible.

Idris had killed someone.

The realisation hit him hard, and he suddenly felt like it was he who was suffering a critical asthmatic attack. His chest tightened and he took deep, unsatisfying breaths.

Murderer.

Idris dropped to one knee, feeling like his legs were unable to support his weight anymore.

'Not often we see The Chemist here, in civvies, so late on,' said a familiar voice, from behind Idris.

Idris had grown up hearing that voice.

Daniel.

'Heard the news on the wire. Came to see if it was true,' said Idris, without standing up.

'Didn't know you cared so much about Jahangir.'

'The man gave me access. Him not being here affects me just as much as it might affect you.'

Daniel used his foot to nudge Idris's body. 'Stand up, Idris.'

The tone was different. Almost accusatory.

Idris struggled to his feet.

'How many years have I known you?' asked Daniel.

'Enough,' replied Idris, realising that Daniel had figured out something was wrong.

'Yeah, enough. And now, here you are standing inside The Mews, within an hour of Jahangir Hosseini's death, on the same day you walk into an armed hostage situation to stop Al-Noor from killing him. A man might think that sequence of events was coincidental. A man like me, though, doesn't believe in coincidence.'

There it was – the loaded statement and an opening for Idris to tell Daniel the truth.

He took it.

'You're right not to believe in coincidences,' said Idris and while it was a measured reply, it felt like he'd removed a crippling weight from his shoulders.

Daniel stepped closer, dropped his voice. 'Whatever you do next, think on it real hard, Idris. I thought growing up the way we did would've taught you to be smarter. Standing here so soon after . . . whatever it is that happened here, tonight?'

'There's no cameras anywhere near The Mews. I'm just as much of a ghost here as you are,' replied Idris, hardening his voice.

'When you're up against it, Idris, you usually get one chance to make a good call. One chance to flip the script. I'm asking you whether this is that time.'

Idris met Daniel's intense stare and held it for several beats then glanced around The Mews, almost feeding off the uncertainty of its residents, an uncertainty which was replicating inside Idris.

What would happen next?

How would Idris distribute Thomas's product within The Mews if the plan with Al-Noor didn't work?

Daniel.

But that was opening a can of worms neither one of them had visited in years. Laying bare secrets and events which were almost as bruising as what Idris had been through that day.

'They've got Rebecca,' said Idris finally, his face cracking into a pained grimace.

'Who has her?' replied Daniel, putting his hand on Idris's arm, pulling him further away from the centre of The Mews.

'I need to get to the pharmacy. They said they would release her if I did what they wanted.'

Daniel stopped walking when they were near the perimeter.

'Who is they?' asked Daniel firmly.

'Thomas Mead,' replied Idris, watching as first Daniel's mouth dropped open and then a rage Idris knew all too well, consumed his face.

'This isn't about you, Daniel. Or . . .'

Idris couldn't bring himself to say a name he hadn't mentioned in a decade. '. . . *him*. It's about Rebecca.'

'The Mead family have her and you don't think this is about me?' he said furiously.

'It's not! It's about Rebecca killing Patrick Mead, trying to save one of the girls she looks after and me helping her to cover that mess up,' snapped Idris.

Daniel turned around, stepped away from Idris, hung his head and took a few beats. To Idris, it felt like an age.

Then he turned around and said, 'When does the meet take place?'

Idris checked his watch. 'Fifteen minutes. At the pharmacy.'

'Just you?'

'Just me.'

Daniel pointed behind him, into the darkness where Jahangir's lifeless body had been found by a Mews resident.

'You?'

Idris nodded.

Daniel looked both aggrieved but also impressed. He closed his eyes, took another few moments to think on things and then said, 'Listen to me carefully, Idris. Very fucking carefully.'

Chapter Forty-Five

Idris parked in his usual space.

He wasn't sure what to do, go inside or wait here in the car until Thomas and his crew arrived.

A message arrived on his phone. Another different unknown number.

Go inside. Keep the lights off. Leave the door open.

Idris got out of his car and walked to the pharmacy, jangling keys in his hand. The CCTV was still not working, meaning whatever happened inside with Thomas would not be recorded.

And they knew it.

Idris raised the shutter, unlocked the front doors and stepped inside. He deactivated the alarm then sat down on a bench.

He glanced around the pharmacy; a place where people came for help.

An environment intended for only one thing: to safeguard and protect the infirm.

Idris needed today to end, it felt like it never would.

He saw a black Range Rover enter the car park, slow down then stop outside the pharmacy.

It was them.

The car disappeared around the corner.

Idris didn't move.

He saw Damon first, undertaking a cautious sweep of the perimeter of the building before entering the pharmacy where he carried out another inspection.

'There's nobody here but me. And you already fucked the CCTV yesterday,' called out Idris.

Damon, satisfied that they were alone, removed his phone, typed a hurried message then calmly joined Idris on the bench.

He hadn't said a word, which was almost as unnerving as his presence.

'Where's Rebecca?' asked Idris.

Damon said nothing.

Outside, another car arrived, flashed its lights then disappeared to park.

A message beeped on Damon's phone.

He checked it and walked towards the doors, waiting patiently.

Sure enough, a few moments later, Idris saw Thomas escorting a weary-looking Rebecca towards the pharmacy.

They entered and Idris immediately went across to Rebecca who seemed drowsy.

Thomas released her to Idris, who led her to a bench, sitting her down.

Damon grabbed the keys and dropped the shutter.

'What did you give her?' asked Idris, looking angrily at Thomas.

'You already know. Relax, it was just enough to sedate her. She'll be fine now you're here to look after her.'

Thomas glanced at Damon who said, 'We're clear. Nobody here.'

'Tell me how you killed Jahangir,' said Thomas, raising his

phone and pointing it at Idris. He heard the recording function being switched on.

Idris remained silent.

It lasted maybe thirty seconds and then Thomas lowered his phone.

Idris spoke firmly, resolute. 'You already have the dashcam footage. That's enough. I'm not giving you anything else. Do what you want.'

Thomas thought on this.

Damon came towards Idris, seemingly intent on handing him another beating but Thomas raised his hand to stop him.

'Enough. He's right, we have more than we need. But now it's just the four of us, no recordings, tell me how you did it.'

'First tell me what you gave Rebecca.'

'Street heroin.'

'How much?'

'Enough that she won't remember the last twenty-four hours.'

'Did you touch her?'

Thomas shook his head.

'If you're lying . . .'

Thomas's mood darkened. 'I'm not. Enough of the backchat. Tell me how you killed Jahangir.'

'I'm a chemist, I poisoned him.'

'How?'

Idris didn't answer.

Thomas smiled, seemingly impressed.

'It is incredible to me, that in twenty-four hours, you managed to do the one thing we have been attempting for years. To kill Jahangir and seize control of The Mews. And you did it like that,' he said, clicking his fingers.

Rebecca was slipping in and out of consciousness. Idris

lowered her body to the floor and put her in the recovery position. He removed his jacket, slipped it under her head.

'You care very much for her and yet you are married to the doctor upstairs?' said Thomas.

'Rebecca is a friend of mine,' replied Idris, knowing full well that it was obvious their relationship went beyond that. 'I did what you asked of me. Now leave us be.'

'Leave you be? Mr Chemist, you and I are now bound,' said Thomas, laughing and smacking his fists together.

He nodded at Damon who removed a kilogram of pure heroin from his pocket and threw it onto the bench beside Idris.

Thomas pointed at it.

'One kee. Pure. You, being The Chemist, are going to cut it with whatever you want using all those fancy chemicals you got back there to produce a thousand ten-pound wraps each week. Each one needs to contain a hundred milligrams – so that kee right there? It's ten thousand doses, meaning your return to me is nothing short of a hundred grand. You spoil some, spill some, lose some? That's on you and you should make it right.'

'I can't run your product throughout The Mews. I'm The Chemist, not a runner.'

'Al-Noor. We know all about him. And today, we hear you did something, inside there,' said Thomas, turning and pointing behind him where the café was. 'Something to get Al-Noor back to The Mews. To . . . us.'

Idris sighed, tired of the games. 'Al-Noor is going to jail. He had a loaded weapon on him. You know, as well as I do, that is a mandatory five-year sentence.'

'Yet still, you went inside. You have a plan, no?'

Idris looked away.

Thomas saw right through him.

'Yes, The Chemist has a plan. Always thinking one step ahead. Tricksy little bastard, aren't you?'

Again, Idris said nothing.

'You do what you need to get Al-Noor back here. You make plans with him, and we see you in a week's time, to collect our money.'

Thomas came closer, crouched to his knees so that he was now at eye level with Idris. 'We own you now, Idris. We know everything about you. Your wife. Your life,' he said, almost hissing in anger.

Thomas tapped his finger on Idris's face. 'You took something from me but with Jahangir's death you repaid some of that debt. Together, we will run The Mews. You show me I can trust you and maybe down the line, your life gets a little easier. Your money troubles go away and everybody wins.'

Thomas stood up, turned to Damon and said, 'We're done here.'

Damon raised the shutter, unlocked the door and stepped outside.

Thomas followed, paused by the door and had a parting message for Idris. 'You brought this on yourself.'

And with that, he walked out.

Idris's focus immediately went to Rebecca. He checked her pulse, felt that it was weak and rushed into the dispensary. He grabbed a box of intramuscular naloxone, the antidote to heroin, and hurriedly prepared a syringe of it.

He moved back to Rebecca, just as Daniel slipped inside the pharmacy, locked the doors and dropped the shutter.

'They've gone,' said Daniel, then made his way across to Idris. 'How is she?'

Idris removed the protective sheath from the syringe and

injected Rebecca through her jeans into the fleshy part of her thighs. 'She's alive. High as a kite but alive.'

'Naloxone?' asked Daniel.

Idris nodded, removed the syringe, re-sheathed the needle and remained where he was on the floor.

'Did they hurt you?' asked Daniel.

Idris shook his head. He nodded to the 1kg bag of heroin on the bench. 'I need to cut that, give it to Al-Noor and get him to sell a thousand wraps throughout The Mews. They're coming back next week to collect the cash. I'm fucked no matter what I do.'

Daniel sat down on the bench, opposite Idris.

'Fucked? We're all born from an act of fucking, Idris. Fucking is what makes the world go round. It's about who gets fucked and who does the fucking. That's it. That is all life has ever been about.'

'I can't do what Thomas is asking. I'm just a chemist.'

Daniel pointed at Idris. 'Just a chemist? A chemist who brought down Jahangir Hosseini like an invisible reaper. A chemist who . . .' Daniel hesitated and then said what he had come here to say, 'who isn't totally alien to this world. A chemist, who if he wanted to, could have very powerful friends in this game.'

Daniel slipped off the bench, sat on the floor opposite Idris so they were now at eye level and said, 'Tomorrow, you know what you have to do. You've known from the moment you tried to cover up Patrick Mead's murder.'

Idris, finally broken from the day's events, nodded. 'I know,' he said quietly.

'You can leave Rebecca with me. I'll take her home and stay with her. What's your next move?'

'Move?'

'You haven't gone this far, Idris, without putting a lot of thought into this.'

'Al-Noor. I need to get him released so he can help me with The Mews.'

'The man held up a café with a loaded gun. He's not going anywhere except prison.'

Idris had a plan, one which required a lot of support from friends he had within the healthcare system but . . . if he was able to pull it off, he would be back in the game.

'What's brewing inside of that big brain of yours?' asked Daniel, seeming to sense there was a bigger plan in play.

Idris told him.

It took all of three minutes. When he was finished, Daniel looked mostly perplexed but also impressed.

'Always said you were the smartest son of a bitch I knew. There's also one other thing you need to do. The one thing you should have done the moment this all kicked off.'

Daniel shot him a knowing look.

Idris finally said the one thing Daniel wanted to hear.

The only thing which gave them a fighting chance.

'Will you do me a solid?' asked Idris.

'What do you need?'

'The barrister; the Scorpion. I need him to get me an audience with Zidane tomorrow. He's the only one who can engineer it at such short notice.'

'I'll make the call. How long has it been since you saw Zidane?'

Idris considered the question.

'The last time I saw him was when I was standing in the dock, as a witness for the prosecution, testifying against him.'

Chapter Forty-Six

Idris awoke to the sound of laughter from downstairs. Of Mariam and Faris enjoying breakfast together. He had slept poorly, not only due to the pain inside his body but also the realisation that this new day brought with it the reality of what he'd done the night before.

Idris immediately checked his phone, dismayed to find no message from Rebecca but there was one from an unknown number.

Idris read it.

Today is the day Chemist. Our partnership begins.

Idris stared at it, anxious, his ribs starting to throb.

He deleted the message, not the number, and moved hurriedly into the bathroom where he had hidden a solitary dose of morphine liquid. He drank it quickly, stared at his reflection in the bathroom mirror and stayed there for several moments, steeling himself for the day ahead.

Idris walked into the kitchen, hearing more laughter, a sound so far removed from what he had experienced recently that he felt as though he were living a parallel life. 'Hey,' he said, approaching Mariam and Faris, sitting down next to them. 'Good morning, Faris. How did you sleep?'

'I slept fine, thank you for asking.'

Mariam topped up Faris's glass with fresh orange juice and said, 'Are you always this polite, Faris?'

'My father always tells me that politeness and hard work open many doors.'

'Wise words,' said Mariam.

'Mr Idris, will I see my father today?' asked Faris eagerly.

Idris stumbled over his words. 'I think . . . maybe,' he said.

'I could come and see him at the hospital?' said Faris.

Idris looked nervously at Mariam who looked away, awkward.

Faris finished his orange juice and stuffed the last piece of Nutella-covered toast in his mouth.

'Would you like some more?' asked Mariam.

Faris shook his head, swallowed the toast and said, 'Are you taking me to school, Mr Idris? I don't know which bus will take me there.'

Idris poured himself a strong black coffee and nodded.

The school run was going to be the easiest part of his day.

He'd received an email from the barrister Daniel had contacted, confirming that a meeting inside Wakefield prison with Zidane was being arranged for later that day and that Idris's availability needed to be flexible.

Idris figured it would be in the afternoon, which meant he had only the morning to engineer Al-Noor's release, something for which Idris was going to need help.

The Becklin Centre, located behind St James' hospital on the outskirts of the city centre, was a place Idris knew well. It was part of Leeds General Infirmary, the largest teaching hospital in Europe, a place where Idris had worked to complete his internship as a pharmacist. He'd been one of forty pharmacists spread across multiple sites, and the most interesting as far as Idris had been concerned, was the Becklin Centre.

It provided secure, inpatient psychiatry services as well as intensive crisis support. Not only had Idris worked here for three years, but he had also been forced to commit Rebecca to the institution after they had lost their newborn son in the most traumatic of circumstances. It had been something Idris had done to try and save his relationship with Rebecca and while it had kept them together for another year, it hadn't been enough to stop their separation.

Inside the reception, Idris signed in and told the adolescent-looking clerk that he was here to see consultant psychiatrist Dr Jamil Kassir.

Idris had called ahead, spoken to Jamil's receptionist, and checked he was working today. Idris knew from previous experience that Jamil's mornings were reserved for reviewing patients who had been admitted overnight. That included Al-Noor, who Idris had known would be sectioned to the unit due to acting psychotically. The police could not have kept him overnight in the cells, knowing that he presented a significant risk to himself.

Idris waited patiently in reception, knowing that Jamil would see him. Not only had they been childhood friends, but they had also travelled around the US together on a summer road trip after finishing university.

Jamil and his fiancée together with Idris and Rebecca.

The innocence and adventure of youth.

Christ, how Idris wished he could return to those days.

Jamil's office was exactly as Idris remembered. *Bloody chaotic, books and research papers everywhere.* And a prominent sign sitting proudly on the desk stating, ONLY IN DISORDER WILL ONE FIND GENIUS.

Idris was sitting on the couch; a cliched shrink's Chesterfield sofa. He'd been told to wait here as Dr Kassir was dealing with an acute emergency. Idris's thoughts immediately went to Al-Noor.

Jamil suddenly blitzed into the room, with his usual pomp and as always wearing an expensive tailored suit.

'Goddamn it, the pharmacist himself,' he said, coming across to Idris who got off the couch and was immediately engulfed in an over-the-top bear hug.

'Easy, easy,' said Idris, pulling away sharply, 'bruised ribs. Feel like I've been hit by a truck.'

Jamil stepped back looking at him concerned. 'What happened to your face?'

'Got into a fight with an addict and he kicked my ass. Just another day in community pharmacy dealing with The Mews.'

Jamil moved across to his chair and beckoned for Idris to also sit down.

'You don't call. Don't visit. Are you here to break up with me? After all we've been through. Those other pharmacists who work here now, they mean nothing to me. You are the only drug dealer I trust. Come on, tell me it's not over,' said Jamil, theatrically waving his arms.

Idris smiled at him. 'I thought the valproate would have stabilised your moods by now. Or are we simply having a manic morning?'

'You're the man with the drugs. What are you selling this time?'

Idris leaned back in his seat, lowered his voice, and said seriously, 'I'm not selling. I'm calling one in.'

235

Jamil used his legs to push his seat away from his desk and towards Idris, with such efficiency that Idris assumed this was something he did frequently with his patients. The men were now facing each other.

Gone were the smiles and relaxed nature of their previous banter. Jamil simply said, 'You're here about Al-Noor.'

Idris was taken aback and clearly Jamil saw it because he went on to say, 'He's in the secure unit, wailing like he's on LSD. Been at it all night.'

'What is he saying?' asked Idris.

Jamil leaned forward, closer to Idris now, his expression sombre.

'Idris, you arrive here, after more than a year, and on the same morning that Al-Noor is admitted. I think it's time you told me what's going on because, brother, the only thing Al-Noor is screaming is your name.'

Chapter Forty-Seven

'Are you insane? What the hell are you asking me?' said Jamil, getting off the couch and walking back to his desk. He stood behind it, arms folded defensively across his chest, staring at Idris, incredulous.

'I need you to trust me,' said Idris calmly but he was already on the back foot, something he didn't like. He needed so much more than what he had already asked of his friend.

'No,' said Jamil.

'Why not?'

'Because I don't buy it. I'm not putting my name to it.'

Idris sighed and having rehearsed his pitch several times in the car on the way over, launched into why he thought what he was asking was reasonable, knowing that with each word he spoke he was reaching, medically speaking.

'Methadone withdrawal psychosis is a documented phenomenon. A study conducted by the International Psychiatric Institute in 2018 proved that for addicts who are regular with their consumption, especially those on more than fifty milligrams, sudden withdrawal of the drug, in the absence of other opioids, can lead to a psychotic state not too dissimilar to that experienced by alcoholics in Wernicke's encephalopathy.'

Idris looked at Jamil uncertain because what he had just said was a crock of shit.

And Jamil saw right through it.

He walked slowly around the desk, perching on the edge of it. When he spoke, his tone was soft, his words measured. 'Idris, we've been friends a long time. Shared a lot together. Been through a lot together. Not sure what hurts more, the fact you think that bullshit you just spouted will wash with me or that you feel unable to tell me the truth about what is going on with you and Al-Noor.'

Ouch.

That hurt Idris, more than he thought it would have.

Seemed that lately he was lying to everyone close to him.

He looked to the floor, felt a sudden urge to burst into tears and managed to stop himself.

'Am I still on your books as being a patient?' asked Idris, without looking at Jamil.

He had seen Jamil infrequently after what had happened to Rebecca and the disintegration of their marriage.

'Well, I haven't officially discharged you, so, yes.'

'Put an appointment in your diary now,' said Idris, removing his phone. He scrolled to his banking app and accessed it. 'I'm transferring two hundred quid to you, for a private psych appointment so this shit is on the books. Documented.'

'What are you talking about?'

Idris glared at him, added some bite to his tone. 'Put an appointment in your schedule.'

Jamil accessed his laptop, typed for a few seconds and a diary invite duly arrived in Idris's inbox along with an invoice.

'Got it,' said Idris.

Jamil turned back to face him. 'We're privileged now. That is, I guess, what you wanted?'

Idris nodded then told Jamil everything except his involvement in killing Jahangir Hosseini. Privilege or not, Idris was taking that secret to the grave.

Twenty minutes later, with it all out in the open, Idris felt better. *Lighter.*

Jamil, however, looked as if he were now carrying that load.

When the silence extended to almost two minutes, Idris said, 'That's why I need you to sign off Al-Noor as being psychotic. Establish that his actions at the café were the result of a psychosis-induced reaction to missing five days of his methadone.'

'Did he miss five days?' asked Jamil.

'The methadone register will reflect that,' said Idris.

'Shit, look at you. Already measuring your words.'

'I'm telling you what the facts will show.'

'Methadone withdrawal psychosis is not a recognised syndrome.'

'I just told you about the international research report.'

'I'm aware of it. But that research was widely discredited. It's just not a thing, Idris.'

Idris slammed his hand on the couch. 'It's psychiatry. Nothing is an exact science. You say that because of Al-Noor missing five days of his methadone, he suffered a psychotic withdrawal, and everyone buys it,' snapped Idris.

'How do I prove that's what it was?'

'Easy. Give him his usual dose of a hundred millilitres of methadone. I have a feeling it will take the edge off Al-Noor's psychosis. In fact, I know it will.'

239

'Because it's not real. It's already in the notes by the admissions doctor that she thinks Al-Noor is faking it.'

'How could she possibly know that?'

Exasperated, Jamil sighed and ran his hands across his face. 'Idris, while you might think nothing in psychiatry can be proven, and can pigeonhole Al-Noor's behaviour as you see fit, it doesn't bloody work that way.'

Idris got off the couch and walked away from Jamil to the far wall, where there were photographs covering almost every inch of it. Most of them were of Jamil collecting awards for academic work. Several were of him rock-climbing, scaling various mountains.

One, though, was of Idris and Jamil, posing in front of the famed Hollywood sign in Los Angeles, not a care in the world.

Idris pulled the photograph free from the wall. 'Christ, I wish we could go back to those times. Nothing to worry about except if we had enough gas in the tank to get to our next destination.'

He heard Jamil arrive behind him. 'San Fran, if I remember rightly.'

'Right. Sourdough bread and movie memorabilia.'

'Had to lend you fifty bucks 'cos you were broke. Pretty sure you never repaid it.'

'I didn't,' said Idris, replacing the photo back on the wall and now turning to face his friend.

'Give me a lifeline here, Jamil,' said Idris desperate.

Jamil took a beat. When he spoke, his voice was assured. 'I will document that Al-Noor missing multiple doses of his methadone may have been a contributing factor to his apparent psychosis. I'll give him his methadone and, as you say, I'm sure he will slip into a remarkable remission. But,' said Jamil, putting his hand on Idris's shoulder and squeezing it gently,

'I won't state that as the primary cause. I can add a little PTSD maybe. And once he's lucid, the police will come and escort him back to the nick where he will be charged with a serious criminal offence. Because that's what happens here, Idris. A psychotic episode does not absolve or negate Al-Noor from the responsibility that he took a café full of innocent people hostage.'

Idris felt deflated, realising that Jamil was right. Idris had overplayed his hand and not fully recognised the parameters of his argument.

'Give you some advice, old friend?' said Jamil.

'I'm not going to the police. Screws me and Rebecca as much as it helps us.'

'Then, Idris, you're going to have to think of something else, because one thing is certain. Al-Noor is going to jail.'

Chapter Forty-Eight

Rebecca woke up to find Daniel sitting in her living room hand-rolling a cigarette. The curtains remained drawn even though the clock on the wall said 11.55.

'You can't smoke in here,' she said groggily.

'Nothing ever changes with you, does it?' he said and added the cigarette to several others he had already made.

Rebecca glanced around her living room, momentarily confused.

Daniel put the cigarette box in his jacket pocket and stood up, seemingly ready to leave. 'You fell asleep on the couch. Wasn't like I was gonna carry you upstairs, was it?'

'Have you been here all night?'

He nodded and wiped clear a few remnants of tobacco from the table with his hands. 'My sleeping pills are in my flat. Not that they really work but without them there was no chance of any kip. Plus, I was paranoid that after so many years of not using, you might vomit and die in your sleep.'

'Blunt as ever. Christ, my head is banging,' she said, sitting up and putting her head in her hands.

'Comedown blues. Gonna kick yer for a while.'

'Yeah.'

'You might need to increase that shitty fifteen millilitres Idris gives you for a month or so.'

'Can't. If I tell the clinic that I used, I'll lose my job.'

'Don't tell them, then. When's your next piss test? Bet you're on three monthly by now?'

She moved her hands away from her head, thought about it and said, 'Yeah. Think it's in a month.'

'Loads of time to clean your system.'

Daniel was clearly agitated, unable to stand still, fidgeting furiously with his hands.

'You OK?' she said.

'Usually get my methadone first thing. Feel like my blood is on fire without it.'

'Go, then,' she said, feeling immediately guilty at the state of him. She stared closer, saw that he was sweating profusely.

'Not until you're up and steady. I promised Idris.'

'Wow. You've not seen me for six months – not even a call – and now you're not going to leave in case I'm unsteady. Go and get your meth.'

Daniel hesitated. Clearly, there was another reason he was not leaving.

'Something else?' she asked, leaning back, and resting her head on the couch.

'You know what else. The shit you and Idris have got yourselves into. We need to talk about it.'

Rebecca massaged her scalp with both hands, squeezed her knuckles into her temples. 'God, not now. Think my head is going to explode.'

'You got some pills here?'

She stared at him, incredulous.

'Pain killers for you – paracetamol – but good to know what you're thinking,' he snapped.

She raised her hand, apologetic. 'Sorry. Just . . . my mind is a mess. Kitchen cupboard, above the fridge. There's a yellow medicine box there.'

Daniel returned a few minutes later with a sleeve of paracetamol and a glass of water.

'Drink it slowly, if you neck that it'll all come up.'

Rebecca swallowed the tablets with some water and placed the glass on a side table.

Daniel retook his seat opposite her and waved a silver blister pack of tablets at her. 'You got an old packet of codeine in that medicine box. I'm having a few, keep me from shaking until I get my methadone.'

Rebecca shrugged.

'What now?' she said.

'For you, it's about seeing how badly you want to use after a couple of days of being high. How long have you been clean?'

'Nine years, six months, four days.'

'Twenty-four hours of using shouldn't screw you too bad. But . . . we won't know until later on.'

'I've no idea what they gave me. What do you suggest?'

'I'd be doubling that fifteen mill you take to thirty. If Idris won't do it, there are . . . other ways.'

'He'll do it. For me.'

'Man's playing with fire. Maybe you two should just go see the pigs and take your chances.'

'I wish we'd done that. Before, it would have just been me who lost everything. Now it's Idris too. I can't do that to him.'

Daniel popped four codeine tablets into his hand and dry swallowed them. 'You think he'll do what I told him last night?' asked Daniel.

Rebecca looked at him, confused.

'The pharmacy. Last night? What he said?'

She remained lost. 'I don't remember anything. I know Thomas brought me there. After that, it's a blur.'

'The plan to help Idris run Thomas's product within The Mews rests on Al-Noor being released from prison but after what he did, there's no chance of that happening. He's not getting bail, not getting anything other than a one-way ticket to Armley until his trial starts, maybe sometime next year.'

A realisation crept into Rebecca's face. 'Without Al-Noor, can Idris distribute within The Mews?'

Daniel shook his head. 'Al-Noor is the runner. Nobody is messing with him 'cos he's covered by Jahangir. Well, he was until last night.'

Rebecca looked at Daniel confused. 'Last night?'

Daniel looked away, suddenly trapped.

She didn't know.

He waited for her to figure it out.

'No,' she said shakily. 'No!'

Daniel grimaced.

'Idris couldn't have. How? When?' asked Rebecca.

'Last night. Don't know how. But . . . he did. Jahangir is gone.'

The colour drained from Rebecca's face. She looked ready to throw up.

Daniel got off his chair, grabbed a bin and handed it to her just as she did exactly that.

He waited until she'd finished, grabbed a box of tissues, and handed it to her, watching her wipe her mouth clean and dispatch the tissues into a bin.

'That was the deal to get you back, remember?' said Daniel gently.

'How could he have done it? Jahangir is untouchable. Everyone knows that.'

Daniel retook his seat. 'He's The Chemist, he found a way.'

'What now?' said Rebecca, sounding more panicked than ever.

'The barrister.'

'Scorpion?'

'Obviously. And then you know where Idris needs to go. To go see Zidane.'

'Zidane?' she whispered, almost as if she were afraid to say the name.

Daniel sighed heavily and said, 'It's exactly what Idris should have done the moment this shit kicked off. Zidane.'

'How do you know that Zidane won't hurt Idris after what he did?'

Daniel replied quietly, his voice nervous. 'I don't, but that's a risk Idris is going to have to face.'

Chapter Forty-Nine

HM Prison Wakefield was a Category A men's secure facility, nicknamed 'Monster Mansion' due to the number of high-profile sex offenders and murderers incarcerated there.

The visitors' car park was mostly empty as Idris waited for the barrister, Reginald Brewster, known affectionately within the criminal fraternity simply as the Scorpion.

Not quite as dangerous as the inmates holed up inside but the Scorpion was known to command a level of respect which meant when he asked for something, usually, he got it.

Which is exactly why Idris had tasked Daniel with calling him the night before and why an urgent visitation order had been signed off.

Which strings Reginald had pulled didn't concern Idris. He simply needed to get inside the prison and hope to learn things which might aid his current situation.

Reginald's car, a gleaming silver Bentley GT Continental, pulled up beside him.

Both men left their vehicles and Idris made his way across to the barrister.

'Long time,' said Reginald.

'Not long enough,' replied Idris bluntly.

Reginald stiffened at Idris's response. 'Do you want the favour or not?'

'Zidane pays your wages, not me. So, this is happening. Doesn't mean I have to like it, or you.'

'As you wish.'

Reginald started to walk towards the prison, Idris falling in behind him.

They didn't like each other, something which had been going on for years and largely because first, Idris had testified against Zidane in open court and second, the fact that since Zidane had been jailed, Idris had ignored all communications from him via the barrister.

Idris hadn't wanted to appear as a witness for the prosecution but had been forced to do so because, he *had* witnessed Zidane killing two men.

Two men whom Idris had intended to kill.

The same men who had assaulted Rebecca resulting in her losing their baby.

The barrister was a facilitator, a gateway to Zidane which Idris had not wanted to reopen. *That part of his life was done with.*

There was a wait at reception as they went through security. Idris was searched, his body scanned and his fingerprints uploaded to the mainframe computer. Idris, under the supervision and guidance of the barrister, then documented the reason for the urgent visitation order – a family bereavement – and handed the form back to the muscular, overbearing warden who gave it a cursory glance then opened the door for them to follow him inside the prison.

They walked militarily down dark, low-lit winding corridors, where every twenty metres or so, bold red emergency panic buttons were chiselled into the walls. The air smelled of damp and dust seemed to swirl around them constantly.

The warden moved briskly, his thick leather boots silent on the cement flooring, unlike the barrister's noisy leather shoes, his heels clicking on the ground in a hypnotic rhythm.

It was bitterly cold, Idris's teeth chattering as he walked. He wasn't sure if it was the hostile environment or the fact that after a hiatus of ten years, he was about to come face to face with Zidane.

Doors opened and slammed behind him, the noise echoing around them as they descended further into the prison, the walls becoming narrow, and Idris started to feel claustrophobic.

They arrived in a corridor, two doors on each side, and stepped through the first one, the warden duly leaving them alone, telling them he would soon return.

It was a barren room, except for one table and four chairs, everything bolted to the ground.

Idris glanced at the ceiling, checking to see if there were any CCTV cameras.

'Not in here. We're blind,' said the barrister, clearly reading Idris's thoughts.

Idris stuffed his hands into his pockets, feeling the chill hitting hard and, try as he might, he could not stop his damn teeth from chattering.

'How long has it been since you've seen him?' asked the barrister.

'Years. You?'

'Few months. Appealed to get him transferred somewhere with a better view.'

'A room with a view. What every lifer wants,' muttered Idris.

'What every lifer wants is regular connection to the outside world. To feel part of something.'

'He *was* part of something.'

'Something bigger than that.'

'There was nothing bigger than that,' said Idris bitterly and his teeth finally stopped chattering as a burst of adrenalin flooded his body. 'Double homicide.'

'*Alleged* double homicide,' replied the barrister quickly. 'Our appeal remains in situ.'

Idris shot him a disbelieving stare. The Scorpion's expression didn't change. Far too cool and measured to show emotion.

'He admitted the charges against him.'

'Under duress. And, *to protect you*.'

Ouch.

That hurt. A truth Idris had buried so deep that he had convinced himself it wasn't true.

'Not sure Zidane has ever been under duress.'

'In this secure, closeted room, I feel I should remind you that he admitted to the charges to spare you having to give any more testimony but also to save Rebecca from appearing in court. Noble, I would say. Honourable, even. While it may not be my place to say—'

Idris stepped to him and cut him dead. 'You're right. It is none of your business, so shut it.'

The barrister, clearly used to such outbursts, nodded, unfazed. 'As you wish.'

The door suddenly flew open, and the warden stepped inside followed by Zidane, dressed in a full-length black bodysuit with cuffs still locked around his hands and feet.

He gave the barrister a cursory glance then a longer one at Idris before he walked into the centre of the room and sat down.

The warden secured the cuffs to the table and the chains around Zidane's feet to the floor.

'You've got sixty minutes,' he said, then left.

Idris remained where he was. His teeth started to chatter again.

The barrister sat down opposite Zidane and waited for Idris to do the same.

He didn't. His mouth felt parched and he really, really wanted to stop shivering.

Zidane spoke, his voice quiet, measured and as calm as Idris had always remembered it to be. He pointed at the barrister and said, 'Give Idris your jacket to stop him from shivering and then, get out.'

The barrister duly slipped off his jacket, left it on his chair and curtly stepped out of the room.

Idris slipped it on, welcoming the feel of the silky interior. He sat down and looked at Zidane who smiled warmly and said, 'Long time, little brother. Long bloody time.'

Part Two

Chapter Fifty

Thomas Mead was alone, sitting on the very couch where they had kept Rebecca Fury hostage.

Had he known what Damon had told him about the footage some peasant named Liam Reynolds was holding, he would have strung her up next to the carcases of dead animals scattered around his slaughterhouse.

Christ knows, he and his brother Patrick had done that to so many others who had betrayed them.

Yet this situation was far more complex.

If it were proven to be true – that Rebecca had murdered Patrick – then Thomas would look weak if he didn't kill her.

That, though, would surely cause The Chemist to stop working for him.

Rebecca was key here – leverage.

Thomas removed his phone, scrolled to his favourites folder and looked at a photo of Patrick, a brother he had worshipped.

But also, a brother who had been reckless.

And the one thing Patrick had coveted ever since he had entered the drugs world had been The Mews. His death had inadvertently given Thomas the keys to that kingdom, something Patrick would have been proud to have seen.

Yet, where did Thomas's loyalties lie?

Revenge for his brother or securing the most prized location within the north of England?

He heard footsteps, Damon walking towards him, clearly wanting to know what Thomas had decided to do.

'I haven't made my mind up yet,' said Thomas.

'I get it. Securing The Mews has always been at the top of our list and if we kill Rebecca The Chemist might stop working for us.'

Thomas looked around at his decaying slaughterhouse. 'Remember what Patrick always said? If you don't continually develop as a business, others will take what you have. Growth and expansion are what keeps you sharp.'

'I remember,' said Damon.

'And we don't know if Rebecca killed Patrick until we get the footage.'

'You want me to do the deal with Liam?'

Thomas sniggered. 'You think we're giving that parasite a hundred grand?'

'Shall I bring him here?'

Thomas shook his head. 'Not yet. I reckon he knows where the hooker, Amy, is. She might be one of his workers.'

Thomas took a slow walk around the floorspace, thinking on his next move.

'Call Liam. Tell him there's no deal without Amy. That if he brings her to us, we can do business.'

Damon looked at Thomas, confused.

'Our team need to know that we punished whoever killed Patrick. I don't know what went on in The Vacants but this hooker, Amy, was involved. Focus on her. Tell Liam we want her first and after that we'll pay him for the footage he's got.'

'A hundred grand?' said Damon incredulously.

'Don't be stupid. That weasel ends up in here with Amy.

But nothing yet. Delay things, keep him sweet, motivated. What we need to establish first is proof that The Chemist is doing what we asked – cutting and selling *our product* within The Mews. We'll know within a few days. Until then, nothing else matters. No complications. No heat.'

'Why not just kill Liam now?' asked Damon.

'Because he runs girls in Beeston. It'll get noisy, difficult to control. We do nothing for a few days. The priority is only making sure Idris is doing what we said.'

Thomas hated the fact that Rebecca would not immediately pay for what she might have done to Patrick.

But The Mews was the most important thing for the survival of their business.

Once they had secured it, Thomas would see to it that both Rebecca and Idris found their way here, to a place where nobody would hear them scream.

Chapter Fifty-One

Zidane looked like a piece of granite, his muscular frame visible through an ill-fitting prison uniform. He had several deep scars across his face and the lobe of his right ear was missing.

Idris was momentarily lost for words. His teeth stopped chattering.

Zidane seemed to realise that Idris was staring at his face. He touched the scars. 'They look worse than they are. This one, though,' said Zidane, touching a deep red laceration across his neck which stretched from ear to ear, 'was a bitch. Nearly put me six feet under.'

Idris said nothing.

The silence lingered.

Idris sat on his hands, which felt colder than ever, searching for an opening gambit.

'Just tell me,' said Zidane, finally.

'Before we get to that, how have you been coping in here?'

Zidane stared coldly at him. 'Shit, man, at least pretend to mean it. Or maybe show me something real, some emotion which comes from inside here,' said Zidane, banging his fist against his chest.

'I don't know what to say to you. After all these years, you're a stranger to me but at the same time, you're my older brother so you can't be.'

'That's what happens when so much time passes. All these old memories hitting you, good and bad, but this face sitting in front of you doesn't resemble the ones in the memories, does it?'

Idris finally smiled and with it released a tension he'd been withholding. 'Something like that. Have I changed much?'

Zidane shook his head. 'Same old Idris. Quiet. A bit lost but behind the eyes, that big old brain is at work.'

'Not so big these days.'

'Thing with genius, Idris, is that it's always there. Born with it same as I was born with the heat that's between my ears,' he said, once again touching the scars on his face.

'Is it, I don't know . . . quieter now?' asked Idris.

'Mostly. You keep yourself to yourself long enough and people start to forget about you.'

Idris stopped sitting on his hands and used one to point at Zidane's neck. 'Was that . . . early on?'

Zidane nodded. 'When they thought I was still a threat. When they thought I still had game.'

'Do you?'

'Do I what?'

'Still have game?'

Zidane frowned at Idris, took a moment. 'All the time I was running gear, you never came anywhere near to asking me that. What kind of shit have you got yourself in, to be here, like this?'

Idris smiled at his brother, as perceptive as ever. 'Still sharp, in spite of being in here.'

'Prison makes you sharper.'

'I should have come to see you earlier. I'm sorry I didn't.'

'First genuine thing you've said. The question is: sorry because you need me now and you're afraid I'll tell you to go fuck yourself?'

Idris felt uneasy, looked away and said, 'You might.'

'Look at me, Idris.'

He did so.

'Do you really think that?' asked Zidane.

Idris shook his head. 'Loyal to a fault. That's you. Always were. It's what got you here.'

Zidane laughed. 'You lose sleep over what I did? You wish those two cunts were in here with me, or dead?'

'Both.'

'You can't have both, Idris. Pick one.'

'In here. Instead of you.'

'Then I'd still be running the game. You'd still be looking over your shoulder?'

'I never looked over my shoulder until the day I had to. Until the day Rebecca had to,' he said bitterly.

'Which is why I did what I did.'

Idris leaned forward and lowered his voice. 'Only you?'

There it was, the one question he had wanted to ask Zidane since the night his brother had killed the two drug dealers from a rival gang.

Ones who had attacked Rebecca, resulting in her losing their baby.

It had changed everything for Idris, Rebecca, Zidane and . . . Daniel.

'Did you do it alone?' asked Idris, probing again, this time more forcefully.

'Complicit or alone. What difference does it make?'

'Never took you for losing your head like that. Always so controlled. Other people, however, not so much.'

Zidane shrugged, let it lie a beat before he said, 'How is the other?'

'Like you. A shadow of what he once was.'

260

'Still using? Seeing you for methadone?'

Idris nodded.

'How's that going?'

'Depends on his mood. Mostly without incident.'

Zidane sniggered. 'Mostly.'

'Daniel is Daniel. Might not command an army anymore but he's still got that rage which makes everyone scared of him.'

Zidane frowned at Idris. 'It's why he uses. A heroin addict is no threat to anyone. If he was clean? Sober? He'd be dead. Hiding in plain sight is the best form of defence. He looks like a down and out. Smells like one too, I bet. Man's just waiting for time to pass.'

'Maybe.'

Zidane leaned back in his chair and checked the clock. 'Time's passing, brother. You came here for a reason. You want to talk on it before the warden comes back. He's a stickler for timekeeping.'

Idris thought about how to tell Zidane what a mess he had landed himself in. The distance between them felt too close. Idris stood up, moved into the corner of the room.

Zidane let him be.

Idris faced the wall, trapped right in the corner, making himself feel small and invisible. He tapped his forehead on it a few times.

'Once you've said it, you'll feel a lot better,' called out Zidane.

Idris took a breath. Then he told Zidane *everything*.

Chapter Fifty-Two

The silence lasted almost five minutes.

Idris remained in the corner of the room, too ashamed to face Zidane.

'Sixteen minutes,' said Zidane finally, his voice heavier than before.

Idris turned around, wanting to be anywhere but here because Zidane was looking at him in a way which made everything he had done feel so much worse. *Disappointment.*

'Sixteen minutes is what you've left me, before the warden comes in here and throws your ass out. Sixteen minutes to figure out how to save yours and Rebecca's lives. Sixteen fucking minutes, Idris,' he said, slamming his fist onto the table and staring at Idris, despondently.

'Don't look at me like that,' said Idris.

'You were the good one, the golden child. University and degrees and shit. How did you go and get yourself messed up in this shit? This world isn't for you.'

Idris closed his eyes, hating the disapproval which was radiating from Zidane, feeling like he was a little boy again. 'You think I don't know that? It's why I'm here, inside the mansion for your help.'

'You're here 'cos Daniel told you to come. You wouldn't have otherwise.'

Idris finally stepped away from the corner of the room.

'I didn't come earlier because I couldn't deal with that look on your face. *Disappointment*. Because for as long as I can remember, it was you who got that look from me.'

'Ego? That's what delayed you coming here before you decided to drop Jahangir Hosseini?'

'Maybe. That and Thomas giving me no time to do anything but what he asked.'

'Goddamn aspirin,' whispered Zidane to himself and Idris thought it sounded like Zidane was more impressed than shocked.

'Tell me how to make it right. How to – I don't know – get out of this.'

Zidane sucked his teeth. He shook his head and muttered something inaudible.

Idris watched as his brother rested his head on the table, and remained there, silent, still for several minutes.

Idris glanced at the clock. Eleven minutes left.

Zidane sat up, rigid. 'And it's definitely DCI Pitchford running point on this?'

'Yes.'

'History repeats itself. The man hunted me like his life depended on it. He isn't letting this lie. Does he know about you and me yet?'

'Don't think so. I changed my surname back to Mum's maiden name by deed poll when you got your sentence. Pitchford will find the connection if he looks hard enough. Depends how deep he dives.'

Zidane glanced at the clock again. 'We need more time.'

'I can get the suit to get me another appointment.'

'You haven't seen me in ten years and suddenly you want two meets in a week? Gets people talking when strange shit

263

like that happens and people talking about you or me isn't what we need right now.'

Idris returned to the table and sat down, tired from all the noise inside his head. 'What can you tell me in eleven minutes to help me?'

Idris saw that his brother had something – or at the very least the infancy of a plan.

It was the way that just for a moment, there was a flicker of life behind his eyes.

And now a wry smile.

'You've got an idea. I can see it,' said Idris, hopeful.

'I know exactly how to help you, and to rig this to not only get Al-Noor back in the game but also, maybe, to get you and Rebecca out of this mess.'

Idris leaned forward, put both hands on the table expectant, eager.

Nine minutes.

When Zidane spoke, not only was his voice authoritative but he had a devilish smile on his face.

'The only chance you've got, is to give that cockroach Pitchford the one thing he has coveted ever since he donned that CID suit.'

Zidane lowered his voice, and in eleven incredible minutes, told Idris exactly what he needed to do.

Chapter Fifty-Three

Al-Noor was sitting alone in the secure, padded safe room of the psychiatric unit, where all new arrivals who were deemed to be at high risk of self-harm were kept.

He was not considered a threat to himself but was being held here because it was also the place patients under arrest were contained until such time as the police arrived to take them back into custody.

Jamil paused outside the room, for the first time in years, unsure of himself.

The detectives working this case had called twice, demanding an update.

Jamil was flummoxed. Never had a seemingly lower-tier resident of The Mews been so actively pursued by so many different people.

Jamil had also heard about the untimely death of Jahangir Hosseini, a name many of his patients had spoken about.

For the briefest of moments, Jamil had wondered if there was a link between what Idris had told him and Jahangir's death but he dismissed the idea as quickly as it surfaced.

Idris might have been playing with fire, but he was no murderer.

Jamil peered through the small glass viewing window, watching Al-Noor resting on the bed. The methadone they had given him had certainly reversed the psychotic effects he had been suffering.

Al-Noor didn't fit the clichéd type of drug addict Jamil often treated from The Mews. He wasn't emaciated, appeared to be generally in good health and now that he was lucid, spoke softly and politely.

He had treated plenty of high-profile prisoners, those charged with murder and heinous sex-crimes, so he wasn't overwhelmed by what Al-Noor had done inside the café. Yet, as he unlocked the door and entered the secure room, he felt more nervous than at any time in his career. Rightly or wrongly, he felt any decision he made here would have significant repercussions for both Al-Noor and Idris.

Jamil left the door unlocked and coughed gently to get Al-Noor's attention. He immediately sat up and remained cross-legged on the bed, arms folded across his chest.

'Al-Noor, my name is Dr Jamil Kassir, and I am a consultant psychiatrist at the Becklin Centre. Do you understand what I am saying?'

Al-Noor nodded and said, 'Kassir. Lebanese, no?'

Surprised, Jamil returned Al-Noor's smile and said, 'Impressive. I don't think anyone has ever made that link on hearing my name before.'

'In Syria, I was an engineer. I travelled far and wide before my country was broken by war.'

'I know that feeling well. Do you mind if I sit down next to you?'

Al-Noor unfolded his arms and gestured for Jamil to sit beside him.

'Lebanon and Syria share many of the same nightmares. People in power looting all the wealth then forcing the population to run to the West for asylum. No?' said Jamil.

Al-Noor nodded heartily and replied in Arabic, 'From your lips to God's ears.'

Jamil, who was also fluent in Arabic, switched to the language and from here on in, the conversation flowed smoothly.

'Idris came to see me this morning. He and I are old friends,' said Jamil and held Al-Noor's stare long enough for him to understand that Jamil knew details which Al-Noor had not expected.

'I thank you for looking after me, sir. I do not know what happened.'

'Idris told me that you had missed some doses of your methadone. Is that correct?'

'Yes. Five days.'

'Can I ask you why that was?'

'I had some kind of illness. I could not get out of bed for days.'

Jamil scribbled some notes in his file then asked, 'Al, why did you take those people hostage at the café? Why did you threaten to kill Jahangir Hosseini?'

Al-Noor dropped his gaze to the floor, and said, 'I don't know.'

'I think that you do.'

Without looking at Jamil, Al-Noor hastily told him that Jahangir had been responsible for bringing his family to the UK from Syria. That they had trusted his organisation and that Al-Noor had lost his wife on their perilous journey and even though Jahangir had not been with them, Al-Noor held him responsible for his wife's death. He had wanted to punish Jahangir, thinking, absurdly that while they had been inside the café, they were in fact on the high seas, on their way to England.

It was a story well told, had all the right beats and emotive emphasis.

Jamil also saw right through it, told Al-Noor as much and asked him again, why he had wanted to kill Jahangir.

When Al-Noor remained quiet, Jamil said, 'The admitting doctor noted on her initial examination of you that you had rectal bleeding. That your undergarments were soiled with blood. And I wonder if something bad happened to you? Something which should never happen to anyone?'

Jamil watched as Al-Noor bunched his hands into fists and cracked his knuckles. For a moment, he wondered if Al-Noor was going to lash out at him but then Al-Noor relaxed his hands.

When he answered, his response was perfect.

The type of perfect which made Jamil think of Idris. He really had briefed Al-Noor well.

'Heroin is a very constipating drug. I always have problems with my bowels. Straining. Pushing. Tearing. This time, it was worse than before. That is why I was bleeding,' said Al-Noor assuredly.

Jamil wrote it down and then said, 'We've had a clinical review of your case, Al. The police are keen for you to return to their custody, and I am in no position to deny that. Your mental health seems to have stabilised and from my point of view, you seem to be no harm to yourself or others. I cannot entertain keeping you here when you are under arrest.'

Al-Noor seemed resigned to his fate.

'When will they come to take me away?' he asked.

'Soon.'

'I have enjoyed speaking in Arabic with you. Your accent is pure. Your words, for a moment, took me back home. To memories of simpler times.'

Jamil closed his clinical notepad, lowered his voice and said, 'Idris said you are a good man. Having spoken to you, I believe that to be true but what he asked me to do for you and him, I cannot.'

Al-Noor cowered into this seat, shoulders slouching. 'I just wanted to protect my boy,' he whispered.

There was a gentle knocking on the door. An orderly popped his head around the corner and said, 'Dr Kassir, the officers have arrived. Discharge is awaiting sign-off,' then duly disappeared.

'Are you ready, Al?' asked Jamil.

Al-Noor nodded.

Chapter Fifty-Four

Al-Noor arrived at Leeds's main police headquarters on Elland Road, just as it was getting dark. He was booked in by the duty sergeant, had his fingerprints taken and was photographed before being taken to the custody cells where he would spend the night, awaiting his appearance in front of a judge the following morning.

The cell was cold, damp and smelled of sweat. Down the corridor, a male prisoner was wailing hysterically, an upsetting sound. In adjacent cells, other inmates were screaming for the prisoner 'to shut the fuck up', but it wasn't having any impact.

Sitting alone, Al-Noor was cold, hungry, and felt utterly broken. Similar emotions to when he had lost his wife.

His one job, the only one which should have mattered was looking after Faris.

Where was he now?

What would happen to him?

No matter which way Al-Noor looked at it, his incarceration, seemingly for a prolonged period, was inevitable.

He wasn't a tough gangster who could navigate the hardships of prison. Moreover, with what he had done to Jahangir, there would surely be prisoners loyal to Jahangir who would be waiting to punish him in jail.

Maybe even kill him.

He slammed his hand onto the bench. Why had he allowed The Chemist to talk him into this plan? It had failed at the very first stage.

The lights in the corridor came on and Al-Noor heard a door being unlocked and the hurried feet of officers. He assumed it was to deal with the hysterical prisoner but instead, an adolescent-looking officer with bleached blond hair stood in front of Al-Noor's cell and unlocked it.

'Up. With me,' he said.

Al-Noor got to his feet. 'Where am I going?'

'Your lawyer is here.'

'I don't have a lawyer.'

'My mistake. You're right. He's not a lawyer, he's a barrister.'

The meeting room was in complete contrast to the custody cells. Warm, pleasant-smelling and more importantly, peaceful.

The barrister, Reginald Brewster, sat opposite Al-Noor, and slid a business card across the table.

Al-Noor read it. The card was silky and had a large picture of a scorpion across it, with the words REGINALD BREWSTER, CRIMINAL BARRISTER etched in gold calligraphy.

'Criminal barrister. I don't have money for that. Are you here by the government?' asked Al-Noor innocently.

'Some quickfire facts,' said Reginald, opening his briefcase and removing a black folder. He opened it and said, 'I don't do government work. I'm the best at what I do which is why my charges are seven hundred and fifty pounds per hour. The minute I walked into this station and told them I was representing you, it told the detectives working your case that you, Al-Noor Qadri, are a *very* important person.'

Al-Noor was perplexed. Had this barrister got the wrong man. 'Me?' he said meekly.

'The reason I am here is that in . . .' Reginald checked his watch and said, 'about twenty minutes time, the detectives . . . Pitchford and Black are going to come in here and if they are smart and have any sense, they are going to release you back into The Mews, tonight.'

'What?'

Brewster slid the file across the table to Al-Noor who looked at it blankly. 'I cannot read this.'

'I know. Just sign it on the dotted line at the bottom.'

Al-Noor repeated the only word he could find. 'What?'

The barrister slid a pen across the table. 'You can leave the date blank,' he said.

'What?'

'Al-Noor, every time you say "what", it costs the man paying your bill more money. I've put an hour on the clock to get this sorted, so I suggest we use less of the word "what" and more of words like, "yes, sir".'

He beckoned for Al-Noor to sign the document.

'Mr barrister, I cannot sign something I do not understand.'

Reginald grimaced and said, 'If I told you that Idris appointed me to represent you and that everything in that document is a plan which he, I and . . . let's just say a mutual associate of ours came up with, does that lessen your fears?'

The fact that Idris was somehow involved lifted Al-Noor's spirits, yet he repeated the same thing. 'Until I understand what this document is, I cannot sign it.'

Reginald, clearly frustrated, sighed deeply, considered how to proceed and then seemed to accept that he was going to have to explain this situation to Al-Noor.

'I will speak quickly, choose my words carefully and need you to accept everything I tell you without question because as I have already mentioned, time is our real enemy here. The longer this takes, the greater the threat of it not working. If we don't get you back into The Mews tonight, this plan becomes much harder to implement. What I am proposing is bold, brave and, to my knowledge, has never been achieved before in this city.' Reginald smiled confidently and added, 'Which is exactly why it is going to work.'

Chapter Fifty-Five

Idris had been parked outside Rebecca's house for the last fifteen minutes but was struggling to go inside.

It was the house they had bought together and lived in before separating.

He hadn't been back since.

It looked the same. Generic black door, faded black paint on the exterior windowsills and, as had frequently been the case when he had lived there, the front lawn looked badly in need of a tidy-up.

He wondered whether their shitty lawnmower was still trapped in the back of the garage. It had always been such an effort to free it from other clutter just to trim a twelve-foot-square patch of grass.

Memories of him and Rebecca gardening, ensuring it was tidy for when they arrived home with their son . . . A son who had never left hospital.

Idris rested his head on the steering wheel and closed his eyes.

History felt like it was repeating itself.

Daniel, Zidane, the barrister, the detectives.

Everything comes full circle, Idris. What we are most afraid of in life, we end up drawing to ourselves.

It was a phrase Zidane had always said to him when they had been growing up.

Idris got out of the car, the words haunting him as he walked towards the house.

Idris felt like he'd stepped into the past. The living room was exactly as he remembered it.

A red checked carpet, contrasting black patterned wallpaper, even the furniture, which he and Rebecca had purchased together, was the same.

He sat on the sofa and accepted a cup of black coffee from Rebecca, sharing a look with her which said it all.

Nothing has changed.

She looked away, sheepish, sitting next to Daniel.

'All good?' he asked Daniel, his voice a touch shaky.

'She's sound. I only left her to get to the pharmacy for my methadone,' said Daniel.

'Is it still standing?' asked Idris, attempting to lighten the mood. The air felt thin, the atmosphere strained.

'For now. How was Zidane?'

Idris looked from Daniel to Rebecca. Clearly she knew what he had been up to.

'He gave me some solid advice.'

Idris perched on the edge of the couch, took a moment and then told them of the unlikely sequence of events that he was trying to put into play with the barrister, and the plan which had come from Zidane.

'Wow,' said Daniel, sounding genuinely impressed. 'Zidane's still got it, I see.'

'He told me prison makes you sharper.'

'Not sure he could have got any sharper.'

'He didn't see what happened to me and Rebecca coming, did he? Either of you.'

Idris shouldn't have said it.

A red rag to a bull.

Daniel was off his seat immediately and snatched his jacket, heading for the door.

'Christ, Daniel, I didn't . . .' started Idris, but didn't get to finish.

'Screw you,' spat Daniel, angrily. 'Every chance you get, you take it, reminding me what happened.'

He pointed at Rebecca. 'Let's get it out in the open, off our chest. I gave her the needle because she was in a bad place, and I thought that a couple of hits would take her away from wanting to top herself. You think that Becklin place did her any good?'

A conversation Idris had wanted to have with Daniel for years now ignited.

'It did her a hell of a lot better than the needle,' snapped Idris.

Daniel stepped to him, enraged, forcing Rebecca to throw herself between both men.

'Stop this,' she said, glaring at them.

Idris ignored her and continued.

'Everyone who ends up on the needle loses,' he replied, locking eyes with Daniel.

'I gave her a few bumps to lessen the pain of what happened. If I'd known she was going to hit it hard, become a junkie like the rest of 'em . . .'

'Like you,' said Idris and immediately received a shove to his chest from Daniel. Idris collapsed onto the couch, rolled over onto his side and released a deep, urgent yell of pain into a cushion.

Rebecca immediately came to him, leaving Daniel standing flummoxed.

'What is it? Are you OK?' said Rebecca, panicked.

Idris wrapped his arms around his body and stayed absolutely still. 'Don't touch me. Don't move me,' he said.

He felt Rebecca's hands on his shoulder and thought that there must have been an exchange of looks between her and Daniel as the next thing Daniel said was, 'I barely touched him.'

'Ribs. Thomas gave me a kicking. Don't think they're broken because I can still breathe but they're sore. Just give me a minute,' whispered Idris.

'I didn't know,' said Daniel, defensive.

'Do you want me to call someone, Idris?' asked Rebecca.

'Just leave me be.'

'I need to go,' said Daniel.

Idris heard him moving.

'You can't. We need to talk on what we're going to do,' said Idris and forced his head away from the cushion. He took a slow, measured breath and cautiously sat up. 'But, if we're going to move forward and help each other, then let's discuss the past and say what needs to be said.'

Things had calmed, Idris making them all a cup of tea, needing the distraction to get his head right. He handed both Daniel and Rebecca a cup and sat down opposite them.

Idris and Daniel spoke about the past, Rebecca remaining largely silent, listening to details she knew but some, she was hearing for the first time.

Daniel spoke calmly, clearly knowing both Idris and Rebecca needed to hear details he had never shared before.

'We never thought the deal would turn out as it did. Was the biggest shipment we had even taken and we had the money. On our end, everything was solid. But the sellers – these European bastards thought they could take our cash and keep the drugs. They tried to screw us, it kicked off and . . . got ugly.'

Daniel took a sip of his tea, twirled the cup in his hands and took a moment.

'I shot the main dealer dead but his two seniors . . . they got away.' Daniel looked at Rebecca now. 'To go to you.'

Rebecca pursed her lips. 'How did they know how to find me?'

Daniel put his tea down, clearly done with it. 'We're assuming they had done their homework on Zidane and me, knowing that they might need an angle in case it kicked off. Honestly, Rebecca, as soon as shit went bad, I tried to get to you first.'

'Why didn't you call and warn her?' said Idris.

'I tried. I called so many times.'

Daniel stared at Rebecca. So did Idris.

She looked away, pained. 'I know. And I've thought so many times how different things might have been if I'd just picked up that call.'

'Zidane got there first, found you and called the ambulance,' said Daniel.

The men who had escaped from Daniel had found a heavily pregnant Rebecca walking through Hyde Park in Leeds and brutally assaulted her, probably meaning to kill her until Zidane had arrived and stopped them. The men had fled, and Zidane had called the ambulance before leaving to gain revenge.

Zidane had found the men responsible and killed them. With or without Daniel's help, nobody had ever confirmed.

Idris asked Daniel the one question he'd always wanted an answer to. 'Were you there when Zidane killed those two men?'

'No,' replied Daniel.

Idris believed him but there was more to it than that.

'What are you not telling me?' said Idris.

'I got there a few minutes after. Saw what he'd done. Left.'

'Zidane tell you to?'

'He told me that I'd need to look after you and Rebecca. I turned that to shit, didn't I?'

Daniel looked away.

'I don't want to talk about the past anymore,' said Rebecca bitterly, with a pain in her voice which made Idris stare at Daniel and shake his head.

She turned away from them both, grabbed the side of a table, seemingly unsteady.

Idris went to her but she pushed him away.

Daniel kept the conversation going. 'What happens now, Idris?' he asked.

Idris kept looking at Rebecca and she nodded for him to continue.

'I need Al-Noor back in The Mews. Thomas has dropped me a kilo to cut and distribute,' said Idris.

'Can you do that?' asked Daniel.

'Only if I have Al-Noor. Without the runner, I'm screwed.'

'Jahangir gone means Elyas and Majid will take charge until one of the Hosseini family arrive to re-establish their control,' said Daniel.

'I can sort Elyas and Majid,' said Idris.

'How?' asked Rebecca.

'I just . . . can.'

Idris felt Daniel's piercing gaze, as if he were looking straight through him.

'Not good enough, you're going to have to tell us how,' said Daniel.

Idris did so. And when he'd finished, for the first time in his life, he saw an expression on Rebecca's face he'd never seen before.

Fear.

Chapter Fifty-Six

Pitchford had read the proposal from the barrister twice and still could not believe it.

What a hand to have played.

What an unbelievable hand.

'This is the longest I've sat with you, and you've not said a word,' said Darcy who had also read the proposal and was busy typing notes into her laptop.

They had an urgent decision to make and had escalated the proposal from the parasitic barrister to the most senior judge they could find and had also engaged with the head of the CPS in their region.

If they were going to do this, the fewer people who knew about it, the better.

'Do you know how long I have been trying to get someone covertly inside The Mews?' said Pitchford to Darcy. He closed the file; nothing more he could do now except wait for the judge to consider it.

'Forever, I suppose,' she replied, continuing to type.

'Exactly,' he replied.

Over 50 per cent of criminal activity occurring in Leeds could be traced back to The Mews and for decades, every senior detective in the city had wanted a snitch who could feed them intel.

They had never managed it.

Pitchford found it as peculiar as he did fascinating. There existed a brotherhood within The Mews which so far had been impenetrable.

Until now.

Until the barrister had presented a proposal so bold, so incredibly outlandish that Pitchford had taken it straight to the judge and asked him to sign off on it.

Not only were they getting a snitch, but they were also getting the goddamn runner, an asset who knew every deal, every addict and vitally, who was a trusted member of the community.

It felt like a winning lottery ticket.

Internally, within HC-MET, the question of Jahangir Hosseini's death had arisen – suggestions about who might assume control of The Mews and whether Al-Noor would be part of this new hierarchy.

Pitchford was willing to take that risk. As he saw it, there were two possible outcomes.

One, Al-Noor would be killed as soon as he re-entered The Mews or two – and most likely – he would slip back into his role amidst the chaos enveloping The Mews over who was going to replace Jahangir Hosseini.

If they were going to put this plan into play, it needed to be now.

The longer Al-Noor was kept in custody, the more people would notice their usual runner was absent.

Another possible mule would take over and then, any chance Pitchford had of gaining robust intel from Al-Noor would vanish. He would become a low-level informant and that is not what this deal was about.

Several hours ago, when the barrister had first presented

the deal to them, Pitchford had been explicit on the level of intel they needed to make the deal work.

Nothing low-level.

They wanted to know who the main players were. Which Mews residents had committed serious crimes. More importantly, though, the deal hinged almost exclusively on HC-MET uncovering the real prized asset, the one thing they absolutely needed to know: *who would become the new leader of The Mews.*

Pitchford thought it likely that a member of the close-knit Hosseini family would cross the border to first, ensure that Jahangir's death had been a tragic accident and second, to ensure that The Mews was protected from being infiltrated by a rival gang.

HC-MET needed to know who the new kingpin was, and Al-Noor could be the man to deliver them that information.

The barrister had played a brilliant hand, knowing full well how badly Pitchford had been coveting placing an informant within The Mews. The fact that Al-Noor had not injured anybody during the hostage situation certainly helped Pitchford's case with the judge. Pitchford had read and presented the psychiatrist's discharge report as part of his recommendation to sign off on this deal. Supposedly, Al-Noor had missed five days of his methadone. The fact that his actions might have been due, partly, because of that could not be discounted and added real weight to the proposal.

Methadone withdrawal psychosis. Not a condition Pitchford had ever heard of but certainly one he intended to research.

There was another thing on his mind, reverberating almost as loudly as the deal the judge was reviewing.

Something told Pitchford that The Chemist, Idris, was involved in this proposal.

He didn't know why or how but there were too many coincidental occurrences. Moreover, how on earth was Al-Noor affording the Scorpion's services? He was either holding a heck of a lot of cash, something unlikely for a Mews runner, or more probably, The Chemist was footing the bill.

Why, though? What linked The Chemist with Al-Noor above and beyond a simple patient–pharmacist relationship?

Nothing had shown up in Idris's records; the man was clean.

Too many questions, though, which Pitchford didn't have answers to. Too little time to get them before the judge made his call.

'Prediction? Yes or no from the judge,' asked Darcy.

'A once in a lifetime opportunity to infiltrate The Mews, the place where we've always been blind, Darcy. Seems like an obvious answer to me but the hostage situation and carrying a loaded weapon makes it difficult.'

Pitchford waved Al-Noor's file at Darcy. 'The psych report casts enough doubt that Al-Noor was not in control of his actions.'

Darcy pointed at Al-Noor's file and said, 'Methadone-induced psychosis. Same thing The Chemist said. Must be a real thing.'

Pitchford emphasised his next sentence. '*Identical to what The Chemist said*. Interesting, no?'

Darcy rolled her eyes. 'I know being cynical is part of the job but come on, the psychiatrist has nothing to do with The Chemist.'

'Both healthcare workers. It's not implausible. See if we can get a work history from Idris.'

Darcy pulled her laptop closer, rolled her sleeves up and

typed on the keyboard quickly. 'LinkedIn. The gateway to every ego,' she said.

Pitchford waited, watching her closely, seeing her eyes light up.

'Well, what do you know,' she said, looking at him and smiling broadly.

Pitchford waited.

Darcy took her time, teasing the answer.

'They worked together,' said Pitchford impatiently.

She nodded. 'Idris Khan, pharmacist, MPharmS, advanced diploma in clinical pharmacy, independent prescriber qualification and, interestingly also a shareholder in a company which formulates and supplies pharmaceutical specials to other pharmacies.'

Pitchford noted that last piece of information on his notepad.

Darcy continued, 'Idris graduated from the University of Bradford in 2001 and completed a one-year pre-registration training at the Leeds Teaching Hospital. He worked for four years there as a pharmacist, undertaking further studies, specifically an advanced pharmaceutical diploma with,' and she looked at Pitchford now, 'a special interest in psychiatric pharmacy. Idris worked for eighteen months at the Becklin psychiatric facility.'

Jackpot.

The link which bound Idris to this.

Pitchford jotted the information into his notepad, his hand now starting to shake a little.

He needed his pills.

'When did he leave the Becklin Centre?' asked Pitchford.

Darcy scrolled down the work history. 'In 2005. He left to work in community pharmacy, looks like he locumed as a freelance pharmacist from 2005 to 2010 and then opened the late-night pharmacy in Headingley, in partnership with a company called Allied Healthcare Limited.'

Darcy typed hurriedly, accessed Companies House, and found the details on Allied Healthcare. 'It's the holding name for the GP surgery above the pharmacy. Directors include Idris's wife, Mariam Khan, and . . . Idris himself.'

'A pharmacist can own shares in a GP surgery?' asked Pitchford.

Darcy shrugged. 'Looks that way.'

'Financial deep dive into all companies Idris and Mariam are involved in. And what was the pharmaceutical specials aspect you mentioned?'

Darcy again used the computer to search for more information.

'Called Granite Specials. Looks like it manufactures unlicensed medications which are not routinely available on the NHS. Wholesale business, it seems.'

Again, Pitchford made a note in his diary and was interrupted by his phone ringing.

The judge.

He answered and listened carefully before hanging up.

'Quickest rejection this year,' said Darcy, sighing. She slammed her laptop closed.

Pitchford, though, was smiling. 'You kids these days have such little faith.'

'You're kidding?' she said, eyes wide and expectant.

'The deal is good. Few minor changes but nothing critical. Three-month trial, a tag on Al-Noor and if he delivers, a long-term deal is on the table.'

'Wow. Just . . . wow,' she said, genuinely amazed that the judge had gone for it.

'Let's get the deal signed and Al-Noor back in The Mews tonight.'

Pitchford slowly got to his feet, feeling for the first time in a long time like the detective he used to be, one who relentlessly pursued cases until they cracked.

'What about Idris? Maybe he *is* nothing more than just a chemist?'

Pitchford paused by the door. 'I wish people would stop saying that.'

'What?'

'That he's *just a chemist* because one thing is certain. Idris Khan is far more than just a chemist.'

Chapter Fifty-Seven

Idris poured his cold cup of coffee down the sink. Even though he'd closed the kitchen door, he could still hear the argument raging inside the living room, between Daniel and Rebecca.

After hearing what Idris planned to do, she wanted to go to the police. Daniel, rightly so, was telling her that it was too late for that.

Idris knew that Rebecca realised it too. This was simply fear swaying her judgement because Idris was about to cross a threshold and take what he had already done to a new level.

He tuned his ear to the conversation, hearing Rebecca's voice, passionate and fierce, saying that, with Jahangir's death, Idris could surely claim some sort of defence. She was standing firm that what Idris and Daniel were proposing with Majid and Elyas was insane.

Daniel countered just as fiercely, pointing out unashamedly that this was the world they were now trapped inside. That there was no going back nor any mitigations for what they had done, neither with Patrick nor with what Idris had done to Jahangir.

Again, Rebecca fought back, only this time she was interrupted by Daniel calling out Idris's name.

He stepped back into the room, to find them both looking flushed, the heat of their argument clear across their faces.

Daniel told them bluntly to both sit down.

Idris slid in besides Rebecca, slipping his hand into hers and squeezed it reassuringly.

'You both talk about how this isn't your world, that you're afraid and out of your depth. But, let me ask you both this.' He pointed at Rebecca first. 'Of all the places you could have got a job, how come it was The Elizabeth Projects, looking after sex workers and drug addicts?'

Then he pointed at Idris. 'And you, Mr IQ university hot shot and passing exams for fun. Look at where you've worked. Why specialise at the Becklin psychiatric unit, full of people with trauma? Then opening your own pharmacy – and where? Near The Mews, taking on all the addicts and wrapping your business around methadone.'

He grabbed his coat, agitated, ready to leave but had a parting message for them.

'You two might kid yourselves that you ain't made for this world, but something inside you both – the estates you were raised on, the worlds Zidane and I ran – has brought you to this point today. Stop bullshitting yourselves that you don't know how to live in this world. *You're both already part of it.*'

Idris and Rebecca were alone now, inside a living room which held years of memories for them both. They weren't focusing on any of those, though, only their current situation.

'Elyas and Majid? Can you deliver on what you've said? It's so dangerous. What if . . . you get it wrong, and Al-Noor dies?' said Rebecca.

'He won't. I've worked out the doses. I'll be close by in case anything goes wrong.'

'Christ, Idris, how did we get here? It's spiralling out of control.'

Idris moved to sit beside her. 'What Daniel said is true, why did we both end up working where we do? Maybe . . . I don't know, on some level, we . . .'

'. . . never wanted any part of *this*,' she said firmly.

'No. But we're not as uncomfortable as you're making out. Are we?'

She shrugged, a half-assed attempt. 'Feels like we're way out of our league.'

'There's more.'

He saw her face tense as she waited for it.

Idris told her about Liam's meeting with Damon.

Her eyes narrowed, jaw tightened and a rage she had just about kept a lid on when Daniel had been with them now detonated.

'I saved Amy's life. How could she do this to me?' shouted Rebecca, furious.

'I know and I promise, I'll deal with it. I'm going to give Liam the money I got from the back of Patrick Mead's car and hope that he goes away.'

'Liam will never do that – he'll blow the money quickly and be back to you for more.'

Idris fell silent. He was out of ideas and focused on the only area where he did have a plan.

'I need two things from you,' said Idris, pushing on, needing to return to the pharmacy where he hoped to soon, reunite with Al-Noor. 'Find Amy. I don't know how but do it. We need her to see reason and tell us exactly who has the footage. We can work with Amy, she's not street-hardened yet and I have a feeling something bad might happen to her. Liam might sell her to the Meads to get rid of her, or worse, kill her himself.'

Rebecca put her head in her hands, took a moment and then without looking at Idris, said, 'What's the second thing?'

'I need you to look after Faris. He can't return to The Mews. Al-Noor won't do what I need if his kid is at risk or anywhere near this.'

Rebecca looked at him, perplexed. 'I can't have him living here with me.'

'What choice do we have? Social services? We know how that will go. If we lose Faris, we lose Al-Noor. I know this is going to be hard for you but please, Rebecca, we need it.'

She moved across the room, staring out of the window. When she spoke, her voice was quieter, full of a pain. 'Do you know what you're asking of me?'

'Yes.'

'There's no spare room here. There's only . . . *that* room.'

Idris made his way to her, stopped by her side. 'Are you telling me the room hasn't changed?'

'I haven't been in there since it happened. Since you . . . left.'

Idris stilled.

The nursery: a room they had lavishly decorated for their child, Ethan.

A room Idris had assumed had long ago been renovated.

Idris pursed his lips, took a breath and felt a sudden jolt of pain in his ribs, his muscles tensing.

'I don't know what to say,' he whispered.

'Nobody has stepped foot in there for years.'

'Do you want me to clear the room with you?'

'No,' she said firmly.

Idris kept his eyes dead ahead, focused on the view out of the window, of a light rain falling on the pavement, and said nothing.

'He can sleep down here. On the couch,' said Rebecca.

'Thank you.'

Idris moved away from her.

She grabbed his arm but he didn't turn to face her, afraid of how she might look at him or what she might ask. They had shared more in the past few minutes than they had done in years.

'My methadone. I'm going to need a bump from the fifteen millilitres without going to the clinic.'

'I'll sort it,' he said and walked away.

Chapter Fifty-Eight

With the deal signed and Al-Noor clear about what was expected of him, he had decided to walk from Elland Road back to The Mews, hoping it would clear some of the noise reverberating inside his mind.

A constant drizzle cooled the side of his face and he looked up at the sky, and opened his mouth which was dry and sticky after all the talking he had done in the last hour.

Truthfully, Al-Noor didn't fully appreciate what he had signed up for. All he knew was that by signing the deal, it had meant that he could return to The Mews and reunite with Faris.

Which brought him to the dilemma currently raging inside his mind and one he had no answer to.

Jahangir may well have been removed, but Elyas and Majid would now step into the role of controlling The Mews, which meant that Faris was still vulnerable.

More than anything, all Al-Noor wanted was for his son to be safe.

Al-Noor had asked the barrister to help him with removing Faris from The Mews as a condition of his agreement but the detectives had argued that any such long-term change would arouse suspicion about how Al-Noor had managed to get Faris into a secure environment when so many other Mews residents had failed.

He walked a little faster, towards Headingley, to the pharmacy where he hoped to see Idris. They needed to speak urgently about just how on earth Al-Noor was going to deliver the intel which his deal depended on.

The detectives had planted a robust secure tag around Al-Noor's ankle, telling him that they would be tracking his movements and that they expected him to be able to account for instances where he needed to leave The Mews. The only exception they had given him was the pharmacy, knowing that he needed to attend there for his methadone. They had also said that they would be speaking to Idris about potentially meeting Al-Noor there, when they needed updating about activities inside The Mews.

The walk to Headingley took just under an hour and by the time Al-Noor rang the pharmacy's doorbell, he was soaking wet and shivering.

He was relieved to see Idris approach the front doors, dangling a set of keys.

Idris allowed him inside, dropped the shutter and turned around to face Al-Noor.

Both men stood uncertainly, eyes on each other, unsure how to proceed.

Al-Noor broke the silence.

'Thank you, Mr Idris. I don't know how you did it. I don't even understand how I am here, but I know you must have done something special to make this happen.'

Idris sat on the bench, thought on how to explain it all to Al-Noor and couldn't figure out where to start.

'Where is Faris?' asked Al-Noor.

'Safe. With Rebecca, waiting for you.'

'I need to see him, but they placed a tag on me,' said Al-Noor, lifting his trouser leg and showing Idris.

'I'll phone Rebecca. Get her to bring Faris here.'

'Please, he will be afraid.'

'He's stronger than you think, Al. He's been . . . resilient.'

Idris removed his phone and called Rebecca, asking her to bring Faris to the pharmacy and some food for everyone.

Al-Noor thanked Idris and sat down on the bench opposite him.

'What happens now, Mr Idris?'

Idris took a deep breath. What they had both been through over the past forty-eight hours had been traumatic but what was to come would be even harder.

'We do exactly what the detectives have asked. You go back to being the runner and we feed the police the information they want.'

'How can I be the runner? Jahangir is dead,' said Al-Noor, his tone suddenly spiteful.

'Elyas and Majid will take over. For now.'

Al-Noor's face soured, the colour draining from his face.

'I cannot work for them after what . . . happened.'

'You need to, Al. They're going to be looking for new supply chains now Jahangir is dead. You're going to go see them and apologise for what you did to Jahangir inside the café, tell them that I have a contact who can supply them heroin but that you need to broker the deal. They'll be interested and want to see the product and you'll tell them you can arrange it.'

Al-Noor looked aghast at the proposal.

'How can you know the drug supply within The Mews will be at risk?'

Idris's thoughts turned to what Zidane had told him but he didn't want to get into those specifics with Al-Noor.

'I went to see someone who used to run The Mews. He told me, so trust me, Al, you need to get Elyas and Majid to entertain you bringing them some product. It's the only way we can get out of this mess and you won't be working for them long: twenty-four hours at the most.'

'What do you mean?'

Idris didn't want to say the next part.

'What happens next, Mr Idris?' insisted Al-Noor.

Idris stared hard at him until he got what Idris had planned.

'Mr Idris, I am not a murderer,' said Al-Noor, reading in-between the lines.

'I'm not asking you to murder them,' replied Idris, still thinking on how to explain it all.

'What happened to Jahangir, Mr Idris?' asked Al-Noor suddenly, abruptly.

Idris couldn't look at him, his gaze once again going to the floorspace where he and Rebecca had been beaten by Thomas. If he was going to make this plan work, Al-Noor needed to know that while everyone thought that Idris was just a chemist, he could, when needed, wield a far greater power.

'I killed him, Al. Just like I told you I would in the café, remember?'

'I don't believe it. You are not a violent man. Killing is not within you.'

'It was within you inside the café.'

'That was different. He . . . pushed me to do that.'

'Thomas forced me. Just like Jahangir threatened Faris, Thomas was going to kill Rebecca. And now, you and I need to run Thomas's product throughout The Mews. It buys us time.'

Al-Noor dropped his head into his hands and sighed

heavily. 'Time to do what, Mr Idris? You and I are gentlemen in a game made only for criminals.'

Idris reached out and squeezed Al-Noor on the shoulder. 'You were an engineer in Syria. *You are an engineer*. Intelligent. Systematic. Calculating. Do you know what these words mean, Al?'

'Yes.'

'Thomas might have muscle but we're smarter than he is. I have a plan. I am sure that it will work but I need you back in the game. I need you to partner with me on this or Thomas will kill me and you will go back to jail. Think of Faris.'

'I am, Mr Idris. Everything I do is for Faris,' he said, his voice shaking with emotion.

Idris told Al-Noor the plan.

For fifteen minutes, he spoke calmly and assuredly about what he and Al-Noor needed to do. The small steps, leading to bigger ones which would give them control over The Mews and then, the final act which would free them both from their shackles.

When he finished speaking, Al-Noor remained silent for a few minutes, digesting it all and then said, 'And Faris? Where does he stay while we are doing what you say?'

'With Rebecca. She will keep him safe. As soon as Majid and Elyas are dead, Faris can move back into The Mews. We're only talking a couple of days at the most.'

Al-Noor laughed, nervously. 'Mr Idris, your plan is . . . a brilliant one. Too brilliant. The kind of brilliance that needs the hand of God.'

'Nobody believed that this chemist could kill Jahangir. Why can he not engineer the fall of Elyas, Majid and soon after that, Thomas? Nobody will see me coming, Al. Nobody can trace what I do.'

Idris moved to sit next to Al-Noor, both men now side by side. 'Bluntly, Al, what choice do either of us have? It's jail for us both or . . . this.'

Idris put out his hand. 'Put your faith in me and together, we will win this fight.'

Al-Noor shook Idris's hand, just as there was a soft knocking on the shutter and the sound of a text pinging on Idris's phone.

'Rebecca and Faris are here,' said Idris, reading the message.

Both men stood up, a final look at each other, a final beat of understanding.

'Mr Idris, I am putting my life in your hands,' said Al-Noor.

Idris shook his head and moved towards the front door, having used a fob to raise the shutter. 'Al, we are putting our lives in each other's. Connect with Elyas and Majid. Get them to entertain you bringing them a sample. If you can do that, leave the rest to me.'

Idris unlocked the doors, and let Faris and Rebecca inside the pharmacy.

Rebecca was carrying two boxes of pizza and set them down on a bench, she and Idris watching as Al-Noor embraced Faris.

Idris slipped his hand in Rebecca's and spoke softly. 'Al-Noor will do what we need. He's in.'

Chapter Fifty-Nine

The leather chair squeaked noisily as Pitchford used his legs to turn it towards the roaring fireplace inside his study.

Marcus had given him his evening medication, a dose of slow-release Sandofar tablets. It would last perhaps eight hours, the effects starting to slowly diminish as he slept. Much as he wanted to increase the dose, he had so far managed to avoid that temptation.

He was already over-using the dispersible tablets he took and each time he did so, it meant that his body moved that bit closer to becoming immune to the effects of the drug. That remained Pitchford's biggest challenge and, his worst nightmare in waiting.

His consultant had told him there was little else to be done. Adjunctive therapy would have a marginal effect only. It was an impending, ever-present death sentence and one Pitchford refused to be victim to.

Assisted dying or not, he would leave this world on his own terms: that was something he was certain of.

The fire crackled nosily, sending cinders across the stone flooring. This, was his downtime, watching the logs burn, seeing them slowly disintegrate. He felt as though it mirrored what was happening inside his body.

*

The walls of Pitchford's office were adorned with papers from one specific casefile, one he had never managed to solve and which haunted his dreams.

The death of six children, by a monstrous gang of four diseased men whom Pitchford had never managed to convict.

He knew they were guilty.

Everyone in the Mews knew they were guilty but Pitchford, the lead detective on the case, had not managed to secure enough evidence to land the prosecution.

He closed his eyes, could see the pages spread across the walls so clearly that he had memorised every piece of intel and circumstantial evidence.

None of that mattered.

Pitchford had over forty years of service in CID, he knew the four men were guilty.

They had even goaded him when the case had not passed the CPS threshold for whether they had enough evidence to prosecute.

Pitchford had never seen evil like it before, and he had seen a lot of evil in his time.

He leaned back, rested his head on the chair, his thoughts now turning to Idris.

A man who had full access to The Mews, a place steeped in malevolence.

Unheard of.

A type of superpower, thought Pitchford, to be able to traverse such different worlds, effortlessly.

And the past forty-eight hours had been all about The Chemist.

The siege at the café, the sudden death of one of the most corrupt individuals known to HC-MET, Jahangir Hosseini – untouchable for so many years, but who died after a routine trip to get his methadone from Idris. Of how The Chemist had looked at the police station; a black eye, hands indiscriminately massaging or, at least, unconsciously protecting his ribcage.

Idris Khan had been assaulted and then lied about it to the police.

Something linked Idris with Jahangir's death, he was sure of it.

Yet, it didn't make sense.

If Jahangir had been the one to attack Idris, then why would The Chemist have put his life on the line to stop Al-Noor from killing Jahangir inside the café?

Something was missing. Perhaps there was another player in this game.

Pitchford was certain that none of these occurrences had happened in isolation.

And perhaps the greatest twist in everything which had happened so far – the release of Al-Noor back into The Mews to act as an informant.

Brilliant.

All orchestrated by The Chemist, of that Pitchford was certain.

The same question continued to needle him – *but why?*

The door to his study opened and Marcus walked in, carrying with him a stack of freshly printed documents. He dragged a small wooden table across the floor and set the documents on it.

'Do you need the lamp?' he asked.

Pitchford nodded and leaned forward to arrange the papers.

Marcus turned on a lamp and moved it closer to Pitchford so he could easily review the documents.

Dim lighting, a crackling fireplace and, the final touch,

something Pitchford knew Marcus was vehemently against: a measure of Glen Grant eighteen-year-old whisky.

Pitchford accepted the crystal tumbler from Marcus. 'How long?'

Pitchford took a sip of whisky. 'An hour, I think.'

He watched Marcus leave, placed the glass carefully on the table and sifted through the documents he had asked Marcus to print. There was the National Institute of Clinical Excellence (NICE) on patient care in community settings.

An informative press release, documenting how pharmacies would soon to be allowed to become independent prescribers, giving them autonomy with regards to treating infirm patients within set parameters.

A case study, the only one Pitchford had found on methadone withdrawal psychosis.

And the most interesting document – the one Pitchford picked up first – a research paper about the most common medication errors which often led to the unexpected hospitalisation of patients, or in some instances . . . their death.

Pitchford grabbed a highlighter, sipped another slug of whisky and started to read.

Chapter Sixty

Idris and Rebecca were inside the medical waste room on the fourth floor. Idris had retrieved the bag of money he had lifted from Patrick's car from the ceiling, and he and Rebecca were now sitting on the floor, counting it all.

'That's all of it; eighty-six bundles of a thousand,' said Rebecca.

'Eighty-six grand. Close enough to the amount Liam is demanding. He won't count it.'

'Are you really going to give him all of this?'

Idris started to replace the money back into the bag, stacking it neatly. 'What choice do I have?'

Rebecca hesitated and then said, 'The kind of choice you had with Jahangir.'

Idris looked at her, thinking that he must have heard it wrong. But the look on Rebecca's face said it all.

'It wasn't long ago that you were solidly against killing anyone else,' said Idris and went back to arranging the money.

'But you've thought about it?'

Idris couldn't lie to her. 'Of course I have. I checked his Abbreviated Care Records but the access is restricted. He must have opted out, or more likely, his file isn't accessible because there's privileged information within it, probably serious psychiatric problems.'

Rebecca started to help Idris with the money. 'Eighty-six grand. How far do you reckon that would get us if we did a runner?'

'Far. But not for long.'

'Do you think they'd find us?'

'No, I think I remember your spending habits.'

She slapped him playfully on the arm. 'Says you, mister. I just need one more golf club. We could have paid off our mortgage with what you spent on those clubs.'

'I haven't played in years.'

'Your clubs are still in the garage.'

Idris placed the last stack of £1,000 into the bag and zipped it closed, wanting to move away from their shared past.

It stung to hear details he had pushed to the back of his mind.

'Al-Noor needs to get back to The Mews and you need to get Faris home. I've a late-night commitment with Daniel, remember?'

They both stood up and Idris unlocked the door.

Rebecca grabbed his arm, stopped him from leaving, and said, 'You and Daniel need to be careful tonight. The Meads might have eyes on you.'

'I've got that covered. I'm going to get us out of this mess, I promise,' he said and hugged Rebecca tightly.

She whispered into his ear, reluctant but needing another favour.

'Idris, I need a bump in my methadone. I'm scared I'll withdraw. Can you help me?'

He kissed the side of her face. 'Of course I can. Come on, Al-Noor and Faris are waiting,' he said.

*

303

Idris and Rebecca were in the dispensary. They could hear Faris crying from here, the boy distressed at being unable to return home with his father.

Idris measured out a 15ml dose of methadone and supervised Rebecca taking it. Then he handed her an additional 30ml to take away with her.

'If you feel the rattle, even after taking the second dose, then you call me,' said Idris.

'How are you going to cover these supplies? You've already given Liam a full five hundred millilitres.'

'Vanessa counter-signed for that spillage, so it's covered. For this . . . I'll think of something.'

There were a couple of ways to do it. If an addict didn't collect their methadone, Idris could book out their dose as having been collected and if that proved difficult then he would simply remove a few millilitres from some of the heftier doses patients were prescribed, and combine their shortages to produce Rebecca's additional dosage.

After everything else Idris had done, this seemed like a minor misdemeanour rather than the serious breach that it was.

Rebecca stepped closer to him, dropped her voice.

'Idris, what you're proposing with Al-Noor at The Mews – killing Elyas and Majid, are you sure there's no other way?'

His face hardened. 'If there was, I'd do it.'

Rebecca nodded towards Al-Noor. 'It's so risky. What if . . . you get it wrong, and Al-Noor doesn't make it?'

Idris had been thinking of nothing else but that scenario.

While what Al-Noor had been through in the past forty-eight hours was horrific, what Idris was about to attempt with him was on another level.

'It can't fail, Rebecca. And, if you respect the chemistry,

there's no reason that Al-Noor doesn't come out of this alive. I need you to focus on Amy.'

'Any ideas?'

Idris lifted the bag of cash and placed it on the bench. 'I'm going to contact Liam, tell him that I've got his money and arrange a meet, somewhere discreet. That will give you a window to go to his house and speak to Amy.'

'And if she doesn't listen?'

'For God's sake, then make her,' snapped Idris, annoyed.

Rebecca took a step back.

'I don't have all the answers, Becky,' he said, using a name he had only ever used when they had been married and having a domestic.

'Becky. Wow,' she said.

Idris took a breath, closed his eyes, feeling an inordinate amount of pressure. 'I'm sorry. Just . . . make Amy realise that Liam is the enemy, not us.'

He felt Rebecca move closer, then her lips on his.

For a few precious moments, they stood as if they were teenagers, having their first kiss, both feeling a familiar heat and electricity.

Rebecca moved away first. 'I'm sorry, I shouldn't have done that.'

Idris pulled her close again, repeated the kiss, slipped his arms around her waist.

This time, they only stopped when Al-Noor coughed, clearly trying to get their attention.

Idris stepped away from Rebecca, composed himself, then looked at Al-Noor, flustered.

'Mr Idris, apologies for the interruption but I must leave to get back to The Mews.'

Idris cleared his throat. 'Of course. We all need to go.'

Rebecca grabbed her coat, and her additional supply of methadone, and without looking at Idris made her way past him towards the front door where Faris was waiting for her.

Idris watched her go: rueful, pained.

'Mr Idris, are you sure Ms Rebecca can look after Faris with everything she has been through?'

Idris had fought with whether to leave Faris with Mariam but truthfully, he wanted Rebecca to do this so that he had another excuse to go and see her.

This nightmare had proved one thing to him; he wanted to rekindle their relationship and escape his loveless marriage.

'I'm sure, Al.'

'What about tonight? With Mr Daniel. You must be careful. These . . . people, the Meads, they are not to be underestimated. I have heard many stories about them.'

Idris smiled. 'The only one who is being underestimated is me. I've got this, Al. You sort The Mews, I'll take care of my end.'

Idris was alone now, everyone else having left.

The first thing he did was to reluctantly take another shot of morphine.

Idris giving Rebecca the extra doses of methadone was one thing. Him becoming addicted to morphine quite another, yet he couldn't function without it, especially if he was about to spend the next few hours with Daniel, gathering intel on the Meads.

Before that, though, Idris had one vital task. Laid out in front of him was the pharmacy methadone register, full of all the entries of supplies which Idris had made.

The pharmacy filled a new paper-based register each

week, Idris refusing to use the electronic system provided by the Methasimple software. The computer hard drive had corrupted soon after he had first purchased the machine and caused him weeks of headaches. He trusted the machine to measure methadone, just not to record it.

The current register was half full; one hundred and fifty entries which Idris now needed to transfer to a new register and manipulate it to reflect that Al-Noor had missed five days of his methadone, thus causing his 'psychotic episode'. It would reinforce the lie he had fed the police and Jamil at the Becklin Centre.

Idris rushed through the entries, annoyed at having to undertake the painstaking, arduous task, especially when he knew Daniel was waiting for him across town. He had texted Mariam that he was working late, and that he was going to the gym afterwards – everything he routinely did to cover his late-night expedition.

It took an hour to complete the new register, his hand aching once he'd finished. Idris felt more exhausted, yet his night was not yet over. He was about to do something his brother, Zidane, had told him to do.

Stop being the victim.

Fifteen minutes after leaving the pharmacy, Idris pulled his car into the twenty-four-hour multi-storey car park next to Leeds General Infirmary. He drove to the top floor and parked in a deserted bay.

He waited, looking around anxiously for any sign that he might have been followed, paranoid that Thomas Mead's goons might have been tracking his movements. This ruse to meet Daniel in the multi-storey car park was to satisfy Idris's paranoia.

Another quarter of an hour later, satisfied that he was indeed alone, Idris texted Daniel and received an instantaneous reply from him.

Saw you come in. Ground floor. Take the stairs not the lift. I'm right next to the stairwell.

Idris got out of his car, moved hurriedly, pulling his sports hoodie across his face.

On the ground floor, he saw an ancient-looking Ford Escort flash its lights and hurried towards it, getting into the passenger side.

'Where'd you get this piece of shit?' asked Idris.

Daniel pulled away from the disabled bay. 'In The Mews as long as you know the right people, you can source anything you need.'

They exited the car park, Idris launching the tracking software on his phone for the device still attached to the underside of Thomas Mead's car.

The hunt was on.

Chapter Sixty-One

Al-Noor had been standing outside Jahangir's apartment for the past half hour, unable to find the strength to raise his hand and knock on the door.

He could hear Elyas's and Majid's voices inside.

They had assisted in Jahangir's vicious assault on him, and now he had to go inside and attempt to make a deal with them.

Al-Noor closed his eyes and forced his mind to shut away what had happened, much like he had done when he had lost his wife on their journey to the UK. He had learned to compartmentalise pain and hatred, something which he did now.

Idris's worlds played loudly inside his mind.

Once you set the meeting, Al, their futures will be over. Trust me.

The Chemist had worked a type of magic, which Al-Noor thought was more akin to witchcraft than anything else.

In Idris he trusted.

Al-Noor leaned in, listened. He could hear Elyas and Majid arguing inside.

There was clearly already a power struggle underway, concerning which of the men would take over The Mews, but also concerns over where the heroin would come from until Jahangir's replacement arrived.

Elyas and Majid were arguing over how much product they would allow to go out into The Mews.

Al-Noor knocked on the door then boldly stepped inside the room.

It smelled of sweat and body odour. Al-Noor did not look to where he had been assaulted, instead focusing on Majid and Elyas, both of whom were clearly high, looking at him in astonishment.

'How are you here? You were arrested,' said Majid accusingly, immediately leaping off the bed and grabbing his gun. He pointed it at Al-Noor. He spoke in Arabic, and Al-Noor replied in the same language.

'They released me,' he said, raising his hands.

'We heard what happened at the café between you and Jahangir. Slave, our leader has died. What you did must have caused it, and now you arrive here for what?'

Al-Noor said boldly, 'I was in jail when Jahangir died. His death was nothing to do with me.'

'How are you here?' asked Majid again, having clearly assumed the role of interim leader.

'The Chemist paid my bail,' replied Al-Noor, hoping that they, much like himself, were ignorant to how the British legal system worked and that bail granted this quickly was an impossibility.

'Why would he do that?'

'Like you, he has a financial interest in The Mews. He does not want to lose his access. Instability makes us weak. The Chemist knows a man, a high-level dealer who can supply us with product, if we are short, now Jahangir is gone.'

Their eyes lit up and even though they tried to be dismissive, Al-Noor could see that he had sparked their interest.

'We do not trust you or The Chemist.'

'But you do. I am the runner. The Chemist is the only other man who has complete access to The Mews. He told you earlier when Jahangir was here that he has money problems. He wants to broker a deal, for ten per cent. Everyone wins.'

'And what do you get, slave?' said Elyas.

'I want to restart my job as the runner. I need the money,' replied Al, desperate, needy and hating himself for sounding this way.

Elyas and Majid looked at one another, suspicious.

Al-Noor could tell what they were thinking, that he was foolish to believe that once Jahangir's replacement arrived, that Al-Noor would not pay for what he had done inside the café with his life.

Al-Noor continued. 'The Chemist says his supplier wants to send a sample. If you like it, he can arrange a few kilos. I thought you would want to hear this offer. The Chemist said he cannot come here and speak this way. It is too dangerous for him.'

Idris had told Al-Noor that not only were Elyas and Majid both genuine drug addicts, but they were also too stupid to really examine what Al-Noor had offered in any real detail.

Greed is all they cared about.

'If you are able to show the Hosseini family that you are able to control The Mews in Jahangir's absence, they would surely look favourably on this and look to keep you both in your positions,' Al-Noor said, floating the idea that they, much like him, were at risk of being ousted by a new boss.

His words landed fully; Al-Noor saw the nervous exchanges between both men.

'I will answer for what I did when that time comes. Until then, I would like to keep my job as the runner. We all must keep The Mews stable, no outside interference. The Hosseini family would be furious if we lost control of The Mews.'

Hook. Line. Sinker.

Al-Noor had managed to turn this predicament on them.

Majid stepped forward, speaking with authority. 'Tell The Chemist to give you the sample he has. Bring it to us here and the price per kilo. We will see if there is a deal to be done.'

Al-Noor nodded graciously then hurried out of the room.

He called Idris, immediately.

'Mr Idris, they agreed. They want to see your product.'

Chapter Sixty-Two

Idris disconnected his call to Al-Noor, delighted to hear that Al had done as he had asked and connected with Jahangir's deputies.

'Slow down,' said Idris, pointing to a house, number forty-two White Chapel Road, an address he had pulled from the tracking software which Al-Noor had attached to Thomas Mead's car. Parked in the driveway was the black Range Rover.

As Daniel slowly drove past the address, Idris used his phone to subtly record the exterior of the modest detached house in Adel, which had clear CCTV cameras covering the perimeter of the property.

They pulled over a quarter mile down the road and Idris took his time analysing the footage he had recorded. The house was unremarkable, but it was the obscene black and gold gates which had caught his attention and the exterior post box attached to them.

'There,' said Idris, using his fingers to zoom in on the footage and showing it to Daniel. 'Stick your hand in the post box and see if there's any uncollected mail. People are notorious for not emptying external mailboxes.'

Daniel removed a can of lager from his pocket. He looked

at the best of times like a down-and-out so playing a homeless drunk wasn't a stretch. He opened the can, took a large sip then got out of the car.

Idris awkwardly moved into the driver's seat and watched Daniel disappear in the rear-view mirror.

The tracking device had given Idris Thomas's address but he needed more details about his life – anything which he might be able to manipulate, ideally medical information – to get ahead in this conflict.

Daniel walked slowly along the street.

Clean pavements.

Manicured grass along the pavements and even separate bins for dogshit.

He looked blankly at the grand houses, each one must have been half a mill, easy.

Private driveways, security lighting and the pinnacle of middle-class security, a sign on the gates which warned of dogs being at the address.

This place was about as far removed from The Mews as Daniel had ever seen. As he walked towards Thomas's house, he wondered how long the residents of this street – aside from those living inside number forty-two – would last inside The Mews.

Or if they even knew places like it existed.

Daniel poured some of the lager across his hand then wiped it across his face, ensuring that if he was stopped by a nosy resident, he would appear and smell like a textbook down-and-out alcoholic.

He approached the gate to number forty-two and scanned for any CCTV pointing directly at him and was pleased to see there wasn't any. He quickly stuck his hand inside the large black post box to the side of the gate, pleased to find it full of uncollected mail. He pulled it free, stuffed it inside his pocket and kept on walking.

Idris had looped the car around the estate and arrived at the opposite end of the street to where he had dropped Daniel. He'd parked in between two lampposts, ensuring the space afforded him a pocket of darkness.

Not perfect but also not particularly noteworthy.

Idris watched Daniel slowly approach, and he lowered the passenger-side window.

Daniel walked by, threw the mail inside the car, and kept on going. They had planned this, so Daniel could loop back around and have another look at the house from the opposite side of the street.

Idris killed the engine and with it the lights. He grabbed the mail, leafing through it quickly. The residents of the house hadn't emptied it for a few days.

He discarded the circulars until he found something useful.

A bank statement.

Thomas Mead.

Jackpot.

Idris opened it and scanned it, a gateway into Thomas's life – outgoings and incomings.

He was surprised to see that Thomas's bank balance was overdrawn.

Idris had expected to see a large cash balance for no reason other than Thomas Mead was a kingpin. He thought about his own situation, seemingly a successful pharmacy owner, yet one who was flat broke.

Daniel looped his way back to the car, threw the can of beer to the kerb and this time got inside.

'Quiet out there,' he said. He turned to Idris. 'Anything useful?'

'Bank statement. Patterns and habitual spending.'

'Anything we can use?'

'Maybe,' he said.

'You're a yes or no type of guy, Idris.'

Idris folded the bank statement and put it away. 'He likes shisha. Twice a week, regular, habitual sessions at a place in Chapeltown. Educated guess, I'd say it's a catch-up session with his senior guy, Damon, or at least some of his crew.'

'Why are you smiling like that?' asked Daniel.

Idris cracked a smile because now he had something concrete he could use. 'Shisha gives me an angle. I need to get back to the pharmacy,' he said and started the car.

Chapter Sixty-Three

Idris was sitting by the pharmacy computer, thinking on how to use the Abbreviated Care Records to analyse Thomas Mead's medical records.

Idris needed an edge and the only way to gain one was to find out if Thomas had any health conditions which Idris could use against him.

Idris launched the pharmacy PMR system and logged on but he needed to engineer a reason to access Thomas's records.

After obsessing over it for almost a half hour, Idris came up with a plan.

He grabbed his iPhone, switched on the VPN – the virtual private network meaning the origin of what he was about to do could not be traced – and then launched the NHS website.

Idris completed an NHS 111 form, inputting all of Thomas's details; completing a health questionnaire requesting emergency medical intervention, specifically help from a pharmacist.

Idris confirmed the request and with a final click of the mouse, he generated an official NHS 111 request, for his own pharmacy to undertake a health consultation with Thomas. Now, Idris had a reason to access Thomas's medical record which he immediately did.

Idris scanned the entries – there were a lot of them; blood

tests, reasons for appointments, medication history, allergy status.

Thomas, it appeared, was suffering from a heart condition: arrythmia; an irregular heartbeat and was taking medication for it: bendroflumethazide tablets, a diuretic to remove excess fluid from Thomas's body, and digoxin tablets to control the cardiac arrythmia.

Thomas had undertaken a blood test at his surgery the month before, to check his U&Es – his urea and electrolytes.

All the results were in range except Thomas's potassium level which was borderline at 3.4mmol / litre of being suboptimal.

Thomas's doctor had made a poor choice of drug for the diuretic – bendroflumethazide, a potassium-depleting drug.

For many patients who were Thomas's age, this wouldn't have been problematic. But Thomas was on digoxin, one of the most dangerous drugs available on prescription. It controlled the rhythm and pacing of the heartbeat and was one of several which had a narrow therapeutic range, working only if the level within the bloodstream was between very specific parameters. Below this, it would not work and above it, the drug could be fatal.

And the one thing which predisposed patients to digoxin toxicity was a low blood potassium level.

Idris again read all the information then slipped off his stool and took a slow walk around the dispensary, thinking on what he had learned, obsessing over how he could use this data to his advantage.

There was something there.

He analysed the bays of medications, reading aloud the names of different drugs, hoping that a moment of genius would occur.

It didn't.

Deflated, Idris did it again because at the back of his mind, there was a kernel of an idea.

Again, he came up short.

Idris kicked his stool over in frustration. It slid across the floor, into a stack of baskets which were full of split packs of medication, sending a variety of drugs sprawling across the floor.

Irritated, Idris took a moment to calm down then picked up his stool and cleared up the mess.

Idris lifted a box of nebuliser solution from the floor, a medication used to help patients with COPD, chronic obstructive pulmonary disease.

He stared at the packet and now from the depths of his imagination came an idea so strong that Idris felt the air squeezed out of his lungs.

He glanced back at the computer, Thomas's medical record still on screen.

Idris removed Thomas's bank statements from his pocket and stared at them.

The shisha bar.

For the first time since Thomas Mead had turned Idris's world upside down, Idris finally felt like he had the advantage.

He knew how to kill the son of a bitch.

Chapter Sixty-Four

Idris was standing outside his pharmacy, having finally locked up at 1 a.m.

He peered at the night sky and allowed a light rain to cool his face.

Idris felt like he now had a chance to escape this nightmare. It was going to take considerable thought and a touch of luck, but he felt resolute about his plan.

Idris walked to his car, carrying with him the bag of cash he intended to use to pay Liam with, when he saw the bastard sitting on the bonnet of his car.

'For Christ's sake,' he whispered to himself, as the morsel of positivity he had just been feeling disappeared.

'Chemist is workin' later than dem girls I run in Beeston. Workin' on gettin' me my money, I bet,' said Liam, laughing. As always, he was holding a can of lager in his hand.

'What are you doing here, Liam?'

'Was in a taxi, drivin' past and saw your motor. Thought I'd see what my friend, The Chemist, was up to so late on.'

Idris waved the bag at Liam, bluffing. 'Paperwork,' he said confidently.

'What's that got to do wiv getting' me my dosh?' snapped Liam, instantly annoyed.

Idris remained calm. 'Accounting paperwork. Got a meeting

at the bank tomorrow. Remortgaging the pharmacy to get you the money.'

Liam slipped off the bonnet of the car, steadied himself and threw the empty beer can away. 'That shit sounds like it's gonna take time, Chemist.'

Idris knew that Liam was too stupid to understand how these things really worked.

'No. It should happen tomorrow if my accounts are in order. That's why I'm working late.' Idris raised the bag again.

Liam seemed to relax, grinning stupidly. 'So, you're reckonin' that I gets my money tomorrow?'

'If not tomorrow, the day after. A hundred large, in cash.'

Liam turned his head to the side, squinting at Idris. 'Are you fuckin' with me?'

'No. I want you out of my life. And Rebecca's.'

Idris needed to engineer a specific meeting time with Liam so that it would give Rebecca a chance to get to Liam's place and speak with Amy. Idris had told Rebecca to float the idea that if Amy offered up the video clip, it would be her who could take the money and start a new life.

Idris felt confident Amy would buy into that.

'I've got your number, Liam. As soon as I have the cash, I'll arrange to meet you. But not here, somewhere discreet.'

'You can bring the money to my place,' said Liam, slurring his words, his balance unsteady. How the hell he controlled a group of girls in Beeston was beyond Idris. Liam could barely stand up straight.

Idris shook his head. 'What if I get seen? How would I explain that? I'm thinking Beckett Park. It's only up the road from here – that good for you?'

Liam considered the proposal. 'It's defo a max of two days?'

'Definitely,' said Idris and pointed to the pharmacy behind

him. 'That place has enough value for the bank to float me a hundred grand.'

'Thought you were broke?'

'I am. But like *you* said, I can get loans and shit.'

Liam grinned and then, inexplicably, hugged Idris.

'Chemist man, you's is all-fucking-right,' said Liam.

Idris broke free of the embrace, desperate to get away from the stink of alcohol. 'I have to go, Liam. I'm back here in a few hours.' Idris checked his watch. 'Five to be exact. Let me go get some sleep. I've a big day with the bank tomorrow.'

Liam grinned and started to walk away.

Idris unlocked his car, got inside quickly. He started the engine when there was a knock on his window.

Liam, again.

Idris lowered it. 'Yes?' he said.

'*Chemist* man, if you're screwin' me . . .' started Liam.

'I'm not,' snapped Idris and drove away.

He had intel on how to solve the Thomas Mead issue.

What he needed now was something he could use to manipulate Liam.

If not, Idris knew there would only be one option.

Daniel.

Chapter Sixty-Five

Idris had managed barely three hours of sleep before he arrived back at the pharmacy at his usual 5 a.m. He had slept poorly, suffering nightmares in which Liam, Thomas and Amy had all tried to kill him and Rebecca.

He had also woken up in a lot of pain and needed another shot of morphine liquid.

He was sitting at the dispensary bench but unlike every other morning, he did not check any medication trays.

Instead, he spent the first hour studying pharmaceutical textbooks, absorbing intricate details about the drugs he intended to use to – in one apocalyptic night – remove everyone threatening his world.

It was an ambitious plan and time was the key factor. The longer Idris waited, the more unknown variables might appear. The Mews was unstable. Yet Thomas and Damon almost certainly felt Idris would be following their orders and distribute their product throughout The Mews. None of them would see him coming.

Idris opened the kilo brick of heroin which Thomas had supplied. Instead of making wraps to sell, Idris instead removed a small quantity of the powder which he intended to use to make an altogether different product.

He checked his calculations a final time then measured the

powder on an electronic scale. Then he walked to the controlled drugs cabinet and removed a packet of fentanyl lozenges.

Using old school pharmacy instruments, a pestle and mortar, Idris ground the lozenges into a fine powder and then mixed that with the heroin, creating a lethal combination.

He packaged the powder in a plastic food bag, secured it and put it to one side.

Idris looked at the empty packet of fentanyl. He was going to have to account for them in the official register and the only way to do that was with a prescription. Idris used the pharmacy computer to search for patients who were on the lozenges.

Only two.

He analysed their medication histories, saw that one of the patients was on Alzheimer's medication and immediately knew how to falsify the records. He checked when the next prescription was due.

Ten days.

Perfect.

Idris would process that prescription and get the medication delivered. Then he would inform Mariam that the patient had forgetfully thrown them in the bin, something which happened routinely with patients who suffered with dementia. Mariam would be forced to give Idris a new prescription and this one Idris would use to balance the shortage in the register.

Feeling buoyed by this plan, Idris was about to take a break and make himself a coffee when the doorbell rang.

He checked the time – 07.05.

Usually, he would have dismissed it, but with everything else going on, he wondered if this was Al-Noor or Rebecca. But they would surely have called him.

The doorbell went again, this time sounding three times in a row.

And now, Idris's phone started to ring.

He removed it from his pocket, stared at the withheld number, his thoughts immediately going to the Mead family.

With a slight tremor to his hand, Idris answered the call.

'Hello?'

'Idris, it's DCI Pitchford. I'm outside your pharmacy and wondered if we might have an early morning chat before you open?'

Idris glanced at the dispensary bench, at the fentanyl, and the brick of heroin, and his notes on how to create the perfect poison.

'Er . . . I'm sorta of caught up with work,' said Idris.

'I totally understand that. To be honest, I had meant to visit you later this morning but then I'd have to interrupt your business – patients might be alarmed – and it would be so disruptive that I thought a quick chat before you opened might be the best way to do this. What do you think?'

Idris paused, thought about how best to get out of this situation.

'It's fine, Idris, I'll come back with a team later in the morning.'

A team?

Christ, surely it was better just to speak to Pitchford alone.

'No, I . . . er . . . can speak to you now. Just give me five to finish what I'm doing.'

'Lovely,' said Pitchford and hung up the call.

Hurriedly, Idris removed the evidence of what he had been doing for the past hour and cleaned the bench.

Then Idris spent a couple of minutes calming his paranoia.

Pitchford arriving like this, alone, meant that he could not

325

have had any evidence to arrest Idris or he would surely have followed protocol and arrived with additional officers.

Deep down, Idris had known this meeting was coming but he still felt uneasy.

His pharmacy had been the scene of multiple crimes. Would Pitchford realise it?

Idris went to unlock the door, raised the shutter and saw Pitchford standing there wearing an oversized raincoat to protect him from the rain.

'Sorry about the delay. I was checking medications,' said Idris, waving Pitchford inside.

'I understand,' replied Pitchford, stepping past him, using his walking stick. He remained on the mat, brushed excess water from his raincoat. 'Good of you to let me in.'

Idris locked the doors, dropped the shutter.

'How did you know I would be here this early?' asked Idris.

'When we took a statement from your staff, Jemma told us that you started here every day at 5 a.m.'

'What if I'd taken a morning off?'

Pitchford unbuttoned his coat. 'Something told me that you're a creature of habit and seeing as this is your own business, I figured that was unlikely. Could you do me a favour, Idris?'

'Try me.'

'Help me take this coat off? My Parkinson's is always worse in the mornings and I'm still a little stiff until my meds kick in.'

'Of course.'

Idris gently helped Pitchford remove his coat and left it to dry on the mat.

'So, my barb about you having arthritis was wrong,' said Idris.

'Feels like it sometimes. Alas, I've an atypical form of the disease – one of only a handful of people known globally to suffer with it – but let's not dwell on my aches and pains,' said Pitchford and followed Idris into the retail area of the pharmacy. 'Are you allowed to work so early, alone?'

Idris shrugged. 'Needs must.'

Both men cracked fake smiles at one another, knowing full well that this exchange was merely a cheap appetiser before the main course.

'I'm guessing you're here about Al-Noor and what happened over there,' said Idris, pointing across the road towards the café.

'Amongst other things,' replied Pitchford, cryptically.

'The Mews, no doubt,' said Idris.

Pitchford smiled at him. 'Smart men chemists. They're very – what's the word I'm looking for? – perceptive.'

'When you treat hundreds of patients a day, you soon figure out what people want without them having to say it. Especially around here with all the students. Communication isn't top of a young person's skillset.'

'Very true. I bet you could tell a few stories,' said Pitchford, laughing.

Idris joined him. 'Patient confidentiality. You hate me saying that, don't you?' he replied, keeping a wry smile on his face.

'Modern-day data protection laws are there to protect people. But yes, sometimes they really tick me off.'

'Tea?' asked Idris.

Pitchford considered it. 'Maybe later. Do you mind if I look around? Don't think I've ever had a behind-the-scenes tour of the inside of a chemist.'

'One condition.'

Pitchford waited for it.

Idris teased his response a little then said, 'That you stop calling it "a chemist". This is a pharmacy. Chemists make pills and potions. I supply medications and advice.'

'Pharmacy it is. Any areas off limits?'

'Not unless you've got fast hands.'

Pitchford raised them. 'Less shaky than usual and certainly not fast anymore.'

Idris stepped aside and said, 'My house is yours. And in the interests of patient confidentiality, if you see medication with someone's name on it, pretend that you didn't.'

Idris was printing out labels for the methadone doses but was constantly distracted by Pitchford who was walking slowly around the dispensary, the sound of his cane tapping rhythmically on the tiles.

Pitchford undertook the same route that Thomas Mead had done seventy-two hours before, finally stopping in front of the detailed estate plan of The Mews, and spent several minutes looking at it.

'How I'd love to take a photo of this,' he said.

'Now, that would be a breach.'

'Unfettered access to The Mews. Impressive. Unheard of.'

'When you bring the drugs, you get all the access you need.'

'How has it been now that Jahangir Hosseini is dead?'

Just hearing Pitchford say Jahangir's name made Idris's heart race.

He had poisoned him yards away from where Pitchford was standing.

'No change yet. The Mews know they need me.'

'And you've never been robbed there? A man carrying all those drugs?' asked Pitchford, clearly impressed.

'Don't jinx me now.'

'How many addicts on your books?'

'All of them. Three hundred-ish.'

'Wow.'

Pitchford pointed to the controlled drugs cabinet. 'Can I take a look inside?'

'As long as you don't nick me for allowing it. Technically, illegal.'

'I won't tell if you don't.'

Idris pointed towards it. 'Be my guest. It's unlocked. Hands where I can see them, though.'

Pitchford opened the cabinet, resting his cane against the wall and carefully raised his hands in the air theatrically.

Idris saw they were shaking. Slight, but it was definitively there.

'Please, I'm kidding. Lower them.'

Pitchford did so, retook his cane and spent several minutes observing the large trays inside the cabinet.

'What are the trays for?'

'They will shortly be filled with methadone doses ready for the addicts to collect. The ones remaining there are uncollected from yesterday – addicts who missed their daily supervision.'

'Does that happen often?'

'Not often.'

'What happens if an addict misses a dose?'

'Depends on the dose. Depends on the addict.'

'Can you generalise for me?'

Pitchford still had his back to Idris, talking to him without looking at him. Idris found it unnerving.

Smart detective, thought Idris, knowing Pitchford was listening for when Idris's tone of voice changed.

'Addicts describe it as rattling,' said Idris.

'Rattling? They shake? Sounds like me,' said Pitchford, laughing.

'It's not really an external thing, they feel themselves rattling inside. The body demands an opioid hit. The receptors in the brain scream for it. Nothing else matters. It's all about the impulse, the urge.'

'And methadone gives them a hit?'

'No. It reduces the craving.'

'Very interesting. I had always assumed – incorrectly I now realise – that methadone was a straight substitution.'

'There's no high with it.'

'Have you ever tried it? Methadone?'

'What?'

Pitchford turned around now. 'Ever tried it?'

'No.'

Pitchford looked around the dispensary. 'Ever tried any of the interesting stuff?'

'Morphine,' answered Idris jovially. 'Regular addict.' He didn't believe that Pitchford would buy it and since he had told the truth, also didn't believe that his voice had given anything away. 'Had a few hits today. You want to try some?'

Pitchford slipped his hand in his pocket and pulled out a packet of pills. 'Parkinson's. I'm rattling as it is. Maybe not a heroin rattle but some days it feels like all I do is swallow pills.'

'Which tablets are you on?'

'All of them.'

'Dispersible in the morning. Slow release throughout the day?'

Pitchford nodded. 'You're good.'

'As everyone keeps telling me, I'm The Chemist.'

'Pharmacist.'

'Touché.'

Idris pointed to the kettle. 'Sure you don't want one?'

330

'Another time. Can you run me through that?' said Pitchford, pointing at Idris's computer.

Idris shook his head. 'Now that would be a stretch too far. To show you how it works, I'd have to select a patient and then all that data protection stuff we love kicks into play.'

Pitchford pulled a white piece of paper from his pocket and waved it at Idris. 'My electronic prescription. I asked my usual pharmacy to return it to me.'

Idris was momentarily flummoxed. The detective really was here to truly understand how everything worked. He came towards Idris and placed his prescription on the bench.

'Can you dispense that for me? Show me how the system works?'

Idris grabbed the script. 'Sure.'

It took only a few minutes for Idris to scan Pitchford's prescription into the computer then label and dispense his Parkinson's medication, all the while aware that he was being watched.

When he'd finished, he handed the parcel to Pitchford.

'And I always thought that it was just sticking labels on bottles,' said Pitchford.

Idris sucked his teeth, exasperated. 'We hear that every single day.'

Pitchford asked Idris which medical information the computer had now stored about his health.

Idris pointed to the parcel he had handed over. 'Just that I gave you those pills.'

'You can't see into my full medical history?'

Idris shook his head. 'Only the GP can do that.'

'And you can't dial into their system?'

Idris did not hesitate and said, 'No.'

'Tell me about methadone supplies,' said Pitchford.

Idris did so. Ran through the whole system.

'Can I see the register? The one which shows that Al-Noor missed five days' supply of his methadone?'

Ahh.

The real reason for the visit.

'No,' said Idris.

'No?'

'This is where I do play the patient confidentiality card. The register is full of the names of addicts I supply. I'd be exposing you to sensitive data on addicts who might be known to you. So, it's a no, I'm afraid.'

Pitchford nodded. 'I can, of course, simply apply for access using the legal route.'

'You'll need to.'

Pitchford remained stoic. 'Seems an awful waste of time when access to the register will be guaranteed.'

'It's to protect me. And the data I hold.'

'Favour for a favour?' teased Pitchford.

A test. Perhaps the only reason Pitchford had really arrived here.

If Idris entertained the favour, he would be showing Pitchford that he was apt to bend rules when he needed to. If he refused, he would be drawing his battle line very firmly in the sand.

'What would you do, if you were me?' asked Idris, trying to push the responsibility for the decision back on Pitchford.

'Well, I guess that depends on how much you like paperwork. I'll get the warrant, come in here with a team, we will photocopy the records, redact them, disrupt your business or – we can simply do it now, off the record and I leave with my curiosity satisfied.'

'Curiosity that Al-Noor didn't miss his methadone?'

'Just curious to see the register. Call it an itch I want to scratch. And maybe down the line, you might need a favour, Idris.'

Idris didn't like the way Pitchford had said that but he also didn't want to seem like he was hiding anything and so far, they had both played nice.

Idris grabbed the methadone register from the shelf. 'I need your word that this never happened,' he said, holding the book just out of reach.

'I will have forgotten as soon as I've seen it.'

Idris handed it over. And in doing so, gave Pitchford everything he needed to prove that he was lying.

Chapter Sixty-Six

Idris saw it.

Christ, how could he have been so careless?

He could see that Pitchford had seen it. Because he had, in front of him, spread out across the bench, previous older registers, all the entries made chaotically, in different coloured ink, black, blue, red.

Yet, in this current register – which Idris had fabricated the night before, doctoring it to show that Al-Noor had missed five days of his methadone – all the entries were neat, orderly but most importantly, the same coloured pen had been used each time.

They were too bloody neat. What a stupid mistake to have made.

Pitchford spent time looking at the register, just . . . staring at it.

Methodical, meticulous.

Absolutely still.

Then he simply closed all the registers, turned to Idris and said, 'Thank you. I got what I needed.'

Idris doubled down, trying his best to show confidence. 'I'm glad. So, what happens next?'

'Did Al-Noor tell you about his deal?'

'He did.'

'Would you be against us meeting him here from time to time?'

'I'd need notice. Ensure that the consultation room is available.'

'What time does Al-Noor usually collect his methadone?'

'Variable.'

Pitchford nodded to the wall where the pharmacy's opening hours were. 'The fact you're open so late is helpful. Potentially, we could meet him here late on?'

Idris nodded. 'Sure.'

Keep your friends close, your enemies closer.

'You've been more than helpful, Idris.'

'Glad to be of service.'

Idris grabbed his keys and was about to show Pitchford out when Pitchford stopped.

'Aspirin,' he said.

Idris stopped dead, his blood running cold.

'What?' he said, only this time his voice was weighted with alarm.

Pitchford turned around. 'Jahangir Hosseini died because he took an aspirin.'

'What?' said Idris again, unable to find any other words.

'We ran a tox screen. Found the usual things we'd expect from someone like Jahangir. But also, aspirin within his system – which I just can't figure out because he must have known he was intolerant to it. He was previously admitted to hospital after taking some.' Pitchford smiled. 'You'll know this – being a pharmacist – that aspirin is a powerful vasoconstrictor and for people with brittle asthma, like Jahangir, it can be fatal.'

Idris, his mouth dry, said nothing.

Pitchford pointed to the computer. 'Does the pharmacy software tell you about things like that?'

Idris shrugged. 'Sometimes, if we've been aware of an allergy or intolerance, we add it to the system.'

'Could you check if you had logged Jahangir as being sensitive to aspirin for me?'

Pitchford turned his back on Idris. 'I won't look to see any sensitive data.'

Idris hesitated. He felt trapped. Letting Pitchford inside the pharmacy had been a mistake. The old-man routine was just an act. Pitchford was on to him.

Idris accessed Jahangir's records on the computer.

'No. We didn't have it listed,' he said, and turned off the screen.

Pitchford turned back to face him.

'Isn't that odd? Or a safety concern? A man who could die from taking something seemingly as insignificant as a tablet of aspirin and yet, it's not listed on your system?'

'Allergy statuses are not legally required to be entered as part of owning a PMR.'

'That should be looked at.'

Idris hated the inference. 'I didn't give Jahangir aspirin,' he snapped.

Pitchford looked shocked. 'Of course not. No pharmacist would entertain that without undertaking due process, correct?'

'Correct,' said Idris firmly.

Pitchford nodded, thought on it a beat. Kept his eyes focused solely on Idris who pushed back, a little harder.

'The thing with aspirin is that it's found in so many different products, ones readily available from corner shops, petrol stations, even vending machines these days.'

Pitchford stepped back and perched on a stool, clearly having changed his mind about leaving.

Idris didn't want to entertain this conversation anymore. 'I've really got to get back to my work,' he said.

'Just a few more minutes, please, Idris. Help me work through something which has been playing on my mind.'

Idris nodded for Pitchford to continue but didn't retake his seat.

Pitchford pointed to Idris's methadone register. 'It says that Jahangir collected his methadone on the night of the incident at the café?'

Idris didn't answer because it wasn't really a question.

'He comes in here. Takes his methadone tablets. Obviously after what happened to him inside the café, he has a headache and needs some painkillers. Yet even though he is inside a pharmacy, with all these different medications around him – not to mention, his regular chemist – he leaves, goes somewhere else and buys some painkillers? Does that sound right to you?'

Pitchford had him. Not quite dead to rights but not far away.

Idris pushed back. 'Who says he bought them? The most common cause of medication-associated hospital admissions is people borrowing drugs from their friends or relatives.'

Pitchford smiled. 'You know, I thought the same thing. And then came across another problem. Care to know what it is?'

Idris said nothing. Waited for it.

'Jahangir was found collapsed, outside his tower block in The Mews. Now, I ask myself, does a man like Jahangir Hosseini pass a stranger or even someone he knows on the street or inside The Mews and just ask them for painkillers? I struggle with that. You?'

The pressure Pitchford was covertly applying felt brutal. Idris locked eyes with him and saw that Pitchford knew what he had done.

Idris smiled. 'I think, detective, that it's time you left. Like I said, I've much work to do.'

Pitchford stuck out a shaky hand. 'Thank you for your help, Idris. It's been invaluable.'

Chapter Sixty-Seven

Idris had not gone to The Mews to deliver his daily round of medications, concerned that with Jahangir's death, his safety was no longer guaranteed.

He had instead come to see Rebecca and found himself, for the second time in two days, sitting on the couch, carefully discussing the most pressing issue they needed to overcome.

Project Liam.

Idris had brought with him Rebecca's usual methadone dose, supervised her taking it and had been relieved to learn that she had not needed the additional supply he had given her the night before.

Idris started from the beginning, working through his plan.

'I'm going to call Liam, arrange to meet him in Beckett Park, and that's your window to go and see Amy, try to make her see reason. Float the idea of the cash.'

'But you're giving it all to Liam?' said Rebecca, sitting by his side, focused, determined.

'I'm giving Liam half now – forty grand – and telling him that he needs to come see me later at the pharmacy to collect the rest, before I go to The Mews to . . . sort out Elyas and Majid. So, float the money to Amy. Trust me, the girl is prepared to work the streets of Beeston, she should snap our hand off for the cash.'

Rebecca removed a piece of paper from her pocket. 'I got Liam's current address from The Elizabeth Projects database. I'll leave here as soon as you confirm your meeting with him is set.'

'Let's do that now,' replied Idris and removed his phone.

He scrolled to Liam's number and made the call.

'Liam?' said Idris, thankful the call connected quickly. He put it on speaker so that Rebecca could hear.

'Chemist man,' replied Liam, clearly expecting Idris's call.

'I've got the money.'

'Fuckin-A man! Bring it ova'!'

'Liam, remember what we said last night.'

'Last night? What you on 'bout?'

'You came to see me at the pharmacy. We spoke.'

There was a short silence. Idris rolled his eyes at Rebecca, gestured that Liam had been drinking.

'Oh . . . yeah, I forgot.'

Idris realised that Liam didn't have a clue. 'Beckett Park, we said. Two hours?'

'Yeah. I can make that. Yo, Chemist, I need more methadone too. I fink I lost that supply.'

Idris sighed, kept his temper in check. 'We can talk about that when I see you.'

'I'll buzz you when I'm in the park,' said Liam and abruptly hung up the call.

'It's on,' said Idris to Rebecca.

She stood up, clearly nervous. 'Do you think . . . I don't know . . . that you should take Daniel with you?'

'I thought about that, but I need Daniel focused for tonight, with Al-Noor.'

'What have I dragged you into?' she said quietly to herself.

Idris stepped in front of her, took her face in his hands,

wanting so desperately to kiss her like they had the night before, but resisting.

'We're all in now. Elyas, Majid, Thomas and Damon, they all have to go. It's the only way we can walk away from this thing unscathed. The only way Al-Noor stays out of prison.'

Rebecca slipped her arms around Idris's body, looked at him in a way which made him momentarily look away.

'Look at me, Idris,' she said.

'We can't do this,' he replied, with little conviction to his voice.

Rebecca pressed her body against his, kissed his neck, then his face.

Idris finally gave in to his emotions and amidst the darkness they were facing, for the next sixty minutes, they relived what it had been like in the infancy of their relationship; heat, passion and, breaking all the rules.

Chapter Sixty-Eight

Liam was sprawled across his couch, half naked, watching the footage of Rebecca stabbing Patrick Mead to death.

That nosy, interfering bitch deserved everything which was happening to her.

But Liam had always thought she was attractive. She had this strict, headmistress-type quality that he thought could be useful.

And seeing her in the clip simply made Liam want to fuck her.

Maybe he'd do that. Show her the footage and see how long it took for her to get on her knees.

He thought about The Chemist now and the call he had just shared with him. The cash was in hand, and they were set to meet shortly.

The daft bastard.

Liam was going to take his cash, then sell the footage to the Meads and double bank what he was making.

Damon had been in touch with Liam, told him that they wanted Amy first, not the footage, and Liam had negotiated a decent price for her.

Liam glanced across the room to where Amy was lying comatose on the floor. He prepared another syringe for her, an increase in the previous dose of heroin he had given her.

She wouldn't be conscious for the rest of the day.

Tomorrow, Liam intended to hand her over to the Meads, take his payday and disappear for a while. Once he was set up somewhere new, he'd return and blackmail The Chemist again and keep doing it until Idris was ruined.

Liam picked up a scrappy piece of paper and an old pencil from the floor. He'd started to create a shopping list of medications which he wanted The Chemist to supply him.

Liam needed drugs to make a name for himself somewhere new.

He needed another bottle of methadone. Then Viagra, pregabalin and most importantly diazepam. It was a drug all addicts loved to take, as it took the edge off their cravings. Liam wanted the good shit too, *10mg tablets*. He could halve them, sell them for £2 a pop.

He knew chemists could get packs of five hundred tablets, having seen them traded on the black market. That would be a thousand doses, which meant a cool two grand for Liam on top of the cash he was already getting from Idris.

Choice man. Fucking choice.

Amy stirred, which surprised him. He'd give her a sizeable hit of heroin.

'Liam, I don't feel so good,' she said, slurring her words.

She could barely hold her head up, eyes squinting across at him.

Liam slipped off the couch and prepared another shot for her.

'No, I don't want any more, Liam. Just gimme some water, please,' she said.

Liam went to her and raised the sleeve on her arm.

'No,' she repeated and tried to push him away but couldn't.

Liam injected the dose into a vein just below her elbow,

pulled the needle free and flung it across the room. He watched her collapse back onto the floor, the back of her skull hitting the carpet with some force.

Crack.

Liam jumped to his feet, excited, taking with him his list of drugs. He stormed out of the house, anticipating his pay day.

As he left, he didn't hear Amy in distress. Or the sound of her vomiting.

Chapter Sixty-Nine

Rebecca got out of her car as soon as she saw Liam leave his house. She walked around the back of the end-terrace property, opened the gate and hurried towards the back door, knocking on it urgently.

She tried the door. It was locked but the damn thing was so badly rotten that it shook on its hinges with each powerful strike of her fist.

She stepped to the side and peered through a cracked window into a chaotic living room space, and saw Amy lying there, vomit across her face.

Horrified, Rebecca kicked the door open – the hinges easily giving way – and rushed inside, through a neglected kitchen, into the living room and immediately turned Amy onto her side.

Rebecca looked for something to clear the vomit with, and grabbed a ragged-looking blanket from the couch. She cleaned the vomit from Amy's face and checked her pulse. It was weak but she was alive.

She put Amy into the recovery position, ensured she was comfortable, then rushed back into the kitchen and started rummaging through the drawers.

On initiation of methadone treatment, drug addicts were also sometimes given a supply of naloxone – an antidote for heroin overdose – in case they used both drugs, something which happened frequently.

She emptied every drawer's contents but found nothing.

Back in the living room, Rebecca was about to do the same thing, when she stepped on a used syringe.

She took a beat and had a slow look around the room.

Unsheathed needles.

A death trap in waiting.

She could only imagine which illnesses Liam was carrying.

Rebecca again checked Amy's pulse and satisfied that she was in no immediate danger, delicately searched her body and found Amy's mobile phone in her pocket.

She removed it and saw that it was an old iPhone. It was password protected, meaning Rebecca could not access it but as it was an older model, the security settings relied on a fingerprint, not face identification.

Rebecca lifted Amy's hand and unlocked the phone using the thumb on Amy's right hand.

She accessed the video files and found the footage of Rebecca killing Patrick Mead.

She deleted it then accessed the 'recently deleted' folder and cleared that also.

Rebecca slipped the phone back into Amy's pocket then rushed upstairs. She saw there were two bedrooms and a small bathroom and searched all three rooms for any naloxone or – as Idris had instructed – anything which he could use when it came to Liam.

The rooms were sparsely furnished, meaning it took only a few minutes to clear them.

Rebecca found no other electronic devices which might have held the footage of her killing Patrick. She did, though, find a box with medications inside and rummaged through them, dismayed to find nothing she could use to help Amy.

Then she lifted a small bottle of pills with an official hospital label on them from the Becklin pharmacy. *Disulfiram tablets.* They looked untouched.

Rebecca didn't know what they were for and left them as they were.

Back downstairs, Rebecca was beside Amy trying to rouse her, but it was useless. She couldn't leave her like this; Liam was clearly intent on killing the girl. She needed to take Amy with her but couldn't carry her to her car; it was too far.

She tried to call Idris, but he didn't answer.

Rebecca moved out of the living room into the kitchen and looked outside. There was space to bring her car around the back and park it maybe ten metres from the house.

She could carry Amy that far.

Chapter Seventy

Beckett Park was full of students, who even in the bitter winter cold were playing sports, football and rugby mostly.

Idris looked at them enviously, the innocence of youth, the world at their fingertips.

He had received a text message from Rebecca that she had found Amy overdosing and taken her back to her house.

Rebecca, whom Idris was now having an affair with. It now put him in the same boat as Mariam, so perhaps the act had – on some level – been inevitable, the final nail in his loveless marriage.

His thoughts were disturbed by the sound of a loud, vulgar wolf whistle and the arrival of Liam who, for the first time since Idris could remember, was not carrying with him a can of lager.

'Chemist man,' said Liam, sliding next to him and immediately kicking at the bag by Idris's feet. 'I remember that from last night. Paperwork or summat, wasn't it? Full of my money now?'

Liam snatched the bag, placed it on his lap and unzipped it.

Idris immediately stood up in front of Liam, concerned that a passerby might see the money.

'All-fuckin'-right,' said Liam, beaming at the cash. He stroked it and started to laugh.

He didn't seem to realise that it wasn't a hundred grand. Idris toyed with not telling him, but didn't want the later aggravation of Liam thinking that Idris had tried to screw him over.

'There's only forty grand there, Liam.'

Liam zipped the bag closed and glared at Idris.

'Relax, I'm going to another bank now to get the rest. It's not easy to get that kind of cash so I've had to split it across different branches.'

'So, when?' said Liam, the greed clear on his face.

'Tonight.'

Liam stood up, removed a piece of paper from his pocket and pushed it into Idris's hand. 'I'll come by later for the rest of the cash, but I need these as well.'

Idris skimmed the list. 'I can't supply you with all this.'

'You will do what I say, Chemist man.'

Idris shook his head, outraged. 'I don't even hold the quantities you've written here. This is thousands of pounds worth of drugs.'

Liam removed his phone from his pocket. 'Sort it or we'll see how the Meads react to this video.'

'We had a deal. A hundred grand.'

'Deals change.'

'Liam, I can't keep doing this . . .'

Liam slapped him, sending Idris collapsing to the ground.

The pain in Idris's ribs detonated and he rolled onto his side, screaming into his shoulder.

'Second time I've had to slap yer,' snapped Liam, vicious, unstable.

Idris took a beat, then glanced around the park, afraid that someone might have witnessed the altercation and would try to play good Samaritan. Thankfully, everyone seemed oblivious to what had happened.

349

Idris struggled to his feet, amazed at what Liam had done, massaging his ribs, carefully.

'What the hell are you doing?' said Idris.

'Remindin' yer who is boss. I'll see you at 8 p.m. and you better have the rest of my money and my drugs,' said Liam and with that, he duly walked away, whistling as he went.

Another message arrived on Idris's phone, again from Rebecca.

Idris read it. I'm home, got Amy with me. Are you coming over?

Idris replied, Is she still out?

Yes. Can you grab some naloxone from the pharmacy? She needs it.

Idris typed his message as he walked back towards his car.

I'm on it.

Chapter Seventy-One

Idris lifted Amy's eyelids, one at a time. *Pin-point pupils*. She was still high.

Idris had swung by the pharmacy, picked up a box of naloxone ampoules and used a syringe to prepare a dose. He administered it to Amy then stepped away from her, walking across to the window where Rebecca was standing.

'You saved her life,' he said.

'I think Liam is trying to kill her.'

Rebecca covered her face with her hands. 'Idris, maybe we should just go to the police and hand ourselves in.'

Idris slipped his arm around her. 'You know we can't. At this stage, we're looking at the lesser of two evils. Us or the Meads.'

'And Liam? Are you going to kill him too?'

'He's going to kill Amy,' said Idris, pointing behind him where she was asleep. 'If you hadn't turned up, she'd be dead already. I just wish Amy could see it.'

'I can see it,' said Amy weakly.

Idris turned to see that Amy's eyes were open and she was looking directly at him.

He went to her, kneeling beside her.

'How are you feeling?' he asked.

'I can taste vomit and I stink of it,' she said.

Rebecca arrived beside Amy. 'You injected too much and vomited while you were unconscious.'

'I didn't inject owt, it was Liam. You's is right. He tried to kill me. Don't need me no more.'

Idris and Rebecca both fell silent.

Amy struggled to sit up. Rebecca helped her, propping a cushion under her head, raising her body as much as she could so that Amy was upright.

'I'm sorry for what I did,' said Amy and started to cry.

And then, just like that, her body flopped to the side, and she slipped into unconsciousness again.

'Shit,' said Rebecca and hurriedly rolled Amy onto her side. 'She's in and out.'

Idris had seen this many times: patients who overdosed would slip in and out of consciousness.

'I think she'll work with us now, Idris,' said Rebecca.

'I agree. But how to get rid of Liam? I don't have any intel on him. I mean, I could, maybe, try something like what Al-Noor and I are going to attempt at The Mews tonight but, really, I need something which feels organic in nature. Which fits with Liam.'

Rebecca came to him and they again both moved towards the window, looking out across the street, watching the world go by, quiet, peaceful.

'I searched Liam's place for the footage – laptop, mobile, anything like that – but there was nothing.'

'He's got it on him.'

'Why can't we just mug him?'

'We could. But then he'd know it was us. There'd be heat on us. Liam might not be Jahangir or Thomas Mead but he's his own version of them. If he wants to hurt us, or the people we care about, he could, especially if he's got a back-up of the footage.'

352

Rebecca tapped her head against the windowpane. 'Crap,' she whispered.

'Did you find anything in the house which might be useful? Medical stuff?' asked Idris.

'He had a supply of something from the hospital pharmacy. Untouched, though. A full bottle of pills.'

Idris turned to face her, immediately interested. 'Name of the drug?'

She grimaced, thought on it and shook her head. 'Shit, I should have brought them with me. They were from the Becklin pharmacy. Does that help?'

Idris felt buoyed, he could engineer getting the intel. He removed his phone, searched for the pharmacy's number and called them.

'Becklin Centre pharmacy, Michelle speaking, how can I help you?' said a female voice.

'This is Idris Khan, superintendent pharmacist at Headingley pharmacy. I've got a Liam Reynolds here requesting an emergency supply of medication which he got from you but he can't remember the name. Says he's lost the container. Can I get a medication history check, please?' he said.

Idris covered his hand with the phone and hissed at Rebecca, 'Try wake Amy up, I need Liam's date of birth.'

Rebecca ignored him, removed her own phone. 'She's out, Idris, but I can get it from my work. Liam is listed on our database.'

Rebecca moved away hurriedly, speaking into the phone as she went.

The lady Idris was speaking to asked him for Liam's address and date of birth.

Idris provided the address. 'I'll get the patient's date of birth,' he said.

Idris rushed across to Rebecca. She held her hand up firmly, listened to the call she was on then whispered to Idris, 'Second April 1978.'

Idris relayed the information and waited.

He listened to the information about Liam's medication and hung up the call.

'Any good?' asked Rebecca.

Idris put his phone away. 'Disulfiram. It's to stop alcoholics from drinking,' he whispered, an idea beginning to take form.

Chapter Seventy-Two

Idris arrived back at his pharmacy and immediately locked himself inside the consultation room. He opened a cupboard and removed several pharmaceutical textbooks, spreading them across the table. He read up on disulfiram, trying hard to ignore the sound of customers and his staff outside the room.

Idris scribbled down some formulas, documenting how he could mix disulfiram to create a lethal solution which he could covertly administer to Liam.

Idris had the ingredients he needed to hand in the pharmacy, the question was one of timeline. Did he have enough time to make the solution?

He thought on what was on his radar for that evening, the ambitious plans he had carefully created.

Liam would be first to arrive at that pharmacy, somewhere around 8 p.m. when Idris would be alone, the staff having left.

Idris estimated he would be free of that situation within the hour. Then, he planned to head to The Mews, to Elyas and Majid for circa 9 p.m. What he needed to do there shouldn't have taken longer than an hour. He had already made the drug cocktail he needed.

It meant that he needed to get across to Harehills, to the shisha lounge where he expected to see Thomas Mead, who according to transactions on his bank statements attended there regular as clockwork. Idris anticipated arriving there at around 10 p.m.

Tonight would be all about a series of targeted hits, all within three hours but most importantly, Idris planned to make it look like a turf war had erupted, opposing clans having taken each other out.

The plan would leave Al-Noor and Rebecca in the clear.

Al-Noor connecting with Elyas and Majid had been key. Idris knew them well and while they weren't on methadone anymore, they were addicts and would manipulate any opportunity they could to make money or assume power.

Getting them to entertain a new supply had been critical but was only stage one of the plan. Stage two involved getting across to the shisha lounge and using a very different type of chemistry.

Idris removed a packet of high-strength potassium tablets from his pocket, which he had lifted from the pharmacy earlier. He dissolved four into a glass of water and drank the solution slowly. Idris needed to raise his potassium level because there was a good chance that at the shisha bar, he too might need to inhale the cocktail of drugs he intended to poison Thomas Mead with.

A poison which would force Thomas's potassium levels to plummet, something which would be fatal, especially with Thomas's medical history.

Idris moved back to his desk and was scribbling down the timeframes for that evening when he heard a raging commotion taking place outside the consultation room. He left his seat and hurried outside, to find an addict, Rico Zimmer, engaging in a furious argument with Jemma.

Rico was towering over her, his six-foot frame and stocky

build an intimidating presence. Not that Jemma seemed to give a shit.

'I saw you put it in your pocket,' snapped Jemma.

'There's no CCTV here anymore. You ain't got shit,' replied Rico.

'Empty your pocket and show me.'

'No.'

'Why not? Got something to hide?'

'You're a cunt, you know that. Where's The Chemist?'

Idris tapped Rico on the shoulder. He turned around and Idris said, 'Get out.'

'Why? You ain't heard my side or anything.'

'I heard what you called her. I don't accept language like that in here. So, you're out. Find a different chemist to get your methadone from.'

Rico pushed Idris away forcefully. 'Jahangir's gone. Who has got your back now?'

And here it began.

The start of blue-script dissent with the removal of safeguards which Idris had always relied upon with Jahangir.

Maybe Idris should have delivered to The Mews today because the residents were all now flooding into the pharmacy to collect medications Idris used to deliver to them.

'Empty your pockets,' said Idris.

'Fuck. You.'

'Rico, not only are you going to lose access to your medications but I won't give you your methadone either.'

Rico stepped to Idris, threatening, a crazed look across his face.

Idris pointed to the door. 'Thirty seconds, or Jemma hits the panic alarm, the cops arrive, and you screw your probation.'

Idris could tell that Rico wanted to hit him but he stood

his ground. The situation with Liam and Thomas had changed Idris and he was no longer willing to accept the usual shit he had previously put up with.

'Twenty seconds, Rico. I'm not playing here,' said Idris.

Rico clearly realised that Idris was not bluffing. He stepped past Idris, shoulder-barging him angrily, and stormed out of the pharmacy, swearing as he went.

Idris turned to Jemma. 'You good?'

She was clearly surprised at how bullish Idris had been, looking at him puzzled.

'You should have delivered to The Mews today. New world order with no Jahangir. I almost miss the idiot,' she said and went back to her work.

Idris's thoughts turned to The Mews, about what he, Al-Noor and Daniel were planning to do.

Jahangir dying was one thing. But once Elyas and Majid were gone, everyone would know The Mews was under attack.

Idris had no idea what the effects of that would be, but one thing was certain, his access to The Mews after tonight would not be possible. And without that, his pharmacy business would surely close.

Idris, though, felt he had a potential safeguard in place. Liam Reynolds would not be needing the cash Idris had given him. That stash was coming back to the pharmacy because without it, Idris's business would collapse.

A message arrived on his phone from Al-Noor.

Mr Idris, are we set for this evening?

Idris replied quickly. See you at 7 pm Al. Everything is set.

Chapter Seventy-Three

Idris had closed the pharmacy and put a sign on the front door saying, CLOSED FOR THE REST OF THE DAY DUE TO AN ELECTRICAL POWER CUT. WE APOLOGISE FOR ANY INCONVENIENCE.

This was where it all started: a five-hour window to bring all the threats Idris, Al-Noor and Rebecca were facing to an end.

Al-Noor was waiting, patiently, inside the pharmacy and today Idris had not given him his usual dose of methadone. With what they were attempting to pull off, he needed to limit the number of opioids in Al-Noor's system.

Idris had instructed Al-Noor to spend an hour mentally preparing himself for a night which would determine both his and Idris's futures.

Idris then prepared firstly, a lethal concoction of disulfiram liquid for Liam and then two syringes of a heroin–fentanyl mixture for Elyas and Majid – and Al-Noor.

Idris also prepared a bag of medications for Liam to take away with him, the drugs he had demanded. Only Idris wasn't giving Liam any such medications. The container might have said diazepam but inside it were simple vitamin D tablets, the same size and shape as diazepam. Idris had done this for all the drugs Liam had demanded, replacing them all with vitamins.

By the time Liam realised he'd been duped, it would be too late and by then Liam would never again be able to blackmail Idris.

Once he'd finished, Idris turned his attention to Al-Noor who was sitting patiently in the retail area. Idris measured out a specific quantity of the heroin–fentanyl mixture he had made, estimating how much Al-Noor could take without it instantly killing him.

Idris called Al-Noor into the dispensary, told him to sit down and showed him the amount of powder he would need to snort that evening.

'But Mr Idris, we always inject heroin,' said Al-Noor.

'I know, but I need the reaction to be instantaneous for Elyas and Majid,' said Idris, pointing at the powder.

He explained that while heroin was not usually snorted it could be if the drug was pure enough. The fentanyl mixed with the heroin was a far stronger opioid but the delivery mechanism of inhalation would deliver first an extraordinarily potent high and then, a few seconds later, start a chain reaction inside the brain which would ultimately result in the user's death. Idris had created a poison so toxic that nobody could survive it.

Including Al-Noor.

Idris went to the controlled drugs cabinet and this time removed a naloxone nasal spray and a packet of naloxone injections. He brought them back to Al-Noor, set them down on the bench and told him to listen carefully and to ask questions as he needed. While Idris thought the science behind what he was doing was simple, to the layman, it was anything but.

Idris had, in effect, created a super-compound which would ultimately kill both Elyas and Majid quickly. But since Al-Noor would more than likely be forced to snort the first line, to prove it was a safe product, it would also kill him.

Al-Noor nodded, following what Idris had said.

Idris picked up the nasal spray and waved it at Al-Noor. 'This is the strongest opioid blocker.'

Al-Noor's eyes narrowed. 'It will stop the effects of the poison?'

'Exactly. You're going to use it literally just before you go and see Elyas and Majid. As it's a nasal spray, it acts quickly and the effects should last at least six hours but because you are going to have heroin and fentanyl swirling around your system, when the naloxone starts to wear off there's a good chance that some of the heroin–fentanyl mixture will still be in your system as the body won't have eliminated it.'

Al-Noor raised his hand to ask a question. 'Eliminated it?'

Idris nodded. 'Our kidneys constantly filter our blood so the level of heroin–fentanyl mixture you've snorted will diminish with each hour that goes by. But once the naloxone is completely out of your system, I don't know what the effect will be which is where this comes into play.'

Idris waved the vials of naloxone at Al-Noor.

'Why can't I use the spray again?'

Idris grimaced. 'It's a large dose, Al. I'm not sure you'd tolerate it and by that, I mean it's not without its own risks. I'm going to prepare three syringes of this lower strength injection and leave them inside your flat where Daniel will be waiting for you and staying with you overnight. If he thinks you are overdosing, Daniel will give you a shot of naloxone.'

'Why not you, Mr Idris?' asked Al-Noor, concerned.

'I need to go to Harehills to see Thomas Mead. Only I can do that part of this plan.'

Idris showed Al-Noor two syringes, full of the toxic heroin he had made. 'This is for Thomas Mead. I'm going to make it look like what happened at The Mews tonight was a turf war between opposing gangs.'

Al-Noor nodded, subdued, afraid.

'Mr Idris, I am scared.'

'So am I, Al. But I trust in the chemistry and so must you.'

'I believe you, Mr Idris. What you have done for me so far is nothing short of the hand of God.'

'We still need that hand, Al.'

Idris pointed to the dispensary bench – at the different drugs he had shown Al-Noor. 'Any questions?' he asked.

Al-Noor pointed to a yellow cylindrical device – an EpiPen. 'What is that?' he asked.

'Adrenalin,' said Idris, a little sheepish.

'Why do we need that?'

Idris went quiet, tried to find the right words. He didn't need to – Al-Noor realised it for himself.

'Is that to be used if my heart stops?' he asked.

Idris nodded. 'Insurance policy, Al. That's all, but we won't need it.'

Idris put all the drugs into a bag and handed it to Al-Noor, just as a loud banging on the shutter outside started.

'Yo, yo, yo, chemist man. I's gonna huff and I's gonna puff and I's gonna blow your pharmacy down,' shouted Liam's delirious voice.

'Time to go, Al. I need to open and let the blue scripts in.'

They embraced strongly and Idris whispered in Al-Noor's ear. 'I've got you on this. Trust me.'

'I do, Mr Idris,' replied Al-Noor.

Idris raised the shutter, opened the door and allowed Al-Noor to leave.

Then, with little choice in the matter, he let Liam Reynolds inside.

*

362

'Chemist man,' said Liam, slurring his words and clearly delighted to see Idris looking so broken as he strode past him, stinking of alcohol and, as Idris had been expecting, holding his usual can of extra-strength lager.

Liam sat down and glared at Idris who switched off the lights and once again dropped the shutter, shrouding them in partial darkness.

'You dimmed the lights, all romantic an' shit. Yer gonna try to fuck me next?' said Liam and started to laugh.

Idris took a beat, silently venting his anger.

You're too stupid to see what's about to happen to you.

Idris retreated into the dispensary and grabbed the bag of medications which he had prepared for Liam, and the remaining cash.

He returned to Liam and dropped both bags at his feet.

'In there is what you asked for,' he said flatly.

Liam put his can of lager on the ground and snatched at the bag. He tipped the contents messily all over the floor and screamed in lurid excitement at the drugs and cash. 'Woo! Right on, chemist man!'

Liam picked up the pot of five hundred diazepam 10mg tablets and opened it, looking in awe at the full container.

Nothing there but multi-vitamins but Liam didn't know that.

Liam lifted a generic white tablet and popped it inside his mouth. Then he lifted his can of beer and took a large swig.

Idris slipped his hand in his pocket, removed a small medicine bottle – the disulfiram solution he had prepared – and loosened the lid.

Liam replaced his can on the floor.

Idris moved to kneel beside Liam and while speaking to

Liam to distract him, poured the disulfiram solution into Liam's can of beer.

'I got your diazes, pregab, and sleepers. Zopi's too. By the end of the week, I'll have the rest. Takes time to get it all together.'

Liam, as Idris had expected, was elated by this.

'Chemist man, you's is done like propa good work here, man!'

Idris feigned gratitude. 'I'm glad you're happy. I want us to work together to keep Rebecca and me safe.'

Liam wrapped his arm around Idris, his body swaying badly. 'You's and I's, Chemist. We's gonna be like, what's them people called? Like, you know that Bonnie character in that show.'

'Bonnie and Clyde?' said Idris.

Liam squeezed his arm tightly around Idris. 'That's the one!'

Come on, Liam, drink your beer.

Idris stood up. 'Liam, if someone sees you in here with all this, or even just with me, it might get noticed. You know?'

Liam hurriedly picked up the boxes of medications and cash and replaced them in the bag.

'Bang on, man,' he said and stood up, unsteady.

Liam started to walk towards the main doors – without his beer.

Idris stopped him.

'Liam? You forgot your beer,' he said, handing it to Liam.

Liam, grinning stupidly, took it from Idris and swallowed the remainder of it in one exaggerated swig before crushing the empty can and dropping it to the floor where it bounced twice on the tiles, before coming to rest.

Yellow clinical waste bin, thought Idris, *that's where that empty can was going.*

Liam belched loudly. 'Shit is good, man. Shit is good.'

'You're going home, right? Don't be walking around carrying those bags. Drugs in there are worth thousands and that cash should be kept somewhere safe.'

Liam gave Idris a military salute, and said, 'Affirmative, sir. Straight home!'

Idris raised the shutter and allowed Liam to leave.

'I loves you, man,' said Liam and duly stormed out, walking unsteadily towards a waiting taxi.

Idris immediately started his stopwatch and grabbed his jacket. He watched Liam's taxi pull away then left the pharmacy intent on following Liam home. Idris ran to his car, got inside and pulled away aggressively.

The drug concentration of disulfiram peaked within forty minutes.

That was how long Liam Reynolds had left to live.

Chapter Seventy-Four

Liam Reynolds did not feel well.

Was it the temperature inside the taxi which was making him feel flush?

'Yo, taxi man, can yer turn the heating off and put the air-con on?' he asked.

Liam saw the South Asian driver frown but do as he'd asked, and a few seconds later, icy cold air started to blow through the vents.

Liam put his face to one, opened his mouth and swallowed the crisp air, then removed a small bottle of vodka from his pocket, removed the cap and took a swig; felt it trickle down his insides, burning, satisfying. He leaned back, his head bobbing unsteadily on his shoulders, his vision blurry.

Shit, maybe he had drunk too much.

No, it was that diazepam he had taken in the pharmacy which was screwing him. It had been a long time since Liam had taken the drug. Maybe it was having a stronger impact than usual.

The taxi pulled up outside his home.

Liam removed a twenty-pound note from his pocket and handed it to the driver, telling him to keep the change.

'Have a good 'un,' he said, hearing his words as if they were being spoken by somebody else.

Liam stumbled out of the taxi, carrying the bags Idris had given him, teetering unsteadily on his feet, his home looking so much farther than it was.

The flushing in his face was back, with a level of severity which made Liam feel like his insides were on fire. Moreover, it was now spreading down his neck, his chest, enveloping his entire torso.

Liam almost collapsed through his front gate, desperate to get inside his home.

Idris was parked a little distance from Liam's house and watched him enter his home, noticing how unsteady Liam was.

It wasn't the booze.

Idris checked his watch: forty minutes had passed, the disulfiram would now be peaking inside Liam's bloodstream.

Idris had prepared a concentrated solution of disulfiram which was a common enough drug prescribed to alcoholics to stop them from drinking alcohol. The side-effects were minimal unless the patient consumed alcohol at the same time.

Then the drug acted like a poison.

At normal dosages, when it was mixed with alcohol, the result would be a flushing of the patient's skin, usually their face, then their body. It was embarrassing and this side-effect was the one which was supposed to strike fear in the alcoholic not to concurrently consume alcohol.

Right now, inside Liam's body, something altogether different was happening.

Combined with the level of alcohol Liam had ingested and the massive dose of disulfiram Idris had covertly slipped inside his drink, there was only one outcome.

Disulfiram would block the metabolism of the alcohol, leading to a variety of symptoms. Right now, Idris thought it likely that Liam was feeling like his insides were on fire. Soon, he would start sweating profusely, vomit and start to hyperventilate.

By this point, the game was over. Even if Liam managed to call an ambulance, he would be long gone by the time it arrived because the next thing which would happen was a severe tachycardic response: Liam's heart racing wildly out of control. This would result in his body slipping into a hypotensive crisis, respiratory depression and ultimately Liam Reynolds would suffer convulsions followed by a massive heart attack.

Idris checked his watch.

Forty-one minutes had passed.

He got out of his car, taking with him some PPE garments and headed towards Liam's house.

In his living room, having thrown up violently, Liam was on his knees, staring at the far wall, seeing nothing but black.

Where was Amy?

He needed the daft bitch and tried to call out her name, but his voice faltered.

Liam could hear his heart racing wildly.

Boom.

Boom.

Boom.

His breath was laboured, short and painful.

The quicker he tried to breathe, the more difficult it became.

With sweat pouring down his body, Liam collapsed to the floor, struggling to remove his phone, and tried to dial 999. But with his hands shaking badly, Liam dropped the phone and then suffered a massive grand-mal seizure: all of the muscles inside his body contracting involuntarily and with such invasive force that it fractured his spine.

Liam died alone, in agony, with his phone beside him, '999' still on the screen.

Idris was standing inside Liam's living room, staring at Liam's lifeless body. Idris had changed into the PPE and entered the house via the back door which was still in a state of disrepair after Rebecca had kicked it open earlier that day.

Not that Liam had even registered that.

Idris didn't bother to check for signs of life, Liam's eyes were open, his pupils fixed.

With PPE gloves covering his hands, Idris carefully searched Liam's body and found his ancient-looking mobile phone. He used Liam's fingerprint to unlock it, scrolled to the videos and found the damning clip of Rebecca stabbing Patrick to death.

Idris deleted it, dropped the phone onto the floor and smashed it with his foot before slipping it inside the pocket of his PPE gown.

Idris glanced at the room, saw the two bags of cash he had given Liam and secured them, intending to take them back to the pharmacy with him.

Deflated, Idris sat on the couch, Liam's body on the floor beside his feet.

He looked at him, for several minutes, reminding himself that Liam had been a toxic, malevolent pimp, who added nothing to society, only inflicting misery.

Idris closed his eyes.

Christ, he was a pharmacist who had spent his entire life doing only good, avoiding the pitfalls his brother Zidane had fallen foul of. Yet now, it was he who had just killed another man; his second of the week. And who would soon engineer the death of Thomas Mead a feat which might actually cost Idris his own life.

Would that be so bad?

How was he going to live with what he had done?

If he did somehow pull off the next part of his plan, four toxic men would be dead, and he would be what exactly? Free?

Idris opened his eyes and looked at Liam.

Freedom was something he might never truly experience again.

Every single day, he would wake up knowing what he had done.

Was it enough that he'd done it all to save Rebecca?

Idris got off the couch, took a final look around the room, picked up the bags of cash then left.

By the back door, he slipped out of the PPE, back into his gym clothes then headed to his car to drive to The Mews.

To a showdown between Al-Noor and Elyas and Majid.

Chapter Seventy-Five

The Mews had changed. Rules were being broken.

As Idris walked towards Al-Noor's tower block, he saw mobile phones openly recording the goings-on.

Until a new warlord arrived here, The Mews would remain unstable.

Idris stayed away from residents, kept his head down and hurried towards Al-Noor's apartment.

Idris had never been inside the flat before. It felt skeletal, simple basics; a couch, an old table in the centre with a kitchenette crammed into the corner. Again, rudimentary, just the essentials – electric cooker, microwave, single fridge, and a kettle. But Al-Noor had clearly tried hard to add colour and his own sense of personality with warm, colourful sketched paintings on the walls, and photographs of his life back in Syria. Idris looked at them, absorbing the life Al-Noor had lived – pictures of him on oil rigs, looking every inch the engineer, surrounded by a group of people who were all smiling.

Idris tapped on a photo of Al-Noor with his arms around a woman.

'Is this your wife?' he asked.

'Rima,' replied Al-Noor, sitting on the couch, head down, clearly distressed.

'She's beautiful, Al.'

'She was the most beautiful woman in our village. She joked that she had married me as her prince because I had a good job and could provide for her and the children we would have. That she believed I would always be able to . . . protect her.'

Idris fell silent, it was such a loaded statement.

'What happened was not your fault, Al.'

'What happens next will be, Mr Idris. Where is Daniel?'

'I've texted him, he's coming.'

'And if he does not arrive?'

'I'm here. I will not leave you alone without someone here to stay with you all night.'

'That will mean that, the . . . other part of your plan, at the shisha bar would not happen.'

Idris moved across to Al-Noor, kneeling in front of him, submissive, small.

'Thomas can wait but I will not leave you alone under any circumstances even though I trust in the chemistry.'

Al-Noor looked at Idris now. 'Chemistry, a science which deals with the composition, structure and properties of substances and the changes that they go through. Or the complicated emotional interactions between different people.'

Idris smiled. 'What are you asking me, Al?'

'I'm asking which of those two definitions you trust in the most?'

'Both. I trust that the drugs will do their job and I trust that you and I are solid enough to pull this off together.'

'I cannot stop thinking about Faris, Mr Idris.'

'I know.'

'No. You do not. You must be a father to understand what I am feeling.'

372

Idris held Al-Noor's gaze and with it, allowed him to see a pain Idris had hidden ever since he had lost his own son.

'You have a child?' asked Al-Noor, seeing the agony in Idris's face.

Idris walked to the window, opened it and looked out across The Mews. It felt more comfortable speaking about painful memories from here, where his words would dissipate into a landscape shrouded in misery.

He saw Daniel leaving his tower block and engaging in conversations with several residents who were all smoking.

Idris spoke softly, almost a whisper. 'I had a son. He died at birth. He was . . . mine and Rebecca's child.'

A deafening silence seized the room.

Idris pushed on.

'My brother Zidane used to do what Thomas Mead does. He was a kingpin, used to work with Daniel.'

Idris wondered how much more to say but needed to get this off his chest. 'We all grew up together on the roughest council estate in England. Daniel and Rebecca were from a notorious travelling family and Zidane was always a rebel.'

Idris spoke for almost ten minutes. How he and Rebecca had eloped, after both their families had been against their marriage.

Idris hadn't cared for any of that.

Only Rebecca.

They had fought hard, sacrificed, and suffered to keep their relationship alive, as both of their families had tried to poison them against one another. It hadn't worked. When Rebecca had fallen pregnant, it had been the happiest time of Idris's life. Yet Zidane and Daniel's world had collided violently with theirs.

Idris turned to face Al-Noor.

'I'm telling you all this because, Al, when you walk into Elyas and Majid's room, the responsibility for making sure that you get back to your son is solely on me and *I will not let you down.*'

In this moment, Idris saw that Al-Noor could see him, *really see* Idris.

Al-Noor removed the naloxone nasal spray from his pocket, and handed the device to Idris. 'It is time, Mr Idris. Show me how to use this,' he said.

Chapter Seventy-Six

Al-Noor paused outside Jahangir's flat, hearing Majid and Elyas speaking Arabic inside the room, bickering as usual.

He pressed his ear to the door and listened, hearing phrases which buoyed his spirit:

'If the product doesn't arrive this week, what do we do then?'

'Jahangir's brother, Mawt Hosseini, will arrive here soon.'

'How soon? We have only two days' supply left.'

'I don't know. The runner is coming now. If his product is good, we can bridge the supply for a few days.'

On and on it went, until Al-Noor finally gathered his courage, knocked loudly on the door and entered the room. It was full of cigarette smoke, the windows closed.

'He is here,' hissed Majid, clearly high, and beckoned for Al-Noor to close the door.

Al-Noor switched to Arabic, the conversation flowing more fluidly.

'As you requested, The Chemist has given me this product for you both to sample. He is keen to do business.'

Al-Noor placed the packet of powder Idris had manufactured on the table.

The poison.

Majid and Elyas stepped to him, and, as Al-Noor had expected, frisked him.

The feel of their hands on his body made Al-Noor angry, visions of them assaulting him still vivid in his mind. He pushed his anger aside, focusing on the bigger picture. If Idris's plan worked Elyas and Majid would soon both be dead.

Satisfied he was not wired, Majid pointed at the powder.

'You first. Tell us how it is,' he said.

Al-Noor could tell they were keen to sample it. Unlike him, they were addicts who loved the intensity and burn of a hit, which was why they could never remain as bosses of The Mews.

Al-Noor had used the nasal spray a few minutes before. Still, as he opened the packet and created a line of powder, his heart was racing, and his legs felt shaky.

'What are you doing?' asked Elyas, waving a syringe at Al-Noor.

'It is a high purity product. I have already tried it. You can inject if you wish but it is so pure that we can simply do this.'

And with that, Al-Noor snorted a line of the powder.

Immediately the effects made his vision blur, and he stepped back, momentarily disorientated. It was the most powerful high he had ever experienced.

He breathed out, deeply, and even though his vision was compromised, he looked towards where Elyas and Majid had been loitering.

'Incredible,' he whispered, feeling like he might pass out at any moment.

He heard the men move towards the table, eager, excited. Their blurry outlines crystallised a little and Al-Noor took another step away and leaned against the wall.

His legs were failing him and his heart racing wildly.

Had The Chemist got this wrong?

Al-Noor sank to the ground, his back sliding down the wall. He did not want to alarm Majid and Elyas, so he spoke excitedly to them. 'This is the best product I have ever sampled in my life. Wow.'

As he sat on the floor, Al-Noor's vision cleared enough that he could now see both men as they leaned across the table, made their own individual lines then snorted the powder, deep, powerful . . . fatal.

Idris had said the effect would be instantaneous.

They were.

Elyas was first, clawing at his throat, eyes wide, disbelieving what was happening.

Majid had a delayed reaction and was staring in horror as Elyas sank to his knees, blood draining from his face, watching as Elyas went into a state of hypoxic shock. Then, he collapsed to the ground, still, silent.

Majid looked to Al-Noor and seemed to realise that he and Elyas had been duped.

He rushed towards Al-Noor, furious, seemingly ready to kill him but stopped short as the fentanyl suddenly flooded his brain, seizing control of his body.

Majid dropped to his knees, staring in disbelief at Al-Noor who used every bit of strength he had to get to his feet. He kept his body against the wall and pointed a shaky finger at Majid.

'I am not the runner. I am Al-Noor, engineer, father, husband and with your death, I reclaim my freedom from you.'

Majid could not speak and had only seconds left to live.

Al-Noor should have conserved his energy.

He didn't.

He stepped forward and using everything he had, kicked Majid in the face.

There was a sickening crack of bone and Majid's body collapsed to the floor.

The ferocity of the blow also sent Al-Noor toppling over. He scrambled back to his feet, fighting for breath but needing confirmation that Elyas and Majid were both dead. He slowly checked each of them for a pulse.

Nothing.

Idris's plan had worked. But Al-Noor's breathing was rapidly deteriorating.

He got to his feet, stumbled chaotically to the door, and walked out, heading desperately to his apartment.

To Idris.

Chapter Seventy-Seven

Idris heard a knock at the door and rushed to answer it, expecting to see Al-Noor or Daniel.

He should have known better – the timeline was too short.

He swung open the door, momentarily shocked to see Rico Zimmer standing there, the addict he had thrown out of the pharmacy earlier that day.

Idris tried to slam the door closed but Rico shoved Idris hard enough that he went sprawling across the floor.

The impact sent painful shockwaves through Idris's body, all of them seeming to peak in his ribs.

Idris screamed and raised his hands expecting a blow which never arrived.

'The thing is, Chemist, your protection ain't here no more, is it? Means, you don't get to walk around here like a boss,' said Rico, slamming the door closed behind him.

'Listen, Elyas and Majid are . . .' started Idris.

'. . . bitches,' snapped Rico, looking around, seemingly for Al-Noor.

'Where's the runner?'

'He's not here.'

Rico pointed at Idris, accusingly, angry, veins pulsing on his forehead, eyes wide and crazy.

'You blocked my methadone today, Chemist, so now, you

and I are going outside where first you're going to buy me some wraps and then I'm going to kick your ass across The Mews where everybody can see that The Chemist ain't welcome here no more.'

Idris could tell that Rico was high on something, his speech rapid, spit flying from his lips.

'Rico, what have you taken?'

'The fuck is it to you. It's 'cos of you I had to score.'

Rico descended on Idris and yanked him to his feet by his hair.

Idris threw a punch, a pathetic attempt which landed on Rico's chin and did precisely nothing.

Rico laughed, touched his face with his finger. 'Go on, Chemist, tickle me again.'

Idris didn't hesitate and raised his palm ninety degrees towards Rico's nose and caught him flush, breaking it.

Rico fell backwards, tripping over the table and crashed to the ground.

Idris looked around for a weapon.

The drugs?

Shit, he had only naloxone and adrenaline. They wouldn't work.

Rico scrambled to his knees, hands now cupped around his nose, blood everywhere.

Daniel.

Idris needed to get to Daniel.

He tried to run past Rico who stuck out a hand, caught Idris's ankle which sent him careering into a table.

Idris landed heavily, immediately winded.

He couldn't breathe.

Couldn't move.

Rico, with blood still streaming from his nose, grabbed

Idris by his hair and yanked him to his feet, marching him down the corridor.

Behind him, Idris missed the slow, mechanical walk of Al-Noor, his body propped up by the wall as he inched his way towards his flat, his breathing laboured and most alarmingly his heart rate plummeting.

Chapter Seventy-Eight

Idris was hurled on the ground by Rico who took great delight in thundering a kick into Idris's side, causing Idris to scream.

There was an immediate metallic taste of blood inside Idris's mouth.

Christ, if his ribs weren't broken before, they must have been now.

Rico grabbed Idris by his feet and dragged him along the ground, like Idris was a dog on a leash, pointing to the far corner of The Mews.

'That's where addicts go, to surrender to their knees for a shitty five-quid wrap. It's your turn tonight, Chemist.'

'Let me go to my car. I've got money in there,' pleaded Idris.

'You'll go there too, Chemist. But first, you're getting the taste of another man down your throat. Puts you right down here with the rest of us, doesn't it? Walking about here, acting like you're all that and now, with nobody to protect you, you're nothing. A nobody.'

'Let him go,' said a firm voice from behind Rico.

Idris knew it instantly.

Daniel.

He turned to see him standing there, calm, hands in his pockets.

'This ain't your business, old man,' said Rico but there was a definite shift in his tone; more uncertain.

'It is my business. You've hurt The Chemist so maybe he decides he doesn't want to supply The Mews anymore. Affects everyone here and for what? 'Cos you got beef with him?'

'Yeah, I got beef with him. And he ain't the only chemist around here.'

'Leave him be,' said Daniel.

Rico shook his head. 'I respect your rep but you gotta be respecting that me and him got shit to resolve. You comin' up all in my face isn't right.'

Daniel removed his hands from his pocket, stepped a little closer. 'Then looks like you and I got our own problem to deal with.'

There it was. A binary challenge, for Rico to either piss off or engage in a shitshow with Daniel.

'Listen, Daniel, you ain't a young man anymore. We dance and you get dropped,' said Rico but he was nervous, his voice shaky, and tellingly, he had retreated several paces.

'Maybe,' said Daniel and removed a packet of cigarettes from his pocket. He lit one, took a drag on it then pointed to Idris. 'Go on your way. You got things to do.'

Slowly, Idris got to his feet.

Rico turned to him distracted and in an instant Daniel descended upon Rico and kicked him fiercely in the balls and then swiftly removed the cigarette from his lips and stubbed it directly into Rico's eye.

'Daniel, no!' shouted Idris but it was too late.

Rico screamed and collapsed to the ground, holding his face.

Daniel, unrelenting, stepped back, took aim, then thundered another kick into Rico's face.

There was a nauseating sound of bone cracking and Rico went silent.

Idris didn't move.

Daniel pointed towards Al-Noor's tower block. 'Be on your way, I'll be there soon.'

Idris limped away slowly, heading back towards Al-Noor's flat.

Al-Noor was on his knees, inside his flat, alone. His breathing was slow, shallow, and his vision fading quickly.

He collapsed to his side, pulling his body into the foetal position and remained still, wanting to conserve as much energy as possible.

Perhaps this would pass.

Perhaps this was just part of the chemical reaction.

He closed his eyes, thought of his boy, Faris.

If these were his last moments of life, he wanted to die remembering good memories, so that he might die with a smile on his face.

Of Rima and their first meeting, at her parents' house where she had been coy and not spoken a word.

Of their marriage, their first night together, the birth of their son, Faris's first baby steps, birthdays and anniversaries.

Al-Noor got what he wanted.

He died with a smile across his face.

Chapter Seventy-Nine

Pitchford was ready to retire for the evening when his phone rang.

DS Darcy Black.

A peculiar thing because this time of night, she knew not to bother him. Which meant it was serious.

Pitchford answered the call and listened intently to a message which made him leave the room.

He laboured into the living room, closed the door and said, 'Tell me that again?'

Darcy's voice was clear and, unusually for her, excitable. 'I'm on my way to The Mews with armed response units. Something's going down. We got a call that Elyas Mansoor and Majid Ansari have been found dead in Jahangir's old residence.'

Pitchford sat down. 'Violent crime?' he said.

'Doesn't look like it. Drugs overdose maybe. White powder in the room. Both with clear signs of fatal intoxication. Just thought I'd let you know.'

'Who made the call?'

'Anonymous resident.'

'Have you called Al-Noor?'

'I've tried. There's no answer.'

For reasons unbeknown to him, Pitchford's thoughts went to The Chemist.

'Your plan?' he asked.

'ARUs secure the area. We go in.'

'You're going to need more than one ARU.'

'Three more are en route from Wakefield and we've got XRAY99 in the sky as we speak.'

XRAY99 – the police helicopter.

'I'm coming too,' replied Pitchford, looking around the room for his pills.

He was going to have to take additional doses.

Pitchford hung up, left the living room and went to get changed, his thoughts on only one thing.

The Chemist.

Chapter Eighty

Idris threw himself to the floor and checked Al-Noor's pulse.

Nothing.

But his skin was still warm, and his face flushed with colour, meaning his heart had only just stopped beating.

Idris hurriedly grabbed the bag of drugs, ignoring the repeated pain inside his own body, and removed the syringe of naloxone and the EpiPen.

He returned to Al-Noor, rolled him onto his back, tore his shirt open and took careful aim.

He had only one chance to get this right.

While the device was meant only for intramuscular use, Al-Noor had a slight frame and the EpiPen had a long-range needle.

A final pause and then Idris hammered the device firmly into Al-Noor chest, immediately above where his heart was.

Bang.

An immediate burst of adrenalin into Al-Noor's heart.

Idris put his fingers under Al-Noor's chin, felt for a pulse.

A delay of a few seconds and then Idris felt it, slight and weak.

He snatched a pre-prepared syringe of naloxone and hurriedly injected it into the fleshy part of Al-Noor's upper arm, through his shirt.

He checked his pulse again – stronger.

Idris remained by Al-Noor's side when the front door flew open, and Daniel strode in, urgent, alarmed.

He opened his mouth to say something, saw the state of Al-Noor and stopped. He reconsidered and said, 'He alive?'

Idris nodded.

'You need to get him up and out of here,' said Daniel.

'Why?'

'Some idiot found Elyas and Majid dead in Jahangir's room. Triple-nined it. Blues and twos are on the way. ARUs for sure. Get him gone,' said Daniel, pointing at Al-Noor.

Idris covered his hands with his face.

'Fuck! Have you been to Jahangir's room?'

Daniel shook his head.

Idris hurriedly searched Al-Noor's body then turned to Daniel, panicking.

'Do it now! Al must have left the spiked heroin there. If the cops find it, they'll figure out I had something to do with this.'

'How?'

'I spiked it. There'll be a trace.'

'You didn't think of that before?'

'I did but I thought Al would bring the drugs back from the room and even if he didn't, that we'd have time to get there and clean it.'

Idris pointed to the door. 'Go or we're all screwed!'

Daniel rushed out of the room.

Idris turned to Al-Noor whose eyes were now open. When he spoke, his voice was nothing more than a whisper. 'Mr Idris, did it work?'

Idris clasped his hands together, as if in prayer, and said, 'You did a brilliant job, Al.'

He put his hands on Al-Noor's chest. 'Brilliant,' he repeated.

'I don't feel so well, Mr Idris.'

'You're going to be fine, Al. If you are able, can you sit up? Can you make it – with my help – to the couch?'

'Let me try.'

Idris scrambled to his knees and gently assisted Al-Noor in getting to his feet.

Al-Noor massaged his chest. 'It is painful here, Mr Idris.'

'I know. Your heart stopped beating. I had to inject it with adrenaline and then give you more naloxone.'

Al-Noor made his way cautiously to the couch.

'Mr Idris, I think that perhaps I need a hospital tonight. I am feeling very unwell.'

Idris was thinking the same thing. There was madness and then there was *this*. After everything Al-Noor had done, Idris needed to get him real emergency medical help. The paramedics would put the hospital admission down to a bad dose of heroin.

Idris removed Al-Noor's phone from his pocket, dialled 999 and handed it to him.

'It's the right thing to do.'

Al-Noor hesitated, eyes rolling, head swaying unsteadily on his shoulders.

Idris told Al-Noor exactly what to say then hit 'dial' and held the phone to Al-Noor's ear.

Al-Noor told the call handler what Idris had instructed – that he had severe chest pains, could not breathe, and had shooting pains up and down his left arm: key red flags for a heart attack and ones which would bump him to the top of the emergency call list.

Idris checked his watch: he needed to leave to get across to Harehills to the shisha lounge where he hoped to meet Thomas and Damon and complete his plan of removing all the obstacles in his life in one fell swoop.

Daniel rushed back into the room, waving the small bag of heroin at Idris.

'Anyone see you?' asked Idris.

'Plenty but none of them are saying shit to the pigs. This is The Mews, remember, and Elyas and Majid were hated just as much as Jahangir was.'

Idris pointed to the bag in Daniel's hand.

'Flush it,' he said, watching Daniel disappear into the bathroom, then turned back to Al-Noor.

'The ambulance will be here soon.'

Al-Noor nodded weakly.

Daniel overheard what Idris had said, the bathroom door open.

'You triple-nined him?' he said, coming back into the room, animatedly.

Idris stood up to leave. 'I tried my best and he's good for now but if he flatlines again, I'm not equipped to bring him back.'

'What the hell are we going to say?'

'Stop overthinking. It's The Mews. Bad shit happens here all the time, dodgy batch, yada yada yada,' snapped Idris.

Daniel looked towards the door, clearly wanting to leave.

'You're staying here with Al, until they get here,' said Idris with authority.

Daniel stepped closer to him. 'I don't do uniform, whether paramedics or coppers.'

'You'll see the blues from here. When they enter the tower, do one. Al will take it from there.'

Idris turned to Al-Noor. 'You tell them you took a bad hit. The police will arrive and figure out that you had some of the same batch that killed Elyas and Majid. Don't talk too much, we'll figure it out tomorrow with the barrister. OK?'

Al-Noor nodded.

Idris turned back to Daniel. 'If I can take down Thomas tonight, the same night as Elyas and Majid, the police will think it was a drug gang feud.'

'But you ain't killing Thomas with illegal drugs, are you?'

'Not initially but I've prepped syringes with the same cocktail which killed Elyas and Majid. If the chance arises, I'll use them.'

Daniel removed a car key from his pocket and threw it at Idris. 'Same Ford we used to track Thomas Mead. It's on the road by the exit.'

Idris nodded towards Al-Noor who continued to look like he might relapse into an overdose state.

'Make sure Al makes it to the ambulance.' And with that Idris walked out of the room, intent on a final showdown with Thomas Mead.

Chapter Eighty-One

Idris drove down Harehills Lane, affectionately known to locals as the Strip, with premium restaurants and cheaper takeaways to both sides of it, most of them with bold neon signs, lighting up the night. Quite the contrast from the nothingness and darkness within The Mews.

Idris was driving the car which Daniel had organised for him. It was registered to an addict in The Mews, had valid MOT and insurance and was routinely used as a run-around for hire.

Idris was certain that if Thomas and maybe even his henchman Damon fell tonight, that the logical conclusion for the police would have been a gang-related incident.

Idris was going to use the nebuliser solution he had specifically made for this part of his plan, but if the opportunity arose, he would also use the prefilled syringes he had manufactured.

Idris drove into the car park, relieved to see Thomas Mead's Range Rover and passed it quickly, parking at the far end. Ahead was a building owned by Thomas Mead. Idris had found the details on the Companies House website. Inside it was a shisha lounge, a place Thomas frequented every Sunday night, details Idris had lifted from Thomas's bank statement.

Idris had thought it curious as to why. Then he had figured

it out. What better place for Thomas to catch up with his cronies than a public space? It had all the hallmarks of a standard cover meet, something Idris had learned long ago when Zidane had been running the game.

There were shadows and secrets everywhere Idris looked, the area overshadowed by the nightmarish ruins of an abandoned industrial mill.

Idris hid the syringes containing the heroin–fentanyl mixture underneath his seat. He couldn't risk taking them inside. They would be for later if he got the opportunity.

Now, Idris removed a packet of dispersible potassium tablets from his bag and dissolved four in a bottle of water before drinking it.

This was risky: Idris was unaware what level of potassium was inside his own body. He'd had a blood test two months before and everything had been within range so he felt confident that he could raise his potassium a little, something he would soon counter once he got inside the shisha lounge.

As a failsafe, Idris removed another drug from his bag of tricks – an injection of calcium gluconate – and administered it to himself. The drug stabilised the heart in the event of a dangerously high blood potassium level.

With that done, Idris got out of the car and headed towards Thomas' car. He needed to remove the tracking device Al-Noor had fitted.

He discovered it fixed to the driver's side of the chassis and pulled it free, stomping on it until it was destroyed. Idris put the fragments in his pocket, intending to dispose of them into a clinical waste bin on his return to the pharmacy.

Now, he headed towards the shisha bar, for a final reckoning with Thomas Mead.

*

The interior of the shisha lounge was a garish space full of neon and flashing strobe lighting.

The perfect place to attempt what Idris was here to do.

The bar was packed, full of people engaging in lively banter, and the room was full of different coloured smoke, depending on the flavour of shisha being consumed.

Idris ordered a pipe and requested a table for one from the waiter, close to the bar, knowing that at some point, Thomas or Damon would have to pass him to visit the restroom.

Idris hoped he wouldn't have to wait long.

Forty-eight minutes passed, each one seeming to last forever, as Idris sporadically smoked his shisha. He didn't inhale much and used the mouthpiece as nothing more than a prop.

It was Thomas who walked past Idris first, did a double take, his mouth dropping open in surprise, his eyes narrowing.

He checked his surroundings, as if suddenly fearful that an attack by somebody was imminent.

Thomas took a seat beside Idris.

'What the fuck are you doing here?'

Idris pushed the hookah aside and said, 'Christ, of all the places, why here?'

'What?'

'What are you doing here? All I wanted to do was smoke a little and relax. Are you following me?' said Idris irritably, playing the best role he could.

Thomas relaxed and smiled. 'This is my place.'

Idris stood up to leave. 'Listen, man, I just wanted a night to myself. I'm not looking for any trouble.'

Thomas told Idris to sit back down.

Idris did just that.

'We can't be seen together in here,' said Idris.

'You think this place has CCTV? That I'm going to sit here with cameras looking at me? This is the free zone.'

Idris sighed, remained looking despondent. 'My hookah pipe's not even working. I was just about to leave. There's some stuff about The Mews I need to tell you – ways you can earn more – but it can wait till next week. You go back to your evening.'

Idris stood to leave again and this time Thomas joined him.

'My table is over there, in the corner. Come on, you can tell me your plan.'

The corner booth was subtly decorated with a dark leather finish. The lower mood lighting made it feel intimate and private. There was one large hookah pipe on the table with two hoses attached to it.

'If we're going to do this, can I get a hose?' asked Idris.

Thomas waved one of the waiters over and ordered an additional pipe and a refill for the water bowl.

A refill – the opening Idris was looking for.

'How is the supply going? You got much left of that brick I gave you?'

'Sold half. It's going well,' replied Idris, lying easily.

'How many bricks you reckon we can sell in The Mews, month to month?'

'I'm not sure. Al-Noor will know more.'

'You were saying we could make more money? How?' asked Thomas.

Idris glanced at Damon who had said nothing, simply looked at Idris with his usual dead eye.

'If I tell you, I need you to help me pay off my debts,' said Idris.

'You're a cocky little bastard, aren't you?' said Thomas and started to laugh.

'The less shit I'm dealing with, the more attention I can give The Mews. If the pharmacy closes because I haven't paid my bills, then this whole operation goes to shit. Look at it as an investment.'

The waiter arrived and put an additional pipe on the table and a new refill bottle full of flavoured hookah solution.

Discreetly, Idris removed the small glass medicine container from his pocket, the one holding the concentrated nebuliser solution he had prepared.

Idris pointed to the hookah. 'Can I top it up?'

Thomas nodded for Idris to do so.

Idris picked up the shisha solution and switched it in his hand with the toxic solution he had made.

He topped up the hookah, knowing the residual liquid left in the reservoir would mask the taste. Then Idris put his pipe to his lips and took a deep pull, while simultaneously slipping the real hookah liquid inside his pocket.

He could taste only mint; clearly Thomas's flavour of choice and it perfectly masked the poison they were all now inhaling.

Thomas and Damon continued to inhale, unaware of the switch.

'Diazepam. Addicts will pay for it. It brings them down when they're not using. Helps them sleep too. A five-hundred tub of diazepam tablets costs twenty-seven quid. Each tablet sells for two quid. That's a grand, easy,' said Idris.

Thomas looked at him, impressed. He took a deep pull on the hookah.

Idris watched him intently.

'Anything else where we can make that sort of margin?'

'Diazepam is easy. Loads of different suppliers and it's not controlled. I'll get one chance to make an error in ordering and it will slip through the system without a trigger warning, whereas if I buy a regular high quantity, it ruins me with audits.'

'What do you need from us?' said Damon, finally breaking his silence.

'Somewhere to store it. If I get a supply of say, fifty pots of diazepam, my staff will return it. There's no reason to keep that quantity on site and I've nowhere to put it. I'll order it in for a late delivery, your boys come and collect it and drip-feed it to me to sell through The Mews. Or you can do whatever you want with it.'

Thomas and Damon took regular, consistent draws on their hookah pipes.

Idris also took another, hoping that each inhalation would nudge his potassium down a touch, mindful of the high-strength tablets he had taken.

'Why are you telling us all this?' asked Thomas.

'Told you. I want a cut to clear my debts.'

'Fifty pots is a hundred large. What are you asking?' said Thomas.

'What are we even having this conversation for?' snapped Damon, unable to hold his tongue.

Thomas glared at him.

'Listen,' said Idris passionately. 'The shit which got us into this? It was Amy who put me here and I'm trying to find her for you. When I do, she's all yours. I don't like what's gone on between us. With Jahangir gone and The Mews open for business, there's opportunity to do something special. You've got the muscle and the street smarts, and I've got The Mews and Al-Noor. I'm not asking for anything other than clearing my debts and maybe a little bump here and there to keep me afloat and make this relationship tight.'

'How much?' asked Thomas.

Idris took a deep pull on the hookah. 'You give me ten per cent and I'll make sure The Mews runs hot.'

Thomas thought on it.

'Layered income. You get nothing for the first hundred thousand we make. After that, ten per cent of the surplus.'

Idris feigned a hurt look.

'Be grateful of that. The diazepam thing? Make it happen or there's no deal.'

'I need money up front.'

'Why?'

Idris pushed his hookah pipe away, again feigned that he was under pressure. 'I told you three times now. Bills.'

Thomas went quiet, thought on it, took another pull of the pipe.

Idris stood up to leave. 'Think on it. I won't spoil your evening anymore.'

He walked away when Thomas called him back to the table.

Idris returned but didn't take a seat.

'I'll pay your loans off. All of them. Know what I get in return? I'll buy your pharmacy outright. You become my employee. That is what happens next.'

Idris stood there, not really allowing the outlandish proposal to worry him.

They kept inhaling on the hookah – that was key.

'What?' he said, pretending to be outraged.

'Makes sense. We're going to be doing this for a long time, Chemist. You got problems, I got solutions. So, I buy you out, business becomes mine. Solves everything.'

Idris said nothing.

Damon pointed towards the door, at the far end of the room. 'Piss off now.'

Idris nodded and sheepishly left the table.

Behind him, Thomas and Damon continued to inhale.

Chapter Eighty-Two

Idris was back in his car, feeling no ill effects from the solution he had inhaled. He had been mindful to inhale only three doses of it and with the potassium he had dosed himself up on, he felt like his body was probably in equilibrium.

An hour passed and still nothing.

No ambulances.

No drama.

Idris felt anxious. He needed to know that Thomas and Damon were dead.

He was toying with going back inside the shisha bar when he saw them both exiting the rear of the shisha lounge, walking towards Thomas's Range Rover.

Only they weren't walking. They were stumbling, slow, unsteady.

Idris's plan was clearly working.

The solution which he had created was an ultra-concentrated mixture of nebuliser solution used primarily to treat people suffering with severe breathing problems, but the drug was also used off-licence for another condition: severe hyperkalaemia, a dangerously elevated level of potassium within the body. The nebuliser solution had the incredibly powerful side-effect of reducing potassium levels in the blood and . . . *quickly*.

Idris had prepared a toxic solution over fifty times the usual dose, containing such a concentrated solution that it would certainly kill Thomas and Damon.

Thomas Mead's chest felt tight. His heart was racing and he suddenly felt incredibly weak. But the worst thing was that he was experiencing the shakes, his whole body feeling like it was about to suffer a seizure.

He looked at Damon, who also looked severely unwell.

'Hey, you feeling OK?' asked Thomas.

Damon shook his head, stumbling with his walk as they arrived beside the Range Rover. Damon collapsed to the ground first, then Thomas.

'I'm shaking, man, like . . . like . . . I inhaled a bad hit of coke,' said Damon.

'Me too. Can't . . . stop. Can hear my heart racing.'

'Same.'

Damon tried to remove his phone but the shake in his hands made it impossible.

'Look,' he said, raising them, alarmed that he could not stop the tremors.

'Something's wrong with us,' said Thomas.

Idris slipped on a pair of PPE gloves, grabbed the syringes from under his seat and got out of his car, having watched both Thomas and Damon slump to the ground.

This was it; *the end game*.

He moved quickly towards them, stopping in front of them both.

Quickly, he injected Damon with a full syringe of the mixture, removed the empty syringe and left it on the ground beside him.

Damon didn't even have time to register what had happened.

The lethal effects took seconds, his respiratory system collapsing.

Damon's body slouched over, and he lay dying on the ground.

Idris turned his attention to Thomas, needing to offload what was on his mind. He waved the second syringe at Thomas.

'Remember, you injected Rebecca?' Idris said, a cold nothingness behind his eyes.

Thomas's body was now shaking so badly he looked like he was having a seizure. 'What did you do? What did you give us?' he said.

'Shisha solution. Switched it for something which makes your potassium plummet. And with your medical arrythmias, and being on digoxin, I'd say that right about now, your dig level is going through the roof. That won't kill you, though, it's the massive drop in your potassium which will do that.'

Idris checked his watch. 'I reckon you've got, maybe, five minutes.' He waved the syringe at Thomas. 'Not that I'll give you that time.'

'Please . . .'

Idris slapped him. 'That's for what you did to Rebecca.'

'Please . . .' said Thomas again but Idris did exactly as he had done to Damon, slipped the syringe in Thomas's thigh and injected him, looking him straight in the eyes, watching as the life leaked out of his body.

Less than thirty seconds later, Thomas Mead's eyes stopped blinking and he sat there, still, silent . . . gone.

Idris forced the syringe into Thomas's hand, ensuring that when the police found the body it would look like a drug overdose.

Then Idris walked away, heading back to his pharmacy.

Chapter Eighty-Three

The Mews was alive – seemingly every resident standing in the courtyard, clearly outraged at the enormous police presence which had flooded the grounds.

Pitchford waited in his squad car, while armed police units tried to secure the area around the tower block.

Reinforcements were being called in from across Yorkshire because one thing was certain, with no Jahangir Hosseini and now both Elyas and Majid dead, The Mews was ready to implode.

Pitchford had cut his teeth policing on this estate before the likes of Jahangir Hosseini had taken over. He knew The Mews from corner to corner.

A cordon had been established around the tower block and a line of police fully suited in riot gear had formed an impenetrable line. In front of them, increasing by the minute, was a growing population of Mews residents. Hooded, mobile phones held high.

Paramedics had been allowed inside the building – an unspoken rule which The Mews had never to this day broken: that medical staff were never hindered.

The police, however, were not afforded such respect. More than ninety per cent of the residents here were known to the authorities, many of them having criminal records.

Pitchford felt more vulnerable than most. The hour was late, and he had taken an extra dose of his Parkinson's medication before covertly leaving the house.

A senior armed officer tapped on the side of the car and waved Pitchford to come with him. He did so, allowing the officer to slip a secure helmet over his head, and fasten a bullet proof vest around Pitchford's body.

Pitchford, escorted now by two armed officers, one of them holding his cane, saw Darcy slip inside the building. He followed a similar protocol as he started his own slow walk towards the tower, past a febrile crowd, feeling like it might rupture at any moment. Abuse was hurled at the police, stones thrown wildly, and profanities screamed loudly.

A small rock hit Pitchford's helmet, another his vest. Christ, it had been an age since he'd been in a situation like this and he felt afraid. He heard the armed officer speaking into a radio, the words 'tear gas' and 'water cannon' mentioned.

Pitchford thought it would certainly come to that.

Elyas and Majid's room was, most certainly, a crime scene.

White powder everywhere.

Two high-level players dead, their bodies lying on the floor, both seemingly having consumed what appeared to be a deadly batch of an illicit drug.

This was no coincidence.

Jahangir, Elyas, Majid.

Someone was making a power play for The Mews.

Pitchford walked around the room, careful not to disturb the scene, keeping the scenes of crime officers outside.

He did the perimeter walk again, slow, methodical, his cane tapping gently on the floor, analysing every inch of the room, which was a chaotic, unsanitary space.

He looked at Elyas and Majid, whom he knew to be high-level players within The Mews.

There was white powder streaked across their faces, and the remains of it on a table where they had obviously snorted it.

Snorted, not injected.

Peculiar.

It made Pitchford momentarily think that it might have been cocaine.

Didn't make sense.

Coke didn't kill people this way.

This was heroin or at least, some sort of opioid.

And yet, they had snorted it, which meant that it's purity must have been high, not some shitty street-level powder.

Ideas were sparking in Pitchford's mind. He continued to ignore the sound of an impatient SOCO team, desperate to get inside to do their work so that they could get the hell out of The Mews.

A high purity powder.

That meant a potential new supplier pitching his product to The Mews, which made sense now that Jahangir was dead. The supply chain would be disrupted until a new kingpin, arguably one of Jahangir's family, arrived to take over.

A new player getting access to not only The Mews but also Elyas and Majid this quickly after Jahangir's death? And in their own flat?

Impossible.

Unless, of course, they knew and trusted the mule who was bringing them the product.

His thoughts immediately went to Al-Noor, who was in his flat on the floor below, being treated for a possible heroin overdose yet, unlike Elyas and Majid, whatever Al-Noor had taken had not killed him.

A coincidence? Pitchford didn't believe that.

And now, it all started to become clearer to him. Al-Noor had been here.

Something had gone down; the specifics of which Pitchford was about to carefully extract from Al-Noor because the runner had overplayed his hand.

He might have thought that he had covered everything. He hadn't.

There was one vital piece of evidence which Al-Noor had overlooked and it was the thing which was about to bring him down.

Chapter Eighty-Four

Pitchford had been delayed in entering Al-Noor's flat because of another incredible development.

Thomas Mead, and his sidekick, Damon Fielden, had been found dead in a car park in Harehills, both killed by what appeared to be the administration of a fatal cocktail of drugs.

Pitchford already knew that it would be a similar, if not the same, product which had killed Elyas and Majid.

A drug feud. Or somebody desperately wanted to make it look like one.

His thoughts went to The Chemist, for no other reason than he hadn't stopped thinking about Idris since he had met him at the pharmacy.

All he knew was, that somehow, Idris Khan had a hand in this. Pitchford stepped inside Al-Noor's flat and told everybody, including the paramedics, to leave.

They were reluctant and undertook some more arbitrary tests, the oxygen saturation levels of Al-Noor's blood, his heart rate and pulse, then left, telling Pitchford firmly that they would be outside and that he only had a few minutes to speak to Al-Noor before they would be taking him to hospital. They left a portable cardiac monitor attached to Al-Noor's body and left the two men alone.

Pitchford pulled a chair towards the couch and sat opposite Al-Noor.

'You look like hell,' said Pitchford.

'I need to go to the hospital.'

'We'll get you there.'

Pitchford looked carefully at Al-Noor, who might have been trying hard to show that he had nothing to hide but there was deceit all across his face.

'What happened?'

Al-Noor shrugged. 'I used. It was a bad batch.'

'Hmm. You heard about Elyas and Majid?'

'Somebody told me.'

'Same stuff, you reckon?'

Al-Noor shrugged, didn't answer.

'Did you see them tonight, Al? Majid and Elyas?'

'No.'

'Are you sure?'

'I'm sure.'

Checkmate. As simple as that.

'Look at me, Al-Noor.'

He didn't.

Pitchford reached across and carefully pulled up Al-Noor's trouser leg. He tapped the electronic tagging device. 'Fifth generation, GPS unit. Incredible technology,' said Pitchford.

A change in Al-Noor. A defensive, involuntary retreat of his body, withdrawing into itself.

'Do you know what the difference between a fourth and fifth generation device is, Al?'

'No.'

'Most of the addicts around here are tagged with third and fourth gen devices. But that one,' said Pitchford, again tapping the device with his finger, 'can tell me, unequivocally, if you've been up and down the stairs and pinpoint you in a building to within a metre of an actual location. It's basically the thing which is going to make sure that you spend the rest of your life in jail for double murder.'

Al-Noor looked at Pitchford, aghast, and in that moment, Pitchford knew that he had him. He nodded, sympathetically. 'We will download the data, analyse it and then I will ensure you go to jail. Faris will go into foster care and then, when he's eighteen, he will be sent back to Syria and you and I both know, Al, where young, impressionable boys end up in Syria.'

Al-Noor looked at Pitchford, horrified. 'Please. You cannot do that to my boy.'

Again, Pitchford pointed at the tag. 'That will do it to your boy. Unless, of course, you tell me exactly what happened here tonight. Give me the one thing our informant deal was based on. Real, credible intel of what is happening within The Mews. What happened to Jahangir Hosseini, Elyas, Majid, Thomas and Damon.'

Another stunned look from Al-Noor.

Another smile from Pitchford, who said, 'Would you like me to help you?'

Al-Noor looked away.

The cardiac monitor started to beep, Al-Noor's heart rate quickening.

'I don't feel well,' said Al-Noor, sounding like he was about to cry.

'If you want to escape The Mews, then this is your only chance. Think of that agreement you signed. If you tell me who has just brought down the two kingpins who control the drugs market in Yorkshire, I will make sure that we honour that agreement. That your boy, Faris, is taken care of.'

Al-Noor closed his eyes and took a beat.

'You're out of your depth here. Help me to help you,' urged Pitchford.

Al-Noor, feeling lost, was thinking of Faris and how to safeguard him. The thought of him returning to Syria was far worse than anything he had suffered so far.

With his heart racing and feeling more unwell than ever before, Al-Noor dropped his gaze to the floor, and said in a shaky voice, 'Idris. The Chemist.'

Chapter Eighty-Five

Having disposed all the evidence which might have connected him to what had happened to Thomas and Damon, Idris was now sitting in the dispensary, a nebuliser machine in front of him with the mask around his face, slowly inhaling a low dose of the nebuliser solution which he had used at the shisha bar, albeit at a safer dose.

He had felt his heart racing and was taking this as a precautionary measure to drop his blood potassium levels.

Tomorrow, he would visit A&E and finally get an X-ray of his ribcage and a full blood test.

He finished inhaling the medication and switched off the nebuliser machine.

He wondered how Al-Noor was and grabbed his phone to call him when the doorbell rang.

The shutters were closed, and it was way past midnight so Idris assumed it to be a pissed-up student who couldn't read the opening times.

He ignored it.

Another ring. And again. And this time it didn't stop.

Twelve chimes and still going.

And now Idris's phone started to vibrate.

He glanced at it – withheld number.

The doorbell stopped ringing.

Idris answered the call but said nothing.

'Idris, it's DCI Pitchford. I know you're inside the pharmacy, I can see your car parked in its bay. I suggest you open the door before I call a squad car.'

Idris hung up the call and remained where he was.

The detective knew.

He must have.

And there was no way for Idris to escape.

His pharmacy, the one place he found solitude, now the place inside which he was trapped.

Idris moved to the retail area, turned on several lights and then raised the shutter, expecting to see blue lights and a melee of activity.

But this was only Pitchford, alone, passively leaning against the door.

Idris allowed him inside, dropped the shutter and retreated to a bench. He sat down and simply waited.

Pitchford inched his way towards Idris, using his cane for support, and took a seat opposite him.

Both men sat in silence.

A minute passed. Then another.

Pitchford broke the silence. 'You look about as good as Al-Noor does.'

Idris, unable to look at Pitchford, leaned forward and rested his head in his hands, eyes rooted to the floor.

'How is he?' asked Idris, defeated, deflated. He heard the jangling of metal and then before he could react, Pitchford slapped a pair of handcuffs around Idris's wrists.

Idris looked at Pitchford in surprise.

'He's alive. Whether or not he ends up wearing bracelets is on you, Mr Chemist.'

Idris looked at the handcuffs. 'Evidence?' he said brazenly.

Pitchford removed his phone, accessed the voice memos and hit 'play'.

Idris's world ended.

A full, detailed confession from Al-Noor, his voice pained, broken and apologetic.

Patrick Mead.

The aspirin for Jahangir.

The lethal drug combination which had killed Elyas and Majid.

'Dead to rights, I think, is the phrase you're looking for, Idris,' said Pitchford.

Idris, in desperation, said, 'That confession you got from Al-Noor, I'm pretty certain it was obtained under duress. He was high, not lucid.'

'Why don't you play the methadone withdrawal psychosis card again?'

Idris shot Pitchford a cold, angry stare. He raised his hands, waved the handcuffs at him. '*If* what you've said is true, do you really think that it's me who should be wearing these? The innocent chemist who might have been in the wrong place at the wrong time?'

Pitchford pointed his walking stick at Idris.

'All those prescription drugs. The utilisation of legal interactions or side-effects to bring down the two biggest kingpins in Yorkshire. Incredible intelligence on your part.'

Idris rattled the cuffs. 'Not intelligent enough.'

'Methadone. The deal with the Scorpion. The fact that you are the younger brother of Zidane Azam?'

Idris remained silent.

'We found the deed poll register paperwork for you changing your name to your mother's maiden name. Smart to

412

have done so, moving away from being associated with such a formidable former kingpin.'

There was a change in Pitchford's voice.

Admiration?

'Why are you looking at me like that?' asked Idris.

Pitchford removed the key to the handcuffs and unlocked them. He slipped them off Idris's wrists.

'I have you, Idris. Yet, for the first time in my life, or, at least, the life I have left, I find myself in a quandary which, you, Mr Chemist, might be able to help me with.'

'I'm listening,' said Idris.

'Maybe I don't arrest you. Maybe . . . this recording I have, which was made only to me, finds its way to a secure location. And maybe the intel from Al-Noor's electronic tag gets corrupted or lost.'

'That's a lot of maybes. But I like the sound of it. Tell me more.'

'For almost a decade now, I've been hunting a gang of four men, residents inside The Mews who did unspeakable things. Who I know are guilty, but I don't have the evidence to convict them.'

Pitchford dropped his gaze to the floor and whispered, 'Unspeakable things. Things which steal a man's sleep and burden his mind when he's lying in bed, frozen from his Parkinson's disease.'

Pitchford looked at Idris now, cold, calculating . . . vengeful.

'How does a man go to his grave knowing that he allowed monsters to go unpunished? That they are out there, still able to do unspeakable things.'

'What kinds of things?' asked Idris.

Pitchford shook his head. 'If we do this, I will show you, not tell you.'

Idris frowned, confused. 'Do this?'

'I want two things from you, Idris.' Pitchford pointed towards the dispensary. 'First, I want you to use your pharmacy expertise and your ability to traverse The Mews to help me bring these four men to justice. To . . . kill them.'

Idris was stunned but keen to entertain anything which kept him out of jail.

Pitchford smiled at him. 'I have, maybe, two years of life left in me before this disease strips away my dignity. I will be meeting my maker and I'm happy to defend what I am asking of you in front of him because the second thing I want you to do, when the time arises, is to help me end my life, *on my terms*.'

Idris grimaced, unsure what Pitchford was really saying. 'What exactly are you talking about?'

'Things which have been on my mind for longer than you know.'

'You want me to help you kill four men and then to assist you in ending your own life?'

'When the time is right, yes.'

'Why?' said Idris, looking at him, perplexed.

Pitchford smiled, rueful. 'One day, but not any time soon, you will arrive at a point where you start to think about how one might finally get to meet his maker. Parkinson's is a dignity-stripping disease and it will remove every ounce of self-respect I have. I refuse to die that way.'

Idris stood up, walked around the retail floor space, stayed in the corner where it was dark. 'Doesn't sound like I have much of a choice,' said Idris.

'You have choices. We are here because of choices you made.'

'I tried to protect innocent people.'

'I admire the way you did it.'

'Really?'

'I have never – in all the years I have been working – met someone as brilliant as you. Had you just stepped back a beat and taken a little more time, not panicked and rushed this plan of yours, you might have got away with it.'

Idris remained where he was, stoic, keen to entertain what Pitchford had offered. 'I'm in. If you make what happened tonight go away.'

Pitchford stood up, stared hard at Idris. 'What evidence did you leave in Harehills?'

'None,' said Idris firmly.

'How can you be so sure?'

Idris thought of the yellow clinical waste bins, which would soon be taken away for incineration. 'I just am,' he said.

Pitchford pointed towards the shutter. 'Raise it. We will connect again soon.'

'Al-Noor? What happens to him?'

'Nothing. He remains in situ once he's been discharged from hospital. He needs to make good with whoever replaces Jahangir Hosseini and keep his position as the runner. It will help us with the cases I told you about – the four men.'

Idris walked towards Pitchford.

'What did they do?' he asked.

'I told you. Some things must be seen to be believed.'

'When do I get to see?'

'We can talk about that later.'

Idris raised the shutter, unlocked the door and opened it, bemused.

Pitchford loitered in the doorway. 'Not everything is as it seems, is it, Idris?'

Idris shook his head.

'The Chemist. I like the name. It suits you.'

'What do I call you from here on in?' asked Idris.

Pitchford thought on it. 'How about . . . The Detective?'

Idris reached out his hand. 'Shake on our deal?'

Pitchford did so. 'I'll be in touch.' With that, he walked away.

Idris locked the door, lowered the shutter and turned off the lights, leaving just the emergency perimeter ones on.

He retreated into the dispensary, sat down on his stool and switched on the pharmacy computer.

Then he typed in DCI Brian Pitchford's details into the Abbreviated Care Records system and hit 'enter'.

Epilogue

One month later

Idris and Rebecca were sitting on the roof of the medical centre, legs as ever dangling over the edge.

Behind them, Al-Noor had released a kite high into the air and was teaching Faris how to fly it. Idris could hear how excited the boy was to be on the roof, so late at night. It was the smallest of treats for Al-Noor, mostly because Idris still felt incredibly guilty for the trauma he had been through.

Idris wrapped his hands around his mug of tea, staring across the city, his focus, now, more than ever on The Mews.

Rebecca finished her dose of methadone, picked up her tea and said, 'Penny for your thoughts.'

'Wondering how Amy is getting on,' said Idris.

'Rehab will be good for her. It was the right call to put that money from Patrick to proper use. Poetic, somehow, that he's paying for the betterment of her life.'

'Wish I could use some of it to pay my bills off.'

'Why don't you?'

Idris shuddered. 'Bad karma.'

She laughed. 'I think you're done there.'

Idris raised his mug of tea towards the sky. 'If I could check the medication history of you, high up there, hiding in the heavens, you'd be in serious trouble,' he said, laughing.

Rebecca pointed at the ground. 'I think we're both heading for a one-way ticket downstairs to see the other guy.'

Idris pointed towards The Mews. 'I wish I'd never set eyes on that place.'

Idris turned his body, so he could watch Al-Noor playing with Faris. His electronic tag was still in situ but as per his informant agreement, the medical centre remained a safe space.

Lately, Idris was seeing more and more of Al-Noor, as together they started to piece together exactly how they might both escape from this nightmare they had landed themselves in. Idris was also using a little of Patrick Mead's money to help Al-Noor and Faris. Again, it felt appropriate, like out of the darkness was born a little light. He was building a foundation for what happened next.

'When does Pitchford engage with you on whatever it is he needs to show you?' asked Rebecca.

'I've taken some time off work, as he suggested. I've got to go to his place during daylight hours when his partner is at work and review whatever it is he wants me to see.'

'Any ideas?

Idris looked at her, anxious. 'He said not to think on it, as nothing would prepare me for it.'

'Do you trust him on this deal?'

Idris shrugged. 'I don't have a choice. Or . . . a plan.'

She mocked him and laughed. 'The Chemist with no plan? Impossible.'

Idris had one, or at least, the infancy of one. 'Pitchford tracked me for no other reason than his own agenda. In everything we've done so far, that might be the biggest twist of all.'

'How do you feel about working with him?'

Idris hated it. He might not have been in prison, but it certainly felt that way, like there would be constant scrutiny over every decision he made. And, if Idris did help, what assurances did he have that he would be free?

His gut, though, told him the detective could be trusted, if for no other reason than what he had done so far meant that Pitchford, too, was now complicit.

He didn't strike Idris as the type of man who would put his reputation on the line unless the outcome of bringing these four men to justice was critical.

Idris was intrigued but also frightened.

'What do you think pushed him over the edge?' asked Rebecca.

'Exactly what he said. He doesn't want to die knowing that justice was not served, but I think the bigger reason he's doing this is his own personal agenda. For me to help him die with dignity.'

Idris removed his phone and showed Rebecca some screenshots he had taken from local online newspaper articles which detailed Pitchford's work within the Catholic Church he attended.

Rebecca shrugged. 'So?'

Idris put his phone away. 'Don't you see? The man's religious. Assisted suicide? Defo a sin, no matter which god you worship.'

Rebecca was more confused than ever. 'What are you talking about?'

'I think Pitchford is worried that his place upstairs is at risk if I help him to end his life. And if he's going to go that way, then he might as well go out with a bang or at least knowing that he left the world a safer place.' Idris nudged Rebecca. 'If you're going to sin, then do it right.'

'Touché.'

Rebecca put her hands on Idris's face and gently turned it towards her. 'Look at me,' she said.

He did so.

'What happens next with us?'

Idris removed her hands, looked away. 'I'm still married, Rebecca, I need to figure things out.'

'I know,' she replied and changed the subject. 'No bullshit. How are you feeling about what you did?'

Idris wanted to tell her that he felt awful about murdering six people, that he couldn't sleep. That, even though his ribs didn't hurt anymore, that he was still drinking morphine liquid. Instead, he simply said, 'Bad things happen to toxic people.'

Rebecca squeezed his hand. 'You, Idris Khan, are not bad people.'

He couldn't look at her because deep down, Idris had come to realise something which he could not share with anyone.

He didn't even want to acknowledge it himself.

Idris had enjoyed what he had done.

The men he had killed had deserved to die.

Now that Idris had got a taste for it, he knew this was simply the beginning.

He relished what was to come, working with Pitchford in a unique way which only Idris could do: through his pharmacy, utilising the drugs, their side-effects and interactions.

Idris glanced towards Al-Noor. He had the runner.

And now, he had the detective.

Idris Khan had found his calling in life.

The Chemist.

Acknowledgements

Firstly, to the community pharmacists and pharmacy related staff (technicians, dispensers, drivers and counter staff) out there. You guys keep the healthcare system in this country ticking over. Underpaid, underappreciated and always doing so much more than we are supposed to. One day (hopefully soon), the funding for our sector will reflect what we do.

To my agent, David Headley, thank you for believing in *The Chemist*, and for your continual support, energy and enthusiasm.

Manpreet Grewal, my supportive and brilliant editor who from day one has championed *The Chemist* with relentless enthusiasm. Many thanks to the incredible team at HarperCollins for bringing this world to life.

Huge thanks to Kate Harwood, for being the first creative to put *The Chemist* on the map. You were relentless in your pursuit of this project and opened so many doors for me. I won't forget it.

To Steve Snow, former DCI in Bradford. Thank you for always being on the end of a phone and for entertaining my queries. Don't nick me yet, Steve, I'm not done and need to keep picking your brain!

To the *Red Hot Chilli Writers* – Ayisha, Vaseem, Abir, Nadeem and Imran. Long may the laughter continue (mostly at my expense). And as for drama . . . well, it keeps life interesting.

MW Craven – for nothing related to this book but as I did indeed forget to thank you in a previous novel for saving it from being binned, I am clearing that debt now. No longer can you use it against me!

Finally, to my incredible wife, Sam. You are the only person I truly write for, and I will end here, in a now familiar fashion: *Keep doing what you do, it makes me do what I do.*

ONE PLACE. MANY STORIES

Bold, innovative and
empowering publishing.

FOLLOW US ON:

@HQStories